DOCTOR WHO

TEN LITTLE ALIENS
STEPHEN COLE

For Jill –
with love and thanks.
The journey's just begun.

Published by BBC Worldwide Ltd
Woodlands, 80 Wood Lane
London W12 0TT

First published 2002
Copyright © Stephen Cole 2002
The moral right of the author has been asserted

Original series broadcast on the BBC
Format © BBC 1963
Doctor Who and TARDIS are trademarks of the BBC

ISBN 0 563 53853 8
Imaging by Black Sheep, copyright © BBC 2002
Schirr designed and built by Mike Tucker,
BBC Visual Effects Dept.

Printed and bound in Great Britain by Mackays of Chatham
Cover printed by Belmont Press Ltd, Northampton

Acknowledgements

Thanks to Justin Richards for many things, not least of which was letting me do this book at all.

Special thanks go to Peter Anghelides for useful insights, valid suggestions and, of course, taken mickey. His generous feedback, pink elephants and spreadsheets (!) buoyed me over the last manic weeks of work on the manuscript.

Those special ones also go to Mike Tucker, who made me a monster just because he thought it would be fun – and because he's my mate.

Many people helped along the way – hello Paul Magrs, Jason Loborik, John and Rachel Boothroyd, Tony, Debbie and Samuel Fleetwood, Tony and Wendy Cole, Sue Cowley, Gary Russell, Simon Gerard…

Finally, apologies to Agatha Christie, but grateful thanks to her charming, helpful and hospitable daughter Rosalind Hicks, who afforded me privileged access to her mother's home and effects in a former working life.

Chapter One
Postern of Fate

I

We're going to take the jump.

The smoky corridor ahead is broken up, a big black gash keeping one end from the other, like a giant's kicked through it. This whole level is dimly lit, the indifferent white of emergency lighting spread too thin. Behind us we hear the low whine of the Kill-Droid charging up its laser.

Hear that and you've got five seconds.

We turn, bring the gun to bear. We're used to something bigger than this pulse cannon, the trigger's so small we can barely fit our finger round it. Makes little odds – there's smoke everywhere, generators are on fire, we can't see.

We couldn't stop the Schirr taking the bridge. We couldn't save the hostages. The *Ardent* had no choice but to take out the whole ship. Good of Haunt to whack out the top section of the *Harbinger* first. Gives us five whole minutes to get back out.

One Kill-Droid floats out of the white mist at last. Cherry-red lasers spew out of its twin barrels. We dive, roll and turn, teetering on the chasm's edge. Our neck tears on puckered metal. We can feel blood but we're too charged to feel the pain right now. The Kay-Dee takes the pulse. Its crystal head cracks and shatters like ice under a boot. Clatters to the ground.

Now we hear footsteps. Reload the pulse barrel, unthinking, just on instinct. Gauge the jump again. We can do it, but we'll need a run-up. Straight into whatever's sprinting for us now? If it's on its feet down here it should be friendly, but –

A tall, dark shape flies out of the fog. *Almost* friendly. Denni. Her eyes narrow as she sees us. Cannon raised, blonde dreadlocks flapping as she spins on her heel, she fires. The mist illuminates like sheet lightning's ripping through it. There's a huge explosion, we feel the heat, smell oil and burnt-out electrics.

'It's you that's drawing the droids here, Shadow,' she shouts over her shoulder at us. 'Your damper's dried out.'

Jesus, we're a droid magnet. 'Where are the others?'

'Lindey's dead.' Denni's voice is terse, like it's all our fault somehow. 'I don't know about Joiks.'

We get up, join her and fire some more into the thick smog. 'Then I'll hold them off here,' we say. 'Get out of here. Pod's that way.'

Denni scoots without another word. She doesn't get far.

'Shadow,' she shouts. 'The ground's blown out. No one can cross this.'

'Sure they can.' We hear the whine of a kill-charge building, and criss-cross the corridor with pulse-fire. 'Look, the pods are just two hundred metres through that smoke. Don't think about it. Go.'

'You're crazy. I'll have to double back.'

'We can *do* it. The pods are waiting. Follow me.'

'No! If you hold them off, then I –'

Fine. So stay. We've got to take this jump. We're gonna prove we can do it. Denni won't take anything on trust from us no more but everyone watching this back on base, every damned one of them, is going to watch us, *feel* us clear this gap.

We push away from the crumpled lip of the floor. In the vids, leaps like this come in slow motion. The thrill stretched out so we can enjoy the long moments of *will we, won't we* clear the gap.

It only takes us a split-second to know Denni's right. We're not going to make this.

We reach out for the twisted edge, helplessly, as the jump becomes a fall. Denni's shouting something, we think maybe she's hit, but we blank her out. We've caught a blackened metal spur projecting from the lip. We're gonna haul ourselves out of here. Our muscles feel like they'll split our skin open as we raise ourselves level with the charred floor.

And we see a Kay-Dee's glassy head, sparkling blue-grey as it blows out of the smoke ahead of us. It waves the stubs of its twin-barrels at us, a victory dance. The guns swivel into position.

The charge kicks in, energy builds ready to take our face off.

Well, we've been through that once. This is where thinking we know best always gets us. We're jinxed. We bellow out curse after curse in frustration. And we drop into the blackness.

Hitting the force mats a hundred metres below.

We lie there, panting for breath in the darkness. Eyes screwed up. *We've* screwed up, again. It's too dark for the webset to function right down here, there's no image to relay. Thoughts cloud up. We can imagine how it is for them watching back in Debrief as we disassociate from these recorded feelings, start to drift.

Something crashes down beside us. Hears us holler back up at the distant patch of white smoke high above. A few seconds later it scrambles over. We're too tired to even react. It's black down here, we can't see anything, but we recognise Denni's breathing from better times in the dark.

'Is your webset off, Shadow?' she murmurs. 'There's something I have to do.'

It isn't. We don't say anything.

Denni spits in our face.

Cheers and wolf-whistles cut through the dark silence. Colonel Adam Shade found he was wiping his cheek when the lights went up in the visual debriefing room. He felt exposed. The rest of his team were going wild with laughter, gesturing obscenely, throwing their websets to the floor.

'Nice jump, Shadow,' jeered Frog, and her pale blue eyes bulged even more grotesquely than normal. 'Maybe you shoulda asked your lovely pretty Denni to give you a push, huh?'

Shade gritted his teeth. Frog's voice synthesiser made her every sentence a fire alarm.

'Or how about a *ride,* huh, Shadow?' She laughed, a metallic buzzing Shade was growing far too used to. 'For old times' sake, huh?'

'Shut it, Frog,' Denni said, shifting uncomfortably in her hard seat, sounding bored. 'And Shade, get me killed one more time and I will see to it you never walk again, do you get me?'

Shade smirked at her. 'Don't I always?'

Denni tutted. 'Those days are long gone, Shadow. Just be grateful I'm still speaking to you.'

'Hey, did you two ever, like, get it together with your websets on?' This was Joiks. Obvious, fatuous, unfunny, of course it was Joiks. He stooped to pick up Denni's discarded webset, displaying the large bald spot that nestled in his short black hair, and spun the slim metal band round his finger. 'Man, I'd pay to see that little vid.'

'I did already,' said Lindey from the row in front of him. She turned to face the audience of twenty or so, her mouth opened in an exaggerated yawn. Shade took a swipe at the tangle of red ringlets that crowned her thin, angular face. She was too quick for him, as usual, bobbing back out of reach.

She got her laugh from the others in the room. Shade wondered how she'd stayed quiet for so long amid so many opportunities to put him down. He shut his eyes to help him wake up, willing himself to drag his feelings free of the sensor net. It was days since the drop now. His team had failed, failed totally. Meanwhile some new guy fresh out of Academy Intelligence had led his bunch to the pods safely and got away to join Marshal Haunt and second and third AT Elite Corps on Central Ship.

As if he'd somehow conjured her, Haunt's face snapped up on to the viewscreen, her salt-and-pepper hair scraped back off her high forehead into a stubby ponytail. She didn't look happy. That was nothing new.

'So you failed,' she said flatly. 'And now you're all dead. A handful more human sacrifices to rid ourselves of another hundred Schirr.'

Shade removed his webset, wishing he could crush the flimsy metal construction. He hated the things. You had to wear them in exercises so that everyone could learn from your many, many mistakes. The rest of his team had lived his part in the mission with him, seen it through his eyes, felt the same frustrations and hurts he'd had for real. And of course, when they got back out they killed themselves laughing about the way he'd got killed himself.

'Your suit's systems were no longer damping your vital signs, Shade,' Haunt remarked. 'You were drawing every droid in the place straight to you.'

'Yes, Marshal,' Shade snapped. His voice didn't seem quite real after hearing the world inside him for so long. His head was throbbing like an old engine.

Haunt kept on staring at him, her thin lips pursed. Once, she might've been attractive, but anything soft or feminine about her had been ground away by the soldier she had become. Her face was lined, and held a permanent look of fatigue; Shade didn't like to think too hard about what she had lived through. Now almost forty, she'd had fifteen years' experience in front line combat before Pent Central had pensioned her off to the training corps.

'You were aware that you were risking the life of a team-mate,' she said, deliberate and clear.

'I thought if I could clear the gap we could reach the pods together,' Shade said, meeting her cold grey gaze.

'It's clear to see what you *thought*,' Haunt snapped. 'You were wrong. What should you have done?'

Shade blinked, opened his mouth to speak.

'Denni told him Lindey was out of the game,' said Joiks. 'Shade *could* have asked Denni for Lindey's last location.'

Frog nodded, absurdly enthusiastic as always. 'He coulda led the Kay-Dees away from Denni,' she said. 'Taken Lindey's suit. Tight fit, but chances are the dampers were still functional.'

Lindey threw up her hands, pretended to gag. 'No! No way!' She looked at Shade and shook her head. 'You're *never* seeing me naked, Shadow. Not even in death.'

'Damned right.' Shade smiled coldly back at her. 'That plan occurred to me, of course. Figured I'd rather take the jump.'

He got his laugh. Lindey pressed her lips into a mocking pout. 'Love you, baby.'

'All right, enough,' Haunt said. 'That's good, Joiks.' Haunt always

5

sounded particularly disinterested when she was giving praise. 'That would've been the best action you could've taken, Shade. In the circumstances.'

Shade didn't want to concede the point. 'Then again, we could be issued with more reliable combat suits.'

The room fell deathly quiet.

Haunt looked at Shade, and he registered the sneer on her face. 'You go in, *Colonel* Shade,' she said quietly, 'and you kill Schirr with whatever you've got.'

Shade nodded stiffly. 'Marshal.'

'And Denni,' Haunt went on. 'I don't know what bodily fluids you may have shared with Shade in the past and I don't want to know, but you don't spit them in his face.' She smiled faintly. 'We have to function here as part of a team. A single unit. One whole.'

Denni nodded. 'Marshal.' Then she blew a kiss at Shade. Amid catcalls and laughter the atmosphere lightened again for a few moments.

'All right.' Haunt's eyes, grey as old stone, stared out at them all from the screen. 'You've got five minutes downtime. Then you'll join the rest of the year in Theatre One for full mission debrief. And Shade…'

Shade shut his eyes and inwardly groaned.

'…*You* will kindly report in full combat armour. Out.'

II

Theatre One stank of sweat and polish. Shade looked around with worried interest at the two hundred-odd faces in the lecture hall, sticking out from the stiff necks of their regimental uniforms. Most of them he'd seen around before. He'd gone head to head with them on various missions over the last year. Now he was dressed for the part again, the only one here in a combat suit. But if Haunt had his humiliation on her mind, he'd settle for standing out. With a face like his, quite apart from being an Earthborn, he usually stood out wherever he went.

And as usual, he was terrified that someone might recognise him, remember him for what he'd done. Might see him in training here and work out something they shouldn't.

A round of fierce applause started up as a long and motley line of Academy Elite training instructors filed on to the stage. These people were veterans of a dozen wars. Once they'd fought for the Empire; now they were glorified Phys. Ed. instructors.

And there was Marshal Haunt. As one of the four Senior Staff Heads, she was almost the last to walk on. Only Principal Cellmek came after her. He'd lost both arms, but refused to get artificials fitted. He believed – and he had told them this so many times – that you had to take what life dealt you. Just take it. Brave and inspirational, Shade supposed, but the man stayed alive by sucking soup up a straw. That was just dumb. Shade had taken some flak from life – his face was full of it since New Jersey – but life had also made him an Earthborn. With that behind you, you could take pretty much anything, and entirely for granted.

Shade hated that. He wanted to do different. But where would he be right now without his connections?

Thinking about it, he could be lying in luxury someplace. Not about to get a rocket up his ass from the one person here he respected.

Cellmek left the line to take up his habitual position at the lectern, and Haunt followed him. He stepped aside respectfully to allow her to take the stand.

'Colonel Adam Shade, A-TE 287645,' she rapped. 'To the front please.'

Shade attempted to saunter to the front, to try to salvage some dignity by making out he was some kind of rebel. But he was too self-conscious to do it well. He probably just looked constipated.

Finally he reached the front of the hall and stood smartly to attention before the podium.

'If I may crave your indulgence before Principal Cellmek begins mission debrief.' Haunt intoned the words like a child saying prayers by rote, but immediately she had the whole audience rapt. She cut an imposing figure, staring them all out from the podium. The Beloved Butch Bitch, Joiks called her. Amongst other things.

'Shade here has queried the reliability – and hence the validity – of the combat suits we issue to our troopers.'

She jumped down from the platform to face him. Shade had never seen her in the flesh this close up. He was surprised to find he was almost a head taller than she was.

'As many of you have witnessed in the viewing rooms, Colonel Shade and his team failed in their attempt to liberate the *Harbinger* from an incursion by the Schirr. Colonel Shade has since blamed his combat suit for his failure.'

She was doing a good job on him, thought Shade. He'd be lucky to scrape through the year with any merits at this rate. Then he noticed movement in the wings. Saw two medics, standing by.

Shade's eyes snapped back to Haunt, alarm bells ringing. She pulled out a pistol and pressed it against his chest. He looked down at it in surprise, just as she opened fire.

The blast knocked him screaming halfway across the hall. He heard the shocked reaction of the crowd. His heart was knocking at his chest like it wanted to jump out.

Haunt spoke calmly over the astonished whispers filling Theatre One. 'The standard-issue combat suit, sculpted from carbon nanotubing, you will observe, gives the wearer more than adequate protection from a direct hit at close quarters.' He watched, helplessly winded, as she strode towards him once more. 'It dampens your vital signs while signalling your location on a secure frequency to your team's scanners – leaving you practically invisible to the enemy. However…' She kicked him savagely in the ribs, then stamped down on his stomach. Shade grabbed hold of her foot, tried to twist it so she'd lose her balance.

She shot him again, in the arm this time. He shrieked in pain, saw a rip in his suit and a livid gash in the flesh, felt a sharp pressure bite into the skin around it.

'Obviously, since the suit must be more flexible around the soldier's extremities,' Haunt went on casually, 'the combat suit is more vulnerable to gunfire in these areas. However, those sitting near the front – and Colonel Shade himself, of course – will note that the fabric of the suit constricts around the wound to staunch blood flow.'

Shade rolled about on his back in agony, like some overturned insect trying to right itself.

'In any combat situation,' Haunt told her audience, 'wear and tear on your suit may lead to the impairment of certain functions. In this eventuality, what do you do?' The shocked silence went on, and it seemed no one was brave enough to break it for fear of being targeted themselves.

'You fight on, Marshal Haunt,' Shade gasped.

'You fight on!' Haunt bellowed. 'Damned right you fight on!' She hunched over him, yelled in his face, grey eyes flashing. 'These are Schirr you're going up against, Colonel Shade. You think a better suit's going to save you?' She turned back to shout at her students. 'Well, the colonel may just have a point. Those pig-faced murderers don't just like slaughtering soldiers. Like the Spooks from Morphiea, they like killing whole cities. Whole planets. Planets they've never been to before, people they've never seen, and none of them given the option of wearing any damned piece-of-shit protection.'

The tirade stopped. Shade wondered if the only sound in the entire theatre was his hoarse, ragged breathing as he fought to ride out the pain, to stay conscious.

'Medics,' he heard one of the other instructors say softly. There were running footsteps. A shot of warmth. The pain lessened.

Haunt pulled him up by his good arm. He saluted her. *Don't you know who I am?* She saluted him in turn.

He made it to a seat in the front row unaided. Every eye was on him. The Earthborn getting his ass whupped. He sat up straight on that ass. Hoped Haunt would think he looked like a man who had just learned a lesson, and who was the wiser for it. Much wiser.

'All right,' said Principal Cellmek quietly, once Haunt had climbed back on to the podium and taken her seat among the long line of grim-faced instructors. 'Playtime's over.'

He nodded to an aide standing impassively beside him. She hit a button on the lectern console, and a picture of the freighter they'd boarded in the simulation swam into view.

'By now you've all of you had your chance to storm the *Harbinger* and get the crew out alive...' Cellmek started his usual waffle about how their performance profiles would be affected by the various tasks they'd encountered during the simulation. All Shade could think about was Haunt. He watched her through narrowed eyes. She looked dead calm now. Just carrying on like her flip-out had never happened. *Don't you know what I could do to you? With just a couple of calls it can all be arranged.*

Cellmek finally got back to real life again. 'The *Harbinger* was on a peaceful mission, with minimal armaments, mapping new trade lines around the Indochina system. The Schirr disciples first infiltrated the lower levels, then secured and held the bridge. Not with weapons. With Morphiean ritual. The AT Elite unit deployed failed to stop them. The real freighter *was* destroyed.'

'Did the unit escape?'

Shade looked across the hall to see who was speaking. It was some guy he'd not seen around. Denni sat beside him.

'Only two men got clear before the Schirr detonated the ship, Creben,' Cellmek announced.

Shade gritted his teeth as the throbbing in his chest grew worse. So this was Creben, known by name to the principal. Only about twenty-five. Short fair hair. Neatly chiselled handsome features. Already he made Shade sick.

'Eight hundred unarmed human civilians on board were lost,' Cellmek elaborated. 'But the explosion took out the *Ardent* too, with the loss of a further thousand. The two survivors drifted for weeks, into the fringes of the Spook Quadrant. We don't know what happened there. But somehow their pod travelled back within the Earth frontier and was reclaimed. By then, both were dead.'

'Then *we* did better than *they* did,' Creben murmured quietly. But not quietly enough.

'You were up against training droids with beta weapons only, Creben,' Cellmek said calmly. 'Those men had DeCaster's fanatics to contend with. Schirr suicide squad.'

Creben nodded deferentially, his head bobbing about like he was looking for a suitable ass he could climb up.

But Cellmek wasn't so easily appeased. 'Perhaps this is a good time to remind all of you that we are not putting you through the most intensive training in the military to make you better people,' he said sternly. 'If the Spooks make good on their threats... If DeCaster and his disciples aren't located and dispatched quickly...'

It felt to Shade like the unspoken threat hung solely over those recruits packed in the hall, not over all Earth's overstretched empire. He checked out Haunt again. The mere mention of DeCaster – to quote Haunt herself from one of her spiels, the 'most wanted pig-faced murdering Schirr bastard in all space' – always got her riled up. He noted spots of colour in both cheeks. Twin targets.

Cellmek finally broke the interminable silence with more cheerfulness. 'You're here because you want to make Anti-Terror Elite. Because you want to hit back at the cowards who commit atrocities like on Toronto, or on New Jersey, or the Argentines. And the final stage of your combat training will be for real. Real ammo, not the peashooters you've been firing off. You've been grouped into tens, each group including one instructor. Your strengths and weaknesses, as extrapolated from the experiential web, have been inputted to Pentagon Central's tactical computers. From this data the most appropriate training program and location will be selected from those in the systems. The e-rag will post your final training groups at twenty-one hundred. But for now – put on your websets.' He paused for two hundred pairs of hands to fumble with the delicate metal headbands. 'The experiences you're about to endure were taken from the two dead men found in the pod. Now we can show you what the unit on that freighter was really up against.'

Shade picked up his own webset and eagerly fitted it in place over his ears. Becoming someone else for a few hours, letting his own feelings, his own pain be swamped by a stranger's impressions would be a blessing right now. The lights in Theatre One dimmed into darkness. He focused on his breathing, in and out, as his senses started to fall away.

And suddenly we're someone else, indestructible. Buoyed up with adrenaline and the camaraderie of our unit, barely waiting for the docking tube to clang home before we rush to board the freighter, to save the ship and everyone on it.

An hour later the tiny detached part of him that still knew it was Colonel Adam Shade was screaming for his own pain, for the lights to be switched back on.

III

'Shade? You get your grouping?'

Shade was woken from painful sleep by the sound of something yelling and kicking down his door.

'Coming along for the greet?' yelled the muffled voice.

He checked the clock; it was gone twenty-two hundred. Rising stiffly, he peeled off the heal-pads from his arm and chest and padded across the cool floor. Hit the green button and watched the door swish open.

Denni was leaning in the doorway. She was smiling, but it was hard to read the expression in her black eyes. 'Sorry, Shade. Looks like we're going to war together.'

Shade half-smiled at her. 'Lindey, Frog and Joiks too, right?'

She nodded. 'Best in squad.'

'Uh-uh. We just need the most work.'

'We must be good. You see who else is with us?'

'I haven't checked the rag,' Shade admitted.

Denni's face softened a little. 'You still hurting?'

'Guess I had it coming.'

'Guess Haunt is an uptight bitch.' She paused. 'She's grouped with us.'

Shade's eyes widened. 'She is?'

Denni nodded slowly. She looked just a little concerned. 'Her and Shel.'

'Haunt's mystery man,' mused Shade. 'Who else we got?'

'Come to the greet, you'll see.' Denni grimaced. 'Sorry. You've not seen the rag. The groups are meeting up. Just so we can see who's going to be watching our backs.'

'Joiks'll be too busy ogling their fronts.' Shade wondered about

12

asking Denni into his room. But there was nothing in her look to encourage him.

'Probably,' she said. 'You know, that big guy, Roba's with us, remember him?'

'Seen him around.'

'And his best buddy, Tovel.'

'The square-jawed hero. Sweet.'

She paused. 'And Joseph Creben, shining star of AT Elite.'

Shade smiled tightly. 'Think I'll give the gathering a miss.'

'You really hurting?'

He looked into Denni's eyes, hopeful she might actually care. No. Nothing there but polite interest.

'I got things to do,' he said. 'Things to arrange, before the off tomorrow.'

'Pulling a few strings on Earth to get the best cabin?'

Shade closed his eyes. He wished there were something warm in the way she mocked him. 'You know that's bull.'

'Whatever.'

'Every time...' He looked at her. 'Why does my coming from Earth have to make a difference?'

She became mock-pensive. 'Because our glorious seat of empire is outmoded and obsolete? Because Earthers stay rich by taxing to death the populations they chucked out into space in the first place? Because...'

Shade felt tired. It was an old argument. 'I'm running from Earth, Denni. I hate it as much as you do.'

'Maybe you'll prove that to me, one day,' she said as she straightened up and stretched, a cat ready to slink off somewhere new. No loyalties to anyone dumb enough to stroke it.

'Oh, I'll prove it,' Shade promised her as she walked away. 'To all of you.'

Big words.

He hit red, let the door swish shut. Looked down at the vidphone. *I got things to do,* he'd said. A single call and he could turn all this around.

Shade sighed, and called up the e-rag. The text played over his wall but he barely took it in, hardly heard the cheesy voiceover making a joke out of everything. He stood unmoving, kept staring at the phone as the minutes slid by.

A-T E—ZINE
23.5.90
supple+mental

POSTINGS ALERT SPECIAL ISH! ++

welcome <u>adam shade</u>. your training group posting is <u>E87</u>.
shortcut yes? no?
yes ++

Breaking the news first as always – then stamping on it, shooting it full of holes and nuking it – your ever-lovin' E-RAG proudly presents your live-ammo training team, <u>adam shade</u> + +

ROBA, Dax   *ATE126673*
Age: 28
Visual: Black male
The big bruiser with the baby face, Roba's had a good semester, scoring **highest KD kill-rate over five simulations**. Just hope he don't give you the evil-eye – Roba was **top marksman** with the Volunteers out in Hunan and the Commonwealth and he's been itching for the live ammo. **Shoot to kill** now, big guy, y'hear?
In his own words:
THE ONLY GOOD SCHIRR IS ++ 'crawling in its coffin right now to save us the effort'

NARDA, Mel (aka FROG)　　　　　*ATE 125735*
Age: 27
Visual: White female
The lovely Frog never got the breaks in life ('ceptin' the one that **broke her face**). Still she's proved herself a **super-soldier** this semester, building on that **scary** reputation she got fighting in the Second-Wave Argentine skirmishes and through the Buenos Aries Pacification Programs of '87-88. She gonna **croak some Schirr** for sure. **Mercy!**
In her own words:
THE ONLY GOOD SCHIRR IS ++ 'a dead Schirr. Or have you had that already? Hey, can I change that?'

JOIKS, Dav　　*ATE 169556*
Age: 32
Visual: White male
Joining A-TE following a two year stint with the **notorious** SMC **Incendiary Division** (African Frontier), Joiks sure must like it when the heat is on. After singeing his fingers over his third and final Academy **caution for misconduct** he's gained a blistering five merits in the last three simulations. Way to go, Joiks – but **don't burn up now, y'hear?**
In his own words:
THE ONLY GOOD SCHIRR IS ++ 'under my boot'

TOVEL, Raiph　　　　　　*ATE 126267*
Age: 30
Visual: White male
Highest-ranking hero of the Dawn Bridge simulation with fifteen merits, about Tovel they say **there ain't a ship in the sky he can't fix and fly**. Come a long way from his days stretcher-bearing with the Volunteers out in the Commonwealth Belt. It's **Schirr stretchers** he's gonna be filling up come graduation day. **Go Tovel!**
In his own words:
THE ONLY GOOD SCHIRR IS ++ 'pacified, kissing Earth's ass'

CREBEN, Joseph   **ATE 200101**

Age: 23

Visual: White male

Creben's not your average Joe. **Acing the braincases** in Intelligence, he's been put on **fast-flight** to join the Big Guns in Pent Central. If he can get through Elite without that **big head** getting **blown off**, that is!

In his own words:

THE ONLY GOOD SCHIRR IS ++ 'More important than blind hatred against the Schirr is the question of why the Morphiean Quadrant has involved itself in a conflict against Empire'

DENNI, Gisel   **ATE 159922**

Age: 25

Visual: Black female

She rose out of the **slums of Paris II**, climbed through the ranks in Stellar Infantry and things are still looking up for **fantastic gymnastic** Gisel Denni, who has received **zero demerits** since starting Academy. She's out to **go far. Far out**!

In her own words:

THE ONLY GOOD SCHIRR IS ++ 'one that toes the line'

SHADE, Adam (aka SHADOW)   **ATE 287645**
                                        [CURRENT READER]

Age: 30

Visual: White male

You saw him **shot down in flames** just this very afternoon, but this Shade ain't no shadow of his former self. 'Course, that's not so hard when you consider he started active service as a **Royal Escort** back on **dear old Mama Earth** before going to war in U.S. Pan-Galactic. Went Elite after ten months in medicare, but **needs serious merits** now if he wants to make the grade... Hey, **have a good war**, soldier!

In his own words:

THE ONLY GOOD SCHIRR IS ++ 'adam shade unavailable'

LINDEY, Stace   *ATE 161662*
Age: 28
Visual: White female

From **humble beginnings** serving in Little Europe with the Lux-dirigibles, the so-called Pauper Fleet, Lindey **rose out of troubled waters** thanks to a scholarship to the Zero-Gs. After five years' combat in low-grav environments, Lindey traded walking on air for dry land when she won an **unheard-of second scholarship** to go Elite.

In her own words:
THE ONLY GOOD SCHIRR IS ++ 'stuffed with frag-grenades and delivered to the Spook Quadrant'

> **SHEL**, Eiji   *ATE 334684*
> *Age:* 33
> *Visual:* Oriental male
>
> Shel joins Academy Elite as **Marshal Haunt's adjutant and science officer** on Personnel Exchange from the **Japanese Belt**, where his exploits have been deemed **C L A S S I F I E D**. Spooky!
>
> *In his own words:*
> *THE ONLY GOOD SCHIRR IS* ++ 'I have no time to comment'

HAUNT, Nadina   *SENIOR STAFF HEAD, INSTRUCTOR*
Age: 39
Visual: White female

Scourge of the Schirr on **twenty worlds** from Idaho to New Jersey, if our beloved Staff Head ever wore all her hard-won medalwear **she'd need anti-gravs just to keep her upright**. Joined Elite after making Marshal following **15 years of front line service**. Served in **every war zone** going, and **survived** everything the Schirr could throw at her. Now she's **throwing YOU back at them**, soldier. Be **worth it**, now, y'hear?

In her own words:
THE ONLY GOOD SCHIRR IS ++ '*Good* and *Schirr* do not belong in the same breath, soldier. They don't even belong in the same *head*. The only possible good in the universe is *absence of Schirr*. Not absent hiding out in some stinking pit in the outer rim, not turning invisible like some damned Spook, but dead, wiped out, *burnt* out. And we didn't start that fire, soldier, but we are going to stamp it out and stamp the *Schirr* out, so hard that in 20 years no man, woman or child will have the first conception of what those stinking, sticky-faced ++
[space exceeded]

GROUP GREET @ 22 HUNDRED ++ THEATRE TEN ++

STUDENTS WISHING TO GRADUATE ARE REMINDED TO STAY ALIVE THRU TRAINING ++

Chapter Two
Appointment with Death

I

Ben looked at Polly and narrowed his eyes. 'You saying I've got a cold wet nose and floppy ears?'

Polly rolled her eyes but she was smiling, her straight white teeth framed by crimson lips. 'You know what I mean,' Polly went on in her *oh-so-frightfully* tones. 'People are either dog people or cat people. And you're a dog.'

'Yeah, well, reckon I know how you'd take it if I called *you* one,' Ben retorted.

'I'm a cat person,' Polly declaimed, running slender fingers through her long blonde hair.

'Thought you reckoned you were just the whiskers on the thing, not the whole moggy.'

'I just mean I make my own way, that's all. Independent.'

Ain't that the truth, Ben thought wryly to himself. They'd shared a few adventures now since leaving London, thanks to the TARDIS's dodgy compass, and throughout it all Polly was always making out she could look after herself all right. No need for Ben to look out for her, oh no. But he knew better. Well, it stood to reason. With the navy he'd seen so much, been so many places, learned how to handle himself. All she'd known were Beaujolais Nouveau parties, poncy nightclubs and finishing school in South Ken until they'd fallen in with the Doctor on his batty travels through time and space.

'You'd be a bulldog.' Polly laughed. 'Or a terrier. Tenacious little Ben, always pulling life's trouser leg!'

'All right, all right,' Ben said a little touchily. He was very aware he was hardly a giant among men, especially since Polly was taller than

20

him by a good inch. 'What about the Doctor, then?'

'Cat person or dog person?' Polly enquired with a wicked smile. 'He's more of an old buzzard, don't you think?'

Her smile dropped suddenly as a door shut loudly behind her.

'This "old buzzard" has excellent hearing my girl, quite excellent, yes,' the Doctor fussed as he walked back in to the console room. The old boy was a real mystery, but it seemed his life was just one long adventure that he was willing to share with his mates. For Ben, that was all you needed to know.

This gleaming monochrome complex was his home. And it suited him. Quite a black-and-white character, the Doctor, Ben decided. Not just his appearance – swept-back silver hair, black frock coat, white wing-collared shirt and grey trousers – but in the way he saw things. A sort of suffer-no-fools and take-no-prisoners outlook that put Ben in mind of an old granddad of his, one who'd maybe lost a few marbles in the trenches.

The Doctor began flicking switches on the pentagonal console. His hands waved uncertainly over various sections before his bony fingers stabbed and twisted at the controls with sudden precision.

The column in the middle of the console's set-up started to slow. The Doctor steepled his fingers and smiled benignly at his two companions, his blue eyes twinkling. 'We should soon be landing.'

'Where?' asked Ben.

The old man's faced clouded in confusion. He turned back to his controls.

Ben turned to Polly. 'Never mind the buzzard, Duchess,' he whispered. 'Reckon he's got the memory of a goldfish.'

II

Shade felt the bridge shudder as the retros kicked in. The vibration made him feel sick, and he put this down to the sleep drug. The 'trip trip', Joiks had called it. Funny.

He couldn't believe they still used needles to inject the serum, or that they laid them on these slabs afterwards like corpses in a morgue. Then again, he couldn't believe an ancient pile of scrap like this lousy space frigate was still being flown by anyone, let alone the military. No quarters – just a bridge and a cargo hold. A ship small enough to blip past any radar, and to drive anyone trapped on board mad in under a week. Especially with Joiks and his one-liners there for the ride.

However they got the drug, Shade thanked God for it. The month had passed in the time it took to close his eyes. That made the worst hangover he'd had in his life a little more bearable.

Now ten of them were strapped into the couches in a punchy silence, staring at the central viewscreen.

Marshal Haunt was in the middle. She craned her head like the rest of them at the dull grey rock that filled the viewscreen. Her skin shared its drab pallor. Both her hands were twitching, like they were still trying to wake up.

'It's been a while,' she muttered dryly as she faced the group. 'Everyone still remember who they are?'

Shade's head lolled back, he closed his eyes.

'Everyone still remember who *I* am?' Haunt's voice hardened a little.

'Think so, Marshal Haunt,' Joiks said. 'Didn't you kick Shade's ass back in Theatre One?'

Shade smiled through gritted teeth at the ensuing round of applause and cheers. All the shock, the violence of the event had been sublimated already into humour. It had meant nothing. Like killing meant nothing to soldiers, provided you killed the right people. But Shade hadn't forgotten. Shade could never forget anything.

I'll show you.

Only Denni didn't laugh. Perhaps she felt as bad as she looked right now.

Haunt didn't seem too amused either. 'I was simply sending a message to everyone in that room,' she said calmly. 'Perhaps you didn't grasp that message. Perhaps I need to demonstrate again.'

Joiks shook his head and did his best to look pious.

'All right. Round the room. Who are you? Why are you here?' She lay

22

back, muttered the words like she'd said them a hundred times before on missions like this, leading her lambs off to slaughter or be slaughtered. 'I don't want your ranks, your full names and life history. And forget I know some of you already. Today you're all school kids and I'm your teacher. Just give me enough so I can yell abuse at your sorry asses with confidence.'

Haunt's latest adjutant began the introductions. 'Shel,' he said. 'Fifth Division Heavy Infantry, Japanese Belt.' He might look oriental but he spoke perfect American. 'Here on interpersonnel exchange program.'

Exchanging what? Shade wondered. What was so classified about his past? He'd barely given away more than the e-rag had in his b-ground profile.

'Next,' rapped Haunt.

'Joiks.'

'We were trying to forget you, Joiks,' Shade interrupted. He got fewer laughs. Figured.

'Yeah, yeah. Joiks. Space Marine Corps. Here so I can kill Schirr scum better.'

'Good,' Haunt said automatically. 'Next.'

'Tovel. Pilot-Engineer with the Peace Keeper Volunteers, Commonwealth Belt.' Shade had forgotten how surprisingly soft the stocky man's voice was since they'd fought droids together in Term One, but not his tufty blond hair and his chin – so square you could fit a palmscreen in it with room to spare.

'For two weeks after the Schirr hit New Jersey I ferried out the dead and dying.' Tovel shrugged. 'Joined the regulars and that's why I'm here.'

A massive black guy lay beside him, his feet dangling off the edge of the couch, a big, taut sack of muscle and attitude. Shade had seen him around – you could hardly miss him. His head was broad and bald, his features bunched up in the middle of his face.

'Roba. Peace Keeper, like Tovel.'

'You two come as a pair, honey?' Frog asked, her jangling voice exploding into the fuggy atmosphere.

'We're close,' Roba said, 'but we never tried that before.'

Frog cackled, leading the fresh wave of laughter. But Shade couldn't relax, couldn't let his gaze shift for long from the lumpy planetoid in the viewscreen.

'You a "pilot-engineer" too?' Lindey asked Roba.

'No. Marksman.' He pointed his finger like it was a gun and fired at her.

'Next,' Haunt said dully.

'My name is Creben.' He smiled and paused like he wanted applause. 'Graduated from Academy Intelligence last year. Need combat experience to rise higher so I've gone Elite. Naturally.'

Shade's initial dislike of the man deepened to loathing.

'Hey Shadow, come on,' Lindey called. 'Your turn to bore us.'

'Name's Shade. Joined up with Earth Ceremonials –'

'Hey, Shadow, you an Earther?' Frog asked, as if this was news to her. Everyone roared with laughter.

'Normally we don't stand on ceremonial,' Joiks added confidentially to Tovel. 'But for him we make an exception.'

'You're funny.' Haunt's voice steamrollered over the laughter. 'Can we finish this before landing please?'

Shade indicated Denni should take her turn. He didn't want to elaborate on his history anyway. It was better this way, even if the new guys thought he was the butt of the squad. Still, Haunt had spoken up for him. That was interesting. Guilty conscience?

Denni, Lindey and Frog all said their snappy little bits. Yeah, yeah, they struggled against the odds growing up on crummy worlds, they were here to save Empire, personally round up DeCaster and his evil disciples and kick Morphiea's ass single-handed; that was what going Elite did for you, right? Who was here for a career, for the housing benefits, for a dacha in the Thai systems when you were pensioned off?

He had all that waiting whenever he wanted it.

'Me, I'm Haunt.' Shade looked up. 'Any of you ever visit Idaho?' she said, her face a pale mask. No one spoke. 'It's a good clean world. I remember when we took it. Tamed the Schirr, brought them into our order. Made them a part of an Empire they could be proud of.'

'Yen, God and Hamburgers,' Joiks quipped. The three pillars of Earth repatriation, as named by some stand-up on the Proxima circuit.

Haunt ignored him. 'So you see, I am a relic of a time when if you saw a Schirr on a vidscreen, it was just some new ugly to point at. To laugh at. See, a Schirr knew its place back then.' Haunt looked round at them. 'Me and DeCaster went into service at the same time. I joined up when the Earth embassy on Idaho was taken out. I've spent fifteen years fighting Schirr and their allies.' She paused for a few moments. Her voice was quieter when she spoke again, the dull look back in her eyes. 'The Army promoted me out of the front line, but I *will* see DeCaster dead within my lifetime. *That* is why *I* am here. Why all of us are here.' She turned to Shel, the faintest trace of a smile on her face. 'All right, where the hell *is* here.'

Shel consulted his palmscreen. 'The planetoid has no name. It's a speck of rock in distant orbit around Vertigan Majoris.'

'Edge of empire,' breathed Lindey. Her tight red curls were plastered to her head with sweat.

Roba spoke up, almost nervously. 'We're as close to the Spook Quadrant as anyone can get.'

'We're several thousand miles within Earth space,' Haunt said, too quickly, too loudly. 'Our rights to be here are universally recognised, you understand that, Roba?'

Shade noticed Denni trying to catch his eye. She whistled silently through her teeth, and he nodded. Roba must be feeling lucky to have raised Morphiea at all, given Haunt's track record.

'I understand that, Marshal,' Roba said quietly.

'You'd better,' Haunt told him. But just for a moment she looked suddenly uncertain, as if aware she'd overreacted.

Shade had never seen her give the slightest concession to what other people thought of her. He caught Denni's eye. She looked oddly apprehensive, like she was really spooked. He tapped his hand against the needle mark on his wrist. 'The drug,' he mouthed.

Haunt seemed to have recovered herself. 'All right, Shel. Mission objective.'

Shel tapped some buttons on the palmscreen: 'Our objective is to locate and secure a Schirr cypher and disable two droids operating inside the planetoid.'

'Two!' warbled Frog in disbelief, grinning round at the others. Seemed the drug hadn't left her with any ill-effects. They probably ingested worse stuff than that at the kindergarten where she grew up. 'Took us four weeks to get here, boys and girls, and we'll be done in an hour.'

Haunt wasn't smiling now. 'These are new droids, still crated up in the hold. Principal Cellmek has advised me that no one's met Kay-Dees like these, in *conditions* like these, on any prior training,' she said simply. 'Consider this active service.'

The words were enough to crush what little ebullience there was in the cramped cabin.

We're not Elite, thought Shade. We're not the best.

We've just survived.

'How did I ever get here,' he whispered to himself, shutting his eyes as he tried to shake the lingering hold of the drug. He wanted to enjoy the dark for a couple of seconds.

But Shel had overheard him. He was consulting his top-secret little pad. 'After turning your back on escort assignment, Adam Shade, you fast-tracked through the ranks in just three years. As an Earthborn, the fact that you were willing to serve at all, let alone out here on the frontier, guaranteed you favourable treatment.' Shel smiled, got up and started showing the pad to every trooper in turn. Interested eyes scanned the text, lips were pursed, heads were shaken. 'You accepted this without question at first – until the looks your squad were giving you finally began hurting more than the hits you were taking off the Kay-Dees.'

Shade listened in horror. He wanted to yell at Shel to stop but his throat was too dry, too tight, the words piled up there.

Denni read some more of his file. Her face filled with disgust.

'So you went all-out to prove you had what it took. You risked everything to make good.'

Creben threw his head back and laughed when the pad was waved under his nose.

Shade stared at the rest of the squad in panic.

'The Schirr assault on New Jersey seemed the perfect opportunity –'

'*That's enough*,' Shade shouted.

Everyone turned and stared at him. Except Shel, who was focussed entirely on inputting some data to his palmscreen, still strapped into his couch like the rest.

'What's enough, Shadow?' asked Denni, a trace of annoyance in her dark eyes.

Shade shook his head, screwed up his eyes, willed himself not to fall asleep and start dreaming again. 'Nothing. Sorry.'

'Shadow's losing it.' Joiks wore a sly smile beneath his crooked nose. 'Hey, stay with us, buddy. We need you.'

'Yeah, any holes in the road, Denni'll let you jump and see how deep they get,' laughed Lindey.

Shade forced a smile, turned away, tried to focus on what was real. He put his hand to his face, felt the hard lumps under the skin that still didn't seem right or normal, even two years on. He listened to the mocking banter of the rest of the unit. Wondered what thoughts went through *their* minds at the words 'active service'.

III

Shel fed the two Kill-Droids their sealed orders and activated their release program from the bridge. The only way Haunt knew that the creatures had vanished into the depths of the asteroid was when the squad viewed the pulverised packaging left behind.

An hour later, Haunt sent her personnel off ship with a blast of orders and threats. Not even she was entirely sure which were which.

They scrambled down the flexible ladders that stretched down from the bright ship into the dark, wet pit of the planetoid's entry zone, their websets recording motion and emotion alike. Haunt led the commandos through the darkness until they came to a large circular chamber. Joiks immediately christened it the bullring. Five further tunnels had been drilled into the rock, stretching away into the dark.

At Haunt's command, the ten quickly split into groups of two. Haunt chose Shel to partner her, and directed each pair to take a different tunnel. The groups sprinted into the pitch-blackness, weighed down with torches and guns.

Haunt checked her scanner. Multiple lights edged through its grids; the peak-level stats of her unit glowing brightly on a secret wavelength as they fanned out through the tunnels.

Somewhere in the dark, things were hiding that wanted them dead.

Haunt beckoned Shel to follow her and set off down the last remaining passageway.

'Do you reckon Haunt's OK?' Denni asked Joiks as they picked their way through the rubble-strewn tunnel.

Joiks came to a sudden halt. 'You're worried about her?' he asked in disbelief, and tapped the metal band round his head. 'You telling me this for her benefit, back at base debrief? Getting yourself some love from above…?'

Denni pulled off her webset.

Joiks stared at her in amazement. 'What's with you? Removing your webset –'

'Brain scramble,' Denni replied. She studied the workings in the band. 'My stats sometimes throw out the frequency, give me migraine.'

Joiks remembered hearing that had happened to Denni once before on an exercise. A freak occurrence Haunt had said. What were the chances of it happening again, and on a live ammo shoot? The webset was off now. Denni could tell a dozen barefaced lies, and who'd know?

She turned to him, cold and beautiful by torchlight. 'Give me yours. I need to fix the frequency.'

'Intermission,' Joiks announced, and flicked the band over to her. 'School's out.' He rubbed his hands through his close-cropped hair. He looked at her slyly. 'So – what's this really about? You don't want the world to know you've always loved me? Everyone knows that, Den!'

Denni grimaced. 'Like I say, it's Haunt. Something's not right. What she did to Shade –'

'Feelin' sorry for your Earthborn ex? Awww.'

'It was a little extreme, wouldn't you say? And the way she blew up at you just for mentioning Morphiea.'

'It's a real-ammo exercise,' Joiks said. 'Aren't *you* a little on edge?'

'Of course I am. But should our CO be?' Denni shook her head, answering her own dumb question. 'We're so close to Morphiean space… Too close. I think it's too much for her.'

'So she hates Morphieans. Hates their Spook guts. Seems a pretty good qualification for fighting them to me.'

'Duh? They *stopped* her fighting them! After what she did on New Jersey –'

Joiks scoffed. 'They had it coming.'

'And the human casualties.'

'We're at war. There gotta be casualties.'

'Most of the ones she fried were repatriated. On our side.'

'Still Schirr, still scum. Back in the Incendiaries we –'

'Enlightened, Joiks.' She kept her cool as usual. 'All I'm saying is, we *have* to follow her orders here. But what if they turn out to be bad orders, Joiks? After what she's been through –'

'What is this, *psychology*?' Joiks wasn't sure if he was amused or disgusted. 'She's too *involved* in all this, is that what you're saying?' He spat on the floor. 'She's a good soldier, Denni.'

'She *was* a *great* soldier.' Denni bunched her slim fists. 'All I'm saying is that her judgement may be shot because of her personal involvement with all this crap.'

'But you're saying it just in private to me, not on the record? Trying to turn us against her one by one, is that it? Gee, that's brave.'

'Jesus, Joiks, she's our CO.' Denni sighed. 'I'm not here just for the ride, I'm going career with the military. I want to *live* long enough to *go* career –'

He took a step closer. Took a chance and put his hands on her shoulders. She gave him a small smile. There was a tiny nervous flicker in her eyes.

'Hey, Den. You got the jitters? Is that what we're really talking about here?'

'No,' she said softly.

'Thought Stellar Infantry were tough bitches?' Joiks went on quietly, caressing her upper arms. 'You know, you got a problem with Haunt, you should've said before we got here.'

'How was I to know we'd wind up training here?' Denni took a step towards Joiks. 'Listen. I'm going to talk to the others. If enough of us lodge a complaint against her… right now… Cellmek would listen to us, I know it.'

So. She wanted something from him. Figured.

'You want out of this mission,' Joiks whispered softly. 'Don't you.'

'I want it led by someone detached. For all our sakes.' She moved closer to him.

He laughed uneasily.

She made eye contact again. Lowered her voice to a whisper. 'See… you don't know what we're going up against here.'

'And you do?'

Denni nodded. 'I reckon so. Bad, bad stuff, soldier.'

Joiks looked at her just a few moments more. Something in her voice sent a chill through him. He let go of her arms and took his webset, held it just over his head.

'If you're done checking your frequency, let's forget about this, OK? Concentrate on staying alive down here.' He paused, chanced a smile. 'And don't worry. I can keep a secret.'

Denni nodded. 'I'm glad. Because so can I.'

He watched her place the webset back over her dreadlocks and followed her into the darkness.

IV

Marshal Nadina Haunt moved quickly and freely, feeling a part of herself coming alive as she angled her gun into every corner of the thick shadows thrown up by her torch beam. But after a few minutes, the tunnel was becoming lighter, she was sure of it.

She checked with Shel, who didn't answer until he'd taken an environment scan. Exactly by the book as usual.

He nodded at last. 'Luminescence has increased by over five per cent.'

'Source?'

'Not known, Marshal.'

Something ahead of them, high up above them, glistened silver in Haunt's torchbeam. She raised her gun.

'What is it, Shel?'

Shel marched over to the side of the tunnel. His own light showed a damp, glistening morass of flat, slab-like leaves edging down the walls from the stone ceilings.

'Some kind of climbing plant is growing here, Marshal,' he reported. 'The leaves have some slight luminous property.'

'Nice to know we're not being left entirely in the dark.'

She moved off down the dank corridor in the rock.

She only stopped when she and Shel came up against a set of ornately carved doors that appeared to have been made from gold.

They swung open soundlessly as if awaiting Haunt's touch. The space beyond was darker, but just as silent.

Shel was looking at her, uneasily. Questioningly.

Haunt nodded. 'We go in.'

Gripping their guns, Marshal Haunt and her adjutant moved cautiously through the doorway.

V

'So where are we, Doctor?' asked Ben as the demented grinding and wailing of the TARDIS landing motors gradually died away.

'I know where we are,' the Doctor announced, 'but I'm afraid I cannot pinpoint our location within that district.' He was still playing with his switches, but vaguely, distractedly now. The way Ben's dad used to try his luck fixing the family motor; when all else failed, fiddling with bits of engine he didn't understand, just in case one of them magically started the car.

Polly sighed. 'Doctor, are you saying that you know we might be on Earth, say, but that you don't know if we're in Africa or Timbuktu?'

'Very neatly put, Polly, yes.' The Doctor bestowed a warm smile on her. 'Except, I'm afraid, we're definitely in a galaxy very distant from the Earth's. Very distant indeed.'

'That narrows it down then,' Ben remarked.

The Doctor didn't find the comment facetious. 'Quite so, my boy, quite so. And we have landed inside a structure of some kind, of that I am sure. The temperature is very cold... and there's no air, either. A vacuum.' He looked up, deep in thought, tapping his chin. 'An asteroid perhaps, too small to retain an atmosphere?'

Polly turned up her long straight nose. 'Sounds like fun.'

'Well, it will be a good opportunity to field test the spacesuits. I've had them in storage for some time.'

Ben frowned. 'Spacesuits?' He couldn't imagine the Doctor in full Yuri Gagarin gear.

'Oh yes, the TARDIS is very well equipped, you know.' He chuckled and turned to Polly. 'And they come in a range of colours, my dear.'

Polly clapped her hands. 'Fab!'

'But we don't know if it's even safe out there,' Ben protested.

'Don't fuss, my boy,' said the Doctor. 'I must take some readings, some measurements for the log... it shouldn't take us very long...'

VI

Haunt turned to Shel. 'Is all this part of the simulation?'

Shel stared blankly back at her.

'You programmed the tactical computers, fed through the droids' orders. You must know something about the testing ground.'

'The location was selected entirely by Pentagon Central,' Shel stated. 'Were I to be given any advance knowledge of the simulation, it would be rendered less effective. I know as much as you do.' He paused. 'However, it seems to me that certain aspects of the architectural style would suggest a Schirr influence.'

Haunt nodded. 'Go on.'

Shel shrugged. 'Ruins found and reconstructed after the destruction of the northern continents share several of the features we have observed here.'

The golden doors led onto a corridor, and were flanked by a set of large bronze double doors; neither of which they had been able to open. The corridor came to a kind of hall hollowed from the slates and silts of the asteroid's mantle, palatial both in size and decoration, like some kind of ancient tomb for long-dead kings. The walls were jagged, gleaming damp and black in the glare of torchlight. Huge stone statues of abstract figures, vaguely humanoid, loomed out at them from the shadows. The fat, thick leaves of the faintly-glowing plant covered the ceilings. From out of the seaweed-like morass, tapestries of cut-glass hung down from the high-vaulted ceilings. They caught the torch beams and fooled with the bright light, passing it from shard to shard.

'It would make sense to incorporate Schirr architecture in the testing ground's design,' Shel commented. 'DeCaster and Pallemar's dissenters are the only significant threat to Earth's empire besides the Morphiean Quadrant. It makes the battleground more relevant.' He paused. 'If we knew anything of Morphiean constructs, Pentagon Central would doubtless have drawn inspiration from them...'

Haunt was no longer listening to Shel. Instead she checked for team vitals on her scanner.

And swore.

The grid, instead of showing four neat pinprick pairs glowing close to those of herself and Shel, was an insane constellation of lights.

She waved it in Shel's face. 'Must be a fault. Try your own.'

Shel scrolled through different screens until the same lunatic pattern of lights appeared. He met Haunt's gaze steadily. 'It would seem this entire place is alive.'

Even as Shel spoke, Haunt noticed a small swift movement by her feet, and froze. For a second she thought she'd imagined it, but then she saw the movement again, arcing past her eyes. A tiny bead of light hopped onto the back of Shel's hand. She slapped her own hand down on the back of his. Then she peered at a pale smear on her palm.

'Some kind of insect,' she remarked. Its body was a translucent sack, half emptied on her skin. 'It hopped like a flea.'

Shel peered at the insect. 'It's like nothing I've seen,' he whispered. 'Must live on the plants. Though how any life could survive here…'

'We're here, aren't we?' Haunt retorted. 'It's just a part of the place. Part of the simulation.' Another grain of light hopped past, fleeting in the corner of her vision. 'A distraction. Here to keep us on edge.'

Shel nodded uncertainly. 'It has to be. In any case, our instruments are picking up their life-signs.'

'And swamping our own team's stats. The scanners are useless down here. We can't track each other.'

Shel nodded. 'Hopefully, neither can anything else.'

Haunt raised the comms bracelet to her lips. 'Creben.'

'Unit One responding, Marshal.' The voice snapped back immediately, cutting tinnily through the dank air. 'Our scanners are all messed up. Thousands of life-signs.'

'Bugs,' Haunt whispered. 'This place is crawling with insects.'

'Marshal. The walls are thick with them.' Lindey's voice sounded shriller than normal. 'There's plant life of some kind on –'

'I know. Check up on everyone else, see if it's the same story. Report back.'

'Marshal.' It was Creben's voice that signed off.

Haunt lowered the bracelet, and she and Shel waited in silence. More and more of the insects hopped and jumped around their feet, on their combat suits, through the air around them. She felt her wrist-comm vibrate.

'Well, Creben?'

'Same story in each direction. Except for Unit Three. They've got some weed, but no fleas.'

Shel frowned.

Haunt spoke back to the bracelet. 'Denni.'

'Unit Three responding.' Denni's voice sounded flat and calm.

'Tell me what you see.'

'It's completely dark here now,' Denni said. 'Marshal, our scanner's useless.'

34

Haunt looked up at Shel. 'The websets won't function in total darkness, will they?'

'Not well,' he replied. 'It's optic stimulation that triggers the record.'

Haunt nodded. 'All right, Denni. Report back if the situation changes.'

'Marshal.'

Haunt indicated to Shel they should move on. More of the dark slate had been piled up into craggy pillars at regular intervals; they looked as if they had grown from the stone. Two of them, monstrously large and each topped with an angular crest, flanked a large circular doorway that seemed to lead from this vast chamber to another.

One of the insects hopped on to the back of Haunt's hand. She brushed it off, crushed it as she did so.

She and Shel walked inside.

VII

More than the fat white insects that flicked around them, the shadows were getting to Lindey. Cast by the gently glowing leaves, dull and shifting over the darker rock, they played tricks on your eyes. Years in the Zero-Gs had left her accustomed to most battlegrounds in space, to fighting in the stark, unchanging light of stars and moons. This cramped gloom and her slow, careful steps made her feel heavy and uncomfortable, like she and Creben were trapped in an endless mire.

She checked her scanner for the hundredth time. She willed the flickering mass of lights on the scanner to vanish, to reveal ten healthy heartbeats huddled close together.

'What the hell are we doing here?' she asked Creben softly.

'Making sure we don't end up as cannon fodder for the Empire,' he answered quietly, barely moving his lips.

Lindey raised an eyebrow, impressed by the honest answer. 'So you make Elite and stay away from the front line?'

'The war with Morphiea won't be like that,' he told her. 'We can't nuke their strongholds, kill their troops, batter them into submission like we did the Schirr. It'll be a cold war. The coldest the Empire's ever known.'

'You have a talent for melodrama,' Lindey told him lightly. 'So, what, it's going to be special operations only in the Elite for you? Counter-intelligence, espionage…'

While Lindey poked her torch beam into random nooks and corners in the rock, Creben's light cut through the darkness with surgical precision. 'I'm going to use my mind, if that's what you mean, yes.'

'So why are you risking your body down here with us, then?' she asked. 'How come you didn't go down the Intelligence route?'

He turned and smiled at her, but the shadows were doing unflattering things with the neat, sharp lines of his face. 'It took me time to realise where my true interests lie.' His gaze lowered from her eyes, flicked up and down her. 'Besides, maybe there are some bodies worth taking risks for.'

She shone the torch straight in his eyes. 'You can stop right there.'

He was about to retort, but she shushed him. 'Hey. Behind you.'

Creben turned, and saw what her torch beam had illuminated. 'Symbols of some kind,' he noted.

Lindey touched the wall with her fingers. 'The rock's been smoothed out…'

'The better to carve into, presumably,' Creben said dryly.

'Forgive my humble stab at military intelligence.'

'Forgiven, and best forgotten.'

She gave him the smallest of smiles. 'There are other ways to get security and prestige, you know. Without risking your body or your mind.'

Creben raised an eyebrow. 'Use someone else's?'

Lindey decided she would have to watch Creben.

'This carving,' he said. 'Perhaps it's a sign.' He smiled, that smug little grin of his. 'Hungry cannons, this way.'

Lindey didn't smile back at him as they continued down the tunnel.

Haunt and Shel pushed on through the chambers.

The next room, and the next, were much the same, except they also contained less stylised sculptures of outsized angels moulded into their ceilings and at the base of each pillar.

In each dank chamber they passed through they found more and more of the strange carvings clustered together as if for warmth.

Haunt noticed Shel was gripping his gun so tightly his knuckles were showing white. 'The increasing numbers of statues,' she said, 'suggests we're nearing somewhere important, would you agree?'

Shel nodded. 'Whatever it is, I think we might've reached it.'

There was a recess in the rock ahead of them. Drawing nearer, they saw a silver door embedded in the slate. Haunt kicked it open to reveal a tunnel big enough for a single person to move through at a time.

'If we go through there and something's waiting for us,' Shel muttered, 'we won't stand a chance.'

'I'll go in first,' Haunt said. 'Wait here and cover this entrance while I take a look. I don't want anything following me in here that isn't you.'

Shel nodded, and Haunt walked away into the pitch-blackness.

VIII

The TARDIS doors opened with the usual penetrating hum, and with the added beeping of some device that was depressurising the control room.

Ben felt a bit of a prat in his new astronaut gear. It was more like a wetsuit than a spacesuit, and made from a dull green quilted material which felt a little too snug for comfort in all the wrong areas. The worst of it was the headgear; like looking out from a crystal ball.

'How do I look?' Polly's voice crackled in his ears over the suit's communicators.

Ben turned and whistled at the sight of Polly in her skintight daffodil-yellow suit. 'Let's just say I hope this bleedin' goldfish bowl don't steam up easily.'

'Come along you two,' came the Doctor's voice, disapprovingly. 'We don't know quite what's out there, so stay close to me.' So saying, he led the way out of the ship, fussing and pulling at his own spacesuit, which was dark blue. It was hard to believe he had his usual clothes on beneath the thermal material; his body looked thin and wasted and his head disproportionately big through the glass helmet as a result. The old boy really did look like a buzzard now.

Ben and Polly followed him out, then the Doctor closed the doors. The comforting light spilling out from the control room narrowed to a slit then vanished altogether.

'Don't lock them, Doctor,' Ben suggested as casually as he could. 'You never know, we might need to get back inside in a hurry.'

The Doctor nodded vaguely.

For a few seconds the blackness was absolute. 'Dark, isn't it,' said Polly. He felt her lightly grip his arm, and gave her hand a comforting squeeze he hoped she could feel through her quilted gloves.

Then the Doctor flicked on his torch. The beam revealed small snatches of the cavernous room they stood in, and from them, Ben tried to build a picture of their surroundings.

The room, or cave, or whatever it was, was five-sided. The walls were built from layers and layers of dark stone, and scaled by ornate metal trellises that gleamed like gold. Above these, what looked to be ducting reached right around the room at the point where the walls sloped up to the high, arched ceiling. Slabs of glass had been set into this roof, hundreds of them, and they winked and signalled back at the Doctor whenever he shone his torch in their direction.

Closer to ground level, banks of weird-looking machinery squatted beneath the trellises. Symbols carved in the slate above presumably denoted the function of each set of controls in whatever language they spoke here.

'Fascinating,' the Doctor said fervently. 'The functionality of a control room but with the trappings of a shrine...'

Ben was considering the ramifications of this when the Doctor's torchlight fell on a cowled shape hunched over a console right beside them, overlooked until now by the far-stretching beam. He felt Polly's grip on his arm tighten and her distorted scream in his ears nearly deafened him.

Ben took a few steps back, instinctively.

A hideous alien face was staring out at him from under the cowl. Its eyes were wide like a fish's, unseeing.

It was lying in a mass of dried blood.

IX

'Come on out, Kay-Deeeeees. I got a mouthful of laser waiting just-for-yooooou…'

'Shut it, Frog.' Roba's gun pointed the way ahead through the darkness. 'You know, I hate your crazy voice already. If you're a frog, swallow some of these damned bugs.' He looked down at her in the gloom, her bulging eyes, stubbly head, her twisted grin. He wondered how she just carried on, as messed up as she was. Then his sympathy snapped into annoyance as she started up her crackling warble again and waved her rifle about.

'We should take out every one of these bugs, Roba.'

'You're crazy.'

'Every one of them.' She slapped a hand over a mass of them quivering on the wall, and wiped it down the curve of her hip. 'Get some numbers on the scanner we can count.'

Roba shook his head again. 'Why'd I get paired with you?'

'Just lucky, honey.'

'*You* ain't.'

Frog shrugged. The half-smile stayed on her lips as usual.

A few metres later, the tunnel ended in big, bronzed double doors.

'Bet they lead someplace bad,' Frog observed.

XI

'What is it, Doctor?' Ben asked, his voice cracking high in alarm. He turned away from the hideous, glistening head of the thing, sickened.

But before the Doctor could reply, a low rumbling note sounded in the cavern, not carried by the spacesuits' helmets.

'There's air in here,' Polly realised, holding on to Ben now with both arms. 'If we can hear something outside the helmets, there must be air, to carry the sound.'

'Indeed,' muttered the Doctor. A faint display flickered over the glass of his helmet. 'Yes, and I believe it's breatheable.'

'But Doctor,' Ben protested, 'you said –'

'– that there was a vacuum in here, yes,' said the Doctor irritably. 'It would seem the situation has changed.'

'It's getting lighter, too,' breathed Polly. The globe of her helmet knocked against Ben's as she looked around.

Ben swallowed hard. 'She's right, Doctor.' The broken glass above them was glowing now, magnifying the light the Doctor had thrown at the ceiling a hundred times.

Another deep, sonorous tone rang out, and the grating of metal on rock.

Polly looked terrified. 'What's happening?'

The Doctor came over to stand beside them, gesturing to the far wall where a pentagonal shape glowed with a cold sodium brightness. 'It would appear a doorway is opening.'

Ben ripped the helmet from his suit and gulped down musty air. 'Something's coming?'

'Coming to get us!' Polly breathed as she took off her own space helmet and gripped it tightly in both hands. 'To get us like it got that horrible thing there!'

'Perhaps,' said the Doctor, heavily. 'And I wonder, did these unfortunate creatures here share in its fate?'

The Doctor was gesturing to a glassy rectangular shape standing on a raised flat dais beside the TARDIS. They'd missed it in the dark. Now, in the rippling sparkle of the growing light, Ben watched transfixed as grotesque nightmare shapes began to form inside the glass. Dark shadows gradually resolved themselves into twisted humanoid figures the same size and shape as the dead thing in the chair.

The space helmet slipped from Ben's fingers and cracked open on the ground.

He was staring at monsters, frozen in glass at the moment of violent death.

Chapter Three
Death Comes as the End

I

There were nine of the creatures. They were massive, alien. The heavy lumpen faces were contorted in pain. Each one was dressed in once-white robes now caked black with dried blood.

Ben turned to Polly. She stared at the waxwork-like horrors for a few moments, then screamed.

The door in the wall had ground almost fully open. Golden light spilled into the chamber through the pentagonal entrance.

'Quiet, Pol!' Ben hissed, grabbing hold of her and turning her away from the gory sight.

'Quickly,' the Doctor rapped, cutting Polly off in mid-yell. 'Back to the TARDIS!'

Ben tried to manhandle Polly, still clutching her space helmet, into the police box. But something was wrong. She wouldn't shift. 'Come on girl, pick your feet up,' he urged her, fighting down the panic rising inside him.

'I can't move, Ben,' Polly cried. 'I want to, but I can't!'

Ben felt his head start to spin, and a noise like rushing water in his ears. He left Polly and turned round to call for the Doctor to help him. The light shining through the doorway lit up the glass that housed the bloody figures. The Doctor was silhouetted against the glow. Slowly, awkwardly, he took a few steps towards Ben.

Ben turned back to Polly and found she'd vanished.

He gaped. 'Doctor? Polly, she's just… gone.'

'Impossible, my boy,' the Doctor said weakly, as he removed his own space helmet and placed it on the ground. 'She can't just have disappeared. We merely did not see her leave.'

'What's the difference? She's gone!' Ben felt stricken. The roaring noise became thicker in his ears. 'And a few seconds ago she couldn't move anywhere!'

But even as he spoke, the noise in Ben's ears ebbed away, as did the dizziness. The Doctor fell into Ben's arms suddenly like a puppet with cut strings. Ben sagged a little under his weight, but the Doctor soon recovered; Ben imagined the furious look the old man gave him was designed to cover his embarrassment at collapsing. A moment or so later his expression softened, and he looked at Ben with evident concern. Then he turned to face the open doorway, shielding Ben behind him.

A burly figure walked out of the light, dressed in a dark grey military uniform, holding a box in one hand and a dirty great gun in the other. The gory display case was between them for a few moments, then the figure moved into plain view, looking around cautiously.

'Stone me,' Ben muttered. 'It's a bird!'

The woman looked in their direction and froze. Light glinted off a sort of metal band she wore round her forehead.

'She's seen us,' murmured the Doctor. He took a step forward, his hands going automatically to where his lapels would've been beneath his suit and floundering as they tried to grip the quilted fabric. 'Madam,' he began, 'forgive me, I do hope our presence here doesn't come at an unpropitious time?'

The woman stared at them in absolute shock for a moment.

Then she raised her gun.

II

Polly stared about fearfully. It was dark. Cold. One minute she'd been with Ben and the Doctor, and the next...

It all seemed a blur. She'd wanted to get away, so desperately, wanted to run headlong from the opening door in the wall. She'd had a feeling of flight, of disorientating movement, and then found herself here, all on her own. The fishbowl-like space helmet rocked gently on the ground at her feet.

It was a cave or something, deep underground. She'd gone to some caves once, nice and safe touristy caves, when she was eight. She'd run about the place in a bright red raincoat pretending she was a lost damsel, that there was no one else down there with her except for dragons. Except then, when she strayed too far from the crowd, when the fantasy became too scary, there was a daddy to rush back to, grown-up hands to hold. Now she was on her own. Not even with any dragons. Definitely no dragons, she told herself.

And kept telling herself.

There was only one thing to do, she knew that. To strike out on her own down these dark tunnels. To try and work out a route back to Ben and the Doctor. She could mark the walls with her lipstick... No, she was wearing this ridiculous spacesuit, no pockets. She could maybe chalk arrows on the wall? No chalk, and it was too dark to see anyway. Then inspiration hit her. She could build a little cairn of stones at the mouth of every tunnel she walked along. That might work.

Five minutes and two chipped nails later, she had made her first marker. Now, lip trembling, wiping her eyes with the back of her hand, she headed into the echoing dark of the tunnel.

She told herself that the whispering voices she could hear in the thick shadows were just her imagination.

III

As Ben opened his mouth to yell at the army woman to stop – a pretty pathetic gesture, but it was all he could think of to do – another soldier ran through the doorway. This one really was a fella, an oriental sort. He wore a headband like the woman, and like her he raised his gun in their direction, but Ben was gratified to see his real attention seemed taken by the figures on the dais.

'Marshal.'

The woman didn't react at the sound of his low, calm voice, but she didn't sound happy. 'I told you to remain where you were, Shel, covering the entrance.'

'I thought I heard you scream,' Shel said, still staring intently at the figures, like they were people he thought he knew.

She snorted. 'You think I'm the screaming type?'

'Marshal, *look.*'

'I am looking,' snapped the marshal. Her gun was still trained on the Doctor. 'These aren't droids. What the hell are these people doing here?'

'We arrived purely by chance,' said the Doctor, beaming benignly. Ben didn't fancy any amount of old-world charm would work against this high-tech old bruiser. He wasn't surprised when she didn't smile back.

'Not them, Marshal...' This was Charlie Chan again. '*These*...'

Only now did Shel's marshal take in the corpse in the chair to her left and the gruesome line-up to her right. After a few seconds her face finally took on some wonder at the sight. 'Schirr bodies?'

Shel nodded. 'They've been chipped. Criminals. Look at the branding on the chests.'

Ben saw from the corner of his eye that the Doctor was slowly edging towards the TARDIS doors. Not wanting to draw attention to the old boy with his eyeline, he swallowed hard and forced himself to look more closely at the bodies on the dais.

They all looked pretty similar. Each had a broad, round head, mottled pink. The eyes were milky-white and bulging, with pupils dilated to dirty red specks. The ears drooped down like melted wax from the smooth sides of the head, and the nose was a fat blob, nostrils thick with bristling hair. The lips were the most grotesque thing about each face, though: full and thick and rubbery, they lent the creatures a sort of obscenely sensuous appearance.

And now Ben came to look at the burst chest of the one on the far end that had taken Shel's attention, he could see that there was some kind of weird symbol burnt into the smooth flesh above the wound. Like a long thin rectangle crossed through with a diagonal line.

'My god,' the marshal breathed. She lowered the gun and looked at Shel, her face a mix of emotions. 'What kind of a trick...'

The two of them stared helplessly at the bodies in utter amazement.

The Doctor had reached the TARDIS doors. Ben clenched his fists.

44

What was he doing, they couldn't go without Polly –

But the doors wouldn't open.

Ben could see the Doctor pushing with all his strength against them. Then he looked round at Ben, furiously, like it was somehow his fault.

'No,' said the marshal, dragging her gaze from the monsters back to the Doctor and looking oddly pleased with herself. 'No, I don't think so.' She raised her gun again, strode closer to them all. 'The corpses of the most wanted criminals in all Earth's empire, just waiting around to be discovered by a military unit on manoeuvres? Not very likely, is it?'

Shel was frowning. 'But Marshal –'

'Oh, come on, Shel,' she sneered. 'This is a live ammo exercise, remember? DeCaster, dead? And here? It's a trap. It has to be.'

The Doctor cleared his throat. 'It may be a trap, yes, it may well be,' he said airily. 'But it is not one set by us.'

'Is that a fact. Just who are you?' the marshal demanded.

'I am the Doctor.'

Ben stood to attention. 'Able Seaman Ben Jackson, HMS *Teazer*. I mean... well, that's my ship, see...'

He trailed off. The marshal's face was darkening with every syllable.

'As I mentioned earlier,' the Doctor said quickly, 'our party arrived here purely by chance, and one of our number –'

The woman glanced over at Shel, casually. 'This is part of a trap. I'm going to kill them.'

'You can't!' Ben protested. 'What have we done to you!'

'This is outrageous behaviour.' The Doctor was clearly bristling.

The woman was unmoved by any of it.

Shel spoke gravely: 'Marshal Haunt, that is in direct contravention of the Codes and Ethics of War.'

'We're on a training exercise,' Haunt pointed out wearily.

'That is an absurd distinction,' the Doctor retorted. 'Now if you'd only listen to us, Marshal... Haunt was it...?'

The name suited her, Ben decided. She was quite a big girl, around Polly's height but stockier, and she could've been the jolly sort.

Instead she had a troubled look about her, a pained expression in her eyes, like she'd taken some bad news in the past that had never got any better.

Shel spoke again, his voice dead calm, like they were discussing the price of tea or something. 'Procedure is to take any civilians into safekeeping.'

'Civilians? On this speck?' Haunt looked unconvinced. Her space-age rifle still pointed their way.

'We are travellers,' the Doctor said. 'You could call us refugees in an experimental craft.' To Ben's surprise he gestured to the TARDIS. 'One that bends the dimensions, passing through solid matter.'

'I don't believe you,' said Haunt simply.

But Shel was nodding. 'In the Japanese Belt such technology is being developed. It *is* a possible explanation. But it's also possible they're part of the team that set this place up.'

Haunt looked uncertainly at Ben and the Doctor. 'Well?' she asked.

'As you observe, we are helpless civilians trapped in this terrible place,' said the Doctor mildly. 'We cannot escape here, and we look to you for protection. So too does our friend Polly,' he added hurriedly. 'She can't be far away but I am dreadfully worried about her. Dreadfully.'

Haunt's face darkened. 'There's more of you wandering about here?'

'Only her.'

Ben wondered what the Doctor was up to, telling these maniacs about Polly.

He spun round as a new voice rang out: 'What the hell…?'

A black bloke strode through the five-sided doorway this time. A huge great geezer, he carried a slim rectangular pack on his back, a space-age kit bag.

'Roba?' Haunt rounded on him. 'What's going on, where's Frog.'

'Outside on guard.' Roba was massive, but Ben could tell Haunt had the power to make him feel two inches tall. 'Our tunnel led to some weird tomb-place. We went through the circles and found them silver doors.'

'All right,' Haunt snapped. 'Shel, brief Roba on…' She broke off. 'On whatever the hell is happening.'

'Yes, Marshal,' said Shel, unfazed.

Ben held his breath as Haunt stalked closer.

Her eyes narrowed. Her finger was still curled round the trigger of her rifle. 'So. Your ship was attacked? You strayed into the Spook Quadrant?'

'I'm not familiar with your terminology for this area of space, though I'm sure you are right,' said the Doctor with a tight smile.

'You have a deathwish,' she said.

'If it is so dangerous, why are you training close by?'

'It's still Earth space.' Haunt smiled tightly. 'Our destiny is in the stars, the pioneers used to say.'

The Doctor raised an eyebrow. 'Well, that's a fine sentiment, yes. Ours too is in the stars, and really, Marshal, look at us.' He tittered to himself. 'An old man, a boy... and somewhere nearby, I hope, a young girl. Can we be much of a threat to you and your men, hmm? Can we?'

IV

Polly checked the rocky mouth to this latest passageway for one of her piles of stones, for some sign she'd been walking round in circles. She would've taken the news as a comfort, that this place wasn't big enough to get truly lost in. But her hands met nothing except cold wet stone, and the tickle of the flea-things that jumped and skittered about in the gloom. They made Polly's flesh crawl, as if they were swarming all over her, just as the glowing weed crowded over the rocky roof above, dimly lighting her way. She felt she could be under the sea.

But as she entered the new tunnel, she realised a new light was seeping into her view. Polly caught her breath. There was a window in the rock. She supposed it must be some kind of glass but it was smearless, free of all distortion. Through it she could see a night sky beautiful and brilliant with stars. They looked like diamonds, like she could stick out her hand and take one in her palm.

Not under the sea then. In space.

'We're definitely in a galaxy very distant from the Earth's. Very distant indeed.'

Polly took a deep breath and turned away from the window, willed herself to stay calm. The TARDIS had brought her here. The TARDIS would take her away again. All she had to do was find it.

Instead, she found two people crossing her path stealthily along an adjoining tunnel: a black woman with the most amazing blonde dread-locks, and a man following on behind her. Both were armed to the teeth.

Seeing the man in profile revealed a nose that had surely been broken a half-dozen times. As he shot a glance up 'her' tunnel, Polly thought she could see the faintest of cocky smiles on his face. She shivered, reminded of the type of bruiser that had hassled her so many times in bars and clubs all over London. So many close calls...

She pressed herself up against the wall, hoping the pair wouldn't notice her in the shadowy mouth of the tunnel. Were they hunting for her? Polly wished now she hadn't chosen to wear what was probably the only spacesuit in daffodil yellow in the universe.

The two figures walked past with only a cursory glance down the tunnel that hid Polly, and she breathed a sigh of relief. She was alone again. All alone. Except of course, for however many others there could be waiting for her down here.

Polly bit her lip. Once she was sure the couple were too far away to hear her, she crossed into their tunnel and crept down it in the opposite direction. Soon she came to a gaping hole in the rock to her right, a side-tunnel that twisted off into the darkness. She decided to take it. The roof was higher than in some of the others, and the abundance of weed made it lighter, less claustrophobic.

But as she moved cautiously through it, a slow, rhythmic sound ebbed into her ears. A hissing, throbbing, pulsating noise, weird and alien.

The walls seemed to shift and shimmer around her. A bright blue light seeped in to the tunnel like water into a sewer, and with it a strange kind of noise, almost like a pressure in her ears. Polly felt giddy, nauseous. For a second she was acutely homesick, remembering late-night London spinning her its sights and sounds, reeling in drunkenness as she staggered with friends in search of a cab, night-life neon reflected in dark street puddles. Moving on to the next party, the logical next step of the night.

This was the sound of something starting.

Polly found herself staggering now, wobbling as if in towering heels towards the blue light.

V

Ben breathed a sigh of relief as Haunt stalked back over to join Roba and Shel by the body in the chair.

'All right,' she announced with bad grace. 'Seems we're landed with some refugees.'

'Refugees…' The black giant, Roba, considered, then nodded. 'State of those 'suits they're wearing, I'll buy that.'

Ben glanced at the Doctor. Under any other circumstances, the look of outrage on his face would've been hilarious.

'Seems the Spooks opened fire on them, here on the fringes,' said Haunt.

Roba nodded. 'Figures. "No human shall feel secure…" Just like they said. Stepping up the terror campaign.'

Shel looked over at the bodies hunched up on the dais. 'While the ones they're after are right here?'

'They *must* be part of the simulation,' Haunt said dismissively.

'This one is branded too,' said Shel quietly, crouching over the grisly alien corpse in the chair. He had raised the bloodstained robe from its shoulder and was indicating something in the flesh beneath. 'Pentagon coding. It's Pallemar all right, he's been chipped. No one can forge these data codes.'

'So this really is DeCaster's Ten-strong? And all dead?' Roba looked at Shel. 'No way. You're kidding me, right?'

Shel shook his head. As he showed Roba and Haunt whatever his handheld gadget was showing, Ben turned to the Doctor.

'We have to find Polly and get out of here.'

'Quite so, my boy,' the Doctor said vaguely. He was looking intently at his surroundings as if taking them in properly for the first time.

'Where do you think she went, Doctor? I mean, how can she just have disappeared?'

'She didn't,' the Doctor informed him curtly. 'There must be a concealed exit here somewhere. This chamber was sealed, airtight.' He sighed. 'In any case… as I said to Marshal Haunt, we require the assistance of our soldier friends if we are to find her. I very much doubt they will let us go looking by ourselves.'

Ben felt sick. 'How come the TARDIS doors won't open?'

'I don't know, my boy,' the Doctor confessed. 'That humming noise that started up when the doors opened… I believe it was some kind of generator, setting up the force field you see around these bodies.'

Ben felt foolish. 'I thought that was glass or something.'

'No,' said the Doctor. 'It's a protective enclosure, triggered no doubt by the rush of air into the room. In the vacuum the bodies couldn't decay. This mechanism was designed to react to anyone entering this room through that doorway.'

'But why?'

The Doctor hushed him. He was listening again to the huddle of commandos.

Haunt was looking at the bodies again. 'We'd better contact Cellmek at the Academy, tell him to let everyone go home early,' she said dryly. 'The Empire's most wanted have saved us the bother of hunting them down. They've killed themselves and kindly put themselves on display for army inspection.'

'What about them two.' Roba scowled at the two strangers. Ben saw the Doctor nod politely as if greeting the vicar.

Haunt raised her comms bracelet to her mouth. 'Frog.'

'Marshal.'

'Join us in here. Move.' Haunt turned to Shel and Roba. 'Frog can take them back to the ship. Meanwhile, we'll warn the others to watch out for this girl, and anyone else out there.'

'Seems this lump of rock is getting awful crowded,' Roba rumbled. 'Ain't it meant to be just us and a couple of droids?'

'And they're still out there,' Shel said quietly. 'Programmed to kill. We can't shut them off.'

Haunt swore. 'Wrong… everything about this is wrong.'

* * *

It didn't take Polly long to find the source of the weird blue light. She came to a tottering halt before a lip of rock jutting out into a huge cavern, staring dreamily at an ethereal cyan sea rolling along both the floor and the ceiling far below.

'Light waves,' she murmured happily.

It was an incredible display. The intensity of the light was growing stronger as the 'waves' grew fiercer. Reaching and rebounding against the far walls of the cavern the light seemed to splash out into the air. The spray from the oceans above and below mingled in the middle and crackled with energy. They were forming shapes, numbers, weird mathematical equations. And although the amount of spray seemed to be growing greater, Polly saw that the value of the numbers was getting smaller.

'Like counting down the hit parade,' she said with a familiar thrill of excitement.

Suddenly she frowned. On the far side of the freaky projection, she saw movement. A figure, blurred and hazy, moved stealthily among the rocks.

Polly tried to focus on the figure but the radio static in her head was growing louder, a near-deafening pressure that continued to build. She leaned back against the tunnel wall. A part of her told her that it wasn't safe to stay here, that she should go back, but while she tried to concentrate on the words they were lost over the raging of the unnatural sea.

Close by, over the noise, she heard a low, powerful whine, like a dozen flashbulbs charging up. She frowned. Was someone going to take her picture? She looked down at herself, saw a smear of dirt on the bright yellow leg of her spacesuit, crouched to brush it clean.

She shrieked as a blast of heat singed her hair and an explosion threw her forward along with half of the wall behind her. She gasped with pain, as the stinging wet slap of her palms against the gritty tunnel floor broke the spell she'd been under. Polly looked up to see a huge, hovering shadow wreathed in smoke from the explosion. Red laser eyes shone into her own, blinding her. With a squeak of terror Polly scrambled up and ran.

She heard the building charge of the flashbulbs again.

Chapter Four
While the Light Lasts

I

Ben joined the Doctor as he walked stiffly over to join the two troopers, raising his hands to show he meant them no harm. Addressing Roba, he nodded back at the monsters on the dais. 'I take it, young man, that you recognise these poor, unfortunate creatures here?'

'Unfortunate?' Roba looked like the Doctor had just spat at his mother. 'What're you talking about, unfortunate?'

'Well, of course, unfortunate only in that... Well, they are dead, after all,' the Doctor blustered.

'Wouldn't have them any other way,' Roba hissed. 'Schirr scum.'

The Doctor looked at him sharply. 'Ah, but the manner of their death. Held in stasis for all to see. What of that, hmm?'

'Keep quiet,' Haunt said warningly.

The Doctor turned to Shel, whose eyes met his own. 'It's bothering *you*, sir, is it not? These creatures are not fake, they are real flesh...' He turned up his nose distastefully at the crimson mess at their feet. 'And real blood, of course.'

Roba clenched his fists. 'Look, man –'

The Doctor raised his voice, losing patience, acting as if the hulk of a man was just some upstart kid speaking out of turn in the old boy's classroom. 'Surely you don't think all nine of these Schirr creatures stood here on their dais waiting patiently to be shot until the last man retaliated, hmm?'

A thought occurred to Ben. 'And what about that stasis field thing you mentioned, Doctor,' he said, pleased to have found something to contribute. He shrugged at Haunt. 'Triggered by *you* lot coming in here, ain't that right, Doctor!'

Haunt frowned. 'What?'

'Yes, it's quite a mystery, quite a mystery,' said the Doctor. He looked almost amused. 'Not forgetting the concealed exit in this room that Polly must somehow have fallen through –'

Shel finally lost his cool. 'That's enough out of you,' he barked.

The Doctor looked furious at the interruption, but then everyone's attention was taken by something else. The echo of approaching footsteps began tripping over themselves as, this time, a small, wiry figure burst into the cavernous hall, dressed again in grey and with backpack and metal headband. Ben was pleasantly surprised to find he was taller than at least one of these space soldiers. But as the bald, scarred person approached...

'Stone me,' Ben muttered. 'It's another blinkin' bird.' Just about, anyway, he qualified to himself. She had a face like the smell of gas.

The woman glanced over at the bodies on the dais, but she seemed far more interested in Ben. He swallowed.

'Frog,' Haunt snapped. 'You're taking these two back to the ship.'

'Yes, Marshal.'

Ben couldn't help himself from smirking at the weird, warbling croak that came from her mouth. As a frog, she was pretty well-named.

Frog continued to stare at Ben. 'Then shall I keep them under observation for a bit?'

Ben stopped smiling and cast an anxious look at the Doctor. He was staring into space, apparently oblivious to all.

'Then you'll join the rest of us at the bullring for an emergency debriefing. Now go. Hurry.' Haunt turned to Shel darkly. 'We need to regroup. Get everyone to retrace their steps, back to the bullring.'

Frog shrugged and indicated with her gun that the Doctor and Ben get moving. They trudged off towards the pentagonal doorway. Ben saw the Doctor cast a wistful look at the TARDIS, their ship and sanctuary, just out of reach.

'Marshal.' Ben heard Shel call over to Haunt, and there was an edge to his usually assured tones. 'I can't raise Joiks and Denni. No contact. Just static.'

'This is how it begins,' murmured the Doctor, just loud enough for Ben to hear him, as Frog nudged them through the exit.

II

Tovel found the wet crunch of his boots on the gritty floor almost comforting in the semi-darkness. Shade marched along beside him. He looked just as concerned as Tovel that Haunt had ordered a recall. They walked on in silence. Tovel tried not to dwell on his concern. It was lucky the websets weren't so good at picking up underlying feelings, the murky background noise during playback; at least this generation of them. For the moment, soldiers controlled their websets and not vice versa; with practice anyone could keep their real thoughts and feelings suppressed. But the technology was getting better all the time. One day the Army examiners would be able to pick up every dissenting thought you ever had – and deal with you accordingly. Tovel imagined that websets of the future would turn their wearers into unthinking, unquestioning machines, designed solely to act and react. Perfect soldiers.

Suddenly he froze.

'Shade.'

Shade stopped dead too. Shadow seemed a good nickname. 'What?'

'You hear that?' A weird whispering sound had started up.

Shade frowned and listened. But suddenly the only sound was that of slapping footsteps on the rock. Something was coming for them, fast.

In the time it took Shade to swear, Tovel had drawn his gun. He aimed it down the gloomy tunnel. The footsteps were getting louder, closer.

'That's no droid,' Shade said quietly. He drew his own gun.

'You heard Haunt, no one's seen these droids before,' Tovel snapped, keeping eyes and gun trained down the passageway. The murky green light seemed a little brighter, a little bluer.

A willowy yellow shape burst into view. A woman. Pretty. Her long blonde hair streamed out behind her like a comet tail.

'Don't shoot me,' the girl yelled. 'Please!'

Tovel turned now to Shade, who was staring at her – up and down and slowly – in amazement.

'There's a blue light,' the girl said breathlessly. 'And a noise, sort of hypnotic. I followed it, to this incredible place, and…' She trailed off, stayed staring at Shade's face. They all did that.

'And what?' Tovel prompted her.

The girl looked at him now with wide, fearful eyes. 'I'm sorry. Please, there's something –'

'Wait.' Tovel could hear the low, flat whine of weapon generators building. In a second Shadow had fallen to one knee and was blasting round after round down the tunnel to where the droid must be coming from. Clouds of white fleas exploded under each impact. The girl threw herself to the ground and covered her head.

Tovel crouched beside her. 'You hurt?'

'No. But guns are so noisy!'

'Keep your ears blocked a little longer,' Tovel advised.

Shade kept on blasting, criss-crossing the tunnel entrance, until abruptly the yellow fire faded. 'Power pack's out!'

For a moment Tovel relived Shade's helpless sense of panic back at the freighter simulation, as the Kill-Droid had targeted him head-on. Then he raised his own gun and took up the barrage. Through the bolts of yellow light Tovel glimpsed burning red, caught coruscations of reflected fire in the body of something big coming out of the darkness.

Shade had thrown down his rifle and released his grenade launcher from the clamp on his back. Now he aimed it down the tunnel and fired. The kickback nearly knocked him over.

The noise of the grenade impacting left Tovel half-deafened. The tunnel mouth was incandescent for a second. Tovel blinked furiously to clear his sight. He had a blurred view of Shade gripping the launcher so tightly it seemed the skin would split over his knuckles. He fired again. Tovel heard the rumbling of rock.

'That's enough!' Tovel yelled. 'You'll bring the roof down on us! We've got to get out of here!' That would be a count against Shade when they got back to base. Poor little Earthborn.

He groped around for the girl, grabbed hold of her skinny arm and yanked her up by it. She squealed as he dragged her away. The ground felt like it would shake itself apart.

A few metres down the tunnel he, Shade and the girl all collapsed together as the impact of several tonnes of rock hitting the ground behind them knocked them off their feet.

Tovel choked as he breathed in dust. 'Nice work, Shade. Were you tired of walking? Wanted to block off that tunnel on purpose?'

The girl glowered at him. 'I'm glad this outfit's quilted.'

'Who the hell are you anyway?' Shade suddenly aimed his gun at her head.

The girl looked up at him. She seemed frozen in fear. Tovel studied her properly: dark make-up around her eyes, a straight, pointed nose that had never seen close combat, the ludicrous yellow spacesuit... she was clearly no soldier. Where the hell had she come from, and what the hell was she doing here?

Tovel gave Shade a look, warning him to ease off. Then he retreated down the tunnel and beckoned Shade to join him, out of the girl's earshot.

'Nice work,' he said.

'Wasted the droid, didn't I?'

'Did you?' Tovel waved back at the blocked passageway. 'And what about *her*? Now we can't go check out her story.'

'What story?' Shade scoffed. 'Blue lights? Incredible places?'

'We'll get more out of her,' said Tovel, 'if she thinks we trust her.'

Shade nodded slowly. 'I guess so.'

'Don't leave me here,' the girl called. She sounded pathetic.

'No chance of that,' Tovel called back as they marched back to rejoin her. 'I think our Marshal's going to be very interested to find you here. What're you called?'

'Polly. Now please, you don't understand...' The mysterious Polly got to her feet. 'I was trying to tell you. There's some sort of countdown going on, I'm sure of it.' She regarded the blocked tunnel with a gloomy expression. 'And now I can't show you where it was!'

Tovel nodded ruefully, though he noticed Shade showed no signs of remorse. 'What do you mean by a countdown?'

Polly gesticulated worriedly with her hands. 'I… I got the feeling we haven't very long.'

Shade looked like he was losing patience. 'Long before what?'

'I'm not sure,' said Polly, 'but *something's* about to happen!'

She was right; Haunt's voice, low and concerned, broke in on their conversation. 'Tovel, respond.'

'Tovel here,' he rapped into his wrist-comm. 'Marshal, I was about to –'

'Shade with you?'

'Right here.'

'Have either of you had contact with Joiks or Denni?'

Tovel swapped a quizzical glance with Shade. 'No, Marshal. But we've –'

Haunt cut him off. 'Get yourselves back to the bullring. We'll meet you there. Out.'

'Marshal, wait,' Tovel said quickly. 'We've had some action here. Clash with a droid.'

'Hit status?'

'Not confirmed. Rockfall came down on us. And something else. Seems we've got ourselves a civilian here.'

There was a pause before the voice came back as heavy as the long seconds that had passed. 'A female civilian?'

Tovel looked at Polly. 'Very.'

'All right, watch her,' Haunt instructed. 'I'm coming to you, you can guide me through from the bullring. I'll be in touch.' She turned to Roba and Shel. 'Come on,' she said, with a lingering look round the cavernous control room, at the bodies on the dais and the corpse slumped in its chair. 'We're moving out.'

She led them out of the chamber, through the tunnel and into the echoing vaults beyond. In a few minutes they had reached the massive gold doors. Then Shel suddenly raised his hand, motioning them all to stop.

'Vibration,' he whispered. 'In the ground, do you feel it?'

'Don't feel nothing,' Roba reported, unimpressed.

'He's right,' said Haunt. 'And Tovel mentioned a rockfall. This whole place could be unstable.'

The tremor increased. With it came a deep rumbling noise from somewhere far beneath them, before both died slowly away.

'Makes sense,' grunted Roba. 'They've thrown everything else at us.'

Haunt looked daggers at the mass of tiny white dots on her scanner, and cursed. 'If we could only pinpoint our location.'

Roba pointed to a set of doors in the rock. 'Me and Frog came through there. Our tunnel led straight to it.'

'Many of the passages must intersect,' Shel remarked as they moved on. 'If you knew where you were going I imagine you could navigate the tunnels quite swiftly.'

Haunt nodded. 'The droids could have the whole place mapped out by now.'

They walked on in uneasy silence until they reached the bullring.

'You two wait here as arranged,' Haunt said, 'let the others know what's going on.'

'Marshal,' Shel acknowledged curtly.

'I won't be long.' She activated her wrist-comm. 'All right, Tovel. Tell me how I get to you.'

III

'The ground gets steeper here,' Denni warned Joiks. The rock sloped down and away into shadows. 'Darker too.'

'Want me to go first?' Joiks mocked her.

'No.'

'Good. Don't want you scoping my ass. Flake.'

'Flake?' Denni said softly.

'Just thinking about what you said earlier.' He chuckled. 'Worried?'

He heard Denni scramble easily down the slope. The shadows got thicker, the darkness pressed in on him as he followed. He couldn't keep his mind focused. What good would it do him to try it on with

Denni now? If he'd reported her straight away, then fair enough, but…

Who cared?

He slipped his hand round her waist. 'Don't think about it,' he whispered.

'Shouldn't that be my line?'

Denni was holding herself very still, acting casual. She didn't pull away. She still needed his support.

He heard his voice, loud in the quiet tunnel. 'It's just bodies.' In the blackness he sounded like a different person. 'The sets don't pick up bodies. Know how they work?'

Denni took a step forward, and he took it with her. 'They're powered by visual stimulus.'

'So focus on the dark. Think of nothing.' His breathing was getting shakier. 'I done it loads of times. Sets don't pick up a thing when you've nothing visual to focus on.'

Denni took a deep breath and released it in a single, stone-cold second. 'Joiks,' her voice slithered into his ears. 'Let go of me.'

'It's a rush,' Joiks urged her. 'I'll help you, you help *me* out, huh? We're safe here in the dark. Nothing can creep up on us here.'

'You reckon,' said Denni. He felt her tense up.

IV

'Don't go so fast,' Ben pleaded with the funny-looking frog-bird as she pushed them along the echoing tunnels that made up this place. 'Can't you see, the Doctor can't keep up the pace!'

'Nonsense, nonsense,' the Doctor muttered, but he clearly had too little puff left to get really indignant.

'All right,' Frog said in her weird grating voice. 'We rest for a minute, no more.'

Ben nodded. 'Thanks.'

It wasn't the nicest spot for a rest. Ben shivered, and only partly from the cold. This whole place was straight out of your worst nightmares. Dark, shadowy room followed dark, shadowy room, and God knew what could be lurking there. Luckily for the moment it seemed to be just fleshy insects hopping about the walls, and swarming all over the slimy, glowing ceilings.

'Fascinating,' the Doctor observed, fingering some hanging strands of the slimy weed. 'I wonder... has this been grown here by the architects of this place so that you can light your way... or so that something else can see you approaching?'

He looked expectantly at Frog. She belched.

'Tell me,' the Doctor tried again more faintly, 'Miss, er... Frog...?'

'Mel Narda. Sergeant.' The boggle-eyes turned on Ben. 'But yeah, call me Frog, honey,' her voice buzzed and crackled. 'Everyone else does.'

Asking why seemed as unnecessary as it was probably unwise. So Ben kept quiet while the Doctor got on with the big questions.

'We've been travelling for some time,' the Doctor said, ignoring her. 'We've become a little out of touch. What can you tell us of the, ah, *rebel Schirr*, hmm?'

'DeCaster and...' the name eluded Ben.

'The Ten-strong?' Frog finished for him automatically, then smiled, apparently amused. 'You never heard of the Empire's most wanted?'

'Indeed I'm afraid not. Remind me, from which planet do these ten terrorists hail?'

'Idaho,' Frog informed them, eyes trained on her watch. 'Outer Empire.'

'A planet called Idaho?' Ben spluttered.

The Doctor ignored him, looked at Frog sharply. 'The Earth annexed the Schirr planet?'

'*Repatriated*,' she qualified with a chuckle that sounded like a rusty alarm clock going off. 'Fifteen years ago. Standard procedure.'

'Yes, of course it is, of course it is,' the Doctor muttered. 'And I suppose the Schirr didn't wish to be so aggressively... *repatriated*, hmm?'

Frog shrugged. 'What we want and what we get, honey, we none of us got a say in.'

'But DeCaster and his mates *want* a say, right?' Ben chipped in. 'Even so, ten blokes against an empire...?'

Frog shook her head. 'Schirr got links with the Spooks.'

The Doctor raised an eyebrow. 'What links might these be?'

Frog shrugged. 'Old, old links. Before the Spooks crept back to their cloud. Old, old magic. And ten's all you need to make the big rituals work.'

'Rituals, not warfare?' the Doctor asked, eyes gleaming now with interest.

'People die just the same.' She raised her gun, suddenly cold and threatening. 'Frog don't talk too much to prisoners, honey. Break time's over. Get moving.'

They did; through a mighty set of doors set into the rock, along a winding, narrow tunnel, on to a large cave riddled with passages.

Then they felt the first tremor.

'Seismic activity on a planetoid as small as this?' the Doctor wondered aloud. His expression suggested he didn't find this likely.

The second tremor sent them staggering into the wall.

'Getting worse!' Ben shouted.

'Soon have you tucked up tight,' Frog told him. 'Here's the dropzone.' And she herded the two of them roughly into a circular chamber, lit with a wide blue spotlight shining down from high above. While the beam was bright and concentrated, it cast the rest of the chamber into pitch blackness. Two flexible metal ladders snaked down the ray of light.

'I imagine those lead through the asteroid's mantle and back up to the docked ship,' the Doctor told Ben.

'But we can't just go and leave Polly and the TARDIS behind!' Ben hissed back, panic rising. The ground trembled beneath him once again as if in sympathy.

'Get climbing,' Frog told them.

The Doctor looked outraged. 'Climb up there? At my age? Preposterous, madam!'

'Yeah,' Ben added, 'you can't expect an old geezer to –'

But Frog wasn't mucking about. She leapt nimbly into the light and caught hold of the ladder. The strength of the light obliterated most of her form, turned her into a pin-man as she scaled a few rungs. She swung out on the ladder, winked at Ben, caught hold of the quilted neckline of the Doctor's spacesuit with one hand, and hauled him off the ground.

The Doctor squawked with indignation as he dangled precariously from Frog's grip. Ben stared in disbelief. Incredibly, the woman was scaling the ladder and carrying the Doctor with her.

''Ere, wait a minute!' yelled Ben.

'Climb the other ladder or I drop him,' Frog called teasingly.

A fresh tremor nearly knocked Ben to his knees, but he recovered and ran into the light without a second thought. A moment later he was clambering up after them. 'Hang on, Doctor,' he yelled, squinting into the blue radiance at the hazy figures above. He could hear grunts of exertion from Frog, the furious fussings of the old boy as he demanded to be released: 'Madam, unhand me at once!'

Then Ben cried out as something small and sharp smacked into his forehead. It was followed a few seconds later by some smaller stinging missiles and a shower of dust.

'Wait!' he shouted, blinking grit from his eyes, disorientated by the blinding light. 'Frog, them tremors… they must be bringing down a rockfall or something!'

V

Polly sighed. Roaming the tunnels had been scary, but at least she might've found Ben and the Doctor. Now she was going nowhere: prisoner of space soldiers, stuck inside a big rock.

Tovel, the bigger and dishier of the two men, mumbled directions into his sleeve to their marshal. The one called Shade pointed his gun at her. There was something wrong with his face. It was peppered with dark markings, like black seeds were trying to sprout from under his skin. The region around his eyes seemed the worst affected, though the eyes themselves glinted a brilliant green.

'You want to know what's wrong with my face,' Shade remarked. His voice was hoarse.

'No!' Polly felt herself blushing. 'I'm just trying to keep my eyes off your gun, that's all.'

Shade shrugged and smiled. 'It's OK. I don't mind.' His voice kept the same gravelly tone, and she realised he must always sound that way. Under different circumstances it might be quite sexy. 'I was clearing some kids out of a war zone. There was this mine…' He shrugged. 'I had to shield the children. My face caught a load of the shrapnel.'

Polly winced. 'Were you all right?'

'They had to stick me in a cryo-tank. Saved my life. But they froze the damage in with me.' He raised his free hand, felt the little bumps and ridges. 'The shrapnel's a part of me now. They offered me a new face entirely but I decided to stick with the old one. Every day… I never forget the scum that did this to me.'

'You were in a war, then?' she asked.

'This was the big Schirr raid, two years ago,' Shade said casually. 'DeCaster and his wannabe Morphieans, they tried to take out the Pentagon sub-router on New Jersey.'

'New Jersey?' Polly seized upon about the only words she'd understood. 'New Jersey in the United States?'

Shade stared at her now like she was mad. 'No.'

Polly jumped as a burly, hard-faced woman strode round the corner. Armed to the teeth, dressed in the same futuristic combat fatigues as Tovel and Shade, this could only be their Marshal Haunt. The woman fixed Polly in her sights and zeroed in without hesitation.

'So.' Haunt swung up her gun and nudged it against Polly's temple. Polly looked beseechingly at Shade. He looked on, stoically; she supposed he was hardly likely to go up against his superior officer over her. 'Here you are, just like your friends said. I suppose it's been you leaving little markers at the tunnel mouths?'

'You've met the Doctor and Ben?' Polly said, trying not to whimper. 'Are they all right?'

Haunt snorted. 'I don't know what they are.' The gun barrel was digging into Polly's head so hard she felt her skull would crack. 'Perhaps you could tell me?'

Polly wished the ground would swallow her up. She scrunched up her eyes tightly as she tried to think up an answer that might satisfy this maniac.

'We've… we've been travelling,' she said.

'Through the Morphiean Quadrant?' Tovel looked at her suspiciously.

'She and her friends here claim they're refugees,' Haunt told her soldiers.

'That's what I meant!' said Polly. 'Please, could you take me to them?'

Suddenly the ground beneath her started to shudder. Polly cancelled her earlier wish.

'We should move,' Tovel warned. He shot a look at Shade. 'We must've weakened this whole area with all that firepower.'

'It doesn't feel like a tremor.' Haunt looked around her, suspicious, as if the answer to the puzzle was somehow staring her in the face, mocking her.

The tremors, meanwhile, seemed to be getting worse. Cracks and fissures were opening in the walls and the roof. Streams of black choking dust seeped from them. Polly wondered how far she'd get if she tried to make a run for it past Haunt, and decided she'd rather take her chances with falling boulders.

Haunt's gaze settled on Tovel. 'What do you make of it?'

'Vibration.' His head was cocked slightly to one side, as if listening to something none of them could hear. 'Like something powering-up.'

'The countdown,' breathed Polly. 'Didn't I tell you something was going to happen!'

Haunt ignored her. 'All right, let's join the others.' She looked Polly up and down. 'I can see I'm not going to learn anything from you.'

How about the importance of moisturiser and dieting for starters, you bullying bitch, thought Polly. If only she could be safe with Ben back in the TARDIS, listening to the engines grind and grate, leaving this horrible place far behind them…

A thought struck her as she was shoved along the passage in the direction Haunt had come from. 'These tremors,' she said, turning to face them. 'I know what they remind *me* of.'

'What?' asked Haunt, looking as if she already regretted asking.

'Our spaceship,' Polly said, 'when it's getting ready for take-off. Only a thousand times stronger.'

'A spaceship?' Shade echoed in disbelief. 'Inside an asteroid?'

'It's not so strange, is it?' Tovel muttered, a surprise ally. 'That's where ours is.'

Haunt, for her part, said nothing. But before Polly was pushed onwards unsteadily through the rumbling tunnel, she at least had the satisfaction of seeing the marshal's face darken into sudden concern.

VI

Ben hung on for dear life as his ladder bucked and almost threw him clear. There was a terrible splitting sound from somewhere above him, and then a shadow fell swiftly over him. Ben twisted and swung on his ladder as a jagged piece of slate the size of a dinner tray hurtled past.

'Doctor!' yelled Ben desperately as he peered up into the brilliant light, and as more and more rock fragments started raining down around him. He felt the ladder lurch sickeningly. A spindly figure was suddenly clinging to one of the rungs above him, the Doctor, it had to be, Frog had passed him over. But then a boot was pressing down hard on Ben's fingers. He gasped and tried to pull them free. 'Get off!' he yelled.

'I'm sorry, my boy.' The Doctor's confused voice floated down with a cloud of rock dust. 'I… I didn't see you…'

The Doctor's boot lifted, and Ben felt his fingers throb, as if about to swell to cartoonish proportions. He ignored the pain, gripped the sides of the rope ladder and slid smoothly down. But when he hit the bottom he found it was like standing on deck in a stormy sea. The ground bucked beneath him. A large boulder tore down from above and pounded into the ground beside him, inches from his foot. He was choking on dust, it was everywhere. The shaft of blue light turned it into a dense luminous fog.

'It's an earthquake, Doctor!' he yelled.

'I don't think so.' The Doctor was crawling, painfully slowly, down the ladder, as showers of pebbles rained down around him. Afraid a more serious rockfall was likely, Ben staggered forward and tried to lift the Doctor clear.

'Put me down, young man,' the Doctor thundered. He disentangled himself from Ben's grip. 'I will not be carted about by all and sundry like a sack of potatoes!'

Ben held up his hands in meek apology.

'Where is our captor?' the Doctor asked, his lined face damp with perspiration. 'She manhandled me on to your ladder, our own was starting to give way.'

Together, trying to keep their balance like surfers riding a wave, they peered about.

'There!' Ben shouted. Frog was on all fours, dazed, struggling for breath. She must've fallen, winded herself.

'Look out, Ben!' the Doctor called back. Grit and pebbles fell like hail from the rocky sky above them. It couldn't be long now before the entire place came crashing down on top of them, and Haunt's ship with it.

Ben dashed forward and crouched beside Frog. 'Come on!' he yelled at her over the sound of the splitting earth, and took her arm. Her muscles felt like steel. She struggled against him, dived forwards and butted him in the stomach. Caught by surprise, Ben folded up and lay gasping beside her.

'You daft cow,' he gasped in disbelief, 'I was trying to help you!'

Frog stared blankly at him. Blood was dripping freely from her nose over her mouth and chin, her teeth were stained gory red. 'Help me?'

'Give over.' Recovering, Ben clambered up and took her arm again, helping her up. This time she didn't argue, resting her weight on him as they staggered away to the edge of the drop zone where the Doctor was waiting anxiously for them. More and more rubble was crashing down from on high. The blinding beam of light had been pulverised to a feeble glow.

Frog wiped the back of her hand across her bloody face and looked up at Ben. '*Why'd* you help me?'

Ben looked away, embarrassed. 'Why wouldn't I?'

'You could've escaped,' Frog said. Then she showed her teeth in a gory smile. 'Could've tried to, anyway.'

'We couldn't leave you to die,' the Doctor muttered.

'Well, you're still my prisoners,' Frog warned them, still dabbing at her nose with her palm. 'When this quake dies down we go straight back up them ladders.'

'You're joking!' Ben angrily gestured to the rumbling drop zone. 'You want that little lot on top of you?'

Frog shrugged. 'The ship'll be safe. It has to be.'

'Even if that proves true, we have no way of getting to it,' the Doctor said tetchily. 'I fear the control room will be the only place of safety. This is no natural earthquake, of that I am sure. It's... that is to say...' His face clouded, and Ben watched him struggle for words that were lost to him like an actor drying up on stage. 'It's something else,' he concluded lamely.

'We'll join the others,' Frog decided. 'And I don't think the marshal's gonna to be too glad to see you...'

As she walked off, Ben noticed she was limping slightly. There was a vivid gash in her calf where a rock or something had ripped through her suit, but it looked like the fabric was digging in hard around the wound.

'You all right?' he asked. 'You've hurt your leg.'

'Ain't you a bleeding heart,' Frog muttered. 'The suit's taking care of it.'

The Doctor perked up automatically. 'Intelligent armour,' he told Ben. 'If the soldier is wounded, the fabric compresses to staunch any bleeding.'

Frog only grunted as she herded them both along the tunnels. 'Gotta get back to Haunt,' she warbled. 'Gotta get back.'

'All right, all right,' Ben complained over his shoulder as Frog's rifle butt dug into his spine for the tenth time, forcing him along the tunnel. 'We're moving as fast as we can.'

She didn't meet his gaze, instead staring suspiciously all around them. The tremors had clearly shaken her in more ways than one. 'Gotta get back,' she said again.

'As I've told you already, Miss Frog,' said the Doctor, marching along beside Ben. 'You will be showing your Marshal considerable initiative if you'll just take us back to the control centre. I must examine the instruments there.'

Frog didn't answer, so Ben did. 'Thought everything was dead in there.'

'Dormant, perhaps,' the Doctor muttered. He looked sweaty and pale-faced. 'A sleeping giant.'

'What,' said Ben puzzled, 'and we've gone and woken 'im up – ?'

Even as he spoke something pushed out from an opening in the tunnel wall beside him, grabbing for his throat.

Ben yelped in surprise. His attacker spun him round. It was a big bloke, with a broken nose and wild dark eyes, wearing a headband like Frog's and yelling in his face.

Over the din and the pressure in his ears he heard the Doctor ordering Frog to do something, and the harsh rattle of Frog shouting. But she wasn't warning Ben's attacker off. She sounded like she was trying to calm the bloke down, as best as she could with her cartoon accent.

When that didn't work, she kicked the man in the knackers. He collapsed backwards, falling on his kit bag.

'Strewth,' Ben gasped, whooping down lungfuls of the dank air. 'Wish you'd kept your mouth shut about them giants, Doctor.'

The Doctor didn't respond, crouching arthritically over the groaning man on the floor. 'Who is this fellow?'

'Just Joiks,' Frog replied. Ben got the impression that belting the man in the jewels hadn't been much of a chore. Frog gestured the Doctor out of the way with her rifle. 'What's up, Joiks? This place made you crazy?'

'Denni,' Joiks muttered. 'She was attacked, in the dark. Taken away.'

Ben thought the bloke sounded a bit South African. He recalled now that Joiks and Denni were the two Haunt hadn't been able to contact.

'I reckon she's dead.'

'Dead?' Frog's bulging eyes narrowed.

'Something came at us in the dark. I tried to hold on to her, but whoever it was just snatched her away.' Joiks glowered up at Ben.

'Must've been this one. What did you do with her?'

'I ain't done nothing to no one since I got here!' Ben protested.

Frog pulled Joiks back to his feet. 'You sure she's dead?'

'Maybe,' Joiks said, apparently without irony.

'Try "maybe not",' Frog said flatly. 'Whatever happened to Denni, it wasn't either of these two. They were with me.'

Joiks looked at her like she was mad. Then he scowled at Ben and the Doctor and clenched his big fists. 'Who the hell are "these two", anyway?'

'These three, you mean.'

Ben shut his eyes and groaned. 'Terrific,' he muttered. 'Marshal Misery's come back to haunt us.'

Her words sank in. Three?

'Ben! Doctor!'

Now Ben spun round in disbelief. Stood bright and beaming next to Haunt was Polly. She was flanked by a right array of bruisers, and her daffodil-bright spacesuit was covered in dirt, but that aside she looked perfect as ever. He rushed to bundle her up into his arms, and Polly ran forward to meet him, managing to snag the Doctor into the clumsy embrace as well.

Ben gently pulled away from Polly. 'Good to see you.'

'What happened, my child?' the Doctor asked.

But before Polly could speak, Haunt put a gun to her head, with a look that warned her to keep quiet. 'Frog, why aren't these two locked up in the ship?' Ben wasn't sure it was possible for anyone to look more peed off than she was.

While Frog started to explain, Ben took in the figures lined up behind her. He was definitely feeling like the odd man out around here. Maybe he should start standing on tiptoes. The two soldiers who'd marched her along with Haunt looked the type you wouldn't want to tangle with. One of them seemed to have weird tribal markings all over his face, which made his otherwise undistinguished features far more formidable. Behind them stood Roba and Shel and two more soldiers, a stocky, sly-looking man and a thin girl who would've been dead tasty if someone hadn't tried to cut her red hair with a lawnmower. All of them carried backpacks and wore the weird headbands.

It was strange, Ben decided. The soldiers could only be around his age, but they seemed somehow so much older. He thought about making a run for it back to the TARDIS, but not for long. Outnumbered three to one, with no weapons and the Doctor's stamina to contend with, how far could they get?

Suddenly it seemed that everyone started talking at once. The soldiers burst out into angry, frightened discussions, with several dark looks in Ben's direction. Haunt began questioning Joiks, whose answers brought fresh mutterings in the ranks. The bloke with the tattooed face looked especially gutted.

And then Frog was pulling Ben roughly away from Polly's arms. He yelled at her to let him go, a complete waste of breath. The Doctor was gripping Polly firmly by the shoulders as Roba and the nimble redhead closed in on them, guns raised. He was keeping her close to him but hushing her questions and protests, taking in each exchange around him with swift movements of his head, like some big worried owl.

Then the biggest tremor yet practically took them all off their feet.

When the rumbling and the vibration finally began to die down, Ben could hear a new noise beneath it. A weird, haunting two-tone melody, a ghost's idea of an emergency siren. As one by one they heard the sound, so each person in the passage fell silent.

'It's coming from the control centre,' the Doctor declared imperiously. 'Marshal Haunt, might I suggest we go there at once?'

She pushed past the Doctor, breaking into a run, Shel at her side and most of the squad falling in behind her.

'Looks like you're getting what you want, old man,' said Roba. He started hustling the Doctor along after them, while the silent redhead steered Polly, protesting noisily, by the arm. Frog motioned that Ben should follow them.

They trooped back through the vaulted cavernous chambers and the flea-ridden ceilings, past the statues and the slates, the ghostly alarm growing louder, more penetrating.

And with it, something else.

A resonant hum growing in power.

VII

'Let go of me, would you?' Polly snapped to the skinny woman who was clearly a lot stronger than she looked. 'You're breaking my arm.'

'And you're breaking my heart.' The skinny woman's cultured voice was like cut glass. She propelled Polly into the control centre.

'Easy on her, Lindey,' said Shade.

'The delicate flower's making *you* wilt is she, Shade?' the dark-haired, neat-looking man inquired.

'She's a civilian, Creben, and there's no need to mistreat her,' Shade said coolly. But he couldn't hide the faint blush beneath his blackened cheeks. Polly tried to catch his eye, to smile and thank him, but he avoided her gaze. Ben, on the other hand was actively seeking it out. He didn't look happy, probably because the squat little witch with the gun was standing so close to him, her hand pressed down on his shoulder. Polly tried to give this 'frog' a look she hoped would show exactly how impressed she was, but the woman didn't even glance up.

Looking away, Polly's heart leapt as she saw the TARDIS, just where they had left it. But she caught sight of the crowd of corpses on the platform, and quickly averted her eyes.

Unlike everyone else. Shade and Tovel, and the man with the broken nose she'd glimpsed earlier, had all noticed the horrible display themselves, and were staring in disbelief. The alarms grew ever louder. Finally Lindey let go of Polly's arm, but only so she could cover her own ears. The noise was almost overpowering now.

Creben turned, pale-faced, dragged his gaze over to Tovel. 'All this is Schirr design, isn't it?' he yelled.

Tovel simply nodded. Then he jogged over to one of the consoles built into the wall. Shade and Creben looked at each other uneasily. Frog and the man with the broken nose stood close together, apparently unmoved by the commotion.

Her whole head ringing with the sound, Polly looked round in panic for the Doctor. Only when the black man stepped aside could she see him standing, head cocked to one side, absolutely still.

'I tried to tell them, Doctor,' Polly shouted. 'Before, there was a noise, a light, a vibration...'

'Quiet,' Haunt snapped. She shouted over to Tovel: 'Can you make sense of the controls?'

'The girl was right,' Tovel yelled back. 'I think some sort of take-off's been initiated, that the engines are starting up.'

Polly noticed the Doctor steeple his fingers and smile almost smugly at the news. His eyes were like dark buttons, gleaming in the oily light.

'Take-off?' echoed the man with the broken nose. 'That's garbage. We're in the middle of a rock, how can we be taking off?'

'A section of this complex has been designed to break free of the main planetoid,' explained the Doctor impatiently.

The oriental man nodded like he understood. 'Those earlier tremors signalled the primary phase of the separation.'

The Doctor nodded vaguely and bustled over to Tovel. 'Can you compute where we are going?'

Polly couldn't hear the rest of his words over the scary whistling of the alarm. But she caught Lindey's breathy voice close in her ear.

'What is this place? Where the hell did nine dead Schirr spring up from?'

Polly frowned, and forced herself to look again at the corpse in the chair and the bodies on the dais, to count them properly.

She screamed.

Though the piercing notes of the alien klaxon had reached their climax, everyone in the chamber whirled round to face her.

'Look!' she shouted. 'The bodies. The alien bodies. There were ten of them when we arrived, now there's only nine. One of them's gone!'

Chapter Five
Destination Unknown

I

The klaxons cut off.

The sudden silence in the cavern was almost physical in its strength. Ben felt a slight stirring in his stomach, the ground pitched a little and he felt a quick pang of homesickness. Motion. They were at sea.

What the hell was happening here?

Lindey turned to Shel. Her voice sounded too loud, unnatural in the silence. 'Could this all be part of the training simulation?'

Shel didn't answer. Ben reckoned he was a bit of a Doctor-type in that he didn't like to commit himself if there was a chance he could be wrong.

Haunt, who had been deep in thought, standing almost statue-like since the klaxons stopped, seemed to come to a decision. 'All right, everyone. Deactivate websets.' Even her best sergeant-major bellow couldn't mask the worry in her voice. 'We can no longer be sure this is a training exercise. Now, I don't want you thinking to make yourselves look good for Cellmek. I want you thinking to save yourselves and your team. No more recording.'

The soldiers gave muted assent. As Ben watched, fingers were placed to a particular spot on the metal band around their foreheads. So the headgear wasn't just for show. The mixed looks on the soldiers' faces as they removed the websets ranged from scandalised pleasure to worried and just downright guilty. It put Ben in mind of how him and his mates had been at school when his older brother taught them how to swear. You were dying to do it but knew it was breaking the rules. And changing you, too, somehow.

Shel spoke up, more confident now he was on familiar ground. 'Regulations state that as senior officers, we remain recording in all conditions of combat, unless our imminent capture dictates we erase all recording.'

'I'm aware of that, Shel,' Haunt said icily. 'Naturally, I exclude ourselves from the order.'

The bloke with the marked face who'd been goggling at Polly was now turning a less enthusiastic eye on the corpses on the platform and the one in the chair. 'Were there nine bodies here before, Marshal?' he asked quietly.

'No, Shade, there were not.' Haunt crossed over to the corpses on the platform. Shel, Roba and Shade immediately followed her. Ben glanced at the Doctor, who was engrossed in some computer readout with that Tovel geezer, and at Polly who was just hiding her face in her hands. He decided to get a closer look at the bodies, and to make sure Haunt wasn't getting ready to blame any of them for this.

Any thought that Polly must be mistaken vanished in an instant. The tableau had clearly changed. There was a clear gap towards the right-hand side. The Schirr had been clutching his bloody head with both hands. Now he had gone, while his two neighbours hadn't moved a muscle. With nothing between them they looked blankly at each other with milky eyes, red pupils fixed in what Ben had taken to be the moment of their sudden death.

'But they can't be, can they,' he said, thinking out loud. Shade looked at him blankly, and Ben took in the black blotches that covered the man's face. 'Dead, I mean.'

'With wounds like that?' Haunt gestured to the guts spilling from one of the bodies, frozen in midfall. 'How could they survive?'

'It's got to be a trick.' Ben wasn't letting this go. 'Special effects.'

'We ran a scan,' Shel told him. He sounded as calm and unfazed as ever as he studied the empty space on the platform where the creature's huge feet had been standing. 'These are real corpses.'

'Don't forget the one in the chair,' said Roba. He spat on it to make his point, and Ben watched the liquid dribble down the huge pink head. 'We can see that's for real.'

'How could a corpse come back to life,' Shade muttered. 'Maybe Ben's right, they're not dead. Maybe this force field is really some kind of cryogenic –'

'They're dead,' Shel informed him flatly, and held out a palm-sized gadget. 'Would you like to check the displays?'

Shade shrugged. 'You're science officer.'

'It's more likely the corpse simply disintegrated when the systems started up,' stated Shel. 'Some resonance in the vibration may have interfered with the stasis field in some way.'

Haunt nodded, perked up a bit. 'Yes. That would make sense.'

It didn't to Ben, but he supposed they should be grateful for any explanation, no matter how incomprehensible it sounded.

'Maybe the force field's there to keep the bodies safe.' Before Ben could be shot down in flames like Shade he quickly carried on: 'You know; they can't bury them, so they keep them up here.'

'So where's this piece of rock going to?' Haunt fixed him with a dark stare. 'Some deep space cemetery?'

'Maybe,' Ben said. 'We don't know nothing, do we?'

'Double negative,' Shel muttered, staring at the empty space between the corpses at the end of the line. 'That would suggest we know everything.'

Haunt looked at him, thoughtfully.

II

'Look at Shadow over there.' Lindey's voice was soft, conspiratorial in Polly's ear.

'Shadow?'

'Yeah.' Lindey plucked her switched-off headband from her buzz of red hair, and tucked it into her belt. Then she spat in her palm and slicked back her tufty fringe. 'Adam Shade the Shadow. Just look at him.'

Polly chose not to look in the direction of the bodies. 'I don't think it's nice to call him names just because of his accident.'

'Accident?' At first, Lindey acted like she didn't know what Polly was talking about. Then she nodded knowingly. 'Oh, sure. He didn't waste much time going for the sympathy vote, did he? But we don't just call him names because of his *accident*. Go on, look at him. Haunt's little shadow.'

'You're soldiers,' Polly said primly. 'Aren't you meant to follow the person in charge?'

'Follow her orders, sure. Not follow her round like a lost lamb. He probably thinks that if he acts like a good little boy, it'll never happen again. But just look at his face.' Lindey smiled, showing a line of neat pointed teeth. 'The one thing he can never be is whiter than white.'

'All right,' Haunt called out to her troops. 'I'll accept a corpse can maybe reduce itself to dust, but not one of my own squad. We need to find Denni.'

'Or what's left of her,' Lindey muttered.

'And while we're searching we can gauge how big a fragment has separated from the main mass of this rock. But first, we need to know if the ship is still accessible.'

'I'm afraid your ship will be quite out of reach by now,' said the Doctor.

'And just how would you know?' growled Roba.

'Surely, my boy, you don't imagine this whole area has detached itself for no reason? That you stumbled upon these dead criminals by chance?' He turned to Haunt and Shel. 'When was this place constructed?'

'We don't have access to that kind of information,' Haunt said impatiently.

'Very well then, by what process was this asteroid chosen for your training exercises?' All the Doctor needed was a barrister's wig, Polly decided.

'I made available to Pentagon Central the experiential records of each soldier in the squad,' said Shel. 'Their computers then ascertained what further training experiences were needed to take the AT squad into elite class, and selected a suitable location.'

'Craphole computers,' Roba snorted.

The Doctor shook his head. 'The computer, sir, is only equipped to take decisions according to the caprices of its programmers.' He surveyed his audience haughtily. 'You were expected here. All this is an elaborate trap that has closed around you.'

'Around *us*, you mean,' said Ben with feeling.

'Yes, quite so.' At once the Doctor's smugness vanished, and he looked suddenly distant. 'I hardly think a means of escape will be left to us.'

'While I'm sure you know *everything*, Doctor,' Haunt said dourly, 'I think we'll check for ourselves.' She turned to her soldiers. 'Shade, Lindey, go back to the ship, check it out. Roba, Frog, get out there and guard that doorway. Anything coming our way, I want to know about it.'

Silently, they obeyed.

'And remember,' Haunt called after them. 'There could be one, maybe two droids still out there in our share of this rock. Watch yourselves.' She turned to Polly. 'You claim you left this room by another exit.'

'I don't *claim* anything.' Polly crossed to stand by Ben's side. 'It's true.'

'Creben. Joiks. Find another door.' Haunt gestured broadly around her with her rifle. She waved it around so naturally, like the thing was a part of her.

Creben moved smartly away and Joiks slouched off to investigate in the other direction, his heavy-set face troubled.

'Tovel,' Haunt went on. 'You're the pilot. Can this really be a kind of ship?'

'Sure it can,' Tovel replied.

Ben looked confused. 'But how can it steer or whatever, if it's just a dirty great rock?'

The Doctor ignored him and turned to Tovel. 'Young man, would you agree that technology of this sort would need some kind of primed navigational matrix in order to move through space?'

Tovel raised his eyebrows. 'Yeah. It's Schirr technology. They load up crystals with cartographic info, all pre-programmed, and burnt into the systems at launch. But the crystals are gone. We've no way of knowing where we're headed.'

'We're on the edge of Morphiean space,' Haunt said. 'Any infringement on their territory could be construed as open warfare.'

'Who are these Morphieans?' asked Polly.

Tovel looked at her. 'So we can take it you had no relatives on Beijing Minor, then.'

'We, er, have been out of circulation, you could say,' the Doctor told him with an apologetic smile.

'Refugees,' Haunt reminded Tovel.

'In a few years we could all be.'

Polly didn't understand what Tovel meant, but found herself shivering anyway.

'The Morphieans are the geezers with the magic, the Spooks,' Ben piped up. 'That bunch on the dais are called Schirr, and they've been ripping off the Morphieans' secrets, see Pol? The Morphieans want them back. And since the Schirr are part of Earth's empire now, the Morphieans are having a pop at *us* for not putting the lid on *them*.'

The Doctor gave Ben a withering look. 'Succinctly put.'

Polly was grateful for Ben's summary, but still confused. 'How did the Schirr get these secrets in the first place?'

'We learned from the pacified Schirr that centuries ago, the quadrant was active in this sector; before their isolationist stance,' Tovel told her. 'Certain Schirr elements still practised the Morphiean black arts, and none better than DeCaster. He's become a hero, a god to these primitives.'

Shel spoke up. 'Over the last ten years he has used Morphiean rituals to commit the most devastating terrorist acts against Empire.'

'Whole worlds,' said Haunt, 'just gone up in flames.'

Polly thought she got it. 'And once the Morphieans realised what was happening, they started reprisals with worse magic?'

'Much worse,' said Tovel.

Polly's voice rose a little in panic. 'And we could be heading straight for them! We can't tell!'

'How can these crystals have gone? We've only just set off.' Ben suddenly clicked his fingers. ''Ere, maybe the stiff did the business while we were all out of the room – *then* he dissolved.' He swung round to face the dais, half-expecting the missing figure to have suddenly sneaked back in.

'Not likely, is it,' said Tovel.

'In any case, the countdown started ages ago,' Polly said.

'According to you,' Haunt pointed out.

'It's true, we told you,' said Ben hotly, his fingers feeling for Polly's hand. 'She just disappeared somewhere!'

Haunt sneered. 'Just like you appeared out of thin air.'

'You can see our craft for yourself, madam,' the Doctor said impatiently, gesturing to the TARDIS.

'Where were you standing,' asked Haunt, 'when you *disappeared*?'

'It was dark, I'm not sure.' Polly frowned. 'Over by the bodies there, somewhere near the TARDIS. I was trying to get away from them.'

'Marshal, these two *were* here when we arrived,' Shel said, his voice flat and emotionless as he looked at the Doctor and Ben. 'It's possible they could have set our destination and then hidden the navigational crystals.'

'Oh, come off it,' Ben protested.

'The systems were dead until you entered,' the Doctor agreed tetchily. 'The area was pressurised, as you well know.'

'But we *don't* know how long you were here before us,' Tovel said, without, Ben was pleased to see, a good deal of conviction.

'We're wasting time!' the Doctor said. 'Even without the crystals I'm sure I can decipher the residual coding in the navigational circuits.'

'You can?' Tovel looked surprised. 'Care to show me how?'

'Wait,' Haunt ordered. 'Scan them, Shel.'

Shel waved some weird-looking device over the Doctor. Then he stuck it in Ben's face. Ben felt dizzy for a few moments.

Shel opened his mouth to speak, but no sound came out. He looked a bit dizzy himself. Maybe it was catching, thought Ben.

'Cl… Clear, Marshal. No power source detected.'

Haunt frowned at Shel. 'You all right?'

'I'll check the girl.' He moved over to Polly as if nothing had happened. But by the uneasy look between Haunt and Tovel, clearly something significant had.

'Nothing,' Tovel observed, and Shel turned away impassively.

'As you see, we were telling the truth,' said the Doctor. 'Nevertheless, you were quite right to check. The crystals must be on board somewhere.' He smiled icily at Shel. 'Concealed by whoever set this vessel in motion.'

'Why can't they be on the part we left behind?' Ben asked.

'Without them,' Tovel explained, 'this ship can't change course. Ever.'

'It's a one-way journey,' said Polly quietly.

'Indeed, that's quite possible.' The Doctor steepled his fingers and turned his eyes to the vaulted ceiling high above. 'But to where are we travelling, hmm? Let us consider the facts.'

Haunt looked at him warily. 'Go on.'

'Firstly, it would seem the Schirr infested this training area and subverted its functions to accommodate their own. If we are travelling under the guidance of their systems it is unlikely we shall be entering Morphiean space. To do so would mean certain suicide for DeCaster and his followers.'

'Yeah, but they're already dead, Doctor,' Ben interrupted.

'Precisely, my boy. But the flight of this asteroid, and the timing of its take-off, would have been determined *before* the bloody conflict that consumed them took place.'

'They've turned this whole place against us,' Haunt breathed. 'They must mean to use it as a weapon.'

Shel considered. 'DeCaster's intent has always been hostile to Earth and Empire. Outwardly, our appearance, size and mass suggests a simple meteor.'

'This rock could steer smoothly into orbit around an Earth world,' said Tovel, catching on, 'then drop out of the sky on any continent before anyone can react.'

Polly just stared at him, horrified.

Ben was still scratching his head. 'But if they had all this planned on the automatics, why stay behind? Why fight among themselves?'

'A power struggle of some kind?' wondered Shel. 'Perhaps Pallemar wanted to take control.'

Haunt nodded, a faraway look in her eyes as if she were somehow watching the bloody events unfold. 'Pallemar was placing the others in the stasis field. They didn't know how long they would have to wait for the next training squad. They planned to use our ship to escape in once the trap was sprung, marooning us here. But Pallemar must've realised that with DeCaster stuck in stasis, he could set himself up as the leader.' She nodded with sudden conviction. 'The scum won't even stay loyal to their own kind.'

'The scenario would seem to fit,' said the Doctor. 'Except for one thing. If such a squabble took place at the end, unexpectedly… why are the crystals not in evidence?'

Tovel clicked his fingers. 'Of course. One of the Schirr must have them! If we can breach that stasis field, we can simply take the crystals back and change course as we wish.'

'Scan the corpses, Shel,' said Haunt.

All eyes were on Shel as he waved the wand-like device around the dais.

And shook his head.

'No power source, Marshal,' he stated.

Polly felt sick as her hopes plummeted. She noticed the Doctor nod his head, just a fraction, as if he'd suspected as much all along.

III

Lindey led the way through the narrow passage in the rock that led to the doorway. Shade wished it was him staying behind to guard it.

'Watch out for dead Schirr,' he called lightly to Roba and Frog.

Roba said nothing. Frog gave him an obscene gesture.

Shade headed off through the glittering shadows of the complex, Lindey just behind him. He felt exposed without his webset, hated having such freedom to think. Without the mission to trammel his thoughts, they were escaping all over.

Half the bullring had collapsed in on itself. The route back to the ship, along with another tunnel, was buried forever. Shade saw that some of the weed had been shaken down from the crumbling ceiling by the tremors. A cloud of fleas hopped round his feet. He watched them jump, fascinated. Going about their business, unaware giants were gathered around them.

'Shadow?' asked Lindey lightly.

He couldn't stop staring.

'You seem a little worked up, Shadow,' she went on.

Shade didn't see the point of arguing the point. 'What if we've got no way off this rock?'

'Haunt will find one.'

'Yeah?'

'You doubt it?'

Shade closed his eyes. He didn't want to doubt it. 'And what about Denni? Do you reckon she's dead like Joiks thinks?'

Lindey shrugged. 'Maybe we'll find her while we're checking out what else is left behind here.'

'You don't sound bothered.'

'She grew up on Paris II, didn't she? Worst cess-pit in Little Europe. She can handle herself here.'

Shade didn't respond. He hated Lindey for being so cool. She was always this way, whatever the spot. She'd *earned* her place here.

'Poor Shadow.'

She may have picked up on his self-pitying mood, but her voice was cold.

'Huh?'

'Always seems to happen to you, doesn't it? Things getting out of hand. Going wrong.'

She knows. Shade cleared his throat, made a big pointless show of picking which tunnel they might take as an alternative. 'I don't know what you're talking about, Lindey.'

'I think that sappy little girl likes you, you know,' Lindey went on, her eyes wide and smiling. 'She must find it so reassuring having a big brave soldier like you around. Someone who keeps his head while all around are losing theirs.' The smile faded. 'Someone who keeps damn sure of it.'

Shade couldn't keep up eye-contact, and studied his palmset

instead. 'Seems there's nothing beyond this rockfall.' He tried to sound brisk and emotionless about it. 'No ship. This is the end of the road.'

'Maybe they'll airlift you out again,' Lindey whispered, her face in shadow. 'Earthman.'

Shade bore down on her angrily. 'What the hell is all this, Lindey?'

But she put her finger to her lips, shushed him, and walked off back the way they had come. 'You know, I wanted you to get through this mission so badly.' Her voice wasn't teasing now. It was strained. 'I wanted you to get merits, to earn your Elite placing. To feel like you'd actually made it, like you'd finally pushed the past behind you.' She paused, enjoying herself. 'Before I buried you with it.'

'Lindey?' Heart sinking, he strode up behind her, grabbed hold of her shoulder.

She spun round, gun pulled and ready, and jammed it into his neck. 'Off. Now.' She sneered. 'You're not in the Royal Escort now, and I'm not just some petty officer in Pauper Fleet – *Earthman*. We're equal. *Elite*, right?'

Shade let go of her. She chuckled softly.

'I know what you are,' Lindey said simply. 'And I know what I could be. So you'd better think of a few strings you can pull for *me* back on Earth. Or a few other people here might have to find out about you too.'

Shade felt his temples throbbing, felt the shrapnel in his face bite at the little good skin left. 'What are you going to do?'

Lindey lowered the gun and tapped the palmset tucked into her belt. 'If we ever get out of this... You'll see.' She blew him a kiss and turned away. 'And then you'll have to be very, *very* nice to me, my little Earthborn Shadow...'

Shade watched her go, clenched his fists. 'Will I,' he muttered.

IV

Polly sighed. The Doctor and Tovel were digging about in the gossamer cables within the navigational console. Haunt was watching them, sullenly. Creben and Joiks were still waving little pieces of machinery around the place, looking for her magic door (Polly hoped they would fall through it and vanish, just as she had). Shel lingered by the grisly display of corpses, staring at them as if he were somehow communicating with them telepathically.

The idea frightened Polly. She edged closer to Ben.

'He's a funny one, isn't he,' she whispered. 'Shel, I mean. He acts more like a machine than a person.'

'Confucius say, he inscrutable,' Ben said cheerily. 'Bet if we looked hard enough we'd find "Made in Taiwan" stamped on him somewhere.'

Polly didn't smile back. 'That's racist, Ben.'

'Come on Pol, I didn't mean nothing by it.'

'No one ever means anything by it, but they still make the jokes all the same. Would you like to be treated like that?'

Ben looked away, hurt. 'We ain't been treated so well by any of them in case you hadn't noticed.'

Polly spoke without thinking. 'Adam's all right.'

'Adam?' Ben didn't look happy. 'Oh, got you. *Shade*. The bloke with the face. Yeah, you and him seem to be getting on pretty well.'

Polly sighed. Jealousy was so childish. 'I don't know why you're so bothered. You and that froggy woman seem to be hitting it off quite well yourselves,' she said, folding her arms.

Ben didn't say anything to the contrary. The rat.

'Look, Duchess,' Ben said finally. 'We're all stuck here, whizzing through space on some dirty great rock with a load of murdered black-magic criminals, a bunch of trigger-happy space marines and God knows what else. Let's not fall out in the middle of this lot.'

'We haven't fallen out,' Polly told him, and was rewarded with a broad grin. She lowered her voice. 'You know what we were saying earlier, about cat people and dog people?'

Ben nodded. 'What do you make of this lot?'

'Well, I suppose they should all be cats. Independent. Tough.' Polly considered. 'Shel's a cat. Creben and Lindey too.'

'Frog's not one or the other. Well, she's a frog, ain't she!' He paused. 'Got to feel sorry for her.'

Polly nodded, forced a smile. 'Adam – *Shade* – is definitely a dog.'

'And you feel sorry for him, right?'

Polly nodded. 'So we're equal.'

'Creben, Joiks,' called Haunt. 'Found anything yet?'

Both men shook their heads.

'As if she needed to ask,' Polly snorted. 'Doesn't she trust them to tell her?'

'She's just trying to keep them motivated, giving them something to do,' said Ben. 'Just 'cause they've got big guns don't mean they're not bricking it like the rest of us. If they feel like she's counting on them, they feel better about themselves.'

The thought hadn't occurred to Polly. 'I suppose that's your Navy background talking.' Then she sighed. 'I really am like a fish out of water round here.'

'Then I'd better watch out for you with all these cats about,' Ben said, patting her hand. 'Especially the big, bad Marshal Haunt.'

Polly shook her head. 'I'm not sure about her. Something in her eyes… She acts really tough, but I'll bet she's been hurt before. Hurt badly. A love affair that went wrong, or something.'

'Female intuition, is it?' Ben smirked.

'She's probably been a soldier forever, but it's like she's not here because she really wants to be… She just doesn't have anywhere else to go.'

Ben raised his eyebrows. 'Getting a bit deep for me, Pol.'

He looked quite relieved when a distraction came along in mutters and grumbles from the Doctor, as he struggled out of his spacesuit. Ben gave him a hand, while Tovel got on with pulling web-like filaments from out of the console. Soon the navy blue spacesuit was a shucked skin on the cavern floor, and the Doctor was resplendent again in his black frock coat, starched wing collar and cravat, somehow none the worse for wear.

'Any luck finding where we're going, Doctor?' Polly asked.

'I'm afraid not yet, my child.'

'Only a matter of time though, thanks to those reducing equations of yours,' said Tovel, and Polly could see he was impressed.

The Doctor smiled wanly, but his face hardened as Shade and Lindey came marching back into the control room with Roba and Frog at their heels. As usual Lindey looked assured and collected. Shade, she noticed, looked less comfortable.

'Half the bullring has collapsed,' Lindey reported. 'There'd be no way through to the ship, even if it was still here.'

The temperature in the room seemed to fall by a couple of degrees. Polly looked longingly at the TARDIS. With the invisible barrier in place it was as out of reach as the soldiers' spaceship.

Haunt took the news stoically. 'Then we sweep this place for droids. We kill anything that can kill us. Then we'll find a way to signal back home. We'll figure something out.'

'Are we *sure* this isn't part of the training simulation?' asked Shade hopefully.

No one replied.

'We could do with finding Denni,' Creben observed. 'She might've learned something that could help us.'

'She's *dead*,' Joiks muttered bitterly.

Haunt overheard him. 'Thanks to you, we don't know that for certain.' Joiks looked up, stung, but said nothing. 'We don't know anything at all,' Haunt went on. 'It's time we did.'

Now, as if under orders to accentuate the positive, there were murmurs of assent from the troops.

Haunt turned back to Joiks. 'Can you guide us back to where you lost Denni? That'll be our starting place.'

He nodded, to Haunt's evident satisfaction.

'All right everyone, we're moving out.'

'Everyone?' Polly squawked.

Haunt turned to her grimly. 'Everyone.'

'Madam,' protested the Doctor, 'surely in light of what has happened here with the missing crystals and the vanishing body, someone should remain here, on guard?'

'I have no one to spare,' Haunt said flatly. 'Besides, what's to guard? The crystals are not in this room, and the corpse fell apart in some kind of power surge when the drives started up.'

The Doctor looked between Haunt and Shel. 'You put a good deal of faith in your adjutant's judgement.'

'We're a team. One unit. All of us,' Haunt said simply. Her gaze swept round the room. 'If we're going to survive, we have to act like one. So congratulations, old man. You and yours just joined the squad.'

'Why do we have to go too?' Polly asked.

Haunt smiled coldly. 'I want you where I can see you.'

V

Ben tramped along behind Joiks as he led them all off to where he had last seen Denni. The Doctor and Polly were separated from him by the mass of marching bodies, straggling at the back of the procession. Now and then he heard Frog buzz some kind of prompt to keep them moving, but whether threat or request, he wasn't sure.

The cold seaweedy cave smell of the asteroid now had the added niff of sweaty trooper. It seemed to be driving the white fleas crazy. They were swarming over the troopers, jumping like ticks in their hair, over their skin, everywhere. The light seemed to shift as they walked along; Ben worked out this was because the weed on the ceilings – fleaweed, he would call it – grew in uneven clumps in these tunnels, rather than the even covering of those closer to the complex.

Why would that be, Ben wondered. What had the Doctor said? *'Has this been grown here by the architects of this place so that you can light your way... or so that something else can see you approaching?'*

Maybe now that something else didn't want them to see *it* coming.

'It was here,' Joiks said, pausing at the twisted mouth of yet another dank tunnel. 'It slopes down and gets pitch black.'

'All right,' Haunt said, pushing to the front of the group. 'We go inside in groups of three. Joiks, take Creben and Frog in there. Tovel, Roba, take the boy here.'

Ben felt his heart beat a little faster. 'I should go with Polly,' he said.

Haunt didn't even bother to look at him. 'The girl can go with Lindey and Shade. Shel and me will take the old man.'

Ben turned to Roba and Tovel. Their lack of enthusiasm suggested that if they'd been picking teams, he might have wound up somewhere else.

'Come on then, fellas,' he said briskly, marching up to Roba with a confidence he didn't feel. 'You've got a spare gun there, ain't ya? Lend us it, will you?'

Roba looked down at him, sneering. 'You're seriously asking me to lend you my weapon?'

Ben pulled himself up to his full height, and even then he was barely level with Roba's shoulder. 'All right, *give* us it, then.'

Roba slowly pulled the chunky pistol from its holster and levelled it at Ben's chest. 'To mess with me,' he said quietly, 'you're either stupid, or else you've got some guts.'

'Don't reckon I'm the brightest in the class,' Ben said, trying to keep his voice steady. 'But I reckon I got plenty of guts.' He put his hand round the gun barrel and gently pushed it aside a fraction. 'And if it's the same to you, I'd like them to stay inside my skin. All right?'

Roba's eyes narrowed, but soon his teeth bared in a wolf-like grin. He opened his palm and allowed Ben to take the gun with sweaty fingers.

'Maybe we could use a man your size around,' Roba told him, slapping down the slab of his hand on Ben's shoulder. 'You can watch my ankles. Let me know if anything's coming to chew 'em. OK?'

'You got a deal, mate.'

Creben and Frog followed Joiks into the tunnel, weapons trained dead ahead of them.

'Count ten,' Haunt instructed them. 'Then move in after them.'

'I'll go in first,' Tovel volunteered. 'Ben, you follow me. Then Roba.'

Ben nodded, and looked over his shoulder at Polly down the dim passage. She was watching him forlornly, peeping over Shade's shoulder. He winked at her, but wasn't sure if she'd see. The Doctor, standing by Shel about ten feet away, inclined his head. His chest was puffed up, as if with pride.

His fingers flexing around the unfamiliar contours of the gun handle, Ben strode after Tovel into the dark, dripping mouth of the tunnel.

* * *

Polly found the darkness almost overpowering. The troopers' torchlight seemed swallowed by it. Occasionally she glimpsed movement in it, a faint flare on a rifle butt, a moving leg or swinging arm. Her imagination filled in the gaps, conjured monsters out of the dark for her to thread her way through. The ground was wet and slippery with scree. She clung on to Shade's arm for support.

'The path splits into three.' Creben sounded as casual as always, even here.

'Me and Denni never got this far,' said Joiks.

'Test your wrist-comms,' Haunt snapped. 'I couldn't reach you and Denni before.'

The squad did as she asked, and everyone seemed satisfied.

'Evidently some sort of energy-source was interfering with your transmissions,' said the Doctor. 'The drives, powering up, perhaps.'

'Perhaps.' Haunt didn't sound interested. 'Joiks, Creben, Frog, push on to the left. 'Tovel, your group follow them. We'll take the middle. Shade the right.'

Polly was impressed by her swift decision making, until it dawned on her that since no one knew where they were going, it hardly mattered who went where.

Except that anything could be waiting, silently, down one of these dark passages.

Footsteps crunched off into the darkness.

'Here we go then,' said Shade. He didn't sound much happier about it than Polly did, and she wasn't sure whether to feel consoled or more frightened still.

Polly stifled a cry as something pushed past her into the tunnel. It was Lindey.

'I'll go in first, Shadow. I don't like the thought of you watching out for me.' She paused, squinted back into the spotlight of Shade's torch beam. 'Not after what you did.'

Still holding on to Shade's sleeve, Polly felt the man start to tremble. From the shaky hiss of his breathing, it wasn't with anger, but with fear.

He pulled his arm away from her, brusquely. Then he followed Lindey into the tunnel.

'What was all that about?' Polly muttered to herself. As she went to follow them, the toe of her boot knocked against something. She cried out.

Shade spun round, gun raised. 'What is it?'

'I don't know. Shine your light here,' she whispered, tapping the protruding object with her toe.

It was a little pile of rocks.

'That's mine!' Polly breathed. 'My marker. I must've come this way.' She frowned. 'I'm sure it wasn't so dark before.' She peered at the little heap of rocks. Beside it was one much larger. 'Here. There's been some sort of subsidence, the tunnel I went through has been sealed off.' She paused. 'I think that weird place with the blue light and the countdown is on the other side of this rockfall.'

'Come on,' Shade said. He sounded preoccupied. 'I mustn't let Lindey get too far ahead.'

Polly shrugged but gave no argument. Their crunching footsteps set a mournful tempo as they set off after her.

'Have you known her long?' Polly asked tentatively.

'What's that supposed to mean?' Shade said with a sideways glance.

'Nothing. I just wondered. With you being a team and all.'

'Well, then, no. I haven't known her long. I haven't known a lot of this crowd long. We're soldiers. What's to know? We fight till one day we die.'

When Lindey's scream tore through the blackness Polly thought her heart would give out.

There was movement in the dark. Now Shade gripped *her* arm, as if not wanting her to run away and leave him.

There was a heavy rushing noise, a pressure in her ears, and Polly's perceptions seemed to skew. She glimpsed something in Shade's torch beam: some grotesque, squat little figure, then a pale face falling away into the darkness like a stone down a well as Lindey, still screaming, was snatched away at unnatural, frightening speed.

Chapter Six
By the Pricking of my Thumbs

I

'We've got to help her!' Polly shouted, Lindey's screams still ringing in her ears.

Shade raised his wrist to his lips. For a few moments he just breathed, deeply and shakily, before speaking. 'Marshal Haunt. Have lost Lindey.'

There was nothing but static.

'Oh no,' murmured Polly.

'Marshal Haunt,' Shade repeated. 'Respond.'

'Maybe…' Polly swallowed nervously. 'Maybe whatever it was got Haunt too.'

The static stopped, replaced by the heavy silence of the tunnel.

'Shade?' Haunt's voice from the communicator made them both jump.

'Marshal, it's Lindey. Dragged off, it was so fast…'

'Get after her,' Haunt snapped. 'I'm on my way. Out.'

'Come on,' Shade said. He took Polly's arm and they ran on together. The torch beam played crazily over the dark and jagged surface. The rock walls were moth-eaten with entrances to other tunnels, gaping open like mouths ready to suck them both inside.

There was a sudden scraping, rattling noise, and Shade ducked down. Polly gave a short shriek of alarm, but a moment later Shade was up again. 'It's all right. I dropped my palmscreen. Let's go.'

They didn't have much further to run before the darkness suddenly gave way to a thick, porridgey light. She and Shade had emerged into a vast vaulted chamber. It had five walls, stacked high with the familiar dark slates, though one was partially obscured by another of the extraordinary glass tapestries. The ceiling was heavy with the luminous weed. It hung down in sticky strands, and here and there on the smooth stone floor it lay in glowing heaps that were clustered with the pale insects. Five tall stone columns reached up from the stone-paved floor like huge candles, each one crowned with a pair of massive stone sculptures. Eerily lit from above, they reminded Polly of Renaissance cherubs grown fat and gone to seed. It must've been a statue of some kind she glimpsed back in the tunnel.

The chamber was otherwise empty and silent, save for the ghostly chiming of the tapestry fragments, disturbed as if by a breeze. There was no sign of Lindey.

Footsteps behind them made Polly jump. She saw Haunt tearing towards them, rifle raised, staring wildly around.

'Where is she?' Haunt demanded of Shade.

Shade shook his head but said nothing.

Haunt glared at Polly. 'Did you see anything?'

'There was no time,' Polly murmured. 'It all happened so fast.'

'Too fast,' Shade agreed. 'She was just… taken.'

'Taken by what, for God's sake? By a droid? By the hand?' Haunt's voice rose a notch, and she slapped a palm angrily against Polly's shoulder. 'By the colour of this stupid spacesuit?'

'There was nothing Shade could have done,' Polly insisted.

Haunt grabbed hold of Polly's chin and leaned in close. Her voice was low and threatening. 'Listen to me. You do not speak for any of my squad. Never.' Her eyes were dark, unblinking. 'You follow me?'

Polly nodded mutely. Shade just looked on, apparently unmoved.

'What is happening here?'

Polly could have cried with relief as the Doctor's voice rang out imperiously around the chamber. Haunt widened her eyes in one more silent warning, then let Polly go.

'There's no sign of Lindey,' Haunt snapped. Polly saw she was ignoring the Doctor and talking to Shel, who stood behind him. 'Could whatever took her have got past you?'

'No, Marshal,' Shel answered. 'We saw nothing.'

'These tunnels interconnect,' the Doctor added. 'We crossed from ours to join yours. I imagine all the passages are joined, it's quite a labyrinth.' He nodded decisively.

'Terrific. So Lindey has vanished, just like Denni. You saw nothing. Shade *did* nothing.'

'Again,' Polly heard Shade whisper. He absently itched one of the black ridges in his face, and quickly screwed up his eyes as if in pain.

As she wondered whether or not to place a consoling hand on his shoulder, she noticed his palmscreen fastened securely to his chunky belt.

And, peeping from his jumpsuit's hip pocket, the shiny corner of an identical computer.

'Are you all right, my dear?' the Doctor had crossed, as quiet as a cat, to join her. Polly steered him discreetly over to one of the stone pillars.

'Doctor,' Polly whispered urgently. 'I think Shade has got Lindey's palm computer thing. She must've dropped it when she was…' Her voice dried up, and she swallowed. 'I think he found it in the tunnel and pretended it was his.'

The Doctor frowned. 'Are you sure, child?'

She nodded. 'So why hasn't he told Haunt?'

'Why indeed?' muttered the Doctor. 'I wonder…'

'And when I first met him… When I was running from whatever that thing was that chased me away from the blue place…' She looked wide-eyed at the Doctor. 'It was Shade who brought the roof down on us, stopped me leading anyone there to see for themselves.'

'You must tell me all that happened, Polly.'

She gladly obliged. It felt good to be able to tell the outlandish tale just as it happened and know that she was believed without question, taken deadly seriously. The Doctor always did that; made you the centre of his world whenever he looked at you.

When she'd finished, the Doctor simply nodded. 'It sounds to me as if you stumbled upon a power source of some kind. Perhaps the very core of this subterranean citadel.' He nodded again with satisfaction at this summation.

'And someone else had found it too,' Polly said, remembering the figure she'd seen through the blue haze. 'Oh, this is a terrible place!' She scratched the back of her neck. 'There's something here with us, I'm sure of it. Something… evil. Watching us all the time.'

The Doctor patted her absently on the shoulder. 'We have eyes too,' he said, 'and we must use them well.'

Around her feet the white fleas hopped mindlessly. High above, the cherubim balanced precariously as if frozen in the midst of some joyful dance.

II

Ben felt like piggy in the middle, stuck between Tovel and Roba. The two men joked to keep their spirits up, but the conversation went right over Ben's head. A good foot shorter than either of them, perhaps it was no surprise, he mused ruefully.

Suddenly the laughter stopped dead. Ben heard a scraping sound ahead of him, then silence.

There was a sound like a generator charging up, and then confused movement about him in the dark as Tovel pushed past to join Roba.

'Keep down, Ben,' Roba shouted. 'Kill-Droid approaching.'

A red glow was creeping round the corner of the tunnel. Then it was lost in the flare of laser fire from the two soldiers. Ben shielded his face as splinters of rock showered over him, smelt chemical smoke from the glowing barrels of the guns. A large stone fell from the ceiling and struck his leg.

'Go easy!' Ben shouted. 'You'll bring the roof down on us!'

The gunfire stopped, as if they'd actually listened to him. The air was thick with dust. For a moment, all Ben could hear was Tovel and Roba's ragged breathing.

'We got it,' Tovel said. 'Sharp shooting, marksman.'

Roba coughed. 'You sure we got it?'

'We must've got it.'

Cautiously they advanced on the bend in the tunnel.

A rush of crimson coloured the walls. Something slammed into the two men, knocking them back.

In the red haze Ben could see a nightmare figure rounding the corner. It was huge, filling the tunnel. Its head was a great glass cylinder, the source of the infernal glow. Its body was the size of a chest freezer, chrome and gleaming, bobbing about on countless spidery limbs that seemed fashioned from tensile steel.

The machine whipped out a metal tentacle that ended in a cruel spike, one that looked easily big enough to skewer two heads in one go. Roba brought up his gun but the robot's spike hooked it from his grip. With a flick, the gun clattered out of reach behind the thing.

Ben scrambled to his feet.

'Here!' Tovel shouted, and hurled his own rifle Ben's way.

Before he could grab it, the robot flung out another tentacle and caught the gun like it weighed nothing.

Ben scooped his own gun from the tunnel floor and fired it, aiming for the thing's head. There was a noise like bullets firing and a lacklustre light flashed out from the gun's tip, but he felt no recoil and the effect on the robot was disappointing to say the least. Ben thought the droid wasn't even going to notice his attack, but finally its head rotated slowly round to face him.

'That thing won't scratch a Kay-Dee,' Tovel gasped.

'We must've damaged it,' said Roba. 'Or else why ain't it firing no more?'

The robot now used Roba's rifle as a club. Ben dived to the floor as the weapon whooshed over his head and smashed into the wall. Tovel and Roba were using the distraction to try and scramble out of the Kill-Droid's way, falling over each other in the enclosed, suffocating space, choking on smoke and dust. When the thing advanced on them, Ben found himself directly in its way.

Desperately he wormed through the robot's tangle of sinewy legs. His skin felt scorched by the fierce heat radiating from the machine's gleaming body. He cried out as something hooked on his ankle and the flesh started to tear. But with his arms at full stretch, he felt the cold, solid bulk of Tovel's rifle. Grabbing it, he jammed its barrel up what he hoped was the part of the Kill-Droid where the sun don't shine.

This time when he fired, the results were a lot more spectacular.

Like a firework going off in a jam jar, the monster's head exploded. A fog of red smoke escaped the shattered glass. Sparks shot out of the blackening neck. The twisting limbs stiffened and then buckled beneath the weight of the great chrome coffin above. Ben tried to work his way clear of the bulk as it teetered and rocked alarmingly above him, but something was still hooked in his left ankle, anchoring the thing to him.

'Don't let it fall on me, for God's sake!' Ben gasped. 'I'll be flattened!'

In the sputtering light of the sparks, Ben saw his own terrified reflection staring him out from the robot's gleaming back. His distorted features grew closer, clearer, as the dead weight of the thing finally fell to crush him.

Inches from his face its fall was halted.

'Get yourself free quickly,' Ben heard Tovel gasp. 'This thing weighs a tonne.'

Ben felt for the hook in his ankle and yanked it out. Raising himself on his elbows, biting his tongue to stop himself whimpering with the pain, he worked his way backwards a few feet along the tunnel.

'All right, I'm clear!' he yelled, but his cry was drowned out by the clang and clatter of the Kill-Droid as it smashed heavily into the ground, inches from his feet.

Ben breathed a long, long sigh of relief. 'Thanks, fellas.'

'Thanks yourself,' Tovel replied, and Roba nodded. Despite the pain in his ankle, Ben felt a giddying rush of triumph. He'd sorted the War Machine's big brother, and earned his place in the barracks. Having the friendship of this pair should make his stay here, and that of Polly and the Doctor, a little easier.

Roba studied the Kill-Droid's inert body. 'This thing's loaded with different weapons, but the charges are all still full. Not a shot fired. Why didn't it use them?'

'It probably heard me telling you the whole roof would come crashing down,' Ben called, gingerly feeling round his injured ankle. It didn't feel too bad now. It just itched like hell.

'You reckon this thing cares about a tonne of rubble on its head?'

Tovel clearly didn't think so. 'No, it must be the one me and Shade met before. We must've hit it.'

'Whatever,' Roba announced, raising his wrist to his mouth. 'Looks like we've got a hell of a trophy to take back to Haunt.'

III

'Good work, Roba. Out.' Haunt smiled in triumph as she swung round to address Polly, the Doctor and Shade. 'Roba reports a Kay-Dee down.'

'No static blocking communications this time,' the Doctor observed quietly.

'Is Ben all right?' Polly asked.

Haunt nodded. 'The droid attacked them in the tunnel.' She paused. 'It must've killed Lindey first.'

Polly saw the Doctor shake his head at this. 'We don't know that for sure,' he said.

'You said yourself, these tunnels are connected.' Haunt stared him down. 'Can you give me an alternative explanation?'

'Very well, if the droids did indeed kill Denni and Lindey,' the Doctor said quickly, 'then that mystery is solved. Will you now accept it is essential we learn our destination with all possible speed, and attempt to find a way of signalling for help from outside?'

Haunt seemed to consider his plea. 'Shel, take the old man and the girl back to the control room,' she said at last. 'I'll contact the others. We'll search on for the bodies of Lindey and Denni and meet you back there.'

Shel looked pale, his face covered in a sheen of sweat. 'Marshal.'

They left Haunt in the vast chamber, alone with Shade, both as silent and still as one of the statues balanced on top of the pillars.

'If it wasn't the droid that murdered Denni and Lindey,' Polly said nervously, 'then what did?'

'Or who?' the Doctor muttered darkly.

Polly decided not to pursue her line of questioning. She was scared enough as it was. She shivered as Shel led them down the same tunnel that she had taken with Shade.

'I do wish you could've seen the blue place, Doctor,' she sighed. 'I'm sure you would've understood it.'

'Maybe so,' the Doctor agreed loftily. 'Young man,' he added turning to Shel. 'Would you be so kind as to attempt to contact someone on your communicator, hmm?'

Shel looked at him curiously but contacted Haunt. Her voice crackled through in response, partially obscured by the rhythmic shushing of the static.

'A test only,' Shel reported. 'Out.'

'The power source you mentioned, Doctor,' said Polly. 'Does that mean it's growing fainter?'

'Perhaps. But without a good deal of excavation, there is no way of retracing your footsteps to discover the truth. We should continue to the main control room.' He sighed heavily, impatiently shrugged off his frock coat. His long white hair was clinging to his damp forehead. 'We must see what is happening back there.'

Polly nodded, and followed after the silent Shel.

Her arms itched. The fleas, she thought. They must bite. She ruminated gloomily on the red lumps that would soon cover her as they trekked back to the control room.

They'd got as far as the bullring when the itching was replaced by a prickling sensation at the sound of flashbulbs charging.

'Doctor!' she yelled. 'That sound...'

'Down!' yelled the Doctor, flinging himself to the rocky floor.

Polly copied him, her cushioned suit protecting her from the gravelly floor. She felt a heat like sunlamps on the back of her neck.

All she could see was a crimson wash filtering into her vision, and the rising whirr of something huge and heavy approaching.

'D– Droid.' Shel reached for his gun.

Polly stared in horror as this 'droid', a chugging red colossus as big as a department store lift, stole into the rocky ring on angle-poised legs and swivelled its heavy glassy head from side to side in search of what it could crush first.

Chapter Seven
The Burden

I

Shel levelled his rifle and fired blast after white-hot blast at the robot. The droid hunched on its many legs like a spider that knows itself discovered, then lashed out a steel tentacle that swiped the gun from Shel's grip. A splatter of blood from his arm slopped onto the floor, but Polly heard no sound of a cry.

The Doctor was back on his feet. He flapped his heavy frock coat at the creature like a matador waving his cloak before an enraged bull.

'Run, Polly,' the Doctor insisted. He looked at her pointedly, sheltering behind his coat. Did he think that if he couldn't see the robot it couldn't see him? 'As fast as you can.'

Polly rose to her feet and prepared to run for the jagged hole in the ring that led to the passageway stretching back to the control room. As she did so, a metal fist punched the Doctor through his coat. Silently he doubled up and collapsed.

The robot sidled up to his prone body. Two flexible probes that ended in gleaming surgical blades emerged from its silvery trunk and hovered over the Doctor, as if about to carve a roast.

Then a grating noise somewhere between an alarm clock and an egg timer burst out into the shadowy bullring. Polly saw the woman called Frog come charging into the rocky arena, screaming. She fired blast after blast from a rifle she clutched in just one hand.

The robot spun round to face her, leaving the Doctor unguarded. Polly swiftly ran over to him, as he lay winded on the floor. She gripped his hand; it was cold, clammy, heavily veined. And as he rose she saw his face. Lined, parchment-thin skin. Eyes like dark beads rolling in his head as he recovered his wits. For a moment she wanted to recoil from him as something almost alien, but he held his hand out to her, a pathetic gesture for help, and she took it. His grip on her arm was feeble as he held on to her, gasping for breath, an ordinary old man again.

Frog had been joined by Creben and Joiks, each firing their guns at the droid, trapping it in a circle of fire, blasting at it again and again until its devil-red haze faded, its movements became weak and clumsy. Unable to resist the hail of fire, its legs splayed and it crashed heavily to the ground.

The Doctor seemed to draw strength from the mechanical creature as it flailed helplessly on the floor. His breathing became more regular, and he smiled at Polly with something approaching pride, as if every breath he drew demonstrated superiority over his fallen foe. He scratched at the back of his neck, reminding Polly she was still itching all over too. Just her luck if the fleas were poisonous.

Shel stared down dispassionately at both the silent machine and at the puncture wound in his arm.

Joiks shot a pointed glance at the Doctor. 'I think he could use you.'

'I am not a doctor of medicine.' The Doctor shook his head wearily. 'However, his combat suit will compress the flesh around the wound, will it not? To stem the blood flow?'

Creben nodded. 'And this should help. Medikit.' He pulled a slim metal box from a pouch on his harness and stepped forward to examine the wound. Shel recoiled, began nursing the injury as if he'd only just become aware of it.

'It doesn't hurt,' Shel informed them.

Looking a little awkward now Shel had rejected his help, Creben discarded the first aid box and turned instead to the droid. 'Is it dead?'

'Looks like it,' Frog gurgled. She prodded the thing with her foot. 'I ain't seen one that size before.' She gave a filthy chuckle. Polly shuddered.

'That was the second droid,' Shel muttered. 'T... Tovel destroyed the first in the tunnels back there.'

Frog slapped her palm against Joiks's in a victorious gesture, her bulging eyes shining with delight. 'Two down, Game Over,' she said with a gappy smile. She scooped up Creben's first aid tin and rummaged inside. 'Celebration time. Got anything recreational in here, Creben?'

'Frog, stop.' Shel shook his head slowly. 'The droid had already k… killed Lindey.'

'Lindey too?' Her voice buzzed out just as loudly, but everything else about her seemed fragile and quiet for a second.

Joiks stared at Shel. 'You saw this?'

'No.'

'Got a body?'

'Her body has not been found.'

'She was grabbed, wasn't she?' Joiks started pacing up and down. 'It just took her, whatever it was. Took her away, just like Denni. No body.' He kicked the droid savagely. 'No damned body.'

Creben pointed to one of the robot's barbed flexible arms, lying uncoiled now like a steel snake. 'If it snagged Lindey and Denni with one of these at full stretch, it could simply have retracted the limb. They'd have been dragged away at quite a speed.'

'But where would it have hidden the bodies?' asked Polly. 'And why?'

Creben tapped a nozzle protruding from the cracked glass façade covering the droid's metal midriff. 'Disintegrator. Nice and clean.'

'You seen something like this thing before, Creben?' Joiks asked suspiciously. 'Thought this droid was meant to be some kind of new secret design.'

Creben shrugged. 'I've come up against disintegrators before. Just never on a droid.'

'Let me see.' The Doctor stooped and delved into a split in the glass to remove a tiny circuit. Once he had finished scrutinising it, he straightened and faced Creben. 'A neat explanation, young man, yes, very neat,' he said, still a little breathlessly. 'But I'm afraid you are incorrect.'

Creben raised an eyebrow. 'Oh yes?'

The Doctor held up his circuit. 'This tells us that the disintegrator hasn't been fired.'

'Then the other droid did it,' Creben countered smoothly. 'It probably obliterated the Schirr body in the control room too.'

'Nah,' Frog buzzed. 'Marshal Haunt said that was *resonance* or something. Vibrations from the take-off.'

'No. Shel said that,' Polly ventured before she could stop herself. She found herself feeling a little guilty to be kicking a man when he was down and bleeding, but she felt things should be set straight. 'Your marshal just agreed with him.'

'You got a problem with Haunt's decisions?' Joiks screwed up his flattened nose. 'Jesus, what is it with you women?'

'I don't got a problem with Haunt,' Frog announced.

Joiks laughed unkindly. 'You ain't a woman, Frog, you don't count.'

'Please,' the Doctor said, cutting across their bickering. 'I am sure you wish to report this, er, victory to your Marshal, and I suggest you enquire as to whether the other Kill-Droid's disintegrator has been used. In the meantime, I must return to the control room, quickly.' He looked beseechingly at Shel. 'Will you not tell them, sir, that Marshal Haunt gave us such instructions?'

Shel looked at the Doctor dumbly for a few moments before recovering himself and nodding slowly. 'There's m… much to be done,' he agreed.

'You need a medic,' Frog said, rattling Creben's tin with one hand and placing the other gently on Shel's injured arm. He pulled away from her, gripped his wound more tightly. 'I'll go with them, Creben,' Frog continued, undaunted, 'and patch up Shel. You and Joiks get back to Haunt and the others with the good news.'

'Two of us for two of them,' said Creben, staring at the fallen robot.

Joiks snorted. 'That's profound, man.'

Creben shrugged. 'Simply an observation.'

'What you saying, that we drew here today? The squad's down by two but we didn't lose more than they did so that's OK?'

'We're alive. So *that's* OK. Now do you want to tell Marshal Haunt we took out the droid or should I?'

Joiks glared at Creben for a few moments. Then he raised his wrist to his mouth and spoke into it. 'Marshal. Met a droid in the bullring.

Hit status terminal, confirmed. No one down…'

Polly turned and helped the Doctor along the rough stone of the passageway. Shel and Frog followed on behind. The Doctor's brow was furrowed in fierce concentration as he walked. Not for the first time, Polly wished she knew what he was thinking.

II

'Pretty strange request, ain't it?' Ben watched Roba and Tovel struggle to lift the panel of thick frosted glass from the droid's heavily-armed torso. 'This is that trophy you mentioned, is it?'

'Gonna look pretty cool stuck up on the wall back at the dorm,' Roba remarked with a huge grin, his teeth white and shiny.

They'd gone wandering on through the tunnel – Ben with a slight limp – until Haunt had come through once again on the communicator, telling them that the other droid was just scrap metal too. She'd ordered them to remove the Kill-Droid's gun panel, then retrace their steps back to where they'd split up from the others. Tovel and Roba had become so bleedin' jolly they didn't even question what G.I. Jane might want the thing for.

'Weighs a bit,' Ben gasped as he helped Tovel and Roba shift the scorched unit.

'It sure is heavy.' Roba looked at Tovel gravely. 'Guess the civilian can't cope. We're gonna have to carry it without him.'

'Reckon we can handle that, Roba?' Tovel asked with mock nervousness.

Roba shrugged. 'All we can do is try.'

Together the two of them easily hefted the gun panel and guffawed as Ben reached up for it, still trying to do his bit.

'Oh, very funny,' said Ben sourly.

'Y'know, Roba, this is just like lifting stretchers again,' said Tovel.

'You still got the knack,' Roba told him with a throaty chuckle.

Feeling himself flush, Ben spoke without thinking. 'Aren't you a bit jolly considering what's just happened to your mate?'

The atmosphere dipped suddenly below freezing. Ben shut his eyes, wishing he could keep his big trap shut sometimes.

'If she's dead,' Tovel said slowly, 'then *we* got the thing that got *her*.'

We hope, Ben thought to himself.

'S'right. We did what we came here to do.' Roba shot Ben a glance. 'You don't think that's something to celebrate?'

''Course I do,' Ben said, looking at the floor. Who was he to tell these blokes how to deal with their grief?

'Didn't know Lindey too well,' Tovel admitted.

'Me neither,' Roba said. 'Some other place, some other time, I'd have liked to.' He smiled. 'Used to see a girl who fought in the Zero-Gs. Fit is not the word. The moves she could pull...'

'What about you two,' asked Ben. 'You know each other, right?'

'Both in the Peacekeeper Volunteers,' said Roba. 'When Beijing Minor went down we were putting out the fires for weeks.'

Ben didn't have a clue if this was a great victory or a crushing defeat. 'I remember Beijing Minor going down. In the third round, weren't it?'

It was the wrong thing to say. Roba dropped his side of the panel and turned on Ben. One shovel-like hand swatted him back against the wall.

'All right, leave off!' Ben protested.

'There were thirty in our unit when we hit Beijing,' Roba hissed. 'Three of us made it back off-world. When Morphiea claimed responsibility for torching the planet, me and Tovel signed up to go AT Elite. Anti-Terror, man. To fight back. To *take* them.' He let Ben go and turned away.

Tovel had watched all this coolly. 'Pretty sweet story, isn't it?'

'Ain't it though?' Roba took a step back from Ben, still frowning, then looked over at Tovel. 'All it needs is an ending.'

'Not just yet, eh?' Tovel grinned.

It seemed that Roba didn't hold grudges except against the Morphieans. Soon he and Tovel were joking around again as they manhandled the droid's weapons case along the tunnel, and Ben felt able to join in again.

'What about the rest of your gang, then?'

'Only really mixed with them at the greet before take-off,' said Tovel.

'A greet? Oh, what, like a party?' Ben smirked. 'Can't imagine Haunt and Shel were the life and soul.'

Roba nodded. 'Haunt stayed five minutes. Shel managed maybe ten.'

'He don't seem too friendly,' Ben observed.

'Friendlier than Creben,' Tovel assured him, gritting his teeth as he shifted the weight of the robot's carcass onto his shoulder. 'Another new boy. Breezed through the ranks. He's got brains, I'll give him that.'

'What about Shade?' Ben enquired lightly. Know Your Enemy.

'He got most of his blown out on New Jersey,' said Roba, and he and Tovel laughed uproariously. Ben laughed too, though he wasn't sure quite why.

'Damn fool threw himself on a Schirr mine, evacuating some kids under fire,' Tovel explained. 'But hey, you can't keep an Earth-birther down.'

'Hey, Tovel. Shade's an Earthman?'

'I believe he may have mentioned that he was, yes, Roba.' Again the two men started laughing.

Ben decided that, if pressed, he'd say he was Martian and hope for the best.

'Earth,' sighed Roba, manhandling the heavy glass plating round to better support it. He sounded half-wistful, half-angry. 'They ship out their poor over half the galaxy, give them a few hand-me-downs and call us pioneers.'

'"There is HEART in EARTH",' Tovel chanted, slack-jawed like a school kid saying the Lord's Prayer in assembly.

Roba suddenly stopped. 'Ben – would you itch my back, man? Yeah, just there.'

'Glad I'm of some use,' Ben sighed. 'What about Frog, what's her story, then?'

'Dunno,' said Roba. 'And with that voice, who wants to hear it.'

'Heard at the greet she was in a shuttle crash as a kid,' Tovel said. He signalled to Roba and they dumped the robot on the ground. 'Joiks told me. Her throat got torn out.'

Roba tapped a spot below his collar bone. 'So they gave her that gadget to buzz her up some voice.'

Now it was Ben's turn to wince. 'And the crash did for her face?'

Tovel shook his head. 'Nope. Her old man did that. She was fourteen, she'd stayed out late, done something she shouldn't. So he took a razor to her. She got it off him and used it right back.'

'You're joking me,' Ben said, wishing he'd never asked.

'Terrible shame, ain't it.' Roba seemed in reflective mood as he and Tovel took the weight of the robot's bulk again. 'Still, can't really blame her old man for trying. Wayward girl like that needs some discipline.'

He and Tovel started creasing up. Ben forced a few laughs himself just to fit in, but he was glad when a few seconds later the endless crunching through the flat darkness suddenly became a climb. They were nearly back where they'd started.

'Welcome back. Finally.' Haunt's caustic voice called to them from the dimly lit passageway ahead. The rest of the welcoming committee comprised Joiks, Creben and a very miserable-looking Shade. He had his fingertips pressed to his face like he was trying to give himself a massage.

Roba and Tovel greeted their squad, gratefully dropped the droid's gun carriage, and spent a few moments scratching themselves all over. It had to be the fleas, Ben decided. He wondered vaguely if his naval malaria jab would cover him for alien insect bites.

'Where's Polly?' Ben asked, darting a quick look at Earthman Shade. 'And the Doctor?'

'Back in the control room with Shel and Frog,' said Creben, already crouching over the discarded panel and digging a knife of some kind into the cracked glass. It split open noisily, and Creben retrieved a tiny circuit. 'The Kill-Droid we came across hadn't fired its disintegrator, but this one...' He tailed off as he scrutinised the circuit.

'Let me guess.' Joiks sounded even surlier than usual. 'This one didn't either.'

Creben only nodded.

Like him, no one said a word.

* * *

III

Frog and Shel led the way back to the control room. With the Doctor too absorbed in his own thoughts to make conversation, Polly set her mind to memorising their path from key parts of the architecture. The golden doors they passed through now she knew led on to the big, tomb-like hallway. The amazing tapestry of glass-fragments hanging down from the cavern roof tinkled softly as it caught some tiny breeze. The weed began to encroach on the ceilings here. Without its fleshy, glowing leaves, the huge abstract stone figures that guarded the final, narrow corridor would remain unseen, looking blindly on the likes of Polly as she passed.

Sure enough, the giant statues soon came into view.

Polly frowned. She hadn't noticed the winged cherubs here, clinging to the great rough heads. Each cherub was the size of a man, but the proportions of the body were those of a pudgy child, with smooth fat arms and swollen stomach. The faces were hard to discern, high up as they were. Polly decided she didn't like the figures; but since little else in this place seemed to be remotely attractive, she wondered if that perhaps was the point.

Everything in the control room was just as they had left it.

Except another Schirr body had vanished from the dais.

Chapter Eight
Cat Among the Pigeons

I

'No,' whispered Polly hoarsely. The hairs on the back of her neck rose. She'd known it even without taking in all the detail; a sense that the place was not as they'd left it.

It was the one at the end, this time, on the left-hand side. The one so soaked in gore it might've drowned in its own blood.

There was a sickly, decaying smell in the room. The corpse in the chair, Polly realised. The air must be getting to it now. But what was getting to the bodies behind the barrier?

Frog swore, dropped the medicine tin and drew her gun. She looked around, uncertain where she should be pointing it.

'No vibration could have caused this.' The Doctor announced, nodding to himself as if he had expected this latest development all along. 'It's interesting, very interesting. Two of them for two of you.'

'Well, if the droids had anything to do with this, then we're OK,' Frog said. 'They're screwed. They can't do nothing else now.'

'Tell me.' The Doctor turned to Shel. 'These killing machines of yours you brought here to fight. How were they transported?'

'In the hold,' Shel answered softly. He staggered over towards the remaining bodies, transfixed. 'The droids were a new design, crated up so we wouldn't see. When Haunt gave the signal, they released themselves into the drop zone to take up pre-programmed positions.'

'So.' The Doctor paused impressively. 'You have no way of knowing if *something else* came aboard your ship with them.'

'And left when they did,' Polly murmured, 'when no one was allowed to see...'

No one said anything for a while as the implications sank in.

'Even say that's true,' Frog said suddenly. 'Sure, they might wanna kill us. But the Schirr are dead already. Why take them?'

Polly shuddered. 'They *must* be dead, mustn't they? Shel, you *said* they were,' she added petulantly.

Shel nodded. 'My instruments informed me that was the case.' He reached for a gadget in his belt with his good hand and waved it in front of the Schirr bodies. Polly was afraid to watch too closely in case they suddenly pounced on him.

He handed the device to the Doctor. 'See for yourself.'

The Doctor took the gadget gingerly, and took a few seconds to familiarise himself with its functions. 'You put a good deal of trust in machines,' he observed, before handing it back with a smile. 'But I prefer to draw my own conclusions.' With that he started to peer at each Schirr in turn, muttering under his breath and occasionally holding a crooked thumb up at arm's length, like an artist gauging a measurement.

Frog looked glum. She scratched the patches of stubble that were all that remained of her hair and stared about, her boggle-eyes wider than ever. 'Who wants to tell Haunt about all this?' she warbled.

'First,' the Doctor suggested without looking up, 'let us be sure of what we are telling her.'

'I should do it,' announced Shel distantly. But he didn't, he just stood there, staring at the bodies, swaying. He tottered forwards and leaned heavily on the nearest control panel, not far from the corpse in the chair, as if about to have a conversation with it.

'Uh-oh,' said Frog. 'I told you, Shel honey, you need a medic.' She pulled something from her pocket, the size and shape of a boiled sweet, and then threw it down on the ground behind Shel. There was a crack like a starter's pistol, and Frog leapt back. A translucent rectangular bubble the size of a couch had appeared out of nowhere.

'Force mattress,' Frog explained with a wink at the Doctor. 'We all carry them, honey. Never know where you might need to bed down for the night.'

Polly watched in fascination as Frog helped Shel, unprotesting, to lie back on the bubble. The force mattress moulded itself to his body like it was made from putty. Her patient in place, Frog retrieved the first aid tin and pulled out what looked like an aerosol. Shel plucked it from her hand and applied the spray to his wound himself.

Frog shrugged and left him to it. She raised her gun again and started swinging it about, pointing it at shadows, making Polly decidedly nervous.

'Come, come,' chided the Doctor, looking up from his studies. 'You're surely not expecting to find our missing friend hiding under the table, hmm?'

'Body's got to be somewhere, don't it?' Frog retorted, still hunting about. 'We saw it here last.'

The Doctor gripped his lapels and nodded. 'And I feel quite certain we shan't see it here again just yet.'

'You think the Schirr disintegrated like the other one?' Polly asked hopefully.

Before the Doctor could respond, Shel groaned loudly. A pale yellow foam now coated his bloodied arm, some sort of space-age bandage Polly supposed. He was pointing with his good arm at something under the control panel beside the dead Schirr in the chair, something only he could see at that angle.

Frog gave an excited squawk as she peered under the control panel herself. 'He's right, look at this! Come and see!'

'What?' Polly asked nervously. Something in the woman's voice put Polly in mind of the horrible boys back at school when she was little, who always tricked her into looking at the dead spiders or slugs they were holding, just to hear her scream. But in the end she relented. The sickly stench from the corpse got stronger as she approached, all Parma violets and rotting peaches.

Polly was relieved to find that the fuss was over little more than a box; a small, bronze casket had been fastened to the underside of the console. A couple of wires ran out of it, lending it the appearance of an ornate junction box. An angular symbol had been etched into one side.

The Doctor came to join her and stooped to see. 'Fascinating,' he said appreciatively. 'It is similar to the symbol burnt into Pallemar here.' His expression hardened. 'Isn't branding a prisoner somewhat barbaric for humans so evidently advanced, hmm?'

'It's done when a prisoner is chipped. Pentagon Central's file on the subject is encoded at the same time into the flesh.'

'And this chipping, as you call it, is not punishment enough?'

'DeCaster and his disciples revived an ancient Schirr religion,' Shel explained. 'They celebrate the physical form as part of their magic, a kind of cult of the body. They've made themselves physically perfect in their own eyes.'

Frog giggled. 'So when we got them, we hit them where it hurt.' She made a hissing, sizzling sound. With the underlying grate of her voice simulator Polly found the noise truly disgusting.

'The mark translates as "dissident",' Shel went on. 'So we can tell. They… They all look so similar.'

'How very enlightened,' said the Doctor. 'But if you had these criminals in your custody, how did they escape?'

'At the time of Pallemar and DeCaster's incarceration, no one had any idea of their significance in the Schirr uprising. The Ten… Ten-strong was able to free itself with ease. And like all Schirr dissidents, they wear their brands as… as a mark of pride.' Shel abruptly switched his focus back to the unit. 'It looks like s… some kind of plug-in module.'

'A good guess.' The Doctor straightened back up with a wince of pain. 'Yes, it's a quite recent addition. I would say it was intended to expand the functionality of this console.'

'How?' asked Frog succinctly.

'It's most interesting, yes,' the Doctor assured them, but wouldn't elaborate further. It hadn't taken Polly long to learn that he could answer the most complicated questions with extraordinary ease – but a simple answer to a simple question was pretty much entirely beyond him.

'Speaking of expanding functionality,' he went on, 'Polly, could you please check the navigational console? I believe the reducing equations I routed into the drive systems should soon be showing results.' The Doctor chuckled almost mischievously. 'We shan't be ignorant of our final destination for much longer, however much our hosts would wish it.'

Polly trotted off to the console against the far wall, eager to put some distance between her and the huge, fleshy bodies. She found herself transfixed by a small display screen. It glowed the prettiest shade of blue that Polly had ever seen.

'Well, child?' called the Doctor a little brusquely.

On the screen was a single eight-digit figure. Polly called it over to him.

The Doctor stiffened, turned away from them all, back to the bodies on the dais. Polly felt her stomach tie a knot in itself.

'What does it mean?' she asked, trying to keep her voice steady.

The Doctor didn't turn back round. 'If Tovel was correct in his placing of our relative spatial position, it seems we are *not* being steered toward Earth's empire after all.' Now he turned to face Polly, and she saw his eyes were agleam, his interest fully engaged. There was even a rueful smile on his face, a chess player acknowledging his being outwitted by a worthy opponent. 'It would appear this asteroid is on a direct path leading into the Morphiean quadrant.'

II

While Creben checked and double-checked the Kill-Droid's circuits, Ben experimented with placing different amounts of pressure on his injured ankle. It seemed pretty well fine, apart from the odd protesting twinge. Even his plates weren't aching too badly with all this traipsing about. In fact, he felt in great shape. He should probably set himself up in business some time. Yeah, that could impress Polly. *You too can have a body like mine. Just go time travelling to lumps of rock in deep space.*

Ben watched as Creben rose from the splintered panel of the robot at last and handed the unhelpful circuit to Haunt.

'No doubt about it,' he announced. 'Disintegrators have not been used. They're fully charged.'

Haunt gave the circuit a cursory inspection in the feeble glow of the fleaweed. She didn't look like she even knew what she was meant to be looking at. Wasn't it Shel who did all the technical stuff for her?

Haunt impatiently tossed the circuit to the ground. 'So. This proves the bodies must still be in those tunnels.'

'We'd have found them,' Shade piped up, hands still pressed to his face.

'He's right,' said Roba. 'If Joiks lost Denni round here, one group would've found her.'

'What do you mean, "if"?' said Joiks. 'This was the place.'

Roba nodded to Shade. 'Same goes for Lindey, right, man? You were right on top of her.'

Shade nodded, and winced as he did so.

'Well, maybe they're not dead,' Ben suggested. 'Maybe they got away, and they're walking about lost, looking for you?'

Joiks shook his head. 'You weren't there. I heard Denni's screams. She wasn't walking anywhere.'

'Same for Lindey,' said Shade.

'They have to be somewhere,' Tovel reasoned. 'In hiding, maybe. Alive or dead.'

Haunt snorted. 'Why would a droid deliberately hide the bodies of its victims?'

'To keep the element of surprise?' Tovel suggested.

Creben looked round at the others, with the crafty look of someone about to put a cat among the pigeons. 'Or maybe it had a use for them.'

'What sort of a use?' demanded Haunt. When Creben didn't answer, she didn't bother to hide her disappointment. 'You're funny. Well, whatever the reason, we need to find those bodies. We're taking them home. And not just that, we need some answers. Denni's webset must still have been recording when she was taken. The information could tell us a lot.'

Ben clocked Joiks. He looked suddenly shiftier than usual.

'So what are we waiting for,' said Shade, pulling his hands away from his face. The black ridges seemed to bubble under his reddened skin in the half light. 'Let's get this finished.'

'You don't look too good, man,' Tovel said.

'I'm fine,' Shade answered tersely. Even Ben, who hadn't known the geezer for more than a few hours, could see that wasn't true. He seemed short of breath, swaying slightly, and his eyes stared wildly out of his sweaty face. 'Come on, let's *do* this. We can do this.'

'You're in pain,' Haunt said dispassionately. 'A lot of it. What's wrong?'

Shade looked like he'd been slapped. 'It's nothing,' he insisted, like a kid on the verge of tears, trying to be brave.

Haunt reached out a hand and pinched Shade's cheek. He screamed.

'You're very funny,' she said softly. 'I've seen people in more pain than you know how to feel, Shade.'

'I'm sorry, Marshal,' Shade said stiffly. 'I don't know… It's my face… Feels like it's bursting open –'

Shade's confession was cut short by Shel's voice bursting through Haunt's communicator.

'Marshal.' There was a tinge of urgency to his usually neutral tones. 'I… I think you should come to control. Immediately.'

'Problems?' Haunt asked.

A pause. 'Something's happened.'

Big problems, then. Ben felt a tingle up his spine. He itched it, like he was itching the rest of his back. It was like he had sunburn or something, a tightness, a tickling soreness of the skin, spreading all over.

''Ere, the Doctor and Polly are all right, aren't –?'

Haunt shut him up with a warning look. 'All right, Shel,' she said quietly to her sleeve. 'I'm on my way. And I'll be bringing Shade with me. Out.'

Shade looked down at his feet, embarrassed. 'Marshal, I don't need special attention.'

'That's enough out of you.' Lovely bedside manner, thought Ben.

She turned to Ben and the others. 'The droids are gone, but there are still a lot of unknowns here. We don't know where we're going, or why. Organise yourselves into groups. Get searching. I'll be in touch.'

Shade followed his marshal into the gloom of the tunnel in the far wall. Ben wished he was going back too. How had he suddenly become part of Haunt's outfit?

'There he goes, Haunt's little shadow,' muttered Roba, unmoved by Shade's suffering.

'What's with Shel and the secrecy?' Tovel wondered aloud. 'Why not just tell us?'

'Môrale, innit,' said Ben. 'He'd rather you heard it from Haunt once she's had a chance to work out the words, than to take it from him off the cuff.'

'Shel was the one who got us into this in the first place,' said Joiks.

Tovel looked at him. 'What're you talking about?'

'Who decided we'd fly to this stinking rock?'

'Pentagon Central.' Tovel gave him the kind of smile you save for simpletons.

'And who programmed the computers with our stats?' said Joiks pointedly.

There was a moment's uncertainty. Everyone exchanged glances.

Roba nodded. 'Like the old man said – the computers only pick a place 'cause of what's fed into them.'

'Well, you're feeding *us* bull, Joiks.' Creben shook his head as if amused by some private joke. 'Since Toronto, Pent-Cent computers are guarded like spectrox. You think it's likely Shel sneaked in and reprogrammed them just so they'd assign this place to us here and now?'

Joiks spat on the floor. 'Is it any likelier that DeCaster and Pallemar show up too, "here and now"?'

'Maybe *they* did it,' said Roba. 'You know. Magic.'

'Leave off!' Ben protested. 'Why would they want anyone to discover them here?'

'There could be a reason,' said Creben. '*They've* discovered a usefulness for us.'

'*They* are dead,' Tovel reminded him.

'But we're all travelling together. And where we're going there could be anything waiting for us.' Creben looked at each of them in turn, eyes unblinking. 'Anything at all.'

A long paralysing pause stretched out like the darkness of the tunnel facing them.

'Are we going to stand around scaring each other stupid,' Ben said nervously, 'or are we going to do what your guvnor told us to?'

Tovel nodded. 'But screw splitting into groups. We stay together.'

'Agreed,' said Creben.

The others nodded, none faster than Ben, and Roba led them off down the gloomy passageway.

III

Polly was staying well away from Haunt. Upon finding another missing corpse from the collection in the control room, the marshal's cosy theory of natural disintegration was strained to breaking point; much like her patience with so many events all beyond her control.

The Doctor was talking to Haunt now, quietly but forcefully outlining their recent discoveries and their position as he saw it.

Polly could see it well enough herself. They were being toyed with by some unknown power. Bodysnatchers, taking the living and the dead. She didn't want to think too closely about the possible reasons for that, nor why Morphiea appeared to be the asteroid's destination.

Nor why Shade and Shel, two soldiers who should've been in the peak of physical fitness, now seemed so sick.

Shel's pain went beyond his injured arm. He was twitching all over on his invisible bed, like a cloud of the fleas outside had followed him in and were biting like devils.

Shade, on the other hand, was lying alarmingly still on the floor beside her. He had collapsed pretty much the moment he'd entered the room. It seemed Haunt had finally lost her shadow. Frog had burst open another force mattress to make him comfortable, but the scanner thing she'd brought out of the first aid box showed nothing untoward.

Polly decided the Doctor was right not to trust these people's machines. The skin on Shade's face was like sticky red polythene stretched tight over dozens of tiny black limpets. His green eyes flickered open from time to time, looked blankly up at her. She couldn't help staring at the tiny computer sticking out of his pocket. *Lindey's* computer.

Frog sat beside Shel, her scarred round head in her hands, looking bored. Occasionally Haunt would raise her voice at the Doctor, incredulous or angry, Polly couldn't tell. And Shade's eyes were closed. She reached her hand out to his pocket. No one would notice now if she took out the palm computer and had a little…

'The Spooks have destroyed whole worlds to try and get their stupid secrets back!' Haunt's voice boomed out like gunfire as her patience reached its limit. Polly retreated from Shade and his secret for the moment as the tirade went on: 'Why would they want to drag a tiny rock with ten soldiers in training to the heart of their empire?'

The Doctor gave as good as he got. 'I am simply postulating, madam, as to why we should be going to Morphiea if not at the Morphieans' behest!' he thundered. She didn't answer back straight away, so the Doctor pressed home his advantage. 'If the Schirr were to be captured by Morphiea it would mean certain death.' He gestured sadly to the bodies behind their invisible barrier. 'Perhaps they saw what was coming, and arranged for their own destruction.'

Haunt nodded, suddenly subdued. 'It's possible,' was all she would concede. 'How long till we arrive?'

'There's no way of telling,' the Doctor announced, shaking his head. 'Now, tell me. How did the Morphieans make you aware that they were responsible for the atrocities they committed?'

'They made…' Haunt's lip curled scornfully, and Polly noticed one hand was clutched to her side. 'They made what our poor little frightened scientists called "constructs". Fleshy things, *animated* somehow. Don't ask me to explain. The constructs were projected direct to Senate. They gloated, threatened us… The Spooks don't care how many of us they kill. We're just animals to them.'

The Doctor looked at her steadily, ignoring her mounting anger. 'They don't have bodies as we do?'

'Flesh is just a tool for their magic.'

'So, the Morphieans have a mindforce of some kind.' The Doctor chuckled suddenly, and turned to Frog. 'I was considering the old, old links between the Schirr and the Morphieans you mentioned. One born, perhaps, from cult of the body on one side, and an elevation of the mind on the other.'

Frog looked less than impressed with the Doctor's theory. Shel, still convulsing silently with his lips bared back over his teeth, almost seemed to be laughing.

'How would that ever bring them together?' wondered Polly.

'Each extreme still needs the other,' said the Doctor. 'Now. So far we only have part of the puzzle. For the bodies to have vanished from this platform, the protective force field must've been breached somehow.'

'By the minds of the Morphieans...' Polly shuddered.

'Perhaps,' the Doctor agreed genially, 'but I'd rather like to try myself.' He crouched down with some difficulty to study the newly discovered junction box beneath the corpse's console. 'Yes, this perhaps could be what I'm after...'

Haunt looked on, rubbing her side more aggressively now. Maybe the insects had bitten her too. Remembering the pale, squashy fleas put Polly back in mind of her own discomfort. She gritted her teeth and resolved not to scratch.

As the Doctor cautiously tinkered with the junction box, Shel suddenly stirred from his feverish shaking. 'No,' he said faintly, then again more forcefully. 'No, stay away from that.'

The Doctor looked up in surprise. 'Young man, I assure you I am perfectly qualified to –'

'Away.' Shel got unsteadily to his feet. His eyes were narrow slits, his breath pushing out in sharp puffs.

He was aiming a pistol at the Doctor.

Polly opened her mouth, but couldn't decide if she should beg him to put down the gun or just scream.

Haunt was looking apoplectic. 'Shel, what the hell are you doing?'

'It's him.' Frog held herself still as a statue, just a few feet away from the gun in Shel's shaking hand. 'He picked this place for us... he killed Denni and Lindey.'

'That's impossible,' Haunt snapped. 'Put the gun down, Shel.'

'It *must* be him!' gurgled Frog.

Shel said nothing. It seemed to be taking all his concentration to keep the gun pointed at the Doctor, crouched before the junction box.

The Doctor gazed fearlessly back at him. 'What is the meaning of this, Shel? Answer me!'

'Put the gun *down*, Shel,' Haunt ordered, her voice rising.

Shel convulsed, his face twisted in pain. There was the sound of a gun firing, and Polly gave a short, high yell. But the Doctor was unharmed.

Haunt bellowed with rage. 'No!'

Frog was clutching her own pistol. She'd shot the gun from Shel's hand. His mouth flapped open and closed now as he stared down at the bloody stumps of his fingers. Frog stared too, apparently fascinated. Polly looked away, sickened.

Now Haunt leaped forward and held Shel in a necklock.

'Be careful with him,' the Doctor advised her.

'Look!' Frog moaned. 'His arm.'

Polly looked automatically, and her hand flew to her mouth.

Metal points stuck through Shel's gory finger-stumps. The skin hung away from a hole in the wrist, too, and Polly saw gleaming silver shafts and coloured wires.

'He's got an artificial arm,' Haunt said, transfixed.

'Away,' Shel croaked. 'Away.' His cheek twitched faster and faster until a tiny metal coil burst through the skin, flecking his face with bright blood.

'It's not just his arm,' Polly whispered. 'It's all of him. He's a robot too.'

Chapter Nine
Nemesis

I

Shel's face twisted with anger. Polly bit her lip as he pulled Haunt's arm from his neck and shoved her backwards with inhuman strength. She rolled over and over across the floor.

'We've been set up! Shel's gonna kill all of us!' Frog brought up her gun and fired again. A spark leapt from Shel's chest. He swayed, then bashed the gun out of her grasp. Frog overbalanced and knocked against the Doctor, who gasped as he tried to stop her falling. He staggered back against the body in the chair, which skittered away on its castors.

Shel swung round to face Polly.

'Don't hurt us,' she pleaded. His eyes were unfocussed, glassy – or perhaps just glass.

'Leave Polly alone,' the Doctor commanded. 'Whatever your purpose here, this girl has done you no harm.'

Shel ignored him. He raised his rifle with his good hand. Polly backed away closer to Shade, who lay still and oblivious.

Haunt was back on her feet. Her own rifle was aimed at Shel's twitching head. 'Put down the gun.'

Shel lowered the rifle without bothering to turn round.

'If you want to live, start talking.' Haunt took a step closer. 'Who sent you?' Another step. 'Who pushed you on to *me*?'

Polly wasn't sure if Shel's mouth was opening with any intent to speak, or if whatever machinery controlled his lips was giving out like the rest of him.

The Doctor slowly advanced on him, his arms raised. 'Why are you really here, Shel?'

'He's here to kill all of us,' Frog whined. 'Whatever's going on, he's planned it all.'

The Doctor looked at Shel more sternly, and swept an arm at the dais behind the console. '*Did* you arrange all this, sir?'

Shel swung the rifle up and fired. The Doctor reeled back instinctively. Polly screamed as a bolt of light shot into the console beside him.

At the same time Haunt opened fire on Shel, who staggered under the impact. He turned and ran for the exit, firing the rifle behind him apparently at random. A blast scorched past Polly's shoulder before she could even react.

Then something grabbed hold of her leg, and pulled. Mid-scream, she went down, as another blast shot overhead.

Shade relaxed his grip on her calf. She almost wept with relief that nothing more sinister had got a hold of her, and wriggled over on her front to shelter beside his force mattress.

'Frog, after him,' Haunt bellowed.

Polly decided it must be at least a little safer to get up now. She squeezed Shade's hand to say thank you and cautiously rose to her feet. She glimpsed Frog as she sprinted through the doorway. Haunt had already vanished. The Doctor stood alone by the shattered console, inspecting the blackened hole carved out by Shel's wild shot.

'That could've been you,' Polly said shakily.

'Yes, I dare say it could,' murmured the Doctor. 'We must find out why. Shel's badly damaged, he shouldn't get far.' He tutted. 'Just look at this vandalism! My dear, would you check our new discovery beneath the console is undamaged, hmm?' He rubbed his back meaningfully.

Polly felt a little uneasy at the way the Doctor could seemingly forget all the violence they'd just lived through to concentrate on a bit of broken technology, but she crouched down obediently just the same. Beneath the console she saw the junction box was scorched and smoking. 'Looks like this has had it.'

'He's managed to fuse the controls.' The Doctor grimaced. 'Dear, dear. And just as I was about to deactivate the force shield and study those bodies!'

Polly looked at him doubtfully. 'That was probably the point, wasn't it?'

Stamping feet made Polly turn. Haunt had re-entered the room. From the look on her face, Shel had got away.

'Where's Frog?' asked Polly.

'Outside, guarding the corridor,' she said. 'We couldn't catch him. He moved too fast, even wounded like – .' She caught herself. 'Even damaged like that.'

Polly wondered how long Haunt had known Shel, how many secrets she'd trusted to him. She shook her head, walked over to the Doctor.

'He was a most convincing human being,' the Doctor murmured.

Haunt snorted bitterly, as if suddenly recognising there had been something blindingly obvious about Shel's deception all along. 'You realise that only someone at the highest level in Pent Central would have access to the kind of technology needed to make a thing like that,' she said quietly. 'Frog's right. They assigned him to my unit so he could lead us into this trap. We have to find him. Find out what he's been planning, and why.' She raised her wrist to her lips. 'I'll alert the others to be ready for him.'

She began by calling Creben.

Nothing but reedy static greeted her in response.

'Tovel? Joiks? Roba?'

Polly felt a chill shiver down her. If anything, the shushing of the static was growing louder, angrier.

Haunt swore. 'Right. I'll just have to tell them in person.'

'You're leaving us here?' Polly asked.

Haunt paused briefly in the doorway. 'Watch the bodies. Watch Shade.'

That said, she turned and left.

Polly waited until she was sure the woman had gone, then ran over to the TARDIS. The door wouldn't budge. She let out a heavy sigh of disappointment. 'If you'd shut down their invisible barrier thing, we might've been able to get back into the TARDIS.'

'Yes, quite so,' the Doctor agreed. 'I do wish I knew what sort of a stasis field is operating here. Until I do, and can find a way to counteract it, I'm afraid none of us are really safe.'

'Safe,' Polly said numbly. The word seemed to have lost its meaning. She leaned back against the police box's stubborn doors and stared up. The endless fragments of glass set into the high ceiling sparkled reflected light at her eyes, and she closed them wearily. 'I do hope Ben's all right.'

'He's a resourceful young man,' the Doctor said, as if this was a talisman against evil and all Ben needed.

Polly's eyes snapped back open as Shade cried out suddenly. She found it hard to believe such a high-pitched, childish sound could come from a man so big. *'Watch Shade,'* Haunt had told them. Polly thought back to her earlier suspicions. They seemed somehow foolish now. Shel was the bad guy, not Shade. Hadn't Shade saved her life when the guns were firing, dragging her to the floor? As she walked back over to the Doctor, her cheeks prickled. She realised she was blushing.

'Are you all right, my child?' the Doctor asked, glancing up at her.

Caught off guard, Polly gave her cheeks a token scratch and shrugged. 'My, er, skin. It feels sore, itchy. Like sunburn.' She smiled ruefully. 'Only I could get a sunburn in the middle of an underground cavern.'

The Doctor could only be half-listening, because he seemed to take her perfectly seriously. 'It isn't the sunburn that causes the itching,' he said. 'That is caused by the skin healing itself.'

Polly politely mulled over this nugget of information until Shade shouted out again.

'Go to him,' the Doctor said softly, still staring at the useless console. 'See what you can do to help.'

Polly nodded, and crossed back over towards Shade. 'What is it, what's the matter?'

'My face,' Shade whimpered as she came close; but by then there was no need for the explanation. His skin had become a sticky black mess. Fresh blood dribbled steadily down into his ears, teeth and hair. His teeth were clenched, every muscle she could see was bunched up with tension, and his body shook as if racked with silent sobs. 'What's happening to me?' he said, grinding out each word. 'My face feels like it's tearing apart.'

It is, Polly wanted to tell him, as her own eyes welled up with tears. She scratched the back of her itching neck. *I think it is*.

II

After all the endless trudging through the dank tunnels, stooped and squashed and single-file, Ben was pleasantly surprised when Roba led him, Joiks and Tovel into some kind of vast vaulted chamber, roughly pentagonal in shape. The luminous weed hung down in thick strands, danced around by the usual attendant fleas. There were even piles of it on the floor. In the far wall was another tunnel, as dark and uninviting as all the others. There had been several narrow channels leading off from the main passage on their journey, but they'd decided to stick to the A-roads first. If they had to double back up a B-road and scarper at any point, Ben wanted to know what they'd be running into.

So for now it was the five towering stone pillars dominating the room that grabbed Ben's attention. They were arranged in the same pattern as the dots on a dice or a domino. At the top of the two columns nearest Ben, there rested duplicate pairs of oversized stone babies with angel wings. They looked like they'd scoffed a few rusks too many. Nothing crowned the pillar in the centre, nor the one behind it to the left. But the final column supported four of the ugly statues, crowded together with their backs to any onlookers, like they were up to something. The overall effect of the design left Ben feeling strangely uncomfortable. There was no logic to it. Modern art, he supposed.

It seemed the others agreed. 'This is different,' said Joiks, without much enthusiasm.

'This stinks,' Roba said more succinctly, and Tovel nodded.

Creben stayed quiet, just walked about and shone his torch diligently into the five corners of the chamber, 'Nothing,' he announced. Then he stopped dead, staring over Ben's shoulder.

Ben spun round in alarm, but while his eyes scanned the wall behind the hanging glass tapestry, he could see nothing untoward.

'Look,' Creben urged the others.

It finally hit Ben.

'The tunnel,' he breathed. 'It's gone!'

Roba folded his arms, with the air of someone not about to fall for a joke. 'How can a tunnel go anywhere?'

Ben walked up to the wall. It looked solid, and when he kicked it, he knew for sure. 'Search me, mate. But it ain't where we came through.'

'We must've come through that one,' Roba said, pointing to the tunnel they could all see. 'We just lost our bearings.'

'Uh-huh. Thanks for that, Roba,' said Tovel dryly.

'It was here,' Joiks murmured.

Creben nodded. 'It must be some kind of secret passageway, one that can't be detected from this side of the wall. These doorways could be littered all over the place.'

'Great,' said Ben sourly. 'So our little search won't be over till we've accidentally gone through every one of them.'

Creben shook his head. 'I imagine we'll have reached our destination long before then.'

'Always there with a cheery thought, ain't you.'

'We'll just have to look harder in the places we *can* see,' said Tovel decisively. 'Starting here.'

Even as Tovel spoke, Ben noticed with a jolt some dark fleeting movement on the pillar behind him. 'What's that?'

Tovel protested mildly as Ben shoved him aside. A thin black trail had appeared on the pillar. It stretched vertically down from top to bottom, where it resolved itself into a sticky liquid pooling round his boots.

'Blood out of a stone,' he murmured nervously, while Tovel just swore in disbelief.

'Where's it coming from?' Creben demanded, unholstering his gun. The others followed suit.

'Up there,' said Tovel.

Ben took a few steps back and several shaky breaths. Whatever was at the top of the column, spilling blood, it was obscured by the huddle of statues crouched over it.

'If we want to see what's bleeding,' Ben said grimly, 'we're gonna have to climb for it.'

Joiks laughed briefly. 'You're crazy.'

'You volunteering?' Roba said expectantly as he knitted his huge fingers together into a makeshift stirrup.

Ben looked round anxiously. 'Well…'

'We've got to know what's there, after all,' Creben said mildly.

'He's right,' said Tovel with the faintest of smiles. 'Reckon you can make it?'

So, it was time to earn his place with the boys again. Fair enough. The column was broad, but there were occasional chips and ridges that could give him footholds.

He put his right foot in Roba's hands and the giant propelled him upwards. The trail of blood smeared against his body as he wrapped his arms round the pillar, holding on tight while he kicked about for a footing. He heard whistles and claps, shouts of encouragement, urging him on. His breath pushed out in ragged gasps through clenched teeth, his heart was racing, but slowly he was scaling the column. The rough stone scuffed and stung his palms as he searched for cracks and ledges he could use to help lever himself further up. His feet caught in crevices, and some were pronounced enough to take his weight. He was going to make it. Then he tried to imagine what grisly scene was waiting for him at the top, and felt less elated.

Far below, the lads still shouted their encouragement. The sounds echoed strangely up here, were almost lost under the rustling of the vegetation, thick with fleas, and the ghostly clinking of the glass tapestry. As he climbed the final few feet, the shadowy statues at the top loomed above Ben. He saw their wings, their smooth stone backs lit with a gentle radiance.

'I made it!' he shouted.

One of the statues twisted round to look down at him.

Ben's pounding heart nearly stopped dead. He wanted to shout out, but the sound died in his throat.

The statue's stone eyes were wide and innocent. Its thick lips were smiling at him benignly.

A scrap of wet, dark material fell from its huge bloody hands, flapping like a bat past Ben's face.

In the thick shadows at the statue's feet he thought he glimpsed a human hand, slender fingers twisted and outstretched.

The smiling stone angel reached for his neck.

Chapter Ten
The Secret Adversary

I

Ben slid painfully down the column as fast as he could go, resisting the instinct to abandon it altogether and take his chances with the fall. He caught crazy corkscrew glimpses of the angel as he spiralled downwards, the pitted rock clawing at his arms and legs. Around him, bolts of energy shot up into the ceiling, pounded into the pillar, caught the statue full in the face. Slowly, the other enormous cherubs reacted to the onslaught. Heads cocked to one side. Arms reached slowly out towards the soldiers. Stone wings began to flap, and the air twittered with movement.

Lazily, the smiling statues launched themselves into the air and drifted down after him, like falling leaves.

Ben leaped down the last ten feet, fell awkwardly. Roba stopped firing long enough to scoop him up and push him towards the mouth of the tunnel.

'Out!' yelled Tovel. The soldiers scattered as the angels drifted after them, pushing through the air like swimmers through water. The air seemed alive with the soft, rhythmic sound of their wings beating.

Ben pelted for the opening in the rock. He was almost there when a bolt of searing brightness shot from out of the darkness. It nearly took his face off. Finding himself under attack again, Ben threw himself instinctively to the ground and landed in a pile of fallen fleaweed. 'There's something in the tunnel!' he yelled, his voice cracking in panic, the pale fleas dancing about him, crawling and jumping over his face. He crawled away, spat them out, saw the grey angels as they floated ever nearer.

Two more yellow bolts whizzed into the room. Then Ben heard a familiar voice, and realised he'd almost been killed by the cavalry.

'What are they?' Haunt was standing in the mouth of the tunnel, brandishing her rifle, looking on appalled.

'They were statues before,' Roba said, backing away until he stood beside her. 'Just statues.'

Haunt's voice was barely audible. 'Constructs. Morphiean constructs.'

'There's a girl's body up there,' Ben said, the words tumbling off his tongue. 'I dunno whose, I only saw the shadow. God knows what they'd done to her.'

The angels bobbed closer in utter silence. Their smiles were compassionate. Their fingers dripped blood.

'Come on.' Joiks led the way out of the chamber, and Tovel and Roba pushed through after him. Haunt stared at the creatures, revulsion on her face, clutching her stomach like she was going to be sick. 'Angels,' she said. She seemed transfixed by the drifting statues. The nearest of them was almost close enough to touch.

'What are you waiting for?' Ben almost screamed. He grabbed Haunt by the arm and dragged her out of the room after him, without looking back.

II

Shade roared with pain as Polly pressed some kind of surgical wipe to his sticky red face.

'This will soothe the skin, make you feel better,' she said shakily, but wasn't sure who she was trying to convince. Truthfully, she'd never seen anyone look so awful. Ordinarily she wasn't too bothered by blood. She'd seen plenty of fights before, living in London. Cuts and bruises dished out down alleyways or outside clubs. She'd even been the reason for them starting once or twice. But looking down at Shade there was no comparison to a bloodied nose, or a cut cheek. Shade's entire face was an open wound. The blood was bright red, watered down with a sticky clear fluid. As fast as Polly could mop it up, it kept squeezing back out. How much more could there be in him?

Her senses felt numbed and she put it down to shock. High above, the slabs of glass in the ceiling winked and glowed with reflected light, disorientating her.

'Pain… kill…' Shade croaked.

'No,' she told him. 'No, you'll be fine.'

'Killer,' Shade said more desperately. 'For pain.' Polly screwed up her nose as she wiped away a miniature mountain range of hard black crumbs from one of his gashes. 'Big hypo.'

Polly got his meaning. She left him for a moment, mumbling apologies, and scrabbled through the medical box until she found something that fitted the description: a sort of metal syringe with odd ends attached. What was she meant to do with it?

She needed a second opinion. 'Doctor!' she called. 'I need your help!'

The Doctor reluctantly left his hole in the console and pottered over to see. 'How is he?'

'Terrible,' Polly said sadly.

She handed the syringe-thing to the Doctor, who studied it for a moment curiously. Then he twisted a dial and jabbed a wide nozzle into Shade's neck. The soldier yelled again, louder than ever, then started to convulse. Polly bit her lip and wondered if the Doctor had got it all wrong. But a few moments later the fit passed, and Shade lay back, eyes closed, his breathing swift and shallow.

The Doctor looked down at Shade and tutted to himself. 'Remarkable,' he murmured. 'His body seems to be rejecting the dead tissue in his face, forcing it out through his skin.'

'Is he going to die?' Polly whispered, in case Shade was listening.

'I don't think so, my child,' the Doctor said thoughtfully. 'No, I don't think so. But his body is reacting to some kind of stimulus…' His eyes narrowed. 'A force of some kind. A force that we have not yet identified, and yet may be all around us.'

'Is that why Shel got sick too?' Polly wondered.

'It could well be, yes.'

'But if he set all this up… how come he didn't make himself immune to this… whatever-it-is?' She glanced over at the Schirr

131

bodies. Had they been immune? Had they killed each other in some terrible madness? A horrid thought occurred to Polly: 'Will the rest of us get sick?'

'I'm afraid I cannot tell,' the Doctor confessed.

The two of them sighed together, which brought faint smiles to their faces. They spent a few moments silently with their thoughts. Gradually, Shade's breathing began to ease.

'The worst of the pain is over for this young man,' the Doctor announced. 'He'll need rest, but he should recover.'

'In time for what,' breathed Polly.

'Now, if you don't mind watching over him alone, my dear, I shall return to…'

His voice trailed off. Something was wrong. As if in slow motion, Polly turned to see. Her heart lurched.

The corpse in the chair had vanished.

So had yet another body from the platform.

'DeCaster,' muttered the Doctor. 'Their leader.'

'How?' whispered Polly. 'The stasis field is jammed on. The console and the junction box are ruined!'

The Doctor seemed not to hear her. 'He is at large again, it would seem.'

Polly grabbed the Doctor's sleeve. 'But *how?* We never left! We only turned our backs on them for a few moments!'

'The one in the chair,' blustered the Doctor. 'DeCaster's most trusted disciple. Shel called him Pallemar…'

'He can't have been dead,' Polly said in a small voice.

'But he *was*. He was dead.' The Doctor sounded furious, like a cheated child. 'I examined the corpse myself. Death has its own posture and appearance…' He shook his head, as anger gave way to bewilderment.

Polly shivered. All the Schirr were scary, but the thought that DeCaster, who had murdered so many millions of people, could be walking about somewhere on the asteroid terrified her half to death.

'Six of them left, now,' the Doctor mused, a little more calmly. 'Only six. But how? How did they do it?'

Polly stared on in disbelief. The frozen expressions on the bloodied Schirr faces seemed to her less representative now of terror and agony, more like those of creatures laughing hysterically, till it hurt, till the tears came rolling down.

III

Haunt pulled her arm savagely from Ben's grip as they ran together down the tunnel. One of the stone figures floated out of the gloomy chamber and into the darkness of the tunnel, trailing after them like a balloon gusted on the wind. Haunt accelerated, beat him to the junction where Tovel, Roba, Creben and Joiks were anxiously waiting with Frog, ready to go. Haunt must've put her on sentry duty here while she went on ahead.

'It's Shel!' Joiks shouted as they approached. 'Frog says it's Shel!'

'Get moving!' Haunt bellowed, eyes flashing. 'Go!' Her moment of hesitation back in the chamber had passed. She was back in charge all right.

They raced down endless tunnels, lit only by the juddering beams of the soldiers' torches. Every shifting shadow seemed to conceal something more sinister, ghostly hands reaching out to tear at them as they passed.

Ben picked up the pace, imagining the gory stone fingers of one of the statues reaching up behind him, groping for his throat.

At last they approached the great metal doors that led to the centre of the complex. Once the threshold was crossed they came to a panting halt, too breathless to speak, making do with mute and frightened eye contact.

Ben saw Roba had clamped one giant's hand around his forearm. There was a tear in his sleeve. 'You all right?' he puffed.

Roba nodded fiercely, but there was a look in his eyes that suggested he was less certain. 'Cut myself getting out,' he muttered. 'It's OK.'

The crowd set off again. Ben gritted his teeth, prepared to make after them, but his legs were cramping up. He felt like one of those

133

marathon runners, he needed someone to run up to him with a cup of weak orange and a big blanket. What he got was Frog, who turned away from the pack, and came back to help him along. She slipped an arm round his waist. His shoulder pressed against her chest. He felt her breath on his face, surprisingly sweet.

Her big bulging eyes met his uncertain gaze for a fraction of a second. Then she looked away, half-carried him along the shadowy path.

IV

Polly's heart leapt as Haunt sprinted back into the control room. She held her side as if she had a stitch.

Polly frowned. It only seemed like a few minutes since she had left.

'Back so soon,' the Doctor observed, as if picking up on Polly's thoughts. He gestured to the empty chair and to the latest empty space on the dais. 'But I'm afraid not soon enough.'

Haunt stared at the bodies. Her face slowly screwed up as if the absences were causing her physical pain. 'DeCaster… Pallemar…' She seemed utterly dumbfounded. 'Both gone? What happened?'

The Doctor looked troubled. 'We turned away for a few moments only. When we looked back…'

More footsteps heralded the arrival of the rest of the soldiers. Polly looked anxiously as first Creben, then Joiks and Tovel, and finally Roba entered through the glowing pentagonal doorway.

'Where's Ben?' she called, her voice higher than she'd intended.

Right on cue, he entered. Half-carried, half-dragged along by Frog. Polly watched sceptically as the ugly little woman helped him over to one of the consoles. He clutched hold of it, smiled his thanks at her.

As the others gathered round the depleted platform of corpses in sullen disbelief, Polly ran over to see Ben. He saw her coming, and made an effort to stand unaided. 'All right, Pol?'

'I'm so glad to see you.' She smiled at Frog. 'Thank you for helping him.'

Perhaps her smile had come out a little tighter than she'd planned.

Frog shrugged. 'All yours now, honey,' she muttered. 'Enjoy.' Then she walked away to join the Doctor and the others as they exchanged updates and information.

Polly half-listened as she waited for Ben to catch his breath; caught occasional words: 'Shade'. 'Sick'. 'Cyborg'. 'Chase'. 'Blood'.

She was grateful of the chance to have a more personal catch-up with Ben. She told him about Shel going mad, and about Shade, who was sleeping peacefully now. Ben blew air out of his cheeks, not sure what to make of it all.

'What happened to you?' Polly asked in turn.

Ben shuddered, leaned back against the console. 'Statues. Dirty great flying things. Came for us, didn't they.'

Polly felt a tingle run down her spine. '*Flying* statues?'

'I swear to you. And they had a body up on their pedestal.' He shook his head. 'Denni or Lindey, I'm not sure which.'

Polly felt her mouth go dry. 'But, Ben, there are statues of the cherubim right outside!'

Ben stared at her. 'I didn't see anything... I mean, I wasn't looking, but I don't reckon...' He stood back up again, felt nervous energy twitching at his muscles. 'Marshal Haunt! Polly says there were more of those things earlier, perched right outside!'

Haunt's head snapped round to face them. Polly prepared to defend her opinion, but the Marshal simply nodded. 'Frog. Joiks. Check it out. Creben, Roba, I want a barricade up outside. See what you can safely rip out of this place.'

'Not a lot.' Creben glanced around at the banks of equipment dotted about, and the ornamental trellises railing in the ducting round the walls, out of reach. 'The console housings, maybe.'

'We don't know what this stuff does,' Roba grumbled. 'What if we disconnect life support or something?'

Creben smiled wanly. 'We put it back together. Quickly.'

'You're funny,' Haunt told him. 'Now get on with it. This is going to be our base, and we're going to make it as secure as it can be. Tovel – see to Shade. Sounds like his face needs stitches.'

'He's asleep,' Polly called over.

Tovel smiled ruefully, tapped the medical kit. 'Not for much longer.'

The soldiers moved to obey, without further question. Polly and Ben nervously joined the Doctor and Haunt.

'I wonder,' the Doctor mused aloud. 'What intelligence is co-ordinating this affair, and to what end?' He nodded, pursed his lips. 'Yes. Yes, that is what we must ask ourselves.'

'It's madness,' Haunt muttered. 'A madman's scheme.'

'I can't believe Shel was a...' Ben trailed off. 'What was he?'

'A cyborg.' Haunt's voice was hollow. 'They're only used for intelligence work. Programmed never to give themselves away.' She looked pained, pale. 'I never knew what he was. My last adjutant was reassigned six months ago, and in all that time I *never* knew...'

'No one could have guessed his true nature,' said the Doctor. 'But now that we do know, we must decide how it affects our judgement of the situation.'

Polly remembered now what the Doctor had been talking about earlier. 'Until both DeCaster and Pallemar vanished,' she pointed out, 'there was one Schirr missing for each *person* missing.'

The Doctor steepled his fingers together. 'Quite so. And the Morphiean sciences – as practised by these Schirr also, let us not forget – place the emphasis on the *body*.'

'What're you saying, Doctor?' Ben asked uncertainly.

Haunt seemed to think she knew. 'That Shel used Lindey and Denni's bodies to somehow reanimate the corpses of DeCaster and his disciples?'

Ben shrugged. 'Figures. Ten of them for ten of you.'

'Before we came along,' Polly pointed out. 'But in any case, there's eleven of us now – if you can even count Shel since he's a robot – and six of them. How does that work?'

'And even with the stasis field jammed in place thanks to Shel's handiwork,' said the Doctor, 'the corpses seem able to come and go as they please.' He considered the problem, his eyes darting from side to side. 'Then there's the sickness. Again, affecting the body. Severely so in the cases of Shel and Shade. I imagine the interface between Shel's flesh and circuitry has begun to break down as the effect increases.'

'Making him crazy?' Polly asked.

'Presumably, having brought you all here and set events in motion, his task is complete…' The Doctor swung round to Polly. 'My dear, do you still itch all over?'

'Well, yes,' Polly said worriedly. 'But I feel fine in myself.' She considered. 'I feel better than fine.'

'Me too.' Ben chipped in, scratching his arms. 'I feel like I could go on forever.'

Haunt's eyes were red-rimmed, her face shiny with sweat. 'You think our own bodies are being affected by something on board?'

The Doctor agreed with her genially, as he might if someone had offered him a sweet sherry. 'Yes, I'm afraid it's possible.'

Polly jumped as Roba leaned in over her shoulder. He looked furious, sweating profusely.

'Who gave you all the answers, old man?'

'No one *gives* me answers, sir,' the Doctor retorted. 'I seek them out for myself, as anyone can.'

'Great, OK – so what's gonna happen to us?' Roba was fidgeting, uncomfortable. 'Seeing as our bodies are being *affected*.'

'I don't know yet.' He half-smiled at Roba. 'But the truth will come in time, I have no doubt.'

'Think you're so smart,' Roba hissed. 'But we still don't know a *thing* about you.'

'No, indeed, you do not.' The Doctor seemed almost amused by this comment.

There was a long tear in the sleeve of Roba's combat suit, and Polly could see a bandage beneath it. He'd been hurt. Maybe that was why he was acting like a bear with a sore head.

Ben scowled at the huge man. 'Ain't you got a barricade to build, Roba?'

Polly looked to Haunt to break this up before it got any nastier. But the marshal's eyes were shut, her lips pressed together. She looked fit to drop.

A second later, she did, clutching her side. Her head smacked into the solid stone floor. Her eyes snapped open, unseeing, and a trickle of blood stained her lip as she bit her tongue. It wasn't enough to stifle her low moan of pain.

Polly turned to Roba, expecting him to lift his fallen marshal. But he just stood there and stared at Haunt in hurt disbelief. Like a child learning there's no Father Christmas, no such person as Superman.

'Dear, dear,' fussed the Doctor. 'We must help her, quickly.'

'There's an airbed over there,' Polly said, struggling to keep calm. She gestured to the translucent rectangle of Shel's abandoned force mattress. 'Ben, help me carry her.'

Tovel rushed over from Shade's side with the medical kit. Creben came over to join Roba, staring on in astonished silence as Polly and Ben lifted Haunt over to the force mattress. Polly felt the considerable muscles in the woman's arms and shoulders twitch and clench.

'Take more than instant sutures to fix this,' Tovel breathed.

'What do you think's wrong with her?' she heard Creben ask behind her.

'A physical malaise of the most extraordinary kind,' was the Doctor's utterly unhelpful diagnosis.

As Ben tried to straighten out Haunt's sweaty form on the mattress, she gave a rattling gasp of pain. He snatched his hand away.

'What is it?' Polly asked.

'Not sure,' Ben said. 'A big lump or something, above her hip.'

'She was holding her side before,' Polly remembered.

Tovel took a scalpel from the kit and cut with difficulty through the damp fabric of Haunt's combat suit. The pale skin beneath was dominated by a huge red swelling, like a mosquito bite gone septic.

'What we gonna do?' Roba whispered hoarsely to himself over and over. He stared down at Haunt, fearfully. 'What we gonna do?'

'Is something inside that thing?' Ben wondered.

The Doctor had by now arrived to investigate, shooing them out of his way as he peered closely at the swelling through Victorian-looking pince-nez. 'I don't think so. It is more likely to be an abnormal growth of some kind.'

'A tumour?' Creben didn't sound convinced. 'She'd never be on active service with –'

The Doctor interrupted him, removing the pince-nez. 'I imagine it has never been detected before. This effect I've been speaking of, it must drive out impurities in the flesh.'

'Like poor Shade's face,' whispered Polly. She glanced at Tovel. 'How is he?'

'Better than he should be,' Tovel muttered. 'Those sutures sting like nothing else, but he didn't even stir.'

Ben, predictably, seemed less interested in Shade's welfare, still grappling with the Doctor's explanation. 'You mean this tumour or whatever is just being...' Ben groped for the right words. '*Pushed* out of her?'

The Doctor nodded. 'It's remarkable, quite remarkable.'

'I'll do what I can for her,' said Tovel, rummaging in the medical kit. 'Jesus, what the hell is happening to us?'

Roba turned, pushed roughly past him. He got back to building his barriers.

V

'I don't see no angels out here,' Frog said, playing her torch beam along the amorphous features of the giant stone figures that flanked the end of the narrow passageway to the control room.

'That means they've gone,' Joiks said. He swung his own torch anxiously from side to side. The fleas squirmed and jostled under the light, worrying away at the fleshy leaves lining the ceiling.

'That's good.'

'It's not good. There were a bunch of them out here. That means they can move too.' Joiks shuddered.

'We're alone out here,' Frog promised him.

Joiks nodded, nervously. 'I guess we'd hear them anyway. They got wings... Make a sound like no bird you ever seen...'

'Weren't no birds where I grew up.'

'Weren't nothing where you grew up.' Joiks swept his torch beam around again, wanting to be sure.

'Listen,' Frog said, and lightly took his arm. 'Stay cool. Ain't no angels here.' She paused, took a step closer. 'And I can prove that if you want.' The words buzzed quickly out of her, as if before she could change her mind.

Joiks turned to face her, lowered the torch until it lit them both from beneath. 'What you talking about?'

'Nothing.' *Don't make a joke out of this, Joiks.* 'Nothing much.' *Just for once.* 'It's…' Frog stopped. She hated her voice. There was some stuff she could never ever say out loud, even to herself, because of how it would sound. She turned off her torch, took the deepest of deep breaths, and concentrated on modulating the words. 'Been a long time, is all. Since anyone…'

Joiks looked at her, realisation slowly dawning. She waited for him to smirk, to burst out laughing that she could even think that kind of thing, let alone have the nerve to act on it, looking the way she did.

He didn't smirk. Just stared at her with a funny expression.

'You wanna get with me, Frog?'

No, she thought. She didn't really. Joiks was an idiot, a bully, she didn't even like him. But people said he really wouldn't say no to anyone, and right now…

She tuned her voice down to a husky whisper, one she could hardly hear herself. 'We could turn the torches off if you didn't want to look.'

He dropped the torch, which fell with a clatter and rolled against the wall. He became a silhouette to her. Too scared to move, she let him come to her. His fingers moved to the zip at the top of her suit, hesitated, then yanked it down. She felt herself start to shake as he slipped his hand under the cold fabric. His palm was rough as it brushed over her skin. That was all she could feel, the roughness. She wanted to open up to him, but it was like her body was dead.

Joiks suddenly pulled his hand away. 'Jesus, Frog.'

'What is it?' Her voice rapped out in fear, a high buzzing gurgle. There was something in his tone, something that went beyond simple disappointment. She pushed her own hand inside her jumpsuit, but still couldn't feel a thing.

Joiks had grabbed his torch. He shone it at her torso.

Frog looked down automatically and saw her pale hand was white

140

against shiny pink flesh beneath. There was a huge patch of it on her right side. Sticky, coarsened skin, like some graft which wasn't taking.

Or which was taking over the rest of her.

She stared up at Joiks, her eyes wide with shock.

He pulled out his gun, grabbed hold of her arm and forced her ahead of him back down the passageway, moaning in terror.

Chapter Eleven
The Road of Dreams

I

Polly heard the sobs ahead of the stumbling footsteps. Creben and Roba both stood up, drew their guns, barely sheltered behind the flimsy barricade they had erected.

She gasped as Frog was marched into view by Joiks. One hand was twisted behind her, tight in the big man's grip, and the other clutched at her gaping suit.

Joiks shouted over the alarmed babble that started up at their entrance. 'She's changing!'

Everyone fell quiet. Polly turned to the Doctor. He was watching closely, his beady eyes narrowed. Ben rose to his feet, glanced uncertainly at Polly.

'Changing?' Creben questioned.

'Her skin. Big patch of it ain't even human.' Joiks looked wildly into Creben's eyes, into Roba's. 'Looks like Schirr skin.'

'Schirr?' Roba's eyes widened.

Frog shook her head mutely, fiercely. Then she hung it.

Joiks tried to force Frog through a gap in the barricade ahead of them. Her thigh caught against a sheet of metal from the back of a console. The clanging it made as it fell woke Haunt from her feverish sleep. She stared round, bewildered. Tovel rested a hand on her shoulder to try to calm her.

'What's your game, Joiks?' Ben shouted. 'You're hurting her!'

'Am I?' Joiks sneered. 'She's changing. How long before she tries to hurt us?'

'Get off me,' Frog shrieked as she struggled, teeth gritted, eyes screwed up. She looked like she wanted to hurt Joiks right enough, and Polly couldn't blame her.

'Show us what you mean, Joiks,' said Creben.

Joiks twisted harder on Frog's arm. She threw her head back and hissed like a cat. He slipped his other arm under her shoulder and brought his hand back round behind her neck, until he held her quite helpless. Frog's suit was flapping open to the waist. Beneath it she wore a cropped grey top, and below the hem Polly glimpsed something sticky and sore-looking.

'What are you all playing at?' Ben shouted. 'Frog's your mate!' The men ignored him. 'She's not well! You can't treat her like that!'

'Hold her still, Joiks,' Creben snapped.

Frog kicked at him as he came closer, so Roba seized hold of her ankles. If his bandaged arm was hurting him he gave no sign. He just stared at Frog, who went on struggling as Creben advanced.

'I must insist you let me examine this woman in a proper manner,' the Doctor thundered, tapping Creben repeatedly on the shoulder.

'Show him,' said Tovel. 'Maybe he can help her.'

Roba looked angry. 'Whose side you on, man?'

Tovel shrugged. 'Frog's, maybe.' Now he looked at her. 'Frog, sweetheart, give it up, OK?'

Polly realised guiltily that Tovel was the only one of them who'd actually talked to Frog like she was still a person, and not some wild dog that needed putting down. 'We want to help you.'

'Help her?' Joiks echoed. His face was pearled with sweat as he clung grimly on to her. 'Look at her! *Look*!'

Creben stepped aside, and now Polly caught a vivid glimpse of Frog's bare midriff. There was an enormous sticky patch of raw, shiny flesh, a deep pink like new skin growing back round a wound. It was puckered with the ridges of strange, powerful muscles, and pulsating like a new heart beat beneath it.

She turned away, feeling revulsed. Joiks was right. The patch of skin was identical to that of the Schirr on bloody display on the platform.

'What do you make of it, Doctor?' she heard Ben ask quietly.

'Well, my boy, well…' The Doctor cleared his throat. 'I would say massive cellular disruption resulting in spontaneous tissue generation. Her genome is being aggressively altered by some alien influence.'

'Come again?'

Creben acted as interpreter. 'She's becoming a monster.'

Polly span round at this. 'No!' she said helplessly.

'What did I tell you,' Joiks spat. Frog finally let herself go limp in his grip. She looked exhausted. Now she was just fighting against the tears that still forced their way out of her.

Ben turned to Tovel. 'Ain't there something in your box of tricks you can give to her?'

'Yeah, Tovel?' Roba joined in. He seemed to have changed his tune. 'We can stop this thing, right?'

'It is a sickness,' the Doctor said, nodding. 'Whereas your leader and Shade have had impurities driven from their bodies, Frog is becoming contaminated in some way.' His voice wavered: 'I am sure we can reverse the process.'

'You don't sound so sure to me,' Roba said, letting go of Frog's ankles.

Joiks sagged under Frog's full weight, almost lost his balance. He shook his head. 'Reckon the only cure for her's right there in Creben's hand.'

For a long, long second, Creben looked down at his gun.

Before he could do another thing, Tovel swiped it from his grip. It skittered across the floor.

'You can forget about using that,' he said flatly.

'What gives, Tovel?' Joiks hissed. 'You marshal now, stretcher-bearer?'

Tovel gave a cheerless smile. 'Well, I don't know, Joiks, are *you*?'

Roba nodded back at Haunt's prone form on the force mattress. 'Someone better be.'

'I should take command,' said Creben stepping forward.

'How'd you figure that, brain boy?' snapped Joiks.

'I graduated to Elite training faster than any of you,' Creben said simply.

'So you got less field experience than any of us,' Roba pointed out.

'What else you got?'

'Gentlemen, please,' the Doctor said heavily. 'Listen to yourselves. Divisive forces are at work here. They seek to spread terror... will you fight amongst yourselves, or will you pit your wits against these forces and defeat them?'

'Do I have to kill you, old man?' Joiks asked like it was a serious question. 'Is that what it's gonna take to keep your mouth shut?'

Tovel stepped in quickly. 'If he opened it to yawn he'd be speaking more sense than you, Joiks. You're not in the Incendiaries now, you got witnesses, OK? So let Frog *go*.'

Ben stood beside Tovel. 'You heard him.'

'Hey, good for you, Tovel.' Joiks laughed mockingly. 'You got shorty's vote. I bet the little girl will be in your gang too!'

'That's enough.'

It was a long way from Haunt's usual bellow, but it arrested everyone like a gunshot. She was facing them on her knees. She looked like death, pale and clammy, both hands were clamped against her side. She swayed slightly, but her gaze was defiantly steadfast. The looks on the soldiers' faces were all identical – like rowdy children caught red-faced and red-handed up to no good.

'Listen to me,' she said. 'No one is killing anybody. We are a team. One unit.'

'One unit?' Joiks spluttered. 'Denni and Lindey, dead. Shel off his head, Shade with his face cracked open, Frog not even human no more... We're in pieces! Don't you see that?'

'I know what I see.' Haunt's eyes locked on to his own. 'Someone so scared he can't even think. Can't even start to think this all out. You know, you're funny, Joiks. You want to quit, is that it? Go back to the ship and go home? Well guess what...' She gasped suddenly, doubled up in pain. Everyone waited for the pain to subside, watched expectantly, in an uncomfortable, funereal silence. It was like waiting for the last words of someone about to die.

'You're all each other's got,' Haunt ground out at last. 'Tovel, you're a good pilot. Turn this thing around. Before... Before...'

Haunt's eyes closed and she slumped forwards across the mattress.

When no one else moved, Polly scrambled over to help her back into a lying position. Haunt's forehead was scorching hot. She seemed short of breath, panting like she was going to be sick. The lump below her rib cage was distended so far the skin was white now under the pressure, seeping a clear fluid.

Polly felt all eyes on her. 'Oh God,' she said. 'I think she's going to die.'

Frog picked her moment well. When she stamped down hard on Joiks's foot she caught him completely by surprise. His shriek of pain died when she jabbed an elbow back into his stomach, turned, and punched him so hard he almost flew backwards, crashing into one of the consoles. He lay still at its base, his eyes closed. Roba lunged for her but Frog ducked past him, sprinting for the doorway.

She never made it. Tovel raised his gun and fired. With a high-pitched electronic squawk, Frog went down hard on the floor.

'You killed her!' Polly yelled. Haunt started and stirred, her bloodshot eyes flickered open for a second. Then she sank back.

'I only stunned her,' Tovel retorted. 'Now if everyone will just calm down so we can *think*… Roba, bring Frog over here. Creben, see to Joiks.'

Polly watched a murderous expression flit across Creben's face at the instruction before he turned to obey.

Roba scooped up Frog from the floor, but he held her away from his body, like he didn't want to catch whatever it was she had. Tovel pulled out one of the magic sweets from his pocket and threw it down beside Polly. She jumped as it instantly snapped into another full size mattress.

Roba dumped Frog down on it. 'Getting like a regular sick bay in here,' he grumbled.

Tovel eyed the unconscious Joiks as Creben dragged him past by his feet. 'More like a crèche,' he muttered.

'Doctor,' Polly gasped. 'Come quickly.'

Ben came too. He wrinkled his nose. 'Cor, dear, what's all that!'

A brown milky fluid was oozing from the lump in Haunt's side.

'Is…' Polly tried not to be squeamish. 'Is that the tumour?'

'Yes,' breathed the Doctor, as he arrived beside them and looked down at Haunt. 'The malignancy has been broken down, rejected through the pores in the skin...' He gave a dry chuckle. 'It's quite ironic of course, but this process may well have saved her life in the long term.'

'How long is long,' Ben reflected moodily.

'That countdown I saw,' Polly recalled. 'It ticked down to us taking off... I wonder if it's ticking down now to wherever we're due to arrive?'

Tovel had rejoined them. 'That blue light, yes... That and machinery of some kind, you said.'

The Doctor considered. 'It sounds like some kind of engine room, wouldn't you say?'

Tovel nodded and looked at Polly. 'And you saw someone there?'

'I think so,' she said self-consciously, hoping people weren't about to depend on the information.

'We need to check it out,' Tovel decided. 'Short of searching this entire asteroid for some sign of Shel, it's about the only positive thing we can do.'

Creben rejoined them, having laid Joiks down beside Shade. 'I agree. Having an achievable goal is better than just searching aimlessly.'

Roba didn't look convinced. 'And what if we run into more of them stone things out there.'

The Doctor looked thoughtful. 'We must attempt to communicate with them.'

'You ain't seen them, Doctor,' Ben said quietly. 'Don't reckon talking's on their mind.'

'If they meant to harm us now, why have they not followed us here? To attack us in our quite considerable disarray, hmm?'

'Well, even if they don't,' said Polly, 'what about Shel? He's still out there, and he nearly killed you.'

'We will take all the precautions we can, I promise you, Polly,' said the Doctor.

'Hang on,' said Ben. He didn't sound too happy. 'We? You mean you're coming with us?'

'Of course I am, my boy.'

'Hey, wait,' Roba scowled. 'Thought you were gonna fix up Frog?'

'By instigating this plan, I hope to,' the Doctor said tetchily. 'And I suggest we attempt to wake Mr Joiks, also. The area is blocked off by a rockfall, and we shall need his strength.'

There was a groan from the other side of the room, right on cue.

'Let's hope Frog knocked some sense into him,' said Ben.

'Indeed, yes. In any case, the rockfall… Once manual labour has cleared that, and the propulsion systems, as we hope them to be, revealed…' The Doctor tapped his head and chortled to himself. 'Then the mind must be put to good use in sabotaging them, hmm?'

Tovel saw what he was getting at. 'We can't steer without the crystals, but we can stop ourselves before we arrive!'

'Precisely,' said the Doctor.

Creben shrugged. 'We might buy some time.'

'And halt the malign influence affecting your friend here,' the Doctor said to Roba, patting Frog on the arm. 'Before it strikes any more of us. Driving out impurities… and yet…' He trailed away, lost in his thoughts.

'What about Pol?' Ben demanded.

Polly had been asking herself the selfsame question. 'I suppose I should stay here,' she volunteered, with a sick feeling in her stomach. 'Look after the wounded.'

'I believe that will be safest,' the Doctor said, smiling at her.

Polly looked down at Frog's unconscious body, and didn't answer.

'What if one of them bodies goes walkabout again?' asked Ben.

The Doctor considered. 'Well, we came to no harm the last time the phenomenon occurred.'

'That was then!' Ben retorted. 'And in case you'd forgotten, there's still a secret doorway into this place that we don't know about.'

'We searched everywhere,' Creben told him. 'Found nothing.'

'Well how come Polly vanished then, eh? Went flying through the wall I suppose, did she?'

'Look, I can't come with you,' Polly said flatly. 'I can't just leave Shade and Haunt here alone, can I? Or Frog.'

'Maybe I should stay,' said Ben.

Yes please, Polly thought to herself, but kept her face carefully neutral.

'The sooner we clear a path, the sooner we can return,' said Creben.

There were nods of assent from the others. Polly forced a smile. 'I'll be fine.'

'Shade's injuries are healing fast,' Creben added. Polly frowned; she found that hard to imagine.

'When he wakes up, he'll be protection for you. Plus you'll be barricaded in, Polly,' Tovel assured her.

Ben didn't look happy. 'You couldn't stop a determined ferret with that!'

'I'll be *fine*,' she told him again, more firmly. 'Go. Go, and hurry back.'

Ben sighed, then forced a smile himself. 'Have the kettle on for us when we get back, eh?'

She rolled her eyes. 'And the best china, right?'

'Then it is settled.' The Doctor looked benignly around. 'Shall I lead the way?'

'Don't push it, Doctor,' Tovel told him. 'Come on, let's go.'

II

Haunt forced her eyes open. She stared straight up at the mirrors pressed into the ceiling, high, high above. No. She didn't want to see herself, to see what was happening to her. She heard the swift clatter of troops marching out of the room. Right now she couldn't imagine what it would be like, to feel so healthy, so strong again. The mirrors reflected gleams of light from the high golden trellises into her watery eyes. She looked to her side instead, but she couldn't focus. Maybe she was falling to fever, maybe to drugs, but everything was starting to distort.

Someone was there, close by, just out of view. She had something important she had to ask, she knew. She had to remember what.

'Frog... Did they kill her?'

No answer, or an answer so quiet it couldn't be heard. Light began to bleed away from her vision, the way starry space always gave way to sunlit sky as planetfall commenced.

Colonel Nadina Haunt was watching it now from the viewscreen of her fighter, the first wisps of the planet Toronto's daylight shining into her eyes. It was a gorgeous, wide-open sky, one fit for angels. A frigid landscape of cloud stretched off to the dense horizon, superimposed over a green sea. The twin landscapes blurred, one into the other, as Ashman took them down more steeply.

'Switching to manual,' he said, and she watched his hands grip the flight gears, the muscles in his forearms clenching as he adjusted their position, taking control himself.

She was twenty-nine, or thirty. Way too old to be feeling the way she did about Ashman.

The targeting grid came up on Nadina Haunt's eyescreen as they cleared the clouds and the flat vista of the sea established its mastery. In the open waters around Labrador harbour, tiny specks of white blossomed into circular blooms. Haunt's mind made sense of them as solar dishes harvesting the power of the twin suns, and it was only when they were much closer that she realised they were actually sails. Each effortlessly caught the stiff salt breeze, skipping the boats over the choppy water.

The sight fascinated Haunt, through the mesh of the targeting grid. She could discern the tiny figures of the ship-crews as they bustled about the wooden decks, netting their haul.

The natives had been allowed to maintain their simple economy, their semblance of culture – it had been a good cover. The Empire was unlikely to house its secret military capital on such a strategically precarious world.

The rich salt-broth seas on Toronto were always thrashing with fish. The natives had only to skim the nets of their fishing boats over the surface for a few minutes to come home with enough food to bloat an entire settlement. And it wasn't only the natives (she couldn't remember their race name) that benefited. The superabundance of marine life enabled the empire to freeze and export billions of tonnes to its outlying colonies. It justified the considerable military presence on Toronto: a dozen worlds really did depend on this planet for food.

It couldn't be helped, Haunt decided as she synched up with the weapons net. The Schirr had crept in and ruined everything. Now human security was at risk. Taken in by their own cleverness, Pent-Cent had got complacent. Ashman had said he was only surprised an incursion hadn't happened sooner.

He banked hard right, the teeming sea and starched sails streaking past beneath them. The harbour compound loomed sheer and white over the still waters. It looked like a glittering block of ice.

Ashman turned to her. Narrowed his indigo eyes and nodded. It was as if the look alone had triggered the pulse in her head. She shuddered as she opened fire, launching her missiles into the midst of the little boats skimming the writhing water. The fighters flanking Ashman's ship followed suit.

'You like your fish well-done?' she asked.

'You're funny,' he told her.

Then she and Ashman were watching the sea and everything in it start to burn.

The Schirr stealth craft concealed in the harbour, pale and fleshy ovoids, sounded like they were screaming as the flames took them. Haunt tried not to gag on the stench of the dying sea, wafting across the compound grounds in a thick salty fog.

'At least one Schirr unit was sighted overground,' Ashman bellowed at his troops. 'Security may have been compromised.'

They would find out together. They were running through the klaxons and emergency lighting of the compound, deeper and deeper underground. There were bodies here and there. Haunt skidded on the slick ground and fell. She'd splashed down in someone's blood. Ashman turned, reached out his hand to her. She took it, felt his strength through the warm stickiness for a moment. Then they were running on. Her wet hair flapped about her forehead in gory braids.

More bodies. A secure zone had been breached. In one room

marked restricted, they saw a woman twisted over a data input, staring at the screen. Her gun lay discarded on the floor along with most of the contents of a medical kit. Blood soaked the whole of one leg black through the fabric of her grey uniform. The woman looked up at them but her shocked expression didn't change.

'They got in,' she kept saying, over and over. 'They got in.'

Behind her was slumped the rubbery corpse of a Schirr, stomach and neck both shot open. Its fat lips bared back over its peg teeth, it looked like it had died smiling.

'Look after her,' Ashman told her. 'I'll screen the corridor.'

Haunt crossed to the woman, stepped gingerly over the detritus on the floor. Saw too late the timer grenade clamped in the Schirr's fleshy grip.

Heat as it detonated. She dived to the floor. The injured woman shielded her a little. What about Ashman, framed in the doorway? He was screaming but she couldn't see for the smoke. And she knew that if she woke up from the sick, heavy blackness coming for her, she wouldn't know how much blood was her own and how much she had slipped in outside.

The heat of the blast wasn't fading.

It was burning her on the inside. Her guts were squeezing out through a lump beneath her ribs.

They would get confused with the Schirr's. Why couldn't she smile in death like it could? Why was she so afraid?

She moaned and opened her eyes and saw a feminine face, framed by long straight blonde hair. The woman who shouldn't be here, Polly. Soothing her. Haunt tried to struggle, hated to let anyone see her so weak. Something hot and molten was stirring sluggishly in her guts.

'What's happening?' she mumbled, almost choking on her tongue.

'Tovel told me to give you something when you woke up,' Polly said. She got up and went away.

'Did they kill Frog?' Haunt said thickly.

'No.' The gurgling voice came to her like she was underwater. 'No, the frog ain't croaked yet.'

'Stay with us,' Haunt whispered, as sound and vision lost all definition again. She felt a hot pinprick in her arm, invasive, bruising the muscle. Shadows came for her again. 'Stay with us, Frog...'

'Wouldn't miss this party for nothing,' Frog muttered.

Marshal Nadina Haunt heard the voice die away.

The darkness swooped and caught her.

III

'She should rest quietly now,' Polly told Frog.

'Great,' Frog retorted. 'What did Tovel say that was?'

'I'm not sure,' Polly confessed. 'Something to break the fever, he said. Help her sleep.'

'What's he want Haunt to sleep for?' muttered Frog. 'Think he likes being in charge?'

'He just wants to help, I suppose,' Polly ventured.

'Nah. He just likes being in charge.' Frog gave a crooked smile. 'Now Haunt's popped that shot, she may never wake up.'

Polly shuddered. 'Don't.'

They listened to Haunt's breathing, a sound just too ragged to be soothing.

'Now give me something to fix me up, will ya?' Frog said brightly.

Polly sighed. 'I wish I could.'

'Sure you do.'

'Of course I do!'

''Cause you feel soooo sorry for me.' Frog narrowed her eyes, spitefully. 'You, with your doll's hair, your long, young skinny body, your clear skin. Bet you grew up under a blue sky and a warm sun. Had yourself toys to play with.' She laughed. 'Where I grew up, *I* was the toy. People picked me up and did what they wanted. Whenever they wanted. Dad. His friends. Anyone.'

Polly stared at Frog dumbly. She couldn't find a thing to say.

'Feeling sorry for me, now?' Frog sneered. 'That always follows. The sorries.'

'What do you want me to say,' Polly murmured, looking away. 'That I'm glad you're sick or something?'

153

'I don't need the sorries. Don't need nothing. I fight, see? The army made me someone. *Something.*' Tears rolled down her scarred cheeks. 'Now I'm being made into something else.'

Faster than you know, thought Polly sadly. Frog's jumpsuit was zipped right up, but a track of the raw and puckered new flesh had crept up to her neck, right up to the small black disc on her throat which must make her voice sound so strange. The normal skin blistered and burnt round the edges of the patch.

Polly couldn't just sit and watch Frog cry. 'I'm going to check on Shade,' she said.

Frog didn't answer. Haunt had begun to snore softly. The sounds were taken by the weird acoustics in the great chamber and twisted, distorted, flung back at her. Polly felt horribly vulnerable. She kept glancing up at the bodies on their platform, counting them over and over. Six. Six. Six.

IV

'You sure you can find this place again?' Roba asked in a loud whisper. He led the way up the passage, rubbing distractedly at his injured wrist.

'There's a bend coming up, then the tunnel should fork,' Tovel hissed back. 'It should get lighter too.'

'Polly had placed a pile of stones outside the relevant path,' the Doctor added. He paused for breath, and dabbed at his forehead with a handkerchief.

Ben waited dutifully beside him, and Creben and Joiks both pushed past. Ben looked nervously around – a pointless exercise, since it was so dark you couldn't see your hand before your face. He was sure it hadn't been so dark before, and had become convinced that the fleaweed on the ceilings was able somehow to shift itself about. Was there nothing that didn't move when it shouldn't in this God-awful place?

In an attempt to avoid unwelcome attention, they'd decided to have just the one torch on, Roba's, leading them on. It was like trailing after a lost little sunbeam in the cold, dark tunnels. Twice they had heard the soft, rhythmic flapping of stone wings in the blackness. Roba had flicked off the torch and they'd stood frozen like statues themselves until the noise had faded back into the shadows.

'Wait a minute, then!' Ben called quietly into the darkness, afraid the others would get too far ahead

'Don't fuss, my boy,' the Doctor told him stiffly, and they started off again.

They caught up with the others in time to see them crouched beside a little slate cairn that marked one of two tunnels. The fleaweed was back, casting its seasick glow.

'Polly must've left that,' said Ben.

'This is the way,' Tovel said.

The passage wound on, getting brighter the further they got. The fleas skipped and scuttled over their faces and hands. Ben brushed them away furiously. Then he realised Roba and the others had stopped – and, a moment later, saw why.

'Stone me,' Ben said, staring out into a star-filled night. 'They put a window in here.'

'Why would they do such a thing?' Creben wondered.

'I wonder, yes,' said the Doctor, making a big show of contemplating the mystery. Ben supposed he was grateful for the extra rest. 'Why one window, and why here?'

'Well, it's not a bad view, is it?' Ben said. The stars were solid points of light, glaring out from the most absolute blackness Ben had ever seen.

'Nothing out there,' Roba remarked.

'Not yet,' Joiks added.

Roba led them onwards

'Can't get no further,' said Roba. 'Rockfall. Time to get busy.'

'All right. Polly said she ran straight down this tunnel from the blue area.' The heavy crack of boulders impacting against floor and wall punctuated Tovel's speech as Roba got his hands dirty. 'If we can clear that lot, we'll be on the way to getting clear ourselves.'

Ben wished he could believe it.

As Tovel helped Roba dislodge the really big stones, Joiks and Creben both began work themselves. While Creben sized up different rocks, looking for those that might bring a number more tumbling down without further effort, Joiks tore at the landslide. He was probably imagining each one was Frog's head. She'd given the berk a right bloody nose; if it hadn't been flattened a dozen times before she'd probably have broken it. Still, it had knocked some of the cockiness out of him and no mistake. He was good as gold and keeping his lip buttoned. Ben almost liked him that way.

Poor old Frog. If there was even a chance they could stop what was happening to her...

'Come on, Ben,' Roba called, as he heaved at a huge boulder. 'You can maybe shift the pebbles, OK?'

'Yeah, yeah.' Ben was glad to see the big man back on side, but a little wary of him too since his acting up back in the control room. He grappled with a chunk of slate too big for him to tackle easily alone, just to show willing. But the thought of Frog had suggested something to him. ''Ere, Roba. That cut of yours. How come your suit's not digging in, staunching the blood or whatever?'

'It ain't working,' Roba grumbled, not looking up from the rockpile. 'Cheap crap they give us.'

They worked on. Just as he was beginning to think that any second now the noise of crashing rock would bring the stone angels flapping back in sympathy, Ben saw a wisp of wraith-like blue light ahead.

'Look!' he called. 'We're almost through!'

V

Haunt stirred, her eyes opened almost involuntarily. The control room snapped back into sharp focus. The fever had broken, and her thoughts had suddenly an awful, fragile clarity. She felt not just the dreadful empty pain in her side and the warm throb of the shot in her arm, but the full weight of her responsibility for the safety and success of the mission. All those lives that depended on her.

She was so tired. Too tired. Didn't they realise that?

Her eyes closed. Just for a moment Haunt thought of Ashman again and wished she could go back there, back then, to that time on Toronto.

VI

Shade had been sleeping silently for some time now; or so Polly had thought. She stopped as she approached him. He was lying facing away from her, curled up.

Lindey's palm-sized computer was gone from his pocket.

Polly stealthily advanced. Now she was close enough to see he was actually using the computer, holding it up to his eyes, entirely caught up in whatever it was showing him.

Polly reached in and grabbed the computer from him. Shade spun round in surprise. Polly stifled a gasp, felt her stomach churn, and the flesh at the back of her thighs go tight at the sight of him.

His face was a mess of half-formed scabs, and streaked with bright red blood. Guilt was written gorily all over him.

'Guess I'm always going to have the same effect on people, aren't I,' he said. 'One look and they scream.'

'This isn't about your face,' Polly snapped. 'Except in as much as you seem to have two of them. Oh, yes, you were so sad to have lost poor old Lindey one minute… didn't stop you stealing her computer thing and keeping whatever it might tell you to yourself!'

She wanted him to deny it. He didn't. She looked at the screen, focussed on the green capitals clustered there.

PRESS OK TO KILL FILES ++

'What's going on, Shade?' she breathed.

'Nothing,' he said, his hoarse voice sounding more choked than usual. 'Give me that palmscreen.'

'I'll get Haunt to show me how it works,' she said defiantly.

Shade stared helplessly at her, his face twisted in pain. For an awful moment she thought he was going to start crying too.

'But if you tell me, I won't tell anyone else,' she added.

157

Shade laid his head back down on the firm mattress. 'I don't suppose it matters much, since we're going to die anyway.'

'What do you mean, we're going to die?' Polly demanded.

'Isn't it obvious?' Shade whispered. His brilliant green eyes seemed to look straight through her. 'Don't you see? It's me, Polly. The reason we're going to die. It's all *me*.'

'What are you talking about, Shade?' Polly croaked, backing away.

'I'm from Earth. You know what that means?'

Polly sort of half-shook her head, not wanting to get sidetracked by unnecessary explanations.

'Privilege. Power. Reward.' He gazed up at her. 'My family could buy the planet that Frog grew up on, and barely notice the expense.'

'So?'

'So I didn't want to be like that. Just about money, and privilege. I wanted to give something back.' He smiled at her, a strained sort of smile.

Give something back. Polly thought back to the New Year's resolution she'd made in 1963, to work in the charity shop for cancer research. Giving something back. But she'd hated the squalor of the grey little store in Notting Hill, standing all day amid the remnants of drab little lives on shelves and hangers. She'd walked out after a week – making her mum ecstatic in the process – and donated a pricey pile of last year's fashions instead to assuage her guilt.

'Go on,' she nodded.

'I joined up. Thought I'd fight for the Empire. Coming from Earth, they made me a lieutenant straight off.' The smile was still on his face, though now it looked like someone had carved it in with a pen knife. 'On New Jersey...'

'You hurt yourself there,' Polly remembered. 'The mine...'

His face crumpled. 'I was squad leader. Schirr everywhere. Walked straight into an ambush.' He contorted his lips over his clenched teeth, trying to keep the words coming.

'That wasn't your fault,' Polly said gently. 'You were helping the children...'

'No. There were no kids. Except the kids in my squad.' He

158

swallowed. 'Didn't fight. Didn't lead. Just left my men to it. They were screaming… I didn't care. So scared I ran straight into a mine.'

Polly looked down at the screen again, at the word 'OK', as Shade kept on talking, so quietly she could barely hear him.

'It took half my face off and stopped my career dead. Without my connections – those same stupid connections I was running from – I'd have been court-martialled and either executed or else given ceremonial duties on some craphole world mid-empire.'

'And instead?'

'Instead I was given an honourable discharge, and allowed to rejoin the following year with a doctored record.' He started to cry, a soft mewling noise coming from somewhere deep inside. 'Every day I look at myself. And I remember.'

I never forget the scum that did this to me, Shade had told her back at the rockfall. Polly looked up from the palmscreen. It was hurting her eyes. 'Lindey found out, didn't she?'

'Someone she knew died thanks to me. Thanks to me believing I could be something I'm not.' He clicked his tongue. 'You've got the files there. I think she was going to blackmail me once I'd made AT Elite.'

'Why?'

'Show me one person who's happy where they are. I've always kidded myself I could rough it out in Empire. She wanted Earth contacts, I suppose.'

'And now she's dead?'

Shade stared dreamily into space. 'All I need do is hit the button, kill the files, and my secret is safe.'

Polly pushed the palmscreen inside her spacesuit. 'I know your secret.' She raised her eyebrows at him. 'What about me?'

'It doesn't matter,' he whispered. 'Thanks to me, we're all going to die anyway.'

'No. That's silly, stop it.'

Shade shook his head, shut his eyes. He seemed suddenly exhausted. 'I can't stop it. No one can. I'm a jinx, see. And the ambush, it's happening all over again.'

* * *

The patch of blue light had got everyone excited. Ben noticed that even Creben had abandoned his methodical knocking out of the key rocks in favour of scrabbling at the pile like the rest of them until the hole was big enough to scramble through.

There was a pressure in Ben's ears, like a sea was roaring and rolling in his head. A glittering indigo filled the wide passage, blissfully welcome after the murk of the tunnels or the sick green glow of the fleaweed. His feet felt like they were barely touching the ground, like he was floating through the night sky in summer. How many warm evenings had Ben looked out at that dark expanse and imagined he could splash out into it as easily as he could the warm, dark sea.

'Ben.' The Doctor's voice was sharp in his ear, and a hand pressed down on his shoulder. 'Ben, listen to me.'

'What?' Ben shrugged off the Doctor's hand. He didn't want to listen. He only wanted to look. They'd reached an outcrop of rock overlooking a dark chasm. Waves of Caribbean blue rolled across roof and floor, translucent sheets of sparkling light that splashed against the rocky walls and out into the air. It was beautiful.

The Doctor raised his voice. Now it sounded like he was addressing a whole crowd.

'Ben, all of you, listen to me.'

Who else was here then?

'We are near a source of great power. A power great enough to distort your perceptions.'

'Quiet down,' Ben complained.

'It wants you to approach with your defences down,' the old man insisted. 'I am sure of it, this place is some kind of trap.'

'Well shut yours then, for starters.' Ben couldn't stay angry for long with a view as gorgeous as this. Just across the sea there was some kind of island, dark filtered through the moonlight. Grainy sand, spiky palms, the perfect desert island. He'd always kidded with the boys on the *Teazer* he'd go AWOL the moment it came along. Now all he had to do was float over and see it for himself. Decide if he wanted to stay.

Ben imagined it was paradise there.

'It is using your memories, your imagination, to reel you in close enough to strike!' Ben felt himself spun round. A craggy old face leaned into his own. 'Think of Lindey, and Denni. Pulled away into the darkness. Pulled apart by winged statues.'

Ben pushed the old man away. 'Leave me alone!' His arms felt dead. The rest of him felt dead drunk. The sky was spinning above him, streaked with stars.

'Think of Polly, alone, back in that room with the sick and the dying!' The old man was back again, back in his face. 'There is evil, here, Ben. Evil that we must defeat if we are to survive. Do you understand me now, hmm?' Ben felt bony fingers digging into his shoulders. *'Do you understand?'*

'Yes!' screamed Ben.

He stood shaking, trembling, at the edge of the precipice. The spell was broken, the rushing static noise in his head reduced to a whisper. As he turned, he saw that the shadowy island was some kind of machinery housed across the divide.

And while Creben stood just a few feet away with his hands pressed against his ears, face twisted in pain as if he was trying to shut out some terrible sound, Joiks, Roba and Tovel had actually walked off the lip of rock into the chasm. Ben stared, woozily, half-expecting the lot of them to look down at any second and, actually *realising* they were walking in mid-air, plummet to the ground like the coyote did in the cartoons. But they didn't.

'Some kind of force bridge, I suppose. Now quickly, Ben, while I deal with Creben, go after them. They must be stopped! None of us know what's waiting for them!'

While the Doctor started shouting at Creben – an easier conversion it seemed, since he was already trying to fight off the influence in the first place – Ben sprinted to the edge of the precipice. With a deep breath, he stepped out into thin blue air. It gave slightly beneath him, but held. He took another cautious step, then broke into a run. Tovel, Roba and Joiks had almost reached the shadowy cylindrical mass Ben had seen as an island. It looked now more like a couple of giant glass

161

cotton reels stacked on top of each other in a rocky alcove. A dark liquid seemed to swirl inside, carried he supposed by the confused junction of pipes coiled all around the structure, disappearing into floor and ceiling.

'Oi, you lot!' he yelled, wondering what each of them was seeing now. 'It ain't safe! It ain't what you think it is!' They ignored him. Soon they would've crossed to the other side.

Then inspiration struck.

'Blimey, here comes Haunt!' Ben shouted. 'She don't look too happy at the state of you lot!'

The three men paused on the slate grey shore of the weird machine's peninsula. They turned, almost as one person. Tovel and Roba looked like someone had thrown a bucket of water over them, stared round in surprise.

But Joiks's face clouded over again. He turned back to the glass cylinder.

'Terrific,' Ben muttered. He sprinted past Roba and Tovel, and brought Joiks crashing down in a rugby tackle. The big man made no attempt to break his fall, and landed like a brick. The shock seemed to bring him round. He rolled on to his back, and looked about him in a daze.

'Hope that didn't hurt too much, Joiks,' Ben said, hiding a smile. That one had been for Frog.

He turned to find the others, the Doctor and Creben included, were standing round him in a semi-circle. Roba hoisted Joiks to his feet.

The Doctor was puffing for breath. 'Well done, Ben, my boy.'

Ben nodded vaguely. He was looking back at the glass tank, and the inky liquid vortex inside. There were occasional flashes of energy from within. Even the air seemed to carry some sort of charge.

'Well, Doctor?' asked Tovel. 'Is that thing part of the drive systems?'

'Part of them? Yes, I believe so.' He drew himself up to his full height. 'We must be very careful.'

Cautiously they advanced. The glass crackled and spat light at them, as if warning them away.

'How is it powering this thing?' Creben wondered. 'The fuel

required for a chunk of rock this size…'

'Hey, what's that?' Roba gestured to a scrap of dirty fabric caught on the rough slate of the wall beside coils of piping.

Ben skirted the glass cylinder to see. The material had been white once, but now it was filthy with grime and rusty stains. 'Could be blood, I suppose.'

Creben took the scrap from him. 'It *is* blood.' He turned to the others. 'It's from one of the Schirr.'

''Ere, wait a minute.' In one of the glass cylinder's more vivid sparks Ben caught sight of something gleaming, pressed into a crack in the rock. 'There's something else down here.'

Creben drew a short-bladed knife and prised out a metal band. 'Webset,' he muttered. He worked more urgently with the blade, forcing the headband out. 'I've found a webset!' he yelled. 'And another beneath it.'

'Right little treasure trove, ain't it?' Ben commented.

'Lindey's and Denni's, they must be!' Creben shouted to the others.

'Why would anyone hide their websets down here?' asked Tovel.

'I say dump them,' Joiks said quickly.

Creben frowned at him. 'What?'

'Come on, who needs them?'

'They must've been hidden here for some reason,' said Tovel.

Then there was a hiss and a crackle like fat on a flame, and then the sound of something heavy slamming into the glass. Ben whirled round in time to see a huge hunk of flesh smeared against the inside of the cylinder, just for a few seconds, until the relentless swirl of inky fluid swept it back into the maelstrom.

It looked to be someone's back.

Ben gagged, turned away.

'Lindey,' whispered Roba. 'That's got to be Lindey. That's why her set's here.'

The Doctor stared at them gravely. 'The secrets of the propulsion system?'

Creben looked properly downcast for the first time Ben could recall. 'It all comes back to the body, doesn't it. Lindey's and Denni's they use for fuel. Frog's is no good so they start turning her into something else.'

'Meat.' Joiks started giggling. 'That's all we are now. Meat.'

Ben turned to the Doctor. 'They're really using human flesh and blood as fuel?'

'For the rituals,' Roba added. 'They're using it for the rituals.'

The Doctor looked down at the floor. 'As a basic material in the energy conversion process, yes, it's possible.'

'Not just human remains.' Tovel pointed to the cylinder.

Pressed up against the glass, along with a mess of dark-brown chunks that looked like dog food, was a bloody medallion of glistening pink flesh. It bore a brand, a rectangle crossed through with a diagonal line.

'Schirr,' he breathed. 'There's Schirr bodies in this thing as well.'

'The Morphieans,' said Creben. 'They're taking back what's theirs.'

'And dealing most conclusively with their enemies,' the Doctor agreed. 'I imagine this centrifuge is where the Schirr bodies on the platform were conjured to.'

'There's six of them left,' Ben said with a frown. 'So why turn Frog into a Schirr too?'

'To maintain some secret balance?' the Doctor wondered. 'Or because Schirr flesh gives a higher yield? Perhaps we will all become Schirr before too long, the impurities driven from our flesh so that it may be changed...'

'And we'll all wind up in there,' said Tovel quietly, transfixed by the cylinder.

'Great,' said Roba. His dark skin was covered in sweat, and he kept licking his lips every few seconds. 'So, how do we stop this thing?'

'Stop it?' Joiks spluttered. 'You want we should get in that thing and pull out the plug?'

'These pipes and stuff. We could pull them out, we could –'

'Young man,' the Doctor said sternly, 'you can see the powers at work there. We dare not disturb that balance without a fuller knowledge of how the processes work.'

'So get learning, *old* man,' Roba growled menacingly.

The Doctor sighed. 'I confess I was hoping to find a more conventional means of propulsion. If I only had more time to –'

'All this time you been shooting off a mouth as big as one of these tunnels,' Roba hissed. 'And now you don't know nothing?'

'All right, quiet, all of you,' snapped Tovel. 'You talk about learning, Roba. We're learning more all the time. We know where the Schirr went, we know where Lindey and Denni went.' He grabbed the websets from Creben. 'And we got these. Denni was still recording when she was killed. Maybe we'll learn some more from watching that back.'

'So, how about we *get* back, then?' chimed Ben. 'Check up on Polly and the others. This place gives me the creeps.'

Joiks suddenly lunged for the websets.

Tovel recoiled instinctively, kept them out of reach. 'What the hell are you playing at, Joiks?'

'What we gonna learn from watching them die? I say we should dump them.'

Roba scowled at him. 'That don't make no sense, Joiks.'

'Don't make no sense to rake over the past, neither.' Joiks laughed nervously. 'What are you people, sick?'

'Something happened down there, didn't it, Joiks?' Creben said. 'When Denni got taken.'

Joiks backed away. 'You're crazy, Creben.'

'Oh, really?' Creben shook his head. 'I think you know something you're not telling us.'

Tovel grabbed hold of Joiks's shoulder. 'We're talking to you.'

'It's nothing!' Joiks pulled himself free of Tovel's grip. 'Denni was saying stuff about Haunt. Didn't think she was fit to lead us on a live ammo shoot when she gets so worked up by the Schirr and all that. She wanted me to log a complaint or something, I dunno.'

'And did you agree?' demanded the Doctor.

'I told her she was crazy.' Joiks paused. When he spoke again, his voice had lost its cockiness. 'But then, you know… she wants something from me, I'm maybe thinking, how 'bout I get something in return?'

Tovel snorted. 'You're filth, Joiks.'

165

'Look, I didn't do nothing! It was dark, when the sets don't pick much stuff up. I put an arm round her waist, sounded her out a little... But she was grabbed right from out of my arms, and that's the truth!' Joiks's voice grew whinier, less confident. 'I tried to hold on to her –'

'Yeah, well, it sounds a sweet little story, Joiks,' said Tovel. 'But maybe we'll view the sets anyway. Just in case they picked up *something*, right?'

'Reckon Denni was lucky she got offed when she did,' muttered Roba.

Joiks turned and stamped off the way they'd come without another word. He teetered on the edge of the indigo abyss for a moment, as if surprised to find it there. Then, with a last glare back at Tovel and the others, he set off across the divide. The rolling blue swell of light swept over and around him. Still it hissed and rustled like the sea.

'We'd better get after him,' sighed Tovel as he secured the two websets to his belt. But Roba was already slouching off, leaving the others behind.

'If you're going to lead us,' said Creben, indicating the two bowed figures as they strode through the blue, 'you'd better *lead* us.'

'Yes, after you, Tovel,' agreed the Doctor absently. He pottered off along the force bridge after Creben and Tovel. Ben followed on behind, trying not to look too hard through the eddying light and down into the depths of the ravine. If whatever was holding them up chose to let go...

They were halfway over when Ben heard the noise of heavy wings flapping, like distant bellows drawing in air and hissing it back out.

He swore. 'Do any of you hear...?'

Tovel and his merry men ignored him and grabbed for their weapons. They'd heard it all right.

Moments later a flight of the fat stone cherubim breezed through the gaping mouth of the tunnel, some six or seven of them.

'They found us,' Joiks screamed.

The apparitions fanned out into the room. Their chubby arms were wide open. The sharp hooks of their fingers flexed and wriggled.

'For all our ignorance,' said the Doctor, glaring haughtily at the creatures as they spun through the blinding blue air, 'I fear we may still have learned too much.'

Joiks opened fire. The others quickly followed suit.

The cherubim bobbed down unharmed through the opening volley of laser blasts. As Ben fired his crummy pistol, he saw the statues' serene smiles growing broader at the sight of the humans huddled beneath them.

'Just meat,' Joiks muttered, as his gun spat bolt after useless bolt.

Chapter Twelve
Murder is Easy

I

Tovel was right, Polly realised. Shade's injuries were healing with incredible speed. The splits and gouges in his face, all puckered by endless lines of tiny plastic sutures, had now practically smoothed themselves out, and he seemed to be sleeping peacefully. It still looked like someone had cut a map of the London Underground into his face, but all things considered, his wounds should've been a good deal worse.

She thought about what he'd said about being a jinx, tried to tell herself it was self-pitying, stupid talk. But what if it was true?

Polly took out the palmscreen from her spacesuit, and studied it. 'Oh no!' she hissed. The screen was blank. She must've knocked the OK button when she hid the stupid thing away. That must mean all Shade's incriminating files were deleted.

Well, good, she told herself. It showed that Shade had some good luck after all, so he couldn't be a jinx. They would all be fine.

Frog's scream nearly punctured Polly's eardrums.

She spun round, and her hand flew to her mouth in shock.

Frog was propped up on one elbow, her combat suit unzipped. She was digging a knife into her shiny pink stomach. There seemed to be blood everywhere.

'What are you doing?' Polly squeaked.

'When you got poison inside you,' panted Frog, her pale staring eyes bulging out of her red face, 'you gotta cut it out.'

'But you can't just… cut out…' Polly wondered if she would faint. 'Cut out all that flesh.'

Frog flashed her a manic grin. 'Wanna watch me try?'

'Put down the knife, Frog,' Polly pleaded. 'You'll kill yourself.'

'Ha!' Frog's mad smile relaxed a little. 'Now why didn't I think of that.' She gritted her teeth and slid the knife along. But another bloodcurdling scream escaped her.

'Frog, you're mad, you're sick,' Polly told her. 'Stop that now, or I'll –'

'You'll burst into tears, sweetie?' Frog's face crumpled in mock-sympathy. 'Look, just turn around and gaze into Shadow's dreamy green eyes or something, OK?'

Polly's resolve hardened. 'Give me the knife.'

'Or you'll do what? Kill me? Go right ahead, honey.'

'Frog!' Shade's husky voice behind her made Polly jump. She supposed it wasn't a surprise he'd woken up. If the first scream hadn't got to him, the second one would've done the trick.

He advanced on her, a little shakily.

'Great, I got an audience,' Frog said. She kept her red-rimmed eyes open. Slid the knifepoint easily into the sticky skin on her stomach. She slipped the blade along.

The eyes shut, the mouth opened.

Joiks screamed.

Ben saw that two of the stone angels had gripped the soldier by the arms. They fluttered just above him, dwarfing him as he ran in panic through the searing blue light that swirled and buffeted all about. Then they lifted him off the invisible ground.

'Concentrate your fire on those ones!' shouted Tovel. Creben and Roba did as they were told. Bolt after white-hot bolt shot through the sizzling air. But the huge, squat bodies of the other cherubim spinning in the whirling sky got in the way. None of them seemed to feel the fire in any case. Joiks was carried further and further up into the blue haze.

One of the giants swooped and landed close to Ben. He fired the pistol into its placid sculpted eyes, its pitying smile. It trotted towards him, like a puppy wanting to play. 'Doctor!' Ben yelled helplessly, still firing.

The Doctor stormed over, a look of helpless outrage on his face.

'Tovel, help us!' he cried as the statue bore down on them both.

But Tovel had problems of his own. Two of the hideous, outsized angels were sweeping about him. One kicked out with a huge stone foot, and his rifle went flying through the air. The other kicked him in the ribs. Tovel yelled out as he fell backwards. Creben and Roba fired at his attackers, but the angels didn't seem to notice.

Ben's pistol was out of ammo. The statue's smile became broader.

'Drop, Ben!' the Doctor shouted as the creature rushed for them. Ben threw himself down, rolled on to his back. But the squat cherub just sailed lazily over them, beat its great stone wings and took to the air again. Stone, for God's sake. How could these things be flying like they were light as a feather?

Tovel helped him back up. The angels persecuting him had flown off too. Roba hauled the Doctor back to his feet. Creben stood a few feet away, panting, staring up into the haze.

The stone angels circled slowly. Only the two that clutched on to Joiks's arms stayed still, hovering like malevolent ghosts, high above the humans. One of them ripped Joiks's backpack away, and let it tumble to the ground. Ben ran for it, scooped it up. He discarded his pistol in favour of the rifle, and tied what was left of the harness and its gear round his waist. But by the time he was aiming back up at the huge stone creatures, he saw he was too late to make any difference to the fight. They had tugged Joiks, teased him, like two cats playing with a mouse, over towards the glass cylinder.

Joiks screamed again, the noise echoing horribly all around. 'They're tearing me apart!'

Ben could see the pain on Joiks's face. The angels were massive, their arms shaped like a plump baby's only fifty times bigger. Their huge hands were digging in to the skin, blood was soaking the dark grey of his combat suit.

'Wait!' shouted the Doctor.

Ben blinked. Everything stopped, even Joiks's screams. Though the frantic sobs that succeeded them weren't a lot better.

The cherubim that held Joiks looked down at him, as if suddenly confused.

* * *

Frog's scream died away, and she looked down at the bloody blade embedded in her skin as if puzzled by it. Dark blood pumped from the gash she'd carved into herself. Now her hand trembled on the knife hilt. Polly sensed she was about to thrust down on it, push it right the way in, to finish this for good.

'Shade, do something!' hissed Polly.

He stepped forward, uncertainly.

The knife twisted a fraction in Frog's hand.

Joiks was still dangling helplessly from the huge stone hands of the angels.

'We can't help him,' Roba shouted. 'Come on!'

Ben saw him and Creben edging for the jutting lip of rock that led on to the tunnel. He glanced at Tovel to see if he would follow suit. But he just stared helplessly up at Joiks.

'Listen to me,' the Doctor called up to the huge angels, his voice booming, unafraid. The creatures floated back towards him, still holding Joiks between them, while their fellows circled with disinterest. 'We mean you no harm. We ask that you release our companion.'

The gruesome cherubim looked blankly at each other. Then they bobbed a little closer to ground level.

'Thank you,' the Doctor said. 'All we wish to do is talk with you in peace.'

'You know her better than me, Shade.' Polly willed herself not to pass out at the sight of so much blood. 'Talk to her!'

But Shade only stood and stared in silence, his mouth flapping open and shut.

'It don't hurt so bad,' Frog whispered. She began to shake. Her grip clearly tightened still harder on the knife.

Then a booted foot swung up under Frog's chin.

Haunt.

Frog's body slammed back into the force mattress.

Haunt sat up beside her. Saw the knife sticking out of Frog's

171

stomach like a lever. Plucked it out of the wound and threw it aside.

'Shade, fetch something to clean this up,' she snapped impatiently. 'Move.'

Shade turned and practically fled for the much-depleted medical kit.

Polly just gaped. She could see new strength in Haunt's eyes. An almost wild look.

Haunt must've noticed her staring. 'Frog *will* be all right,' she said. 'I give the orders. No one dies round here without my say-so.'

Joiks shrieked one final time as the two stone angels tore his arms from his sockets.

'No!' Tovel yelled.

Ben saw the rest of the creatures swoop down on Joiks's body. They tore the corpse to pieces in mid-air, all seven of them in a silent frenzy. Joiks's blood sprayed over their beatific stone faces, soaked the sharp fingers.

The Doctor stared on, appalled. 'You are intelligent creatures,' he cried. 'Why this senseless killing!'

'Move out!' Tovel yelled.

Ben turned his back on the scene. He took the Doctor by his elbow and steered him away, back across the shifting blue landscape towards the way out, urging him on as fast as he could.

The Doctor was still mumbling to himself, shaking his head, shell-shocked. All prepossession gone. He looked about him nervously, not with the usual air of the brilliant academic, but as a bewildered, frightened old man. Ben practically had to drag the old boy along to where Tovel was waiting grimly on the jagged slate promontory. Behind him, in the shadows, stood Roba and Creben.

Creben's face was white as dust. 'We have to get back to control.'

'Please, a moment, please,' the Doctor muttered hoarsely, trying to catch his breath.

'It's all right, Doctor,' Ben told him, with a hesitant backwards glance over his shoulder. 'It's all right, they're not coming after us.'

'But if they choose to do so, my boy,' the Doctor whispered, 'as inevitably they shall... How will we fight them?' He gripped Ben's wrist, stared chillingly into his eyes. 'How can we resist such evil?'

II

'So,' said Haunt stiffly. 'You lost Joiks.'

Tovel, standing rigidly to attention before her, nodded once – though to Polly, from the story he'd told, it hardly sounded like he was responsible. 'For a few moments I thought the Doctor was getting through to them, that they were going to let Joiks go...'

'They were like ruddy great kids,' Ben chipped in, slumped between Creben and Roba against the barricade. 'Just playing about.'

'Not kids,' said Roba, scratching his neck furiously. 'Animals.'

The Doctor tapped his chin. Polly saw he was looking a little more his old self now, and shuddered to think what they all must've been through in the blue cave. 'The wielders of any kind of power are animals, seeking to dominate animals less fierce.'

Haunt didn't look impressed. She fiddled uncomfortably with the bandage around her waist. 'What are you talking about?'

'Power flourishes because people respond to talk of freedom but prefer not to be really free,' the Doctor informed her. 'They seek the comfort of acceptable strictures in their societies, of a ruler to govern them, of set territorial boundaries that enable a tribal identity to exist.'

Ben grimaced. 'You've lost me.'

'And so the people with power in these tribes, these factions, seek to extend their territories.' He jabbed a finger at Haunt. 'Your kind sought, for example, to assimilate the Schirr into your culture. To assert your power over them.'

'A pacifist,' Haunt said with all the disgust she could muster.

'So we are the animals,' said Creben, yawning midway through. 'Is that the banal point you're making?'

'No, sir, it is not.' Polly was glad to see the gleam in the Doctor's eyes had returned. 'I am merely observing that the Morphieans are acting in a similar regard. Wielding superior strength, attempting to assimilate us since they consider us less fierce. Ergo, they are animal

173

also, for all this unhelpful talk of disembodied mysticism and magic – and therefore they are fallible. They *can* be beaten.'

'Yeah, but how?' said Shade gloomily. He was stronger now since his illness, but all the act of the perfect soldier had gone out of him. He stood beside Polly, glanced at her now and then, perhaps hoping she would return Lindey's computer to him. She hadn't told him she'd accidentally wiped the incriminating evidence on his behalf. She didn't like to just yet.

'Well, we must give the matter some thought,' said the Doctor. He gave Polly a comforting smile.

'Great,' Roba said. 'We've got so much time to sit around thinking.'

'The websets we found may tell us something useful,' said Tovel.

'Shade, you take one,' said Haunt. He nodded, and retired back to his couch, almost gratefully, it seemed.

Haunt paused, then handed the other set to Polly. 'Give this to Frog.'

'Frog?' Roba scowled. 'She ain't one of us now, she's one of them.'

'She remains a part of this team,' Haunt said icily, quashing all other possible resistance to the idea. 'She is currently incapacitated but will contribute to our war effort for as long as she is able.'

That might not be long at all, thought Polly fearfully as she approached Frog's makeshift bed, dragged into a gloomy corner of the pentagonal room. The blood had stopped flowing from her stomach, but it still looked a dreadful mess. Shade had covered the gashes in some sort of plastic skin; it sat like white custard on the tacky raw pink beneath. The alien flesh now covered her chest and neck, and was creeping under her chin.

Polly noticed Frog's black voice-disc had fallen from her neck and rolled away across the floor. She retrieved it, and studied it blankly. It had been embedded in Frog's skin, but the Schirr flesh had rejected it.

Polly felt in a bit of a spot. What use was it, Frog viewing something back if she could no longer tell them about it?

The woman stared helplessly up at her. The scars on her face seemed less livid in the gloom. She looked younger. More vulnerable.

'Hey. I can't feel a thing from the neck down…'

Frog's voice died away in her throat. Her big eyes grew huge.

Her *voice*.

'What... the... hell...?' Frog whispered each hoarse word carefully, a proper whisper. Her natural voice. She had a soft American accent. 'Is this me talking?' Her face split open into the biggest smile Polly had ever seen.

'She can talk!' squealed Polly in excitement. 'Frog can talk!'

Everyone turned to stare at her, bewildered.

'Of course she can talk,' said Haunt patiently, 'which is why she can give us a full analysis of the experiential report on that headset.'

Polly shook her head. 'No, you don't...' She broke off as she felt a hand clamp round her leg.

Frog was shaking her head, urging her to keep quiet.

'Sorry,' she concluded lamely, and crouched back down to see Frog.

'What you telling them I can talk for?' she whispered huskily. 'I can tell them myself, now, when the time comes. Right?'

'Of course,' said Polly.

'But they won't trust this,' Frog said urgently. 'The old Frog couldn't speak.' She closed her eyes, a blissful expression on her face. 'Speak, speak, speak.' She stretched the word out, enjoying it like chocolate: 'Speak. It's this stuff, this stuff inside me, putting me right, putting me back together again.' Her eyes blinked back open. 'If Haunt knew, she wouldn't trust me. Understand?'

Polly nodded uncertainly.

Frog took the webset. 'Wait till I have a report ready for Haunt. Then I'll tell her. Then they'll all hear me.' She gave her habitual chuckle, but now it was a warm, playful sound and not an electronic belch. 'I'll yell it at them. I'll sing it at them! What a blast.' She laughed again.

Polly felt uneasy.

Frog was like a child at Christmas with a longed-for gift as she eagerly put on the headset and closed her eyes. 'This is the only place I ever belonged,' she murmured, as she put her fingers to her temples. Polly wasn't sure if she meant with Haunt – in the army – or inside her head.

She walked briskly back to the others, in time to catch Creben calling out a new set of numbers from the navigational display.

Tovel and the Doctor looked gravely at each other. 'We have moved several parsecs through space since our last reading,' the Doctor reported.

'Into the heart of the Quadrant,' muttered Tovel.

Haunt chewed her lip, said nothing.

'She all right?' Ben noticed Polly standing with a troubled look on her face. He got up and walked over.

'As she can be,' said Polly neutrally. She felt like official confidante to the unit with the number of secrets she was keeping. What about the others? Tovel seemed pretty straightforward, and Haunt seemed fairly cut and dried, but Creben seemed far too much a cat sort of person to ever seek the camaraderie of the army. Too smart, too independent. Polly wondered what secrets he might have to tell. Her glance moved to Roba, who was sweating and scratching in a heap against the barricade. She decided she wasn't in a hurry to learn his particular story. She sighed, she'd had too much time to think. She longed to actually do something.

The Doctor seemed pleased. 'The local knowledge these websets can provide could be very valuable. But what of the bigger picture…?' He pottered off towards the wrecked stasis console, and peered inside it. 'I do wish my eyesight was better,' Polly heard him mutter.

'Let's consider the facts,' said Creben. He sauntered over to join the main party, leaving Roba slumped alone against the barricade. 'Three of us are dead,' he said coldly. 'Shel is missing, and presumably the one responsible. Pallemar was dead, we all saw him outside of the stasis – and three Schirr, including DeCaster, are missing too, presumably chopped up and thrown in that power drive.'

'Quite so,' said the Doctor. 'And for Shel to have been placed here, we know our enemies must be working with a human collaborator, and one in a position of quite considerable authority. But collaborating with the Schirr, or with Morphiea, I wonder?'

'Does it matter?' Haunt said. 'They're all scum.'

'Of course it matters,' the Doctor snapped, 'if we are truly to understand our predicament. The Morphieans may have taken control… But what did the Schirr need us for?'

176

'All right,' Haunt said. 'Enough talk. While we're waiting for Shade and Frog, I suggest we hold an examination.'

Ben yawned. 'Multiple choice, is it?'

'A physical examination,' said Haunt. 'Something's attacking our bodies. If Frog's body is changing into Schirr it can happen to any of us.'

Now Roba got groggily to his feet. 'What, you don't trust your own squad now, is that it?'

'I trusted Shel,' she said simply. 'Now come on. We pair off, examine each other for any sign of the changes.'

Polly fingered her long hair. It felt soft and luxuriant, like she'd just stepped out of a salon. Her skin, too, felt soft and well-moisturised. She thought of Frog's voice box healing, of Haunt's tumour, Shade's face... her stomach churned. They were like turkeys, being fattened up for Christmas.

'This is most demeaning,' fussed the Doctor.

'Just get on with it,' Haunt said. 'You and Tovel. Creben, take the boy. Roba, you're with Shade when he's finished his movie show.'

Polly glanced over at Shade. He was lying on the force mattress, oblivious to all. His body was rigid, limbs twitching like a cat's when dreaming.

Roba crossed his massive arms. 'I ain't doing it.'

'You have a problem, Roba?'

Roba pulled out his gun. 'You're damned right I do.'

For a single sickening second, through the tear in his suit, Polly glimpsed a patch of mottled pink against the dark skin of his wrist, peeping above the dressing on his wrist.

'He's changing!' she yelled, and pointed.

Roba fired three warning shots at the ceiling. Pieces of the mirrored glass lodged in the rock shattered, rained crystal dust over them.

'That cut of his,' Ben said, grimacing. 'He reckoned his suit wasn't working. I should've worked it out!'

'Roba,' Haunt thundered. 'Just put the gun down.'

'So you can have *me* put down? Huh?' Roba was breathing quickly, sweating more than ever. 'No way.'

'Then let us help you,' the Doctor implored him. 'By close study –'

'Study Frog all you want,' Roba shouted. 'I'm finding Shel. Gonna make him put a stop to whatever's doing this to me.' He backed away towards the exit, fired off another couple of laser bolts into the floor in front of them as he squeezed through the barricade.

'We'll find you, Roba,' Haunt yelled.

'Or the angels will,' Creben added.

'Anyone comes looking for me knows what they get.' Roba fired one more blast, high over their heads, and ran from the room.

Tovel started to follow. 'No,' said Haunt. 'Let him go. Let him calm down. Then we'll go after him.'

Ben looked worried. 'I wondered what was up with him. Don't reckon he'll ever calm down.'

'He will, when he realises it's hopeless.' Haunt gave a sideways glance at Frog. 'And besides. This proves the need for those examinations.'

Polly saw the Doctor nod thoughtfully. Haunt led her off to behind the depleted row of frozen Schirr corpses, a grisly audience to watch them undress with sightless eyes.

III

Ben looked enviously at Creben's toned, muscular body. He was a regular Charles Atlas on the sly. There wasn't a mark on him.

Creben returned the favour with an unenthusiastic inspection. 'You're clear.'

Ben turned to the Doctor, who was doing up his shirt, and gave him a thumbs-up. The Doctor nodded cheerfully, so presumably he had passed muster too. Now he motioned that Tovel should undress.

'You want to check Shade?' Creben asked.

'Not a lot.' Then he saw Shade was rising from his couch. If he looked too far to his right, he could probably see Haunt and Polly giving each other the once over. Well, he'd soon fix that little game.

'Kit off, sunshine,' Ben said cheerily, positioning himself carefully so Shade was looking well away from the bodies on view. But Shade wasn't showing much interest in anything. There was a frown on his face deeper than his few remaining scars. 'What's up? Didn't like the film?'

'The webset was Lindey's,' he said, and tapped his fingers distractedly against the metal band. 'Her trip through the tunnels. Nothing that could help us.' He fixed Ben with his green eyes. 'You should've seen her there. Every move was textbook, every decision... She had a smart mouth, sure, but the way she carried herself... She never even had to try...'

'What're you talking about?' Ben asked.

Shade looked like he was going to start blubbing, but for himself or for Lindey Ben couldn't tell. 'I thought we hated each other, me and her. But I guess we each just wanted what the other had.'

'Yeah, well,' Ben said awkwardly. 'You'd better show me what you've got now, Haunt's orders. And don't worry, I'm not about to hold anything and ask you to cough –'

'No. Not me too.'

The anguished voice was barely recognisable as Tovel's.

'I'm so very sorry,' the Doctor said, holding up his hands in a calming gesture. 'So desperately sorry.'

Tovel was topless, hugging himself. Ben saw straight away the patch of globby alien flesh on the small of his back.

'Marshal Haunt,' Tovel shouted, between loud, shuddering breaths.

Haunt bobbed around the corner of the macabre exhibit of alien bodies, Polly – kit on again – right behind her. At least *she* was all right.

'It's happening to me too.' Tovel offered his hands to Haunt as if expecting her to handcuff him.

She didn't move to take them.

'You should restrain me,' Tovel insisted.

Haunt shook her head emphatically. 'Just make sure you hold on to yourself, Tovel.'

'No need for cuffs if you wait a while, Tovel,' a new voice called.

Ben stared in amazement as he realised where the call had come from. 'Frog?' He jogged over to her shadowy corner of the room, the others, Tovel included, close behind him.

'Soon you won't be able to move at all!' The voice would've been Doris Day's if she'd grown up in the Bronx. It couldn't belong to a knockabout like Frog.

'She can talk again!' Polly said quietly.

Ben grinned broadly. Until he actually saw Frog. He tried to keep the smile fixed in place for her, but it was hopeless.

The skin on her hands, neck and chin had turned shiny and spongy. Beneath her combat suit her body had grown bulkier. It was pressing up against the material, pulsing all over. But her face was the worst. While the scars had faded to soft, pale channels in her skin, her features were coarsening, growing larger. Like her face was an inflated mask over the real thing.

'I've got this to look forward to.' Tovel's voice cracked as he spoke, leaving the words midway between timid question and bleak statement.

Ben looked dead ahead as Tovel pulled on the top part of his combat suit, hiding the diseased flesh from view.

Frog's thickening lips twitched in a coy smile as her eyes darted from face to face.

'Kill me before it comes to this,' Tovel whispered. Ben hoped that was more of a general prayer than an instruction to any of them.

'Don't be scared, Tovel,' said Frog.'I'm not. Not any more. This thing is healing me.'

'Stop this,' Haunt warned her.

'I can't move, but I think I'll be able to, soon. It's making me strong.'

Ben told himself this was Frog's cheerful optimism, though it sounded more like a threat coming from this bloated creature.

'You didn't think so before,' Polly reminded her.'You wanted to... to hurt yourself.'

Frog nodded. Her new double chins wobbled like jellies. 'Yeah, well... swings and roundabouts, I guess.'

'My dear,' said the Doctor. He alone was acting as if everything was fine, with no cause for alarm. 'I can see you're excited, but you're really not well, no. Not well at all. You should be resting.'

'So you don't wanna know my news, then?' she said, almost shyly.

Everyone waited expectantly. Ben could tell Frog was savouring this, the centre of attention at last.

'This webset. It ain't Lindey's…'

'Duh,' said Shade. 'I had hers.'

'…but it's not Denni's either.'

Ben felt a tingle drive up his spine.

Frog chuckled. 'It's Shel's.'

She got, Ben imagined, her desired reaction. Everyone stared first at her, then at each other, transfixed.

'Shel's?' Haunt's face was stony.

'Uh-huh.'

'But he's a cyborg, an artificial intelligence,' Haunt argued. 'How could he wear the web like the rest of us?'

'He didn't,' said the Doctor. 'Such enfeebling devices reduce the whole tract of human experience to a digital impression, a stream of ones and zeroes.' He chuckled. 'Since Shel's mind functions digitally also, I imagine he would interface with the webset far more efficiently.'

'Think you mean, *used* to interface,' said Frog, with a crafty smile. 'He's dead.'

Creben stared. 'Dead? How?'

'He was ripped to shreds by the statues and flushed down some big glass toilet.'

'So they got him too,' said Polly.

'Good riddance,' muttered Shade.

Frog tutted. 'Oh, but was it?'

'Could you just skip the mystery theatre,' Haunt snapped. 'Say what you've got to say.'

'He didn't put a foot wrong. Not once, from start to finish.' Frog seemed to have sobered up suddenly. Her fingers stroked the webset. 'Being Shel was weird. Boring. No feelings, no thoughts, just reactions, decisions. Then he got sick, confused… couldn't speak.' Frog looked at the Doctor. 'That panel he wasted. I think he was trying to tell you something. And he didn't run far before they got him. They were hiding in the dark, a whole bunch.'

No one said anything for a few moments, trying to make sense of the revelations.

'But…' Haunt looked like her view of the world had clouded over. 'But if he wasn't here to set this up, what was he doing here?'

The Doctor, who had remained surprisingly quiet, broke in at last. 'There still remains the issue of the well-placed traitor in a position of authority. Perhaps Shel was in fact *investigating* that person.' His eyes narrowed. 'Or one of their agents.'

Agents? Ben looked nervously around the huddle of soldiers.

'That's enough.' Haunt sounded a little shaky as she plucked the webset from Frog's forehead. 'We'd better watch this for ourselves.'

'You don't trust me?' Frog said coldly. 'This is still me, you know.'

For how much longer, thought Ben gloomily, scratching the back of his neck. How long till nothing's left of any of us?

The cheery thought led to another.

'So where's Denni's webset then?' he asked aloud. 'If she died first, why wasn't nothing of hers hidden away down there with the others?'

'Maybe it was, and you just didn't find it,' Polly suggested.

'No wait…' Creben looked at Haunt. 'If Shel's not behind this –'

'– Then Roba's chasing after the wrong person,' finished Tovel.

'That's not what I meant,' Creben told him coldly. 'If Shel's not responsible for bringing us here, somebody else is.'

Haunt swore. 'And who went conveniently missing right at the start of all this, without a trace? Who's been moving about freely as a result ever since, making this nightmare happen?'

'It fits,' said the Doctor. 'Yes, it fits.'

Ben stared at him. 'Denni.'

Chapter Thirteen
They Do It With Mirrors

I

Polly felt she could weep with frustration. Just as she thought she was getting things straight in her head, another suspect came to light. She came over to Ben, leaving the others to talk worriedly among themselves.

'If only we could just get into the TARDIS and leave,' she said bitterly.

'The Doctor'll –'

'Oh, don't just say that the Doctor will think of something, Ben!' Polly snapped.

He looked like she'd just slapped him round the face.

'Sorry, Ben,' she sighed, and he shrugged. Polly glanced up at the Doctor. He was back rummaging inside the damaged console. Couldn't stay away from the thing. 'It's just, sometimes I wonder what he –'

The Doctor clapped his hands. 'Yes! Yes, of course, that is it. Time! It explains everything. Time held still.'

Ben shot Polly a knowing glance. 'What are you talking about, Doctor?'

'The stasis field. The bodies there are caught in a single moment of time.' He pulled out some components from the charred guts of the console. 'I've seen circuits like these in the TARDIS systems.'

'Then the Schirr aren't dead, only frozen in time?' Polly peeped round nervously at the corpses. 'What about when Shel scanned them?'

'The bodies are outside our own time frame. To the scanner they would have no relevance – and so appear entirely inert. Dead. But as you say, that is not necessarily the case.'

'Then those navigational crystal things we need to turn around could be in there too!' Polly realised.

'Very possibly,' the Doctor agreed. He paused, took hold of his lapels, looking oddly pleased with himself. But by this time, Haunt had come over with Creben, Shade and Tovel, and she didn't look happy at all.

'We haven't got time to waste on any more speculation,' she said heavily.

'This isn't speculation, it is fact.' The Doctor generously included the newcomers in his explanation. 'Frog said she believed Shel was trying to tell me something. Indeed he was.' He gestured to the console. 'These controls do not operate the stasis field. They cannot, the connections have been severed.'

Haunt frowned. 'Damage from the explosion when Shel –'

'That's what I thought, at first. But the severance of the circuitry is too precise to have been caused randomly.' He turned to Ben. 'Would you be so good as to prise open the metal box beneath the console for me, hmm?'

Shade offered him a knife, like the one Frog had used on herself, and Ben crouched beneath the console, baffled. 'Dunno what you expect to find, Doctor. Looks like a bomb went off here.'

'What is inside?' the Doctor asked, looking up at the ceiling.

Ben re-emerged holding a large, thick chunk of what looked like yellowish glass.

'That's all?' asked Polly.

'That is all that is needed,' said the Doctor, still staring upward, an evangelical expression on his face. 'Look up at the roof. Look.'

'More glass,' said Tovel.

'That is how they send the signal,' the Doctor said triumphantly.

'What are you talking about, Doctor,' Creben scowled.

'The stasis field is operated from the platform. It has to be.' The Doctor seemed to be trembling with excitement as he stalked over to the display of Schirr bodies. Their albino eyes seemed to glare at him, full of hate, as he examined them. 'It must be concealed above.' He waved a hand frantically. 'Will someone please examine the Schirr bodies from *above*?'

'This is ludicrous,' Creben complained, but Haunt waved him into silence.

Tovel offered Ben a bunk up. He didn't look happy, but he took it, and started to scrabble up the invisible wall like a French mime.

'There's nothing,' Ben reported when he reached the top. 'Just a lot of bald heads.'

'But there must be something,' the Doctor insisted.

'Wait…' Ben tapped at something none of them could see. 'There's a tiny bit of glass here. Can't shift it, it must be frozen too.'

'That is it,' the Doctor hissed in triumph. 'The relay they have been using.'

'But it's titchy, it looks like it just dropped here or something!'

'It is all they need to turn the stasis field on or off. Somehow they can transmit power through this material… a signal.' He nodded to himself, certain of what he was saying. 'Of course, there would almost certainly be some spillage…'

'Spillage of what?' Creben looked at him dubiously. 'Of *time*?'

'Quite so,' the Doctor told him.

'So that's why we can't get inside the TARDIS,' Polly heard Ben mutter. 'We don't have the time!'

'And why Pallemar seemed to be dead, but wasn't,' Polly whispered back. 'He must've been caught up in it too!'

Even with all this, the Doctor wasn't ready to stop astounding his audience yet. He addressed Haunt directly. 'Can't you see? Whenever the stasis field is activated or deactivated, it must have a curious effect on our own perception of time.'

'That's how DeCaster and Pallemar vanished without us noticing?' asked Polly.

'Precisely.' The Doctor beamed at her. 'What took them many minutes, passed for us in just a few moments, yes.' He turned back to Haunt. 'It seemed to us you had been gone only a short time when you returned – but in fact, a good deal of time had passed.'

'So why didn't the Schirr use this time difference to attack us?' Haunt inquired.

The Doctor gestured over at Frog. 'Clearly they have a use for us.'

'Well then, how come I ended up in the tunnels, right when we arrived?' Polly asked, hoping her head could handle all of this.

'A hidden doorway in the rock?' wondered the Doctor. 'Yes, again, if it's frozen in a single point of time until used, no one would be able to detect it.'

''Ere, Tovel,' Ben said. 'That room where we went up against them statues for the first time…'

He nodded. 'We seemed to come right through the rock.'

'And there were pieces of that glass hanging down there too,' Ben said triumphantly.

'They're all over the place,' Haunt realised. 'So the Schirr can move around safely with no chance of being discovered.'

'And Denni, it would seem,' Creben added, grudgingly accepting the supposition.

'But you said the Schirr had been put in the engines of this thing,' Polly complained.

'Whatever was supposed to happen to us here,' the Doctor said thoughtfully, 'it appears we have become mired in a struggle for power between Schirr and Morphieans…'

'Look out!' yelled Shade.

Polly's heart leapt. As she turned, the control room was plunged into blackness. Blinding blue current sparked and spluttered along the golden trellises that snaked round the walls. The ducting smoked, and the air filled with filthy fumes.

In the sputtering light she saw the stark silhouette of a giant angel, flying towards them.

II

Roba staggered down the dark, dank tunnels with a familiarity that made him uneasy. He was becoming at home here, a new creature that belonged to the shadows.

The fleas bugged him more now than ever, though, as they hopped and crawled over his skin. He tried to keep his Schirr hand covered, but the insects seemed drawn to it.

He paused, panting for breath, and held it up. It was alive with the creatures.

Roba smacked it into the wall, as hard as he could again and again, grunting with pain. He heard his knuckles crack and break, and took a bitter satisfaction. If something wanted to take his body, he'd mess it right up for them first.

He only stopped when the pain swamped his stung senses. Sobbing, he took a long, miserable look at the broken hand. The fleas had gone, shaken loose, hopped away.

Two heavy footsteps ground into the scree that carpeted the tunnel floor.

Roba looked up to see one of the stone cherubim towering above him, still as a statue. He yelped and fell backwards, retreated on his elbows, gazing up into the cold, blank face of the creature.

In two more steps it caught up with him. Roba had backed himself up against a wall. The angel reached out for his chest, its fingers curved hooks, ready to tear him open.

But instead it reached for the webset dangling uselessly from his belt.

Roba barely dared to breathe as the monstrous angel plucked the headband away, studied it a moment. Then it smiled serenely, leaned in close to him. Its stone fingers were cold as old bones as it gently fitted the webset around his forehead.

Its blank, wide eyes looked into his own. Roba kept closing his, hoping it would go away, a child's wish: *I can't see you, you can't see me.* But each time he opened his eyes a fraction it was there still. Maybe it would think he was asleep, or dead. But every time he sneaked the glance the angel hadn't moved. It was right up close and it was still smiling.

Roba heard dragging footsteps. Something was lurching down the tunnel towards him. He and the angel waited for it to arrive, together.

III

'Open fire!' Haunt roared, as the colossal winged creature drifted closer through the smoke and the shadows.

Polly saw the thing lit up in yellow flashes as Tovel, Shade and Creben joined their marshal in firing off blast after blast from their rifles. Its pallid, inhuman face glared emptily at her, as incapable of fear as anything else. It had been built grotesquely from some mysterious flesh that did not seem to feel the gunfire that should've charred it to ashes. She willed the rifle-fire to hurt it somehow, to send it flapping round the room like a caged bird looking for release. But it only drew closer and closer, resisting all attempts to drive it back.

The Doctor ducked down so as not to obscure the line of fire and scuttled over to Polly. They clung to each other, looking up helplessly together.

'Your launcher,' Tovel shouted at Shade over the fizzing cacophony of the rifle fire. 'Use your grenade launcher!'

Polly remembered the way the weapon had brought down the roof when the robot had been chasing her. She felt a sudden surge of hope. 'Yes, Shade, come on, you can do it!'

But Shade ran past her in the opposite direction, and was swallowed up by the darkness. She stared after him in shocked disbelief.

'Come back,' the Doctor demanded, outraged. 'Come back at once, sir!'

To Polly's amazement, Shade did – carrying the grenade launcher.

'I left it back there,' he explained curtly, and dropped to one knee. He aimed the launcher.

Polly looked up into the elongated, colourless mask of the giant cherub's face. It began to smile.

Then she clamped her hands over her ears as Shade fired the grenade.

The angel silently exploded into a billion pieces.

A billion *insects*.

Polly choked as the black, smoky air became thick with fleas. She tried to hold her breath but they were everywhere, falling like hard rain, crawling and hopping in her hair, over her face. She thought she would be sick.

'What the hell was that,' yelled Frog from a pitch-black corner. 'I know none of you wants to look at me, but...'

'The fleas,' the Doctor called out urgently, cutting her off. He lit a match, and Polly saw his pale face flicker into focus. 'They are the life from which the Morphieans fashion their constructs! The weed must sustain them when they're not in use...'

'They really did turn this place against us,' said Haunt. 'Shade, check on Frog and fetch some light. The rest of you, stay wary.' In the thick gloom Polly watched as Haunt brushed a mass of the insects from her face, spat out a mouthful. 'Doctor – wherever those things are, they can swarm into angels?'

'Yes, I'm afraid so,' the Doctor told her. He cupped a hand round his match.

'What's to stop them reforming right now?' Polly asked, fingers pulling dozens of the things from her hair.

'It would seem the creature came here to deliver a message,' said the Doctor. 'Now it has done so, it is no longer needed.'

'Message?' Ben looked at him like he was raving mad.

The Doctor gestured to the flickering screens with his free hand, right the way around the room.

A single angular symbol, a kind of spiral, was glowing on each.

Then a bright, white glow spread through the control chamber. Polly flinched from the sudden light. Shade had placed some kind of high-tech lantern on the ground between them all.

'What kind of a message is that?' Tovel said in a strained voice.

'It means "life",' said Haunt.

Everyone turned to look at her. Polly noted the surprise on the Doctor's face. He blew out his match.

'Seen it a thousand times. The symbol denotes a Schirr life on their combat scanners.' She gave a crooked smile. 'See one of those wink out, you got another dead. Sweet as blowing out birthday candles.'

'OK. So what does it *mean*?' asked Shade.

'Life support, maybe,' Tovel suggested. 'Those sparks, the lights going out...'

'Those things have decided to stop mucking about then,' Ben said.

'But there are so few of us now,' said Creben. 'If they wanted us all dead why not just attack us in force here?'

'Maybe they knew we had the grenade launcher,' Tovel said. 'Seems to be the only thing we've got they're vulnerable to.'

Ben sighed. 'So they cut off the life-support systems.'

'Surprised you didn't recognise the sign yourself, Creben,' said Haunt. 'You saw it only a matter of hours ago.'

Creben looked uncomfortable. 'Marshal?'

'You and Lindey. I viewed it through her eyes, on her webset.'

'I didn't really study the carvings in any detail,' said Creben. 'Back then we were looking for Schirr cyphers and droids.'

'Seem almost cuddly now, them robot things,' joked Ben to Polly.

'Then if you've seen the carving, you can lead us to it, hmm?' The Doctor's gaze flicked between Haunt and Creben.

'We approached it along a tunnel close to the ship,' Creben said, 'but the tunnel caved in when our section separated.'

'All these tunnels interconnect.' Haunt looked around at her troops. 'We'll just have to find it, that's all.'

'That could take us days,' Ben argued.

'And we're getting closer to Morphiea all the time,' whispered Polly.

Haunt shrugged. 'We'll have to split up.'

'Move through these tunnels alone?' The Doctor looked sourly at her. 'With the constructs poised to destroy us?'

Ben agreed. 'Not to mention Denni roaming about, a Schirr or two and poor old Roba off his rocker.'

'We'll cover more ground faster,' Haunt said flatly. She hesitated. 'But I have an idea of how we might be able to watch out for each other.'

The Doctor looked at her shrewdly. 'The websets?'

Haunt nodded. 'It's been done before. In the pacification riots on Idaho it saved the lives of our entire squad. Instead of using the websets to record what we saw, we used them to *transmit* to the other wearers. See and communicate from each other's perspective.'

Creben raised an eyebrow. 'How?'

'Practice,' said Haunt dryly. 'But if it's a technical answer you're after...'

Polly was almost amused to see Haunt turn hopefully to the Doctor to provide one.

'May I study a webset, please?' The Doctor held out his hand, and Haunt gave him Lindey's. He pulled a jeweller's glass from his pocket and scrutinised the circuitry in a metal band. If he was aware that all eyes were on him he remained entirely unflustered. 'Yes… Yes, it's quite straightforward really. Any receiver can be turned into a transmitter, of course, it's a simple matter of reversing certain polarities…' He slid open a compartment in the headband that contained what looked to be tiny tools, and removed one.

'How would we switch between different viewpoints?' asked Creben. 'If you turn our brains into transmitters, we've no way of regulating the strength of the signal. Any one person's perspective could swamp the others.'

'I imagine it's more likely the reverse would occur,' said the Doctor, using the tool to expose the webset's circuitry. 'We would have to concentrate a great deal to receive any signal from the network thus created.'

'We have the wrist-comms, too,' Haunt said. 'It's better than nothing.'

The Doctor looked up at her. 'My dear woman, it's a most excellent idea. A masterstroke, one might say, yes.'

'Have we got enough of them?' asked Tovel, a new urgency in his voice. 'For everyone, I mean.'

'There's Lindey's and Shel's spare,' said Shade. 'That's two of you covered.'

'Joiks's must've been destroyed when the constructs killed him,' said Creben.

'I took his backpack, remember? Might it have been in there?' Ben ran off to look for it. 'I dumped it round here somewhere…'

Polly bit her lip and crossed her fingers.

'Could always give him Frog's,' said Shade.

Haunt shook her head. 'She's helpless. Completely vulnerable. I won't leave her alone. She can be our eyes here.'

Ben jogged back over into the circle of light, a forlorn expression on his face. Polly's face started to crumple in dismay when he produced the webset from behind his back. 'Gotcha!'

The Doctor looked up from his inspection and beamed at him. 'Well, I believe I can make the necessary conversions to everyone's equipment. It's a fairly simple procedure.'

'Good.' Haunt looked relieved, actually smiled at him with some warmth. 'So get on with it. We don't have long.'

The Doctor gave her a hard stare. Then he returned to his work.

Ben winked at Polly. 'So, I'll be able to see the world through your eyes! A rough dog like me always wondered what it would be like to be a pampered puss.'

She pulled a face, trying to jolly herself up. 'I'm not sure I want to be inside your head, Ben Jackson...'

Shade came and stood beside her. 'It'll be like each of us is in eight places at once. A proper, organised force.' He smiled. He had quite a nice smile, Polly thought.

As the Doctor worked, Haunt called a council of war for her squad. Polly and Ben listened in. Despite the dark, the idiot insects and the urgency of the situation, Polly felt the general atmosphere had taken an upturn. They had something to do. A path forward.

She forced herself to concentrate on Haunt, and told herself she didn't believe in omens when the monitor screens, still glowing with their alien symbol, flickered and went dead.

IV

'The adjustments have been made,' the Doctor assured his little audience. 'As I said before, the webset is essentially quite a straightforward apparatus. Its processors read and preserve certain information transmitted through the brain. You see, fibres in our skulls transmit light – projecting the images of objects – from the retina along the optic nerves, into the cranial cavity and through the *dura mater* until they cross at the optic chiasma. As our brains interpret this optical data it triggers an emotional response, which is also read by the webset...'

Polly slowly lost his thread. She was never one for technical explanations. As long as something worked, what did it matter *how* it worked?

Everyone had gathered solemnly around Frog's force mattress, in the glare of the lantern, their websets in place. Polly couldn't help smiling at how the Doctor looked with the little headband stretched over his high forehead. Frog, on the other hand, looked terrifying. She lay there muttering to herself in a world of her own, a dreamy smile on her face as she listened to the stream of words she was making all by herself. Now her forehead had swollen up the webset barely fitted across it.

The Doctor finished his explanation. No one looked much the wiser.

'Ain't never used one of these before,' Ben said with a nervous glance at Polly.

'Neither have we, in this way,' said Tovel.

Ben rolled up his eyes like he could see his webset. 'I feel like a real Nelly in this thing. What do we do?'

'Close your eyes. Try to clear your mind,' Haunt instructed, closing her dark eyes. 'Feel your way into the signals.'

Polly shut her own eyes, tried to get into the swing of it. But the stuff Haunt was saying only reminded her of an idiot she'd met once at a party at Kensington Roof Gardens. He'd told her that acid was the ultimate trip, waving a piece of blotting paper in her face with just such facile advice.

It couldn't work, she felt too stupid, couldn't relax in this atmosphere, so many strangers. But even as she was trying to stop thinking of the man she heard Ben beside her give a soft chuckle.

'Who's that bloke I see you with, Duchess? What's he waving at you?'

Polly's eyes snapped open. She stared at him. 'You can see my memories?'

'Whoah!' Ben shouted. 'That's me! You're coming through loud and clear!' He opened his eyes. 'This is amazing. If I shut my eyes, I can see meself.' He did so, and ran his fingers through his short fair hair as if combing it in front of a mirror. Polly looked away, annoyed with herself for not being able to use the webset properly.

'Think of the person whose eyes you want to see through,' Haunt told her, her voice surprisingly tender. Was Haunt in her head too?

Polly closed her eyes and saw a bleary image of herself, from half a dozen perspectives. There was a noise like static in her head. Hushed voices. They must be thoughts. Some of them must be Ben's, so she thought of him as hard as she could. It was amazing; the other voices grew quieter, and his rose in volume through the static. She couldn't get precise wordings, but the impression of his feelings was clear enough: he was simply excited. She smiled. Ben even thought in a cockney accent.

She winced in a wave of dizziness. She was finding it hard to mix sound and vision. Vision was much stronger.

'It should grow easier with time,' she heard the Doctor say in her ear, 'as you grow used to it.'

She nodded, and tried to think of him. To see what he was seeing.

It was like she'd touched a naked flame –

For a single violent second it felt (terror) to her that her flesh had aged a thousand years. We are (*we will not waste a second of our life*) still young, vital, but trapped inside this awful, ancient (frustration) corpse of a body –

Then inexplicably, a picture – an old, strange-looking bicycle, a penny-farthing or something – resolved itself from the chaos in her mind. And she heard the Doctor chuckle as the image faded, though this time he spoke in her head. It felt like he'd poked her brain with a stick.

'No. No, Polly my dear, you may not eavesdrop on *me*, I'm afraid.'

Polly opened her eyes. She felt confused and sick. She had to fight the urge to rip the webset off and hurl it away.

'It's all right, Polly,' said Shade. He put a hand on her shoulder and smiled. 'It *will* get easier.'

'I can't seem to get you, Doctor,' Ben said.

The Doctor smiled knowingly and shook his head. Polly shivered. *I don't get you either,* she thought quietly.

'It's possible to block your mind to others,' said Haunt, with a glare at him. 'But the whole point is that we can all check on where we are.

194

It's in all our interests to be as open as possible.'

'Of course, I agree with you.' The Doctor didn't seem fazed by her evil eye. 'But I dare say we all have our secrets.'

'Well, in any case, we can't delay,' Haunt said, rising. 'So listen to me. All of you.

'You know what we have to do.'

Chapter Fourteen
Spider's Web

WEBSET ONLINE INFORMATION SYSTEM ACTIVATED

*To switch between different viewpoints within the neural net,
select the relevant section numbers as instructed.*

*Do not attempt to read all sections in a linear fashion, or the
dataflow will not make sense. Go forward or back depending on
which viewpoint you wish to access.*

*Join the neural net by first tuning in to Haunt's viewpoint.
Turn to section 1 on page 197*

1
Haunt

'All right listen,' we say. Best bullying tone, it comes unbidden when we open our mouth. Like we're back in the field. Going in, taking the fight to the enemy. It's a good feeling.

Or it always used to be. Now we feel just a little sick as the adrenaline pumps round us.

The unit is scared. None of these people want to go back out there but they know what'll happen if they don't. It's all or nothing now. A shot at life, or certain death.

The hole in our side is killing us. Or more accurately, it was. Now it just hurts like hell.

'Doctor, your party doesn't have communicators, so you'll just have to pair up with those who do. Doctor, with me. Ben, you go with Tovel.' We look at Tovel, at the filthy Schirr carcass he's becoming. 'And watch him.'

'I'll watch *out* for him, if that's what you mean,' the boy says, fiercely loyal but hopelessly naïve. Once, he might've made a good soldier.

'Shade, take the girl.'

We can feel Shade respond to this, strongly so. The girl's less sure. We keep out of all that. Keep distance. Concentrate on what needs to be done.

'We'll go out together to what's left of the bullring. From there we'll fan out, looking for the symbol you saw before.' We concentrate, bring it shining into our minds. There's a wave of fear, apprehension. Seems the neural web is holding together well. But we can't afford to get cocky.

'One of us should be able to find our way back to the carving,' we say.

'And if we don't have the tools?' asks Creben. Practical as ever.

'I'll have them.' We smile. 'And I'll come running, believe me.'

They keep watching us, like we're going to give them some miracle to get out of this. We wonder if the troops we left behind to the Schirr on New Jersey looked at us in that way. Looked up at the missile incoming and understood that miracles only come at a cost.

Do we have to physically herd them out there into the darkness like sheep?

'Move out,' we bellow.

To continue in Haunt's viewpoint, select section 9 on page 209

To switch to Tovel's viewpoint, select section 4 on page 200
To switch to Polly's viewpoint, select section 6 on page 203
To switch to Shade's viewpoint, select section 21 on page 231
To switch to Ben's viewpoint, select section 25 on page 239

2
Creben

We're sick of this labyrinth. Of having to choose the turnings. When we scouted this area with Lindey we were working to a pattern of course. But since the cave-in, it's hopeless to compare our position. We trust to blind luck and…

Well, well. We've found the very spot.

The symbol glares out at us, a square stone eye unwinking in our torchlight.

'Creben. You've found it.'

The Doctor's voice sounds over the wrist-comm. We're surprised. We did not detect his presence here in the network.

'It appears to be carved in solid stone,' we tell him, and anyone else who's listening in.

'I know. I am sharing your sight, Creben.' He laughs without a good deal of humour. 'I do hope you don't begrudge me.'

'Well it's here, as you can see. But there's no sign of any machinery nearby.'

'Run your fingers over the rune,' the Doctor says.

'You think it's touch-activated?' We trace the eye's outline. 'Sorry. Nothing. No life here.'

'Wait.' The Doctor sounds suddenly urgent. 'Look behind you.'

We turn. There's a bare wall facing us. Weed hangs down from the ceiling, a thick coverlet.

'Move that aside,' the Doctor says impatiently. We do so.

There's another eye carved in the stone, looking back at us

'Move aside, boy,' the Doctor roars, in our head this time, not through the wrist-comm.

We do as he says, scowling. The two eyes look across at each other. They start to glow. The light gets stronger, blazing hotter until a red haze stretches between the two symbols.

Then a complex schematic resolves itself in the air before us, its lines and vortices a deep crimson.

'Seems the tools will be unnecessary,' we say.

'Quite so, Creben.' The Doctor pauses. 'Your fingers are all we shall require. Reach out. Touch the schematic.'

We do so, gingerly. Our fingers press against the blood-red lines. The fingertips tingle. The floating lines feel solid, like wires.

The Doctor chuckles again. 'Quite a feeling is it not? You can grasp and connect these ethereal filaments as though they were real. And so repair the systems.'

'Please, Doctor. I must concentrate.' He senses how uncomfortable we are at his presence. Retreats.

When he speaks again it is through the wrist-comm. 'Tovel's had some experience of the way these Schirr circuits work. Let us seek his help. Then the two of us can advise you.'

We study the schematics, brooding. We have never much appreciated the advice of others.

There's only silence as we wait. Then, stealthy footsteps. The sound of something coming.

To continue in Creben's viewpoint, select section 18 on page 227

To switch to Haunt's viewpoint, select section 11 on page 215

3
Frog

What you looking at? Ain't nothing going on. Except kilo on kilo of fresh Schirr meat on our bones. So unfair. You know we only joined the military to lose some weight? That and to get away from home. Maybe find a home. While we still had half a face.

Wonder how much of it we got left now.

Don't wanna think. Just gonna lie here and talk aloud. It's a good voice we got now. Sexy, you know? Swear we're turning ourself on here, even saying prayers. Just lying real still, praying.

I'm gonna go on feeling sorry for myself, you know. You should go somewhere less dull.

Haunt's found something you might find kinda interesting.

Switch to Haunt's viewpoint. Select section 5 on page 202

4
Tovel

Step after step on pins and needles down the tunnel. We can't stop looking at our hands. Knew a pilot in the volunteers who lost his hands once. Not from any war. Accident. All he could say was, 'I'll never fly again. I'll never fly anything ever again.' We felt so sorry for him. We knew what it would be like if it happened to us. Not just to lose a part of us, but the part that *made* us what we were.

Now we look at our hands and we keep telling ourself, 'I'll never fly again.' Not through pity. Because we're scared if we take us some ship up out into the skies it's gonna be Schirr. A Schirr ship. And the Schirr'll be our best buddies and we'll take them wherever they want to go.

'You all right, mate?' Ben says quietly. He keeps looking at us. Thinks we don't see him doing it. Thinks we can't feel him sneaking inside to check this miserable tunnel looks the same through our eyes. But we don't blame him. He's only scared, like we are.

'Tovel?' Ben prompts us.

'I'm a good pilot. Did you hear Haunt say that?'

'Yeah, course.'

We shake our head. '"Turn this thing around," she said. Do you remember back in the control room? "Turn this thing around before…" She never finished.' We stop for a second. We don't quite know how to cry with our face the way it is. 'And I couldn't finish it for her either.'

Ben's silent for a few moments. Then he says: 'It ain't over yet.' He sounds optimistic.

We listen to him and we want to believe it. But it feels like a part of us is just drifting away. Watching the changes happen from somewhere far away. Cut off with no way to get back.

And then we can't walk any more. Our legs won't respond. We stare at them. Ben calls our name but we barely recognise it. We start to beat our legs with the hands that aren't our own. We shout at them.

But we shut up when Ben starts yelling in our head. He's telling everyone we've fallen. That we can't go on any more, and he doesn't know what he should do. We hear other voices but they're vague, quiet.

It's so dark. No sign even of that stupid weed. Pitch dark. We're shouting to Ben. Shouting that we're all right. That we'll be all right in just a few moments. That we'll beat this thing.

We feel his hand on ours. He squeezes our wrist. We know, even by that simple touch, he understands. Strangers, practically, us and him. But we feel like we might be something more now.

He's leaving. Maybe he's just scouting ahead. We shout again, but he won't answer back. We can hear his footsteps as he backs away and rounds some unseen corner.

To witness these events from Ben's viewpoint, select
section 25 on page 239

To switch to Haunt's viewpoint, select section 9 on page 209

5
Haunt

'Doctor, wait. Someone's up ahead.'

They're propped up in the shadows. The fleas look like they're feasting on them, whoever they are.

'It's Roba,' declares the Doctor.

We see he's right. Sort of. This twitching thing used to be Roba. His dark skin is mottling, falling away to the shiny new flesh of a Schirr. His head looks like someone's pumped it up. His features, still focussed in the centre, form a scabby little continent in the waste of a dark sea.

'He's wearing his webset,' the Doctor observes.

'Angels put it there,' whispers Roba. His eyes look fearfully up at us. He ignores the Doctor. It's us he responds to.

'Showed me things in my head,' he says.

'What things?' asks the Doctor slowly, like Roba doesn't speak the language.

'What are you bothering to ask him for?' We tap the metal band clamped round his sweaty head with our gun. 'Fix up his set. Let's see in his head.'

He fiddles with the metal band. We breathe in sharply, close our eyes. Roba's here with us.

Only he's someone else, and he's back in the control room. We realise we're seeing the place as it was before we came. Our skin starts to crawl.

'Everyone,' we snap into our wrist-comm, and yell inside our heads. 'Tune in to Roba. I think you'll want to see this.'

Switch to Roba's viewpoint. Select section 13 on page 219

6
Polly

We were uneasy, here alone with Shade in the gloom of the passage. Oh, we're scared to death as well – whatever we find out there it can only be bad – but this feeling of uneasiness is something separate. It's our first time alone with Shade since we talked together about his past. Except we're not alone any more. Our head's like a revolving door with all these people going in and out any time they choose.

We wonder if Shade feels awkward too. We could probably look inside and see, but it doesn't feel right to even try.

He looks at us. 'You haven't told anyone, have you,' he says. 'About any of it. Not even your friends.' He's not asking a question. It's a statement. And he's right, of course.

'Maybe there's more important things to talk about right now than your guilty conscience,' we say.

He thinks this over for a while as we go. Looks almost wounded.

'Besides,' we add. 'I keep secrets.'

'So do I,' he whispers. 'Keep them for so long, I can't ever let go of them.'

We break off our march, look into his eyes. They seem to glow in sympathy with the mossy ceiling. 'You should see your face,' we tell him. The skin is barely marked, looks baby soft. 'It's like nothing ever happened.'

He bites his lip. 'It happened.' He places a finger on the outline of Lindey's palmscreen, visible through our grimy yellow suit above the hip. 'It's all there.'

We turn away from him, unzip the front of the spacesuit, pull out the tiny computer. Then we hand it to him.

'Gone?' he whispers, staring at the display. 'You wiped it.' Then he looks at us. So many guys have looked at us that way over the bar in the Inferno at the end of the night. They're tired, and all the possibilities of the night have flounced out in mini-skirts and high heels in someone else's arms. They've cried on our shoulder and when we give them the right answers they want to take us home and get them through the night. The Florence Nightingale of Covent Garden, the girls used to call us. Except in the morning, those poor lost lambs would only want us to get them a cup of tea and shut the door on our way out.

We don't know what to say. Yeah, we wiped every last scrap of evidence – by accident, not because we're on your side. Yeah, you're a cheating hypocrite who pulled strings to get himself a second chance. Yeah, you never meant to get those people killed, you just panicked, but they're dead anyway now and are you going to blame yourself forever?

He could be hearing all this. Looking in our head. We try to think hard of a penny-farthing like the Doctor did, but it's no good, it just falls to pieces. A pink elephant appears out of nowhere behind the wreckage. We like that. Think of pink elephants, pink elephants...

'It's wiped,' we agree. 'OK, so it's not like it never happened. You'll see to that, by never letting it happen again.'

'It's happening now,' Shade says. 'Happening to all of us... Denni wants us all dead.'

'You won't... be like before. You're not running away.' We squeeze his arm, just a touch. 'You're coming after Denni. And you're looking after me. I don't think you'd run out on me.'

We're saying all the right things. He's quiet. Maybe working out how much of this night is left, whether we'll see another morning.

The passage forks into two snaking tunnels, and we recognise one of our little cairns. We lead Shade down that path.

'You knew Denni well?' In our minds we can hear the bouncers calling for the swingers to drink up and do their swinging outside in the street.

'We were together for a time,' Shade admits. 'I could never work out what it was she saw in me. I guess since my face got me noticed, hanging with me marked her out too. She liked being talked about.' He gives a nervous laugh. 'A woman of mystery, that's Denni. No one could work out what someone who looked as good as her saw in a guy with a burnt-out face.'

The lights have come up, and oh dear, he's laying this on a bit thick.

'Woman of mystery is right,' we say, avoiding the wallowing stuff. He smiles at us suddenly. It's not like he's not gorgeous now. We think for a moment of how the two of them might've been together. Just for a moment. 'Why would she do something like this? How could she?'

'I can't believe it. That she'd turn on us all like this. I mean, she always had problems with Haunt…' Shade shakes his head. 'And I guess she always had ambition and a whole load of attitude too. But to do all this…'

'It's evil,' we whisper.

'Her *temper* was evil, sometimes,' he says cautiously. 'But *her*… I can't believe this of her.'

We thought he wanted us to take his arm and face up to the chill and the drizzle outside together, but now… he's thinking about Denni all the more. He looks upset, eyes darting about in all directions, like he's picturing the things they used to do and trying his hardest not to.

We should maybe tell him about the pink elephants, but we can't say we're not tempted to try to see his thoughts properly for ourself. Something sweeter, all together safer than this miserable world of tunnels and fleas and seaweed and death and…

We move through a narrower section of the passage together and Shade's arm brushes against ours, closer than it needs do.

I wonder if we're saying goodnight, or else maybe walking out together. The night big and black above us, the stars bright and close enough to touch.

Like a chaperone, the face of the Doctor swims into our view, unbidden. He's saying something about Haunt. Something we should know.

To witness these events from Shade's viewpoint,
select section 21 on page 231

To switch to Haunt's viewpoint, select section 9 on page 209

7
Polly

We walk along beside Shade in silence, listening to the way we take three steps for each of his. Whatever he thinks, and whatever we say out loud, *we* can believe this of Denni. She's in the Army, for God's sake. What woman wants to join the Army? Wants to go around shooting people or whatever? Women like Haunt. Case rested.

Denni sounds like a real cow.

We suddenly twig that Haunt might've heard what we were thinking, and we blush. A pink elephant comes to our rescue.

But Haunt's not listening.

She's screaming in our ears. Desperate. Scared.

Her words are shot through with the dead grey pallor of the angels. 'Do all you can. Work together. Keep the neural network open. That's an order.'

The voice cuts off. Our head goes silent, the unsettling silence you get when some background noise you didn't even know was there suddenly switches itself off.

'Doctor!' we scream out loud.

'I'm still here, my child,' he says, his voice strained. We can hear strange undertones, like he's talking to someone else at the same time. 'Marshal Haunt ran on ahead, we saw someone…'

'Denni?' we ask.

Shade starts to say something. We shake our head, shush him as we try to listen.

'It seems highly likely, yes,' says the Doctor. 'I was too far away to see clearly.'

'Is Haunt dead?'

A pause. 'I'm afraid I can no longer detect her in the neural network.'

'Haunt's dead,' rasps Shade. He looks lost.

'What about everyone else?' we say. We're thinking of Ben.

'They are well. I am keeping a close watch on everyone. Be careful, my dear. I shall be back in touch soon.'

His voice ebbs away in our head.

Shade looks as if he might start crying. We go to him, open our arms. Hold him, as he holds us back, shaking softly.

'Who's going to get us out of this now?' he whispers, and we want to say the Doctor will, we're sure he will. But in the blackness, straining to catch the murmuring presence of the others as they creep along dark passageways, we can't imagine ever getting out.

We cling to Shade and we feel no bigger or better than the fleas that leap and skip about us.

If you have not yet witnessed Marshal Haunt's severance from the network, review section 11 on page 215. Then return here and select another viewpoint

To witness these events again from Shade's viewpoint, select section 8 on page 207
To continue in Polly's viewpoint, select section 12 on page 217

8
Shade

We peer ahead into the darkness, our ears full of the crump, crump, crump of our feet on the stony ground, and straining to catch the first whispers of anything that might be lurking ahead of us, licking its lips at our approach.

When Haunt screams it nearly deafens us.

She's lodged somewhere deep in our head, we feel a stab of pain behind our eyes, stony fingers clawing at – no, *inside* – our shoulder.

'Do all you can,' she yells. 'Work together. Keep the neural network open. That's an order.'

And every trace of her is gone.

'Doctor!' Polly yells. Even right in my ears, the scream feels muted in comparison. We stagger back a few paces, still reeling from the power, the *pain* of Haunt's presence.

'I'm still here, my child,' says the Doctor. 'Marshal Haunt ran on ahead, we saw someone…'

'Denni?' asks Polly.

'What's happened to her,' we start to say, but Polly shakes her head, fiercely. Her long hair splays about over her face.

We hear another voice inside us. Our own voice: *jinx*.

Haunt made a fool of us in front of the whole academy, dressed us up in a combat suit so she could dress us down. *Shoot* us down. And didn't we wish her dead? Didn't we stare down at the vidphone and think about calling in friends and favours that would make Haunt disappear from our life forever? She must've known we could do that, but she didn't care. She knew that when it came to it, we just wouldn't have the guts.

We told Polly all this was our fault.

'It seems highly likely, yes,' says the Doctor. It takes us a few scared seconds to realise he's saying Haunt must've chased after Denni. 'I was too far away to see clearly.'

'Is Haunt dead?'

A breathless pause. 'I'm afraid I can no longer detect her in the neural network.'

'Haunt's dead.' We can barely bring ourselves to say the words.

'What about everyone else?' Polly says.

It's only a matter of time, we think. If Haunt's dead, with all she's lived through… how can the likes of us go on hoping for miracles?

The Doctor gives her a kindly answer, and says how he'll be in touch. Will it be him next, shouting and screaming in our head as the angels close in on him, as the Schirr come stealthily for him out of the shadows?

Polly's looking at us. She looks like she might burst into tears. She holds out her arms to me. We shamble over and clutch her close to us.

'Who's going to get us out of this now?' we whisper. Our face is clear, unmarked, like the past never happened, like we've never fought our own battles before.

And Polly has nothing to say to us.

*If you have not yet witnessed Marshal Haunt's severance
from the network, review section 11 on page 215.
Then return here and select another viewpoint*

*To continue in Shade's viewpoint, select section 24 on page 237
To witness these events again from Polly's viewpoint,
select section 7 on page 206*

*To switch to Roba's viewpoint, select section 22 on page 234
- then return here*

9

Haunt

We trudge about in the dark, playing out this stupid sick game. We can feel Schirr here. Out in the darkness.

The Doctor holds us up. He feels useless, we don't need to try to spy on his head to get that signal. We have to keep stopping for him to rest.

We're back thinking about Ashman. Listening to the Doctor's old-man-breathing here in the chilly darkness brings us crashing back to Toronto. Nothing else to do while he catches breath but look back. Try to warm ourselves round that inner image. Maybe others are looking in. Let them.

After the Schirr blast, we came round in the shattered data office an hour or so later, woken by the sound of screaming. We couldn't swallow. Our head felt like someone was slamming it in a blast door.

It took us a few minutes to realise the screaming was Ashman's. In combat his voice had always rung with calm authority. In pain, he sounded like a hysterical woman. The noise was coming from outside the room. Most of the ceiling had fallen inside it.

We wanted to help him. We tried to push ourself up. That's when we found our arm was broken, and we joined our CO in the shrieking.

'Haunt,' Ashman shouted, when he heard the noise. 'Haunt, are you all right? Can you move?'

The concern for us in his voice left us stunned. We even forgot the pain for a few seconds. 'I'll live.'

'For God's sake you've got to help me,' Ashman moaned. 'Get to me. For God's sake get to me.'

We crawled past the remnants of the data inputter, and the leering mask of the Schirr. Incredibly, the medikit was intact. And Ashman and us, we were both alive. Lucky.

A slick of blood poured suddenly out of our mouth, over our chin and onto the floor.

Bewildered, we checked our neck and found a jagged piece of metal sticking out there.

Ashman was still screaming for help. But we knew that unless we helped ourself first we would both die.

We ripped a length of charred material from the dead woman's shattered leg. Gathered a handful of pills from the floor around the medical kit, tried to fathom them. Gave up and swallowed the lot.

We didn't dare pull out the piece of metal from our neck straight away. We didn't know what else it might pull out. But we worked out the metal was probably from the back of the monitor housing, and just knowing that made us feel a bit better. Crazy. Ever since we were a child, we always felt we could handle anything as long as we understood it. Got it. Weren't floundering about, out of our depth.

'You'll never fall in love, then,' our mother used to tease us.

There was a small hole in the ruined doorway. We wormed through. Ashman was lying in the corridor. His body was bent all wrongly. It looked like it was only his combat suit that was holding it together.

His face was a sticky red-black where the blast had stripped his skin away. But he must still be able to see through the eye that hadn't melted into the flesh, because he fell silent when he saw us.

It was one of those stupid, slushy moments when you look at each other and you feel the electricity. Power there, between two people. Like in books. He started shaking, trembling for us as we crept towards him. He wanted us. Needed us. He would die without us. We could feel it, and we shivered.

'Are...' It was tough to talk with the metal in our neck. 'Are you OK?'

'You're funny,' he said. Like normal.

We held out a handful of painkillers. He lunged for them like they were diamonds. But his hand was shaking too much to keep hold of them. They fell and scattered on the floor. We picked up each one and tucked it inside his mouth. He moaned, like we were feeding him strawberries dipped in chocolate. He coughed pathetically as he tried to swallow them down. His eyes stared blankly at the metal stuck in our throat, but he said nothing.

Finally, his shaking hand gestured to his comms unit, just out of reach. 'More Schirr, they said,' he muttered. His voice was hoarse. 'Unit came down outside. Took most of us out.'

'Did we beat them?'

'Don't think so.'

Neither of us said anything for a while. We listened to Ashman's breathing grow gradually easier. Ours got worse. Throat felt like it was closing up. We coughed and felt something hot flood out the back of our nose. There was nothing to break the silence now. The shadows were thick and coal-black. One emergency light still flickered half-heartedly.

We fixed up our neck as best we could. Lay down beside him, careful not to get too close. We wanted to but we knew somehow that would hurt us more.

'They might come for us,' we whispered.

'Who?'

'Help.'

A pause. 'I thought you meant the Schirr.'

'No.'

'If the Schirr won, they might want to get back down here,'

Ashman said slowly. 'Finish off whatever they wanted to do.'

We didn't answer. We felt so tongue-tied this close to him, seeing him so vulnerable.

What could we say? Someone who'd been so strong, weak like an old man, catching his breath.

Like the Doctor now, who can't even make a crummy mile in the dark.

That feeling, the fear and resentment and the sorrow, never left us over the days that followed. We painfully built the rudiments of a nest about the two of us. The rest of the dead woman's clothing made a cushion for Ashman's head. A half-melted plastic covering draped over one of the ruined banks of equipment served as a blanket for us both. It was freezing now in the silent, shattered corridor.

Somehow, under Ashman's direction, we manhandled the ruined monitor into the corridor. There was no power supply, but Ashman told us that by crossing some of the wires inside, we could generate enough current to heat up the casing, and so warm us in the chill of those fitful days and nights. But Ashman was wrong. We crossed every wire in the machine, every possible combination methodically, but it remained cold. Dead. This was a ritual we had to go through every day; sometimes several times in a day. Our failures incensed Ashman. He insisted it was possible if only we could do it right. And when we didn't, he laid into us, ordered us away in disgust. He'd only call us back when he couldn't last a minute longer without the painkillers we would ease into the dry split of his mouth.

He was getting worse. We felt like we were dying with him. Light-headed, we would glare for hours at a time at the broken bulk of the useless monitor.

Then finally, days later, once life had dwindled to little more than a cold, painful sleep punctuated by rummages through the dregs of the medikit, the comms unit squawked into sudden life.

The voice was heavily distorted, but it sounded like a woman. It said something about victory, and about help.

Ashman stared at it dumbly, and we felt a stab of pain in our hungry stomach. They would come for us. They would help. They would help Ashman like we never could.

He grunted at us. We turned. He was looking straight at us with his good eye.

Holding out his hand to us. It wasn't shaking so badly now.

Can you feel it now? How our quiet shrivelled little heart quickened? We even dared to smile back at him. We reached out our fingers to his, touched them, entwined them. Everything seemed too hot. Our breath steamed out into the dank air like a warm kiss to him.

He pulled free, smacked our hand away, threw out his palm again.

'The pills, you stupid useless bitch. I need more of the pills.'

We froze. Froze everywhere. Then we reached into our pocket for the painkillers and we hurled them away as far as we could. Like our senses, scattered to the shadows.

Ashman bellowed like we'd stuck him with a knife.

'Forgive me.' The Doctor's voice in the dark. 'I'm ready to go on, now.'

We jump like a current's just been put through us.

The Doctor's looking at us expectantly. Was he in our head watching the show or was he…

We slip back there for just another moment before we have to go on.

This was the moment. When everything changed.

Our good hand was groping around in the dust and the dark for the pills. We despaired of finding them before help came. We pictured the rescue party in the ruins outside doing much the same as us. Hunting round uselessly in the dark for tiny, meaningless things.

It's as dark here.

The Doctor's set off again, breathless along the tunnel.

We feel our side. It's sticky, pink and gleaming in the torchlight. We knew it was coming but still we're shocked. Repulsed. And we know this is just a tiny taste of what the future holds.

The Doctor beckons to us. We have to pick up the search.

To switch to Frog's viewpoint, select section 3 on page 200
To switch to Creben's viewpoint, select section 20 on page 230

10
Ben

Tovel really puts us through our paces, fixing up the light-wires for the life support. We're grabbing this, tracing that back…

'Whoever done this knew what they were doing,' we mutter to Creben.

He nods. 'They did. They certainly did.' Then he takes my latest bundle of laser spaghetti and buries them somewhere lower down in the grid. The red links flare brighter and then the lines merge.

'This should be the last of the links,' he says.

'Good news, my friends.' The Doctor's whisper starts up from somewhere deep in our head. 'Polly and Shade have the crystals. We can reset the coordinates and steer ourselves far from Morphiea's noisome influence.'

We want to yell and cheer. But the Doctor's shushing us, frantically.

'We should not make this known to all in our network,' he says, his voice low and urgent.

'As we saw the Schirr through Roba's eyes,' Creben says, 'you think they can see through his?'

'And Tovel, and Frog, too, are no longer dependable,' mutters the Doctor.

We want to protest. But we remember the change in them, their bloated, twisted bodies, and we just nod. One sensible thing our old man used to say: careless talk costs lives.

'I think we were allowed to complete these repairs,' Creben says. 'Denni could have sent a hundred angels to take us here. She's been waiting for something… Just keeping us busy…'

'Perhaps so. But Denni won't have expected us to find those crystals. Hidden most ingeniously, most ingeniously, yes.' He chuckles. 'Those little gems may yet give us the advantage in this struggle. Once you've finished here, head for the control room. Be on your guard. I shall join you.' With that, the Doctor breaks radio contact.

Creben stands back from the glowing red maze, pleased with himself.

'All done and dusted?' We can't believe it. Life support's fixed up, and we've got back the crystals. Maybe, just maybe, we stand a chance of getting out of this.

Creben nods.

'Let's get back to the control room, meet the others.'

'Yes, I think we –'

Before he can say anything else, the other voice comes booming out at us all. Sounds like a woman... but with some edge to it we can't place...

To switch to Polly's viewpoint, select section 19 on page 229
To switch to Shade's viewpoint, select section 26 on page 241
To switch to Tovel's viewpoint, select section 23 on page 235

To witness these events from Creben's viewpoint, select section 15 on page 223

Or you may withdraw from the neural net – but only after experiencing Frog's perspective. Select section 27 on page 241

11
Haunt

'You can discard those tools,' the Doctor tells us. 'They won't be needed.'

We shrug. He knows what he's talking about, we've worked that much out about him. We drop the tool kit to the cold ground.

Goal one will be achieved – to get life support back on line. Provided Tovel and the Doctor can make sense of the Schirr systems, that is. The Doctor says he can. We see he's resolved to win out here, just like us.

At the point we're standing in, the tunnels cross. We catch movement up ahead. Something swift and stealthy, dodging past.

'Did you see that?' the Doctor's asking. He's sharp, pointing ahead into the gloom.

'I saw it,' we say. We start in pursuit, run off along the tunnel. The fleas flick off our bare face and hands as we go.

'I will wait for you here,' the Doctor calls.

We're sprinting away. We reach the intersection and take the left.

It's there. The figure. Not running anymore. Shrouded in murky shadows from the ember-glow of the ceiling, facing us.

Denni. Can you glimpse her there in the dark?

A hand slaps down on our shoulder. Heavy as stone. We turn, catch a glimpse of one of the cherubim, standing behind us.

We shrink back but it's got hold of us. Digging in its fingers.

Another one forms from nowhere in front of us.

'Do all you can,' we bellow, so loud that everyone in the web can hear, however far away they are. 'Work together. Keep the neural network open. That's an order.'

The stone hand clamps down on our face, its wide palm scrapes our skin, rough and cold. Its fingers pull

Marshal Haunt has been severed from the network

To switch to Polly's viewpoint, select section 7 on page 206
To switch to Shade's viewpoint, select section 8 on page 207
To switch to Ben's viewpoint, select section 14 on page 221
To switch to Creben's viewpoint, select section 18 on page 227

Or if you were instructed to return to the section you came from, go there now

12
Polly

We didn't stay hugging Shade for long. We were both too jumpy. So we moved on, out through these endless, endless tunnels. Denni's out here somewhere. And angels. And Lord knows what else. Once we found glass on the ceiling, half-hidden by weed. It made us dizzy. Brought us through to a new tunnel, one of those concealed entrances Ben mentioned. So what do the Schirr hide here?

'Look,' we breathe. Our feet crunch into the scree as we stop suddenly. 'There's light up ahead.'

Shade pulls the heavy grenade launcher from the harness on his back, and checks it over. He tries not to let us see his hands are shaking, and he goes ahead first, slow and cautious. We wonder, if it came to it, if he would run off and leave us here, alone, to whatever Denni's sending after us now.

He stops. Turns back to us and smiles. 'Come on.'

The light, white and harsh but beautiful all the same in this world of darkness, is nothing to be scared of after all. It's only starlight, from that window in the rock we looked out through an age ago.

'It's beautiful, isn't it,' we say, as the two of us stare out at the star-speckled night. We hear his breathing, slow and steady behind us.

'"Our destiny is in the stars", my ancestors used to say,' Shade murmurs.

'On Earth?' we ask softly.

'Where everything began.'

Our soldier's becoming a priest. 'I thought you were running from the Earth?'

He pauses for a second. Sighs. 'I guess it'll always be my home.'

Ours too. A sigh escapes us as we think of all we know and love back in London, in our own time. Black cabs. Cocktails. Parties on roof gardens. 'I'd give anything to see the Earth right now.'

'I'd give anything to take you there.'

He places both hands on our shoulders. Thinks his ship's come in.

The thought of Ben comes to us, loud and clear.

Ben missed his ship that first night we met. He looked at me across the bar, miserable as sin. Not calculating. Not weighing up his chances.

We've tensed up just a fraction.

'I always wanted to reach out and touch the stars,' we say, and the subject is changed, Shade is waved off alone into the cold window of night before us.

We reach out our hand to the glass, as if to caress and capture the brightest stars in this sky.

Our hand tingles and passes through the window. We're touching something hard-edged and cold. Pulling out a handful of stars from that amazing vista.

We're staring dumbly down at three crystals in our palm.

'The navigational crystals,' Shade breathes. 'They have to be. Hidden where a bunch of soldiers would never think of looking.' His hands tighten on my shoulders. He flips us around like we were a rag doll and grins stupidly into our face. 'Polly, you've done it! You've *done* it!'

We burst into giggles, stare at the crystals in wonder, as if they're made of ice and might melt away.

'Doctor,' we say, closing our eyes. 'Doctor, can you hear me?'

'Gracious, my child,' comes his voice in our head. 'What is it you have there, hmm?'

We let him work it out for himself. We feel warm all over as he starts to chuckle.

'Hidden in the stars,' we whisper.

'You know, I believe we stand a real chance now, my dear. Yes, Denni won't have expected such resourcefulness. Those crystals were hidden most ingeniously, most ingeniously indeed.' He titters to himself. Then his voice hardens. 'I shall contact the others and inform them. Don't be tempted to broadcast this good news across our little network. Remember, the Schirr infection is intensifying in Roba and Tovel, and poor Frog. If they overhear... so might others.' It's strange, we can hear an echo of his voice in our mind, but it's other words that are sounding. As though he's having other conversations too, even as he speaks to us. 'Those little gems may yet give us the advantage in

218

this struggle. Once you've finished here, head for the control room. Be on your guard. I shall join you.'

Shade's just looking at us, the smile gone from his face. He's puzzled. We realise the Doctor was speaking to us in private. We tell Shade the gist of what he said.

'It doesn't feel right, keeping this some sort of secret,' he says. 'You heard Haunt. We're supposed to work together. A team. If we don't trust each other…'

He tails off, looks at us, pained. 'The Doctor wouldn't have told us to keep it secret if he didn't think it important,' we say. 'We should go straight to the control room like he asks.'

Shade nods doubtfully. We press on regardless.

To witness these events from Shade's viewpoint, select section 24 on page 237

To switch to Ben's viewpoint, select section 10 on page 214
To switch to Creben's viewpoint, select section 15 on page 223

13
Roba

We're –

We're looking through Schirr eyes, at our friends, our fellow disciples lined up on the platform in heroic golden light.

We all feel so old. Relics. Old and hollow as human threats. Empty promises.

Pallemar has betrayed us all and the master knows it now.

He towers over the traitor, covered in blood. He's bludgeoned Pallemar's body, torn his flesh open as if looking for a thing in him that has turned him from our cause.

How much Pallemar has told the humans we can't know. Enough to buy his life and diplomatic immunity. He thought the master's ambition too overreaching. In contrast his own stretches no further now than to be allowed to live. He wriggles in his chair, begging. Ten make the rituals strong. Pallemar must live. It must be ten.

Like him we watch his deep dark blood spurt out sluggishly from the holes the master has torn in him.

It doesn't matter that Pallemar will die. The master has learned something new. He says we will become more than ten, many more. All we need shall be supplied. The plan *will* go ahead.

Puny, we stumble and blunder up on the stage. With the others we take our places. The master speaks of unexpected saviours.

He teaches us our lives will go on even as he blows open our bodies with his gun.

The air begins to hiss out of the stronghold we have fashioned here. It will not fill this room again until salvation is at hand. The master will be waiting, ready. For time will touch us soon and put us to sleep. We may know rest now while he will go on, surviving his single endless moment of death. When we are all dead he will stand alongside us and turn his gun on himself.

A shard of glass hovers charmed in the air to our left. The master's key. An escape switch to be thrown the day new life shall come to us. Time will run back. Our wounds shall be undone and we shall live again.

The others are screaming out as they die. Our nose twitches in pleasure at the sweet smell of their open flesh. The master's gun fires. We scrabble with both hands for our precious guts as they dribble out, feel heat and darkness. The last of the air seeps from the room leaving only death, only darkness as time stops.

Blackness. Cold.

Blackness.

To switch to Frog's viewpoint, select section 16 on page 224
To return to Haunt's viewpoint, select section 17 on page 226

14
Ben

There's a red haze up ahead in the dark, like neon. This could be an Amsterdam sidestreet in winter. Except we doubt some leggy blonde with some bad English is waiting round the corner.

We grip poor old Roba's gun as tight as we can.

Through some maze of red lines floating in the air, we see it's only Creben. Not quite the blonde, but we're less likely to catch something nasty. Probably.

'Creben. I'm glad to see you.' The red lines look almost like some floating net, waiting to catch anyone who comes by. 'You all right? What's all this?'

'It's what we came here to fix. That's all.'

We look at him. 'That's all? This is it! We'll be all right!'

'We'll be able to breathe for a while longer, certainly. But since Denni brought us here with the intention of changing us into something else, it was never likely we were going to suffocate before that happened, was it?'

That told us. Take down the bunting. 'One of them fleas got up your jacksie, did it?'

He's not listening. Looking at us, dead suspicious. 'Where's Tovel?' he says. 'Weren't you with him?'

Yeah, but we just left him on his tod to get on with it. We don't want to have to tell that to Creben.

'He's not good. I had to leave him.'

He's probably poking about in our head, checking us out. 'Did you now,' he says sceptically.

'Yes, I did.' Like he'd have done any different. 'He can't move, Creben, all right? He's half-turned into one of them.' Just the thought of it makes us feel sick. We shut our eyes, try and reach out to him, but it's a no-go. We're just not good enough at this caper. 'Anyway, the Doctor *said* I should leave him. S'pose it makes sense. You know, try and help the rest of us before going back to help him.'

'And what can you do?' Creben asks. Smug basket.

It's not actually a bad question. But we don't have to answer it, because suddenly Haunt's screaming in our head: 'Do all you can.' We glimpse heavy stone. 'Work together.' Hooked grey talons reaching out for our face. 'Keep the neural network open. That's an order.'

Her voice just stops.

'She's out of the web,' Creben mutters.

'Dead?' He doesn't reply, and there's my answer. 'But the Doctor was with her!'

'I'm still here, my boy.' Thank God. 'Marshal Haunt ran on ahead, we saw someone…'

'Denni?' we ask.

The Doctor's thinking stuff through, we can tell. 'It seems highly likely, yes,' he says.

Wonderful. Still out there, still psycho. Haunt's dead, now. 'Thought this network thing was meant to help us watch out for each other?'

'And through each other.'

That's Tovel. For a second we look at our communicator, like he's talking through that, but of course, he's banging on inside our ears.

'You all right, Tovel?' We're still looking at the communicator. Maybe it might boost our voice or something, make us less faint.

'Comes and goes,' breathes Tovel. At least he's not just staring into mid-air. Stay on side, mate. You can do it. 'Now listen,' he says. 'Forget Haunt, you have to. Concentrate on the circuit display. If the Doctor's right, it'll take two of you to make the repairs on that thing.'

'Tell us what to do,' says Creben quietly. He's staring at the glowing red maze, dead intently, like it's some group palm and he's reading all our lifelines.

He's got that prissy little smile of his back on his face.

*If you have not yet witnessed Marshal Haunt's severance
from the network, select section 11 on page 215.
Then return here and select another viewpoint*

**To witness these events from Creben's viewpoint, select section 18
on page 227**

To switch to Polly's viewpoint, select section 7 on page 206
To switch to Shade's viewpoint, select section 8 on page 207

15
Creben

The work is routine. The repair process is perfectly logical. Once you express the sum of the integers as a –

'Whoever done this knew what they were doing,' says Ben.

'They did,' we agree. They knew they had to make it simple enough even for the likes of him. 'They certainly did.'

We take the last fizzing bundle of cables from his sweaty hands. 'This should be the last of the links.'

Before we can make the final repair, the Doctor's voice sounds in our skull. 'Good news, my friends. Polly and Shade have the crystals. We can reset the coordinates and steer ourselves far from Morphiea's noisome influence.'

We hesitate, unsure how to react. To us, this scarcely seems possible.

'We should not make this known to all in our network,' the Doctor goes on.

'As we saw the Schirr through Roba's eyes,' we say, 'you think they can see through his?'

'And Tovel, and Frog, too, are no longer dependable,' mutters the Doctor.

Not just them.

'I think we were allowed to complete these repairs,' we say. 'Denni could have sent a hundred angels to take us here. She's been waiting for something… Just keeping us busy…'

'Perhaps so,' the Doctor concedes. 'But Denni won't have expected us to find those crystals. Hidden most ingeniously, most ingeniously, yes.' He chuckles. It's strange, we can hear an echo of his voice in our mind, but the words are different. We wonder how many

223

conversations he's having at once. 'Those little gems may yet give us the advantage in this struggle. Once you've finished here, head for the control room. Be on your guard. I shall join you.'

We plant our handful of red vines deep in a misty circle of amber light. They glow contentedly. The last of the harm is undone.

'All done and dusted,' the boy says strangely. 'Let's get back to the control room, meet the others.'

We start to agree. Then the voice of a Schirr purrs out to us. A voice we know straight away from a dozen gloating broadcasts system-wide after the dust has settled on each new ruined world he's left behind.

To witness these events from Ben's viewpoint, select section 10 on page 214

To switch to Polly's viewpoint, select section 19 on page 229
To switch to Tovel's viewpoint, select section 23 on page 235
To switch to Shade's viewpoint, select section 26 on page 241

Or you may withdraw from the neural net – but only after experiencing Frog's perspective. Select section 27 on page 241

16
Frog

Thank you and goodnight, Dax Roba. He's still there, you know, his head bubbling quietly away. Like us. We had the same kinda story bubbling under a while back. Some other Schirr's view. Same kind of ending though.

Can still feel how it was to have our guts blasted open. If we could lift our head, see over our chins, we imagine we'd find that hole gaping there now. All the life, just slipping away.

You know we seemed happy before, when the others were gathered round? You probably think we're such a flake. One minute we've got the knives out ready to carve us right up, and the next we're giggling like a kid on her first date.

Well, we've been making sense of stuff, or trying to. A part of us was thinking, we had our voice taken away ten years ago and now it's come right back. Luck, see. The kind of luck we've never had in our life. So, we might be changing but so's our luck. And we ain't never had looks neither, so losing them ain't so bad.

Weird thing is, all this time we've wished we was Denni, or Lindey, or anyone 'cept us… the moment we started to change it seemed all right. But we want to hold on to us now. We're not a frog. Not now we can speak. So we don't wanna croak now.

We remember… we remember when we came down on some dead village on a sun-scorched world in the outer Argentines. Forget its name. But the Schirr had done a good number on the place when Empire hadn't pulled out of Idaho by the deadline, and there was nothing there alive when our squad scooted down in the shuttles to check it out. Nothing 'cept this stupid bird.

It was all white, white all over. Sturdy looking thing, too. A swan, or a goose maybe, can't remember which, we ain't been on too many nature trails in our time. But the damned thing kept following us around, and honking and stuff, and there was no one round any more to feed it and water it, and it'd be alone once we'd buried the dead and shipped out. We kind of felt sorry for it.

And the bird kept following us around and making this stupid bird noise. So in the end we shot it.

Just a reflex, that was all. Put it out of its misery. But it didn't know nothing about misery. Maybe it might've stayed alive somehow if we'd not been around down there, and all sick with the stuff we'd seen. You know, we can still see it now plain as a hot clear day. That beautiful white bird turned all red and messy. Regretted the shot as soon as we fired it, but what can anyone do? What's done is done. One hit.

We was gonna kill ourself but we didn't. Haunt saw to that. Why she's a marshal and we ain't making Elite in a hurry, we guess. We feel like that white bird now. Except we bled, and then we got healed. A second chance.

225

So we lie here and we hold on. We're holding on. We're gonna keep on honking like that swan-goose thing. Only, it's a sweet songbird voice now.

No one to hear it now, in this empty place. No one to see us neither, to tell us what we look like. Floating above the floor on our little bubble looking up at the glass on the ceiling. Holding on.

What you still doing here? I just got the verbal craps. Get out of here.

To switch to Creben's viewpoint, select section 2 on page 198
To switch to Roba's viewpoint, select section 22 on page 234
– then return here

17
Haunt

We snap out of Roba. Clutch hold of ourselves, to know we're still here. Still us.

'Well, well,' says the Doctor.

'We should kill him now,' we say.

'He's truly becoming one of those Schirr,' the Doctor says, as if he's impressed or something. 'I've seen cultures where consumption of a person's flesh resulted in the eater taking on certain memories, certain characteristics... but this is an altogether more invasive process. The subject is helpless to resist.'

'So we're all going to turn this way?' we ask, though we know it's true anyway. 'Each of us into one of them?'

The Doctor nods grimly. 'And I think DeCaster wants us to know. He wants to feed our fear, to keep us off our guard. To stop us from thinking clearly...' He gestures at Roba's bloated, distorted body beneath the fleas. 'Hence this somewhat graphic demonstration of possession.'

'Then we *should* kill Roba, shouldn't we?' Creben's voice sounds over the communicator. Now we can feel him, trying to watch through our eyes. He's learned to use the network quickly and well. An adept. We can feel the strength of his mind.

'We should just kill him,' he says again, 'spare him all this. Stop DeCaster's plan.'

'I agree,' we say.

'But what is DeCaster's plan, hmm?' The Doctor addresses his question to our wrist for want of something better to focus on. 'What will killing this poor man achieve?' The Doctor shakes his head. 'And where should we stop? Should we take our own lives now, simply give up?'

Creben remains silent. We feel him sulking at the back of our mind.

'OK,' we say. 'Then let's move on. He lives. But we leave his webset on so we know what he's doing.'

'A wise precaution,' the Doctor agrees. 'You know, I feel quite distracted and disorientated after that experience. I wonder how the others are getting on, hmm?'

To switch to Creben's viewpoint, select section 2 on page 198
To switch to Frog's viewpoint, select section 16 on page 224

18
Creben

We feel we've been here for an age, body pressed hard back against the rock, trying to conceal ourself. But the glow bleeding from the stare of the carved eyes makes everything too bright.

We're noticed the moment the furtive figure rounds the corner.

It's Ben.

He's relieved. 'Creben. I'm glad to see you.' He frowns at the schematic. 'You all right? What's all this?'

'It's what we came here to fix. That's all.'

'That's all?' he says. 'This is it! We'll be all right!'

'We'll be able to breathe for a while longer, certainly. But since Denni brought us here with the intention of changing us into something else, it was never likely we were going to suffocate before that happened, was it?'

He glares at us, mutters something we don't understand.

We realise he's alone. 'Where's Tovel? Weren't you with him?'

'He's not good. I had to leave him.'

We look at him suspiciously. 'Did you now.'

'Yes, I did. He can't move, Creben, all right? He's half-turned into one of them.'

He's indignant. We feel it's genuine.

'Anyway,' he carries on. He even closes his eyes like he might start crying. We believe he actually feels guilty. 'The Doctor *said* I should leave him. S'pose it makes sense. You know, try and help the rest of us before going back to help him.'

'And what can you do?' we ask politely.

It's Haunt's voice that answers. Screams at us.

'Do all you can. Work together. Keep the neural network open. That's an order.'

We catch a whiff of something old and decaying. Glimpse the cold empty face of an angel. As we do so, Haunt's voice spirals off into nothing.

'She's out of the web,' we say quietly.

'Dead?' We don't answer him. 'But the Doctor was with her!'

'I'm still here, my boy,' comes the Doctor's answer. He sounds troubled. 'Marshal Haunt ran on ahead, we saw someone…'

'Denni?' Ben asks.

'It seems highly likely, yes.'

Ben laughs, a brief and bitter sound. 'Thought this network thing was meant to help us watch out for each other?'

'And through each other.'

Now we hear Tovel. Whispering inside our head. Perhaps the communicator has snapped off his bulging wrist? No. It's there on the boy's arm. He seems a little self-conscious about it for some reason.

'You all right, Tovel?' asks Ben. He's half-talking into his wrist, the idiot, forgetting whose gear it is. The pressure's getting to him.

'Comes and goes,' breathes Tovel. 'Now listen. Forget Haunt, you have to. Concentrate on the circuit display. If the Doctor's right, it'll take two of you to make the repairs on that thing.'

'Tell us what to do,' we say. We want to get this over with. So we can breathe again, until we figure out what to do next.

We're taking Tovel's orders again. The irony is, it's almost easier to swallow now he's no longer competition. Now he's becoming a Schirr.

The situation's quite ludicrous. Absurd. And here we are, stuck in it up to our necks.

If you have not yet witnessed Marshal Haunt's severance from the network, select section 11 on page 215. Then return here and select another viewpoint

To witness these events from Ben's viewpoint, select section 14 on page 221
To switch to Polly's viewpoint, select section 7 on page 206
To switch to Shade's viewpoint, select section 8 on page 207

19
Polly

We set off back down the passage. It wasn't so far from here we took the blue-lit tunnel. The tunnel that led to the place where Joiks –

Our thoughts crash up against a voice.

It's high like a woman's but there's a harshness, an anger, that puts us in mind of a man.

Dimly we feel Shade grab hold of us, his arm round our waist, dragging us along.

There's nothing special about the contact now.

We can't feel a thing, except that voice there deep inside us.

The crystals in our hand rattle together as we start to shake.

*To witness these events from Shade's viewpoint,
select section 26 on page 241*

To switch to Ben's viewpoint, select section 10 on page 214
To switch to Creben's viewpoint, select section 15 on page 223
To switch to Tovel's viewpoint, select section 23 on page 235

*Or you may withdraw from the neural net – but only after
experiencing Frog's perspective. Select section 27 on page 241*

20
Creben

We trek along these tedious tunnels, endure the jumping touch of the fleas as they swarm in great clouds around the weed above, the great dull lamp we see by. We can feel others trying to get into our head. They can't reason things out so they want our answers. They want to use *our* mind to light *their* way. We prefer not to listen.

People always seek to use us. It's been the same all our life. Our parents gained licence to have a further child once they'd made us demonstrate our prodigal intellect. Our university's reputation was so enhanced by our achievements that its Chancellor received special commendation from the Paris authorities and a bursary. We were not rewarded.

Cheats do not prosper. Our mother miscarried twice before our brother was born. He grew up a criminal and a stupid one. He got caught burning down the Chancellor's library.

He tried to protest it was our idea.

Always used. We're thinking this through now because we're trying to work out if Haunt's used us. We don't think she ever has. Brains are a disadvantage in her scheme of things, we suppose. Adaptability, that is what the modern soldier needs. Haunt couldn't adapt so they threw her out under the guise of honouring her, and left her to train others according to programmes and guidelines and principles that weren't her own. An insult. She must've seen it for that. And still she stayed. Because she believed in the Army, even after all it did to her.

We were honestly just another person to Haunt back at the Academy. She couldn't fathom us, so she stuck to her job. Trained us. Gave to us, or tried to.

Now we're all she's got.

When the time comes, we hope it's us who kills Denni.

We stop. We hear Haunt's voice in our head. Something's happened.

Switch to Haunt's viewpoint. Select section 5 on page 202

Switch to Haunt's viewpoint. Select section 5 on page 202

21
Shade

So Haunt's put us with Polly. That's good. We need to talk with her.

We can't believe we told her all that stuff. That was when we thought we were going to die. It's like we've given away everything we own because we thought it was the end of the world, and now there's been a stay of execution.

Except that she can still end the world for us now, any time she wants.

She doesn't look so happy to be with us.

We hope it's the location and not the company; the usual flea-ridden shadows abound here, masking the jagged slates piled up to the soft-glowing ceiling. The dead weight of the grenade launcher on our back is actually a comfort.

As we lead the way, we narrow our eyes. Try out this web, try to dip a toe in her head. She's on edge. Stuff's going round and round, but one thing we read loud and clear.

'You haven't told anyone, have you,' we say 'About any of it. Not even your friends.'

She shrugs her shoulders. 'Maybe there's more important things to talk about right now than your guilty conscience.'

We suppose she's right. She can't know how deep this goes, how we can be thinking of this at the same time as thinking of anything else. Anything else at all.

'Besides,' she adds. 'I keep secrets.'

'So do I,' we whisper. 'Keep them for so long, I can't ever let go of them.'

She stops walking. We check she's OK. 'You should see your face,' she says. 'It's like nothing ever happened.'

'It happened.' Our eyes wander down her body to her hips. There's Lindey's palmscreen, tucked away on her left. We tap it through her suit. 'It's all there.'

She turns away, reaches a hand into her suit. Pulls out the palmscreen and hands it to us.

The display is still glowing, waiting for our next command.

We realise the files have been killed.

'Gone?' we whisper. We stare at the display. We could've wiped Lindey's painstakingly collected files the moment we found them, but we didn't. A part of us *wanted* to let the truth come out. That way it'd all be over. No more fighting against it, no more guilt at hiding our guilt.

'You wiped it.' We look at her.

There's no coming clean now. All the easy evidence has gone. We're safe in our lies. The second chance still stands.

'It's wiped,' she agrees. 'OK, so it's not like it never happened. You'll see to that, by never letting it happen again.'

She sounds serious. Like she believes we can change now the files are wiped clean, now the mess has gone from my face.

Can't she see we're still marked for life?

'It's happening now,' we tell her. 'Happening to all of us.... Denni wants us all dead.'

'You won't... be like before. You're not running away.' She touches our arm, squeezes softly. We guess the blushes will show in our clear cheeks, and wonder if we'll live long enough to get used to that.

She takes her hand away. 'You're coming after Denni,' she says. 'And you're looking after me. I don't think you'd run out on me.'

We follow down the passageway after her, but we don't say a word. We picture stone angels humming down the tunnels towards us. Imagine us standing our ground.

The passage forks. Polly leads us to the left.

'You knew Denni well?' she asks.

'We were together for a time. I could never work out what it was she saw in me. I guess since my face got me noticed, hanging with me marked her out too. She liked being talked about.' We give a short laugh. It sounds too high. 'A woman of mystery, that's Denni. No one could work out what someone who looked as good as her saw in a guy with a burnt-out face.'

'Woman of mystery is right,' Polly says. As she speaks we feel she's picturing our old face, all black and mottled, but she's struggling. She can't get the way we look now out of her head. She likes it! And now she's trying to focus again on the idea of Denni and me together. She doesn't know what Denni really looks like, of course, and she's got a mental image of me kissing some big, butch-looking white girl. Then this huge, bright pink animal with a long nose appears out of nowhere. We bail out of her head before it can get any weirder.

'Why would she do something like this?' Polly says. 'How could she?'

She's upsetting herself. We linger in her mind for a moment longer, to see if maybe she'd like us to hold her or something. Why are we so scared, why can't we just reach out to her? But she doesn't want us now, anyway. She's scared for herself and for her friends. Scared of Denni.

'I can't believe it,' we say. 'That she'd turn on us all like this, I mean. She always had problems with Haunt...' We shake our head, remembering back over the last three years. Haunt got her screaming mad sometimes. 'Guess she always had ambition and a whole load of attitude too... But to do all this...'

'It's evil,' she whispers.

We just can't believe that.

'Her *temper* was evil, sometimes,' we say, non-committal. 'But her…
I can't believe this of her.'

It's like the image of her in our mind is becoming faceless,
dangerous, the woman in Polly's head. Makes us want to shout out
loud.

The passage narrows as we walk along, and we brush against her
accidentally. She doesn't shy away. We sneak a sideways glance: her
body looks so slim in that silly yellow suit, she's so soft, so unspoilt.
We think of Frog, and Roba, and Tovel… think of how the changes
will tear through us too. Why shouldn't we hold Polly close to us? Feel
her slender arms wrapped tight about our neck, before all of us
change?

We walk along beside her. Scared of dying, and just as scared of
being alive.

We sense the Doctor is trying to tell us something. Something about
Haunt.

*To witness these events from Polly's viewpoint, select section 6 on
page 203*

To switch to Haunt's viewpoint, select section 9 on page 209

22
Roba

We don't see so clear. It's dark, we know, but we couldn't even tell you
that. Our eyes are burning up. That thing, that walking dead Schirr
that came down the tunnel to get us, to mess with our head…

Now we keep catching sight of things we shouldn't see.

Like we're walking around inside different people. When we were
a marksman, starting off, we used to see people through our sights.
Night vision, snow vision, infra red. It was like seeing things through
different eyes. Like someone else pulling the trigger.

Now we can't control what we do no more. Just feel the fingers pulling through our guts, tugging at our eyes, arms and legs.

Seeing what works what, and how it can work for them.

So if we come for you. If we come to kill you. Know it's not us.

We just wanna go home.

Return to the section you came from and select another viewpoint:

To return to Shade's viewpoint in section 8, turn to page 207

To return to Frog's viewpoint in section 16, turn to page 224

23
Tovel

We're guiding human hands over the glowing paths and junctions of the schematic. Ben twists and bundles the damaged filaments, Creben routes them through to new circuits. We guess this sabotage is Denni's work. It's clumsy, easy to fix. And the schematic, it's not designed for fat, swollen pig hands like ours. Like Schirr. It's for small, dainty little hands, like Creben's, to put right.

We twitch as a fresh burst of pain flows through us. Feels like our veins are full of slush ice, sticking on its way round our body, watering down our blood. We try to open our eyes, but it's hard. The lids are like clamshells, tight shut, the eyeballs just pieces of grit lodged inside, changing to strange pearls.

We find we're wondering what Haunt looked like when she died.

'The work proceeds quickly,' we hear the Doctor say. 'Almost complete.' He sounds rattled. We get the feeling he felt just a little of what I did then. So he's checking I'm still here. Trying to distract me with pleasantries.

'Where are you, Doctor?'

'On my way to meet Polly and Shade back in the control room.'

'Why?' We sense something's happened he doesn't want to tell us. We slip through different viewpoints, shadowy figures all around us, hear a babble of voices. For a second we glimpse a field of stars, and a girl's hand stretched out to them.

'I, ah…' The Doctor falters. 'Polly wishes to go back to safety, and I am escorting her.'

Creben has almost made the last of the links. We watch him through Ben's eyes as he finishes the work.

'It's all gone too well,' we think back at him. 'We've been allowed to do this.'

'Perhaps.' The Doctor sounds preoccupied. 'After all, as Creben says, why instigate the change in us, then let us die before it takes hold?'

'The damage to life support,' we hiss. 'What if it's just been a decoy, taking our attention from something else?' We wince as the slush ice scrapes through our bloated veins again. 'If only we had those navigational crystals.'

The Doctor pauses. 'A decoy. Yes, of course, something must be happening in the control room!' We feel a sense of urgency, but whether it's the Doctor's or else something inside us desperate to take charge, we can't tell.

'Frog. Frog, my dear,' the Doctor shouts urgently. 'Can you hear me?' But it's not her we hear.

It gets black again. We can't move.

Something in us shifts, comes alive, as a Schirr speaks in our head.

To switch to Ben's viewpoint, select section 10 on page 214
To switch to Creben's viewpoint, select section 15 on page 223
To switch to Polly's viewpoint, select section 19 on page 229
To switch to Shade's viewpoint, select section 26 on page 241

Or you may withdraw from the neural net – but only after experiencing Frog's perspective. Select section 27 on page 241

24
Shade

We've come through one of those hidden pathways now. What's waiting for us here?

'Look,' Polly whispers, and her hand grips ours. 'There's light up ahead.'

Carefully, we reach back, slip the launcher from our harness and prime it. We cradle it and creep into battle.

The light's coming from a window in the rock. Outside there's just space. We call to Polly, 'Come on.' We want her to see this with us.

'Beautiful, isn't it,' she says, and pushes past to see it more clearly.

We shrug behind her back. We've looked out on a million views like this one from thick, scratched safety-glass in ships of all sizes. '"Our destiny is in the stars", my ancestors used to say.'

'On Earth?' she whispers.

We nod, almost fondly. 'Where everything began.'

Polly sounds surprised we should sound so tender. 'I thought you were running from the Earth?'

'Maybe you'll prove that to me, one day,' we remember Denni saying that last day at the Academy.

'I guess it'll always be my home,' we answer.

It's not just a line. We're not Elite, not the best, we've always known that. We've just survived. Maybe we've survived so much, for so long, that we've outgrown the questions we were trying to answer in the first place. We look out on that window of timeless, endless space like we're understanding distance for the first time.

'I'd give anything to see the Earth right now,' Polly murmurs.

'I'd give anything to take you there,' we say, without even thinking. Then we place both hands on her shoulders. Not afraid.

She tenses under our touch.

'I always wanted to reach out and touch the stars,' she says, like it's something she wouldn't want broadcast. But the real intimacy is gone from her voice, and she's self-conscious as she reaches out her hand to the glass.

She freezes for a moment.

When she pulls it back she's holding three bright, round gemstones in her palm.

'The navigational crystals,' we realise. 'They have to be. Hidden where a bunch of soldiers would never think of looking.' We spin her around, feel a smile stretching back our cheeks further than we've ever known. 'Polly, you've done it! You've *done* it!'

We both start to laugh as we stare down at the crystals cupped in her palms.

'Doctor,' she says, and she shuts her eyes. 'Doctor, can you hear me?'

We wait for his ponderous old voice to start up. There's only silence.

'Hidden in the stars,' Polly whispers, eyes still closed, smiling to herself.

We watch her as she nods and cocks her head to one side... The Doctor's talking to her, he must be. Her eyes open at last and she seems surprised we've not been included in the conversation. When she tells us what was said – about keeping the news off the network, about how we shouldn't trust Tovel, and Roba and Frog... it sounds like the Doctor has taken charge of us all.

'It doesn't feel right, keeping this some sort of secret,' we say. 'You heard Haunt. We're supposed to work together. A team. If we don't trust each other...'

We tail off. *Trust*. How can we even say this? We've lied to everyone from the moment we joined the Academy.

'The Doctor wouldn't have told us to keep it secret if he didn't think it important,' Polly insists. 'We should go straight to the control room like he asks.'

We nod uncertainly. But her faith in him is absolute. Could she ever feel that much faith in us? We feel sick.

To witness these events from Polly's viewpoint, select section 12 on page 217

To switch to Ben's viewpoint, select section 10 on page 214

To switch to Creben's viewpoint, select section 15 on page 223
To switch to Tovel's viewpoint, select section 23 on page 235

25
Ben

We can't hear the footsteps of the others anymore. Polly and Shade have been swallowed up by the tunnel opposite. Hope they find the holy grail quick. Something tells me Tovel don't have too long.

Hold up, he's looking at his paws again. They look like they'd fit round our neck a treat. Nice one.

We have a quick butchers at the world according to Tovel. It's getting a bit misty. You can't be optimistic with a misty optic, our old mum used to say. And she never even wore glasses, daft cow.

What we wouldn't give to see her now.

'You all right, mate?' we say, keeping the noise down. Tovel keeps looking at us like he don't really see us. 'Tovel?'

'I'm a good pilot,' he says suddenly. His voice, which used to sound quite posh compared to the others, is getting rougher. Like he's not working his tongue so well. He's like an old man suddenly, going downhill fast. We hope he isn't noticing all this kind of stuff as he goes. 'Did you hear Haunt say that?'

'Yeah, course,' we say. We can't remember to be honest.

Tovel shakes his head, like he can work loose the Schirr patches, send them flying off like bits of blancmange. '"Turn this thing around," she said. Do you remember back in the control room? "Turn this thing around before…" She never finished.'

He stops still. Looks like he might lay an egg. Finally, he just takes a big, deep breath: 'And I couldn't finish it for her either.'

We don't know what to say. What can we say to that? 'That's because you were turning into a ruddy monster, mate?' The Doctor would have something clever to say, we reckon, but no chance of reaching him.

'It ain't over yet,' we say finally.

In a whole load of ways we wish it was. But you've got to keep plugging away, ain't you? Go the distance. Jeez, now we're quoting our old man.

Tovel don't say nothing. We don't even know if he's heard us. His eyes, piggy under his big brows, have sort of glazed over. He don't look too steady on his big pins. Then he falls.

We yell his name, try to pull him back up. Feel how clammy, how *dead* all this new skin on him feels to the touch. We can't shift him.

Time to close our eyes and tap the ruby slippers. 'What do I do?' we yell with our head. Nothing comes back to us. Try again. 'Tovel's collapsed. He's not right. I can't move him.'

The Doctor's there. His voice is crackly like an old record.

'You're very faint, Ben.'

'So are you. Listen, Tovel's fainted, or something.'

A pause. Has he gone, or –

'He's fighting against the infection, my boy. You can't help him.'

'So what do I do?'

'Go on alone,' the Doctor says, like it's no big deal. 'But take Tovel's communicator. You may need it.'

'What if *he* needs it? He's helpless ain't he?'

'Don't argue my boy. We have to find the life-support systems, and find the navigational crystals. We're doomed if we do not. You are able bodied and Tovel is not. You must leave him.'

We know the Doctor's right. Even before he's finished his spiel we crouch beside Tovel and slip off his little bracelet. It takes some doing, his wrist has swollen up and the communicator doesn't come easily. Tovel doesn't even notice, just stares into space. The lights are on but nobody's home anymore.

We get back up, put on the wrist thing. 'Be lucky, Tovel,' we mutter. 'We'll soon have you moved back in.'

Then we're off, on our own again.

We don't know why but we're thinking about Haunt.

Switch to Haunt's viewpoint. Select section 9 on page 209

26
Shade

Polly bouncing along beside us, we set off back the way we came.

Then a voice presses down on our senses. Seductive and sibilant, proud and gloating. A Schirr voice, powerful, it's like it's trying to crush our thoughts into the ground.

Polly's staring round, wide-eyed. We grab hold of her, pull her on down the tunnel.

We can't just stop here when she's got our one and only chance of escape in her hand. We have to keep moving, *moving –*

To witness these events from Polly's viewpoint,
select section 19 on page 229

To switch to Creben's viewpoint, select section 15 on page 223
To switch to Ben's viewpoint, select section 10 on page 214
To switch to Tovel's viewpoint, select section 23 on page 235

Or you may withdraw from the neural net – but only after
experiencing Frog's perspective. Select section 27 on page 241

27
Frog

We hear something. Something soft, a whirring kind of noise.

We stop singing.

Our eyes are stinging. Watering. We think that's why the ceiling seems to be blurred at first.

No.

No, there's something pretty weird happening. All the glass is sparkling. Around where Roba shot at the stuff. You try and look at a piece and it shifts, becomes another piece. Like there's a blindspot somewhere in our vision, and God knows, there probably is by now.

But then we see the angel come swooping into our field of vision and we know we ain't just imagining all this.

We can't move. Even if we could we'd be too scared stiff to move a muscle. We're helpless. That angel thing knows it. Behind it there's a crack in the wall that was never there before. A black split, in and out of focus. Secret passage. But it can't keep our eyes off the angel.

We watch, stuck like we're made of stone as it hovers just above us. Its wings flap. We feel the breeze they make, it's like a summer wind. The angel shifts just a little. We follow it with our eyes, wishing we could fly too. Is this us thinking, or is this what we're becoming, but the angel thing's kind of beautiful.

It hovers above the bodies. Reaches out to what looks like a frozen drop of water sparkling in mid-air just above one of them pool ball heads.

The lights take a dip. And the Schirr on the platform start twitching like they got a few of them flea bugs under their nightgowns.

We wanna run screaming but we're stuck here watching.

And we hear the scary bitch voice of one of them speaking loud. We hear it in our head before we hear it in our ears, and then the echo of the voice after it. Like there's more than one Schirr talking. We're feeling like there's all kinds of stuff hiding in this web that we never knew about. And we wanna scream or something, but we know we'd never be heard over these words.

'Please remain still,' the Schirr says. *DeCaster* says. 'You're not going to die, humans. You're going to live forever.

'*We* are going to live forever.'

WEBSET ONLINE INFORMATION SYSTEM DEACTIVATED

You exit the neural network
Now turn the page

Chapter Fifteen
Partners in Crime

I

The Doctor paused outside the control room, trying to focus. Frog, of course, must be trapped inside with the emerging Schirr. He had tried to contact the others in the network, but without success. Still, he had done all he could for them. If they weren't here already, he knew they soon would be. Where else could they go?

Steeling himself, he strode with all the dignity he could summon into the pentagonal chamber.

It seemed to have come alive. The golden trellises high in the walls glowed like neon, and the light was caught and reflected all ways by the glass in the ceiling, brightening the place considerably. The air was warmer, and shot through with a sickly-sweet stink like dustbins left unemptied for too long.

'Well, well,' the Doctor said. 'Quite a gathering, I see.'

The Schirr corpses on the sullen stage were heaving for breath, laboriously. They looked weak. Their pink-white eyes rolled in their sockets as they acclimatised to life again. It seemed to pain them.

In front of them stood DeCaster, an altogether more powerful creature in long white robes. His fleshy brows were knitted together in a dark frown. The red pinpoints of his pupils fixed on the Doctor. The nose was a jammed-up snout, like a pig's, except it waxily joined a huge, broad top lip that drooped down either side of his face. The chin was dominated by a thick, trembling lower lip.

Beside him, easily as tall but more massive than the Schirr leader, stood one of the Morphiean constructs. It stood still as the statue it resembled.

'Of course.' The Doctor chuckled darkly with satisfaction. 'You didn't steal the secrets of the Morphieans' dark sciences. They were supplied to you.'

DeCaster said nothing, but he watched the Doctor closely.

'Well, what of Denni?' the Doctor asked, stepping closer. 'As your accomplice, should she not be present here, at the end, hmm?'

DeCaster's fleshy lips stretched back into a wide smile. 'Denni,' he said. His voice was like that of a woman's, sensual and soft. 'Human female. She was offered in ritual, fed to the propulsion drives.' He pulled something from his robe and threw it at the Doctor's feet.

Blonde dreadlocks, still attached to a bloody slice of scalp.

The Doctor nodded sadly. 'I suspected she would be dead. I suppose she had outlived her usefulness.'

As he spoke, a long crack appeared in the far wall, behind the platform and the TARDIS. The secret door became visible to the Doctor as it opened, its edges blurred with strange energies.

Through it, silently, stepped Marshal Haunt. She raised a finger to her lips.

DeCaster's mouth quivered. 'Denni's usefulness was as meat.'

The Doctor endeavoured to appear undistracted. 'Er… Come now, surely you undervalue her contribution to your cause?'

Rifle raised, Haunt stole closer behind the Schirr.

'She has, after all, manipulated events very much to your advantage, has she not?'

Haunt circled the platform and crept right behind DeCaster and the construct.

But DeCaster must have heard her. He whirled round, bore down on her.

And turned back, his smile even wider.

Haunt pointed the gun at the Doctor's head.

'What is the meaning of this,' the Doctor demanded hoarsely.

'Can't you guess, Doctor?' Haunt spoke without any sense of triumph. 'It was me who arranged all this. Not a training mission. A *rescue* mission.'

There was a sudden clattering of feet from the narrow passageway outside the control room.

DeCaster's long, twisted ears twitched. 'The humans should all be paralysed,' hissed DeCaster. 'We transmitted the disabling pulse along the network. How can they still move?'

Haunt looked uncomfortable. 'I don't know. A mistake in the ritual?'

'Impossible,' hissed DeCaster.

The Doctor tutted. 'I'm afraid you got rather ahead of yourself, didn't you.'

'You?' DeCaster's brow furrowed further as he stared at the Doctor. 'This is your work?'

'Over here, Doctor,' Haunt snapped. 'Or I'll blow your head off.'

The Doctor didn't move. He gave her a pitying smile. 'But you've expended so much energy to keep enough of us alive... I really don't think your master would be pleased if you killed me now.'

DeCaster blasted out a hiss of breath from his snout, and stamped towards the Doctor with alarming speed.

The Doctor shrank back instinctively, but a moment later the Schirr's huge arms had clamped around him. He was twisted about to face his friends as they ran in to the room: Ben, Polly, Shade and Creben. The others must still be lying in dark corners, changing, unable to move.

'Be still,' DeCaster snarled, his breath hot and wet in the Doctor's ear. 'Drop your weapons or I kill this one.'

'No!' shouted the Doctor. 'He won't do it!' Damp, fleshy fingers pressed down on his mouth and nose. He could barely breathe.

'Haunt!' Ben yelled, his amazement at finding her alive clear on his face. 'Can't you do something?'

She fired just above their heads. A yellow bolt of laser fire smashed into the wall behind them.

Ben looked shocked. 'Not quite what I had in mind.'

'Throw down your weapons like the Schirr says,' Haunt bellowed. 'And raise your hands!'

The soldiers obeyed, bewildered. Ben hesitated, but Polly looked at him imploringly, and he followed suit.

'What *is* this?' Creben snapped.

The Doctor managed to twist his face free of the thick, sticky hand.

'Your marshal has betrayed the people of the Earth and their empire,' he shouted. 'She has used you all.'

He heard the Schirr's rumbling laughter behind him.

II

Polly stared in horror at the tableau before her. Haunt pointing the gun at them. The stone angel as it floated forwards and trampled the soldiers' weapons into scrap. The dark bulk of what used to be Frog, lying silent in one corner. The huge Schirr bodies *moving*, swaying, breathing in and out, and the frail form of the Doctor caught in the grip of the biggest one of all.

Shade was trembling beside her, his eyes fixed on Haunt's. Creben was speechless. Polly wondered how it must feel for them, such a total betrayal.

'Used us?' croaked Shade. 'Why?' He still stared disbelievingly at Haunt.

Haunt regarded them coldly. 'I have my reasons.'

'Our bodies have been weakened by the rituals,' DeCaster said. The contrast between voice and appearance made him all the more repellent. 'Worn out, unable to heal. We need…' He smiled again, bared huge square teeth. 'We need your assistance.'

'You're taking our bodies to replace your own?' Creben demanded. 'One for each of you?'

'No wonder she said no one dies without her say so,' Polly murmured.

'We *appreciate* human flesh,' DeCaster told him, and licked his lips. 'We have groomed your bodies, healed them, made them pure. Now we each shall be as one. Two of my disciples – you may have noticed their absence – they have been casting the prelude to the joining ritual. It is now complete.' He grinned over at the motionless stone cherub. 'A lengthy piece but a most satisfying one.'

'That's the reason for all this deception,' Creben realised. 'The tableau, the mystery… once we were here, you needed time to prepare yourselves for us.'

The Doctor nodded with some difficulty. 'So they stayed hidden in plain sight… fooling us all.'

'I thought you needed ten to make your magic work?' Ben challenged. 'You bumped off your mate. What happens once you get past the warm up and the match kicks off?'

'We do not need the traitor,' DeCaster hissed. 'The neural network has united your minds. When we join with you, *our* minds will absorb yours. It will give us the power of many… enough for our purpose.'

Polly felt brave enough to speak up at last. 'Purpose? What is your purpose?'

Haunt shook her head. She wasn't saying.

'So,' the Doctor said, crumpled in the big Schirr's crushing grip. 'You always planned for the real-time neural network to be in place.' He looked pitifully dejected. 'And I made it possible for you.'

'I had Shel marked out for that task,' said Haunt. 'But yes, Doctor, you were an excellent replacement.'

'Well, we know how to balls up your little game, don't we?' said Ben, and he pulled at his webset.

It wouldn't shift, no matter how hard he tried.

'You're doing this!' Polly shouted at DeCaster.

He laughed and nodded. 'You cannot remove the websets now.'

'And your ritual cannot proceed unless I allow it,' the Doctor said. His composure had returned, it seemed, and with it his innate sense of authority. 'You said yourselves, these people should be paralysed by your powers. They are not.'

'What have you done, Doctor?' Haunt demanded.

'You expect me to tell you when so much is still a mystery to me?' He chuckled. Then he winced, struggled feebly against the monster's tightening grip. His simple bravery made Polly well up as she watched. 'The moment I tell you, I have nothing to bargain with.'

'There is no bargain to be made.' DeCaster pressed his upturned snout against the Doctor's cheek and inhaled. 'Your mind is fresh, but your body is old. It is *alien*.' He glanced over at the statue, his pale eyes betraying a flicker of annoyance. 'The Morphiean constructs should really have deliberated more carefully over who they culled.'

Polly stifled a cry as the stone cherub moved smoothly into life, swivelled its head round to view DeCaster. 'Our instruction was to bring the numbers down to nine.' The statue's voice was brittle and dry. 'This we have done.'

'There is much you must learn about the body, Morphiean,' DeCaster said, turning his attention back to the Doctor. He caressed the translucent skin of the old man's cheek. 'About the nature of *flesh*.'

'So the Schirr gain Morphiea's powers of the mind, and Morphiea regains the pleasures of the physical form.' The Doctor laughed hollowly. 'Is this your exchange? Hmm?'

DeCaster abruptly released the Doctor, who gasped in pain as he hit the floor.

'Your sabotage is negating the onset of the ritual,' the Schirr leader hissed. 'Tell us what you have done.'

'I will not,' the Doctor insisted, 'until I know the truth. I will not be a catspaw in your game.' His voice became sly. 'But tell me and I may willingly assist you.'

'Doctor!' Ben protested.

The Doctor wouldn't look at him. 'There's nothing more we can do, my boy.'

Haunt looked at DeCaster for assurance it was OK to speak. 'All right,' she said uneasily. 'I came here with two doctored droids, neither able to kill, and nine personnel. Ten of us for ten of them. I didn't know Pallemar had been executed until I got here. Whatever he told Pent Central about this place, or my involvement in setting it up, it must've been enough for them to check it out.'

'They sent Shel,' Polly whispered.

'But when you arrived, one of your squad was considered surplus to requirements and executed,' the Doctor deduced. 'Poor Denni. Fed to the propulsion units I suppose.'

'You can't have been happy when we turned up,' Ben said cockily.

'The presence of any excess organisms in the complex would destabilise the ritual,' DeCaster said in his flesh-crawling voice. 'Three more had to die.'

'It might've been Frog if she'd managed to kill herself,' Polly murmured. 'But when Haunt saved her, you killed Joiks instead.'

Creben turned to Ben and indicated the giant angel. 'Lucky for your party those things couldn't distinguish between us and you.'

Haunt nodded, her voice still devoid of any feeling. 'Denni's webset was destroyed with the rest of her. I didn't think we'd need it.' Now she actually addressed Polly directly: 'When the construct took Lindey instead of you, I made sure we kept the webset safe.'

'And once it became apparent that Shel was an artificial intelligence, he was next to be slaughtered,' the Doctor said, looking sickened. 'A cyborg simply wouldn't do.'

'It turned out well that the three of you came here from nowhere,' Haunt admitted. 'You could wear the web as well as anyone else.'

'And a good thing for you that the cleansing process happened to drive out your cyst, hmm?' Haunt didn't react, but the Doctor nodded. 'You fell desperately ill. A most ingenious way of diverting suspicion away from you. Yes, you've been very clever,' he proclaimed graciously, as he painfully stood back up. 'But are you really so keen to give your body to one of these creatures, hmm?'

'There's been no going back for me, Doctor,' Haunt said coldly. 'Not for a long, long time.'

The Doctor clicked his tongue, then turned his back on Haunt and addressed DeCaster as he would a waiter who had given poor service. 'But isn't all this a little small-scale, hmm? I can believe your ragged band of Schirr dissidents might need to skulk in the shadows like this, but the Morphieans have the might of an entire quadrant…' He tailed off, a wily smile on his face. 'Only they don't do they?' He turned to the construct, gripped his lapels and tipped back his head. 'You're dissidents yourself, aren't you!'

The cherub looked at him blankly.

'The old links between our peoples never truly died,' said DeCaster. 'Certain factions in Morphiea have been pressing for the expansion of the Morphiean empire on a corporeal level. We have let them taste the feel of flesh. Naturally, they want more.'

The Doctor would not look at him. He concentrated on the giant stone baby. 'Will you not speak to me, sir?'

'Our rulers are not mindful of the Earth's expansion.' Polly shuddered at the return of the angel's dry, dead voice. 'They would let humans seed the entire Quadrant, content to operate on the intangible planes.' The statue's face remained blank – clearly the Morphiean hadn't got much of a handle on emotion – but it made a horrible crackling sound, like bones breaking, that Polly took to be laughter. 'We shall not surrender all claim to the physical for all eternity to make way for animals.'

'There, you see?' The Doctor looked at Polly and the others. 'It is some wayward faction only that has been making these terror attacks on the Earth. In league with the Schirr all along.'

Creben had already cottoned on. 'The rest of Morphiea couldn't give a damn about us.'

'This complex will travel to the heart of the Quadrant,' DeCaster continued in his purring voice. 'We will use the renewed strength your lives will give us and the amplified power from the joining ritual to crack the Morphiean mindforce wide open, to suck out its secrets…' He licked his lips with a fat leathery tongue. 'With our allies then in dominance over all Morphiea we shall begin our assault on humanity in earnest.'

Polly saw two more Schirr had appeared in the new doorway behind the TARDIS, their raw, shiny skin gleaming in the bright light.

'The prelude to the ritual is complete,' said one.

As if this was some ominous signal, the rest of the Schirr shifted down from their platform, slowly and painfully, eyes sunken and white. They tramped past Haunt, who did not flinch, and took up positions at the various consoles. Polly held on tight to Ben's hand, shrank in to him as the creatures lumbered by.

The closest of them, staring at some sort of scanner screen, piped up in a rasping, forty-a-day voice: 'We are nearing closest approach.'

'Our time is at hand,' said DeCaster. 'Our powers reach their zenith. Doctor, we cannot delay.' His pink eyes grew redder, and his voice rose. 'With the work we do this day, we take the first step to liberate all Schirr from the ghettos, from the barbaric constraints of Earth repatriation. We shall have the means to take human stock and make them Schirr, then drive out their minds to give Morphiean intelligences a physical provenance.' He paused, gloating. 'Your empire shall be *our* empire.'

'So, Doctor,' Haunt said quietly. Polly saw she looked almost uncomfortable. 'Will you let this end now?'

All eyes were on him.

He bowed his head and nodded. 'Take me to the propulsion chamber.'

'Why there?' DeCaster demanded.

'I will show you,' the Doctor said tartly, 'when we arrive.'

'You can feel its pull, can't you, Doctor?' Haunt studied him closely. 'Even here. Hypnotic, isn't it?'

DeCaster nodded. 'We controlled the tremors to block off all visible approach to the chamber,' he hissed. 'We feared its pull would lead you all to a premature death feeding its hunger.'

'It almost did,' Ben muttered, turning to Tovel. 'That weird hypnosis thing when we broke through the rockfall –'

He was cut off as the room echoed with a crazed, high-pitched shriek.

'Frog? You all right, girl?' Ben started forward, but Haunt fired another shot over his head, warning him back. She looked round in alarm.

Polly saw the corner where they'd left her was empty now.

Frog could move again. She was coming to their rescue.

One of the Schirr lurched to one side, fell face down on the floor. It choked and retched, it was dying. Polly's heart leaped, Frog's counter-attack had begun.

Only when it turned over, arching its back, thumping the floor with swollen fists in pain and frustration, did Polly realise the fallen Schirr *was* Frog. There was little that was human about her now, all but consumed by the blistering alien flesh.

'See,' DeCaster told his brethren over Frog's whimpers of agony. 'It is fascinating, is it not, to compare the differing speeds with which the metamorphosis occurs.' He grinned evilly at Polly. 'But you will all fall to us in the end. You have no choice.'

Polly, still holding tightly on to Ben's hand, felt a creeping feeling under her palm. She looked down and screamed, let go of Ben like he was red hot.

'My hand,' whispered Ben, staring in horror. 'Crikey, Pol, look at my hand! I'm changing!'

Polly didn't need to look. She had felt the slimy, dead texture of the Schirr skin that coated it. She hugged herself tightly.

The Doctor looked anxiously back at them. 'Fight it, my boy!' he shouted. 'You must fight, *all* of you.' He looked meaningfully at Polly. 'It is not yet the point of no return. We can still reverse this, hmm? Turn it around?'

Polly, her senses still numbed with shock, stared at him blankly.

'No more talk,' rasped DeCaster. He pushed the Doctor towards the secret door in the wall. Haunt was already walking through it, leading the way.

'No, Doctor, come back!' yelled Polly. She wanted to run after him, to somehow get him back, to explain exactly *how* they could turn things around. But he was already gone.

'The old man will not delay us long,' DeCaster announced solemnly at the threshold. 'We shall return. Construct: see that the two humans in the tunnels are gathered and brought here. They are nearly turned to us. The joining shall be all the quicker.' The stone angel nodded, and DeCaster turned his attention to his disciples. 'Guard the humans,' he instructed, and a smile almost split his face open. 'Your new, exquisite bodies stand before you. Gloat over their good, clean flesh.'

The glass in the ceiling glowed brighter as he passed through the doorway. The split in the rock lingered on behind him.

The chamber fell quiet, save for Frog's choking sobs, and the laborious breathing of the Schirr. Slowly, arthritically, the creatures shambled closer. The cherub looked on dispassionately, a statue in the centre of the room.

'I'm changing,' Ben said again in disbelief, his voice cracking. 'What am I going to do? I'm *changing*.'

'We're all changing,' whispered Creben. 'The effect's speeding up, the closer we get to the heart of Morphiea.'

'No!' Polly insisted, tears rolling down her cheeks. '*I'm* not changing. I'm *not*!'

'It's on your neck,' Shade croaked. He turned away from her, and she saw a clump of sticky pink flesh smeared over the back of his head like putty.

Polly threw her arms round Ben, crying for them both as the Schirr lumbered closer.

Chapter Sixteen
Towards Zero

I

'Keep away,' Shade shouted in warning, as the Schirr dragged themselves closer.

Ben could see why their pale, bloodshot eyes held such a hunger. Their skin was baggy and pallid, muscles all over their bodies twitched uncertainly. They were weak, so they were going to take strength from him and Polly, and the others.

'Ben,' Polly murmured breathlessly in his ear. 'I just realised what the Doctor said, about still being able to turn things round.'

'Oh yeah?' he whispered back. He shut his eyes. He just wanted to enjoy holding her close for as long as possible.

'He meant I still have the navigational crystals,' said Polly. 'We can turn this whole *rock* around, literally. If we were travelling *away* from Morphiea, maybe the infection would fade.'

'Where do we need to put the crystals, then?' asked Ben, looking over his shoulder now at Creben and Shade.

'Tovel's the pilot,' said Creben. 'I understand the basic principles, but…'

'Even if we did know, we wouldn't stand a chance,' Shade muttered. 'D'you think they'll just stand there and watch us try?'

'What have we got to lose?' Ben kept his voice low. 'We can either die for these things or die fighting against them.'

'Wait – they *can't* kill us, can they?' Creben reasoned. 'Or there won't be enough of us to go round.'

'You cannot die,' said one of the Schirr, its voice a wet hiss like air escaping a punctured tyre. It may have been old but it wasn't deaf. 'Our cellular hold on you is too strong.'

'Well then,' said Ben, glaring at the exhausted creature. 'There's nothing you can do to us, is there?'

'But you can feel pain,' said another, the one with the chain-smoker's voice. 'Terrible pain. Must I slit you open, right down the middle? Force you to watch your wound as it slowly, agonisingly heals?'

The stone angel padded lightly towards them. Ben froze. He felt like *he* was the statue under its cold, blank stare.

'Pain,' the cherub said, its voice dry as deadwood as it leaned in closer to Ben. 'Yes, we enjoy the study of pain.'

Ben flinched from the cold bulk of the angel, picturing its face covered with Joiks's blood. As he pulled back, he heard the sinister sound of stone wings scything through the air, getting closer. Seconds later, two of the cherubim swept into the room through the pentagonal doorway. One held Roba in its arms like a sleeping baby, the other dangled Tovel by his arms. But Ben was only able to tell them apart by the colour of what little human skin remained. The shiny, hairless sticky flesh of the Schirr had swamped them, bulged through rips in their combat suits.

The angel turned away, distracted by the newcomers. Tovel and Roba were placed gently on the ground.

'That settles it,' said Creben savagely. 'You think we stand a chance with three of those things in here?'

'There's got to be a way,' said Ben. But he saw his right hand going the same way as his left, swelling, his fingers like frying sausages filling with hot fat.

Polly shook her head. Ben saw her face was getting bloated, her lips thickening to the size of slugs. 'It's no good, Ben,' she slurred. 'Not this time.'

Ben didn't want to believe it. He looked over at the grisly remains the angels had brought in with them. Roba was lying in a twitching heap on the floor, but Tovel was on all fours, staring around dumbly.

'Oi! Tovel!' hissed Ben.

The soldier looked up at the sound of his name, and Ben breathed a sigh of relief. There were still human eyes beneath the thick brows. Tovel shuffled over on his hands and knees. The Schirr, and the angels, watched him go. They seemed fascinated, like children watching where a clockwork toy will go next.

'Tovel,' Ben whispered, as he crouched to help him up. He realised he couldn't even feel his hands anymore. 'Listen. Those navigational whatsits, can you still work them?'

Tovel stared at him blankly. Ben signalled that Polly should show him one of the gemstones. She wriggled her sleeve and one fell into her palm.

'We've got the crystals, do you remember?' Ben whispered. 'If we make a distraction, you can steer this rock out of here!'

Tovel looked at Ben helplessly. He was hairless and mute, his features distorted beyond all recognition. *That's me,* thought Ben. *That's going to be me, any time now*.

Then Tovel nodded. His eyes were gleaming.

That's going to be me, Ben thought again, determined now. *Never giving up*.

II

Haunt looked dead ahead as she led the Doctor along the secret tunnels that branched off to the propulsion chamber. She'd spent so much of the last day scurrying around these pitch-black passages. Doubling back on herself, setting the asteroid complex in motion, hiding the navi-gems as instructed... wishing sometimes that she could hide too. But no matter how dark a corner she found, there was, predictably, no escaping from herself.

Nor, it seemed, from the Doctor's questions.

'You've explained what you have done,' he said to her, 'but not why.'

Haunt didn't turn round. She could hear the heavy, measured tread of DeCaster following on behind them. 'Does it matter?'

'It seems that nothing matters to you. Nothing at all. Can that be true?'

She walked on in silence.

'You're betraying billions of lives. You know that, and yet it would seem to make no difference to you. I'm curious as to why.'

257

It wasn't much further to the propulsion units.

'I witnessed your entombment on Toronto,' the Doctor said gently. 'I couldn't help but overhear.' He sounded tired, strained, not just in the way he struggled for breath, but in his speech. She found she slowed her pace a little to let him draw closer. But she kept her gun cocked and ready.

'It wasn't the Empire forces that tunnelled down and rescued you, was it?' he murmured. 'It was the Schirr.'

She nodded, and let out a long breath she didn't realise she'd been holding. 'Ashman died of his injuries. I was close to following him. Took the last of the pills as an overdose. But they found me.' She stopped for a moment, tried to swallow down the tight band that constricted her throat. Heard the heavy footsteps and set off again.

'The woman, there. Killed when the grenade went off. "They're in," she said. She didn't mean there were Schirr in the building. She meant they were inside our computer systems. Setting up this rock, everything, even then, ready for this time. And they needed someone on the inside to make it happen.'

'You agreed?' the Doctor asked her.

'I was dying. Their physicians seemed to heal me, then they let me go. They never explained anything, never spoke. Just put me back in the ruins of that place.'

They went on, step after heavy step.

'How could I tell anyone I'd been saved by the Schirr? That I'd let them kill my Ashman –' She clenched her fists, closed her eyes. 'That I let them kill my commanding officer, and then allowed them to put me back together again? They'd have court-martialled me.' Now she turned to the old man, angry at the memories, angry at *him*. 'And I wasn't through. Not with the army, not with the Schirr. I tore through those bastards on twenty worlds. I made sure they'd regret keeping me alive. I killed thousands of them.'

'And yet it was never enough,' the Doctor said, like he understood, like he was some kind of shrink or something.

Step after step in the darkness. DeCaster trudging on too, getting closer.

'When I took out New Jersey,' Haunt whispered, 'when DeCaster and his stinking Spook sciences had us beat and there was no way out. When I pressed the button and nuked the planet... I wiped out a million. Just like that.'

'How many of your own kind did you kill in the process?' the Doctor murmured.

She ignored him. 'The Army couldn't condone it, of course. But I was too high-profile to be tried. They made me a marshal and retired me to training duties with the minimum of fuss.'

Haunt recognised the blue tinge of the propulsion units bleeding into the blackness, quickened her step slightly.

'War changed,' she went on, 'I *watched* it change. No more battlegrounds. No more front lines. Just terrorists. Anywhere, everywhere. And who dies, in their thousands, every time? Not the soldiers. Not the enemy. The innocents.' She laughed mirthlessly. 'How can we stop that? We can't stop that.'

They turned a corner in the passage. The light was deepest blue, shot through with a harsh brightness like sunlight.

'But a war,' said the Doctor, his voice harsher now, 'a good old-fashioned war, with a foe you can see, an enemy you can touch and kill... That is acceptable, is it, hmm?' He seemed furious. 'That is desirable?'

Something in Haunt finally broke. She muscled him up against the jagged slate of the wall and leaned in close. 'If the Spooks want bodies, let 'em have bodies,' she snarled in his face, mindful of DeCaster getting closer and closer. She realised she had her hand round the Doctor's throat. 'Least we can see them, then. Least we can *kill* them. They can burn just as well as us.'

'That's no justification,' he said, fighting for breath. 'You know very well it isn't.'

'I know your kind,' she spat at him. 'I knew it from the moment we met. The lump of butter that won't melt in your mouth. The roses you come up smelling of every time.' She sneered, shook her head. 'I was damned the second the Schirr saved my life.'

'No,' the Doctor gasped as he clawed feebly at her hands, his eyes

259

tightly shut. She slackened her grip. 'No,' he said more firmly. 'You lost someone dear to you and never let yourself recover. You withdrew into yourself, withdrew from life, until nothing mattered at all. The Schirr didn't cause that change in you. You did it yourself.'

'Oh, you're funny.' She stared at him, breathless. 'You think I didn't know there'd be a price for my life? That they'd want something from me in return? It's so obvious.' Her hand slid down to her side.

The Doctor stared at her. 'The cyst?'

'It was theirs,' she whispered. 'They grew it in me. Malignant. No way to remove it save the way you saw.'

He met her gaze, grave and unflinching. He acted like he understood now. Like he wasn't afraid. 'And over the years it's slowly taken control of you. Led you to this pass.' His bony hand gripped her wrist and he spoke urgently. 'But it's gone from you now! Now you can fight their conditioning, prevent this evil –'

DeCaster was approaching the tunnel bend. Coming into the light.

'No, Doctor. It's for the best, all this.' She let her forehead rest against the Doctor's chest. 'When we're all a part of them… We'll start a real war. A proper war, one we *can* win.' She couldn't suppress a sudden smile. 'And even if we don't… I won't be scared any more.'

'You're mad,' he said quietly in her ear. 'Quite mad.'

She heard the rasping breath of DeCaster as he rounded the corner. Straightened up, but a fraction too late. His pink eyes looked furious, the pupils dilated to red specks.

'Has he explained what he has done?' the Schirr enquired.

'No,' she said, 'he hasn't.'

The Doctor looked up at the Schirr and smiled weakly. 'Through here,' he croaked. 'I will show you, sir.'

'Why so feeble,' DeCaster wondered. His voice was sticky, seductive. 'I smell youth in you. Can the body be so frail when the mind is so…?' He trailed off mid-sentence. Then he seized the Doctor by his coat and lifted him off the ground. 'Yes, of course. I see it now.'

'What?' Haunt asked nervously. 'What is it?'

'He is holding back the paralysing pulse with his *mind*.'

Haunt stared at the old man. 'It's not possible.'

'Such power we shall have in this little creature when he is ours,' breathed DeCaster. 'But look at him now, he is so tired.'

The Schirr dropped the Doctor to the tunnel floor. He scrambled up, a pathetic figure, limping along towards the light, trying to get away.

'Let go, little creature,' DeCaster shouted after him. 'Let go, and the joining can be completed.'

Haunt saw two of the Spook constructs stride up out of the blue mist that swirled through the propulsion chamber. They towered over the Doctor.

'I asked for them to appear as angels, Doctor,' she called out to the old man, 'and they did. I could never understand God. But angels are different. They can be evil as well as good, can't they?'

The Doctor staggered back from the constructs. They caught him with ease.

Haunt watched him as he struggled to hold on. Watched the Spooks as they pushed and pulled at his feeble body. 'I wanted angels,' she told him, 'to guide us to our rest.'

III

'We need a distraction,' whispered Ben, mindful of the oversized ears of their Schirr captors, and unsure the constructs were really so detached from all this as they seemed. 'Creben, Shade, if we can lead them away from here, through that secret passageway, Polly and Tovel can have a go at fitting them crystals and getting us out of here.'

Polly glanced down at Tovel. She crossed her fingers, and nodded.

Creben and Shade looked more doubtful.

'It's the only chance we've got,' Ben insisted. 'Cheer up, this is the easy bit. Once we've done that, we've got to save the Doctor.'

Creben looked away. 'Forget it.'

'You just gonna wait till you turn into one of those things?' Ben hissed furiously.

'You're only prolonging the inevitable,' Creben muttered, not turning round.

Ben nodded to himself. Polly glared at Creben, but he was too wrapped up in himself to even notice.

'Shadow?' Ben asked, eyebrows raised.

'Shade,' he corrected. 'All right. I'm in.'

Ben saw Polly's fattening face light up with a smile.

'Thank God for that,' said Ben gratefully. 'Next question. Any ideas?'

He saw Shade staring at what looked like boiled sweets that had fallen from Roba's torn combat suit. His eyes met Polly's. She scooped a couple up discreetly, pretending to check on Tovel, still slumped on the floor beside them.

'Not hungry, ta,' said Ben, bewildered. But Shade reached into his own pocket and pressed one into the puffy, blistering flesh of Ben's hand.

'Follow my lead,' Shade said. 'Polly, can you act sick? They'll be less bothered about guarding you if they think you're like Frog and Roba.'

Ben glanced at the two of them, spreadeagled on the floor, misshapen and twitching. Roba's milky eyes met his own. He turned away.

'All right, I'm ready when you are,' he said.

Polly gave a pitiful, sobbing cry, and collapsed to the floor, thrashing about beside Tovel like she was mental.

'Now,' yelled Shade. He threw the boiled sweet down at the floor between two Schirr. *He's missed,* Ben thought for a sickening moment. *The silly sod's missed.* But a second later, with a bang like a cap popping, a long rectangular bubble appeared, one of those things Frog and the others were lying on. Three Schirr went tumbling backwards as the thing expanded and knocked them off their feet.

Ben ran up screaming to two of the stone angels and threw down his own instant mattress. It sprang into full size. One of the creatures fell heavily to the ground, the other flapped away in surprise, like a dirty great startled pigeon.

Now every second counted. Ben sprinted for the door in the wall, raising a fist in triumph at Shade, who was matching him for speed across the control room. A big, pink, Schirr fist.

He halted in the doorway, looked back. One of the angels was already drifting across to catch them. The hunched-up Schirr lumbered after them like amateur Lon Chaneys. And behind them, unnoticed, Polly was helping Tovel into a kneeling position, helping him towards the navigational console.

'It worked,' Shade panted. From his tone, the gormless grin on his face, you'd think nothing he'd done had ever worked before.

'Yeah, like a charm,' said Ben wryly. 'Every ugly in the place'll be breathing down our neck.'

'Let's go.' Shade led the way down the passageway like he was John Wayne all of a sudden.

'Terrific,' Ben muttered, and ran to catch him up.

The beating of stone wings echoed eerily down the tunnel behind him.

IV

Haunt watched the Doctor collapse to his knees, clutching his head. The constructs had toyed with him for a few minutes, spun him in dizzying turns through the air and batted him about between them. She sensed he couldn't stand much more.

DeCaster did too. His eyes had narrowed to white slits in his great livid face. 'He is falling,' the Schirr muttered. 'The barrier is giving way.'

Then he convulsed with giggling laughter as the Doctor screamed out in pain and dismay.

Haunt felt herself trembling. This was it then. The moment she'd been saved for.

DeCaster swaggered up to her. She looked deeply into his glistening white eyes, ready to be taken. 'I accepted the new life you gave me,' she whispered. 'Now I accept your new death.'

'You were ours from that moment,' he murmured soothingly, tilting her head back. 'We knew all you were and foresaw all you could be.'

You understood me, she wanted to say, wanted to smile, but DeCaster had pulled open her mouth.

'And we always reclaim our own.'

A flood of sour saliva fell into her mouth, choking her, as the Schirr pressed his open lips against her face in a kiss. He crushed her body against his own. She couldn't move. Distantly she could hear the Doctor shouting out, but she couldn't hear the words. Surely there was nothing left to be said?

The Schirr's flesh scalded her own. She wanted to scream but he didn't wish it, so she stayed silent. His mouth opened wider, sucked in her whole drenched face, his teeth tore her hair from her bleeding scalp. She was breathing his air, big whooping gulps too big for her lungs, so she used his. He bit off her head and it went rolling down his black throat to melt in his guts. The body she left behind was a bag of old blood and bones, drying in his heat, more desiccated with each new beat of their heart.

There was no fear, no sorrow as the last splashes of Haunt bled away. Only strength as their mouth, DeCaster's beautiful wet mouth, moved in the chanting of the ritual.

264

Chapter Seventeen
The Unexpected Guest

I

Polly had fitted the crystals into the console. They sparkled in the light like Hatton Garden's finest. Her puffed-up fingers hovered indecisively over the tactile controls. Tovel was trying to tell her which buttons to press by nodding his oversized head at them. The muffled grunts of alarm he made when she went for the wrong ones left her wondering what would happen if the course correction sequence got snarled up. She tried to follow his gaze across to a small lever beside the screen full of numbers.

Tovel groaned again, more loudly.

'Well which one is it then?' she snapped at him.

'For God's sake, let me.' Creben pushed her aside and hit a switch below the lever.

Polly looked at him as she felt a faint rumble from somewhere deep beneath her feet. 'Thanks for joining us,' she said.

'They won't kill us – you might,' Creben retorted. But she could tell by the embarrassed flush of colour in his cheeks that he wasn't helping for that reason.

Tovel started to gurgle and groan again.

'I'm not even pressing anything,' she protested.

She realised he wasn't looking at her.

Three of the Schirr had come up behind them, one each. Polly almost gagged on the stench of them, a sickly reek of sweat, perfumed soap and filled nappies. The one zeroing in on her, wrinkled and wheezing, was smaller than the others but broader. It reached out for her face.

She tried to twist away, out of its reach. But she was frozen to the spot, paralysed, unable even to scream as it touched her with its sticky hands.

II

Ben kept running. His footsteps ricocheted around the tunnel walls like gunshots as he pelted through the darkness, the whooping and rustling of the massive angel's wings getting louder, closer. Ahead of him he could hear an eerie chanting, a litany of hard sounds against a background noise like cats yowling at enemies, ready to pounce.

Then Ben's legs locked. He collapsed to the ground, face and hands stinging from the impact. Blue light from down the passage shone in his eyes. He couldn't close them.

Shade had fallen too. His body was lifeless, his arms stretched out stiffly to the light.

The creature that had chased him here landed lightly close by and crouched silently to inspect him. Its expressionless face came up close to his own.

It couldn't close its eyes, either.

Behind him he heard heavy, dragging footsteps. He strained every muscle he had to try and move, but it was useless. The Schirr were coming, for him and Shade, for the Doctor. To destroy them.

III

The webset seared the Doctor's fingers as he tried to tear it from his head. It was no good. He couldn't shift it. Blocking the pulse for so long had left him exhausted. Now that it had slipped past him, torn through the neural web as fast as a thought, he felt his muscles stiffen and cramp as the paralysis hit.

The Morphiean angels watched him. Their mouths were open, o-shapes in the hard grey flesh, and a noise somewhere between singing and screaming issued forth. DeCaster's body made a giant X, all but silhouetted against the fierce blue of the propulsion units. Nothing remained of Haunt save for the dark stain smeared on the Schirr's

266

billowing robes. The half-words and whispers he chanted reverberated in the Doctor's head, whipped up the sympathetic Morphiean energies in the glass cylinder to a crackling incandescence.

Then another Schirr peeped into the bright blue light, started to slouch over to where the Doctor knelt, ready to take his body. But he was spared the doomy image. It vanished as DeCaster's mystical babble summoned up a darkness in the Doctor's eyes more profound than any he had known.

He willed himself to hold on to consciousness. The network contracted, gathered the nine of them together. The Doctor felt them all around him, vague digital impressions scattered about, brushing against his senses as they were slung like mud into the blackness. Ben and Polly were fretting for him even as they dwindled and died. Shade and Tovel wished only for a little more time. Frog, who didn't think of herself as a Frog any more, hung on for grim life to the person she could be. Creben and Roba were both buried deep within themselves, so it might hurt less when the last layers of self were peeled away.

And he felt Haunt's presence, all that was left of her, crushed to a pulp of ones and zeroes at the epicentre of the joining. The digital vortex swept the Doctor down too, dragged him closer and closer to the point of no return as the ritual neared its peak.

Then he became aware of something else.

Someone else, hidden there in the dark.

'It's you, is it not?' the Doctor heard himself whisper. 'Shel? Can you hear me?'

There was a sluggish shifting of sensation. The Doctor gritted his teeth. 'Shel, a trace of you remains. Reach out to me.'

He could feel Shel's presence hovering close by, a still point in the storm as skin and spirit began to to pare away.

'Join me here. Stand with me.' The Doctor steeled himself for one last, despairing try. 'Stand with me against *them*.'

Shel let himself be found.

DeCaster felt it at the same moment. He choked on the hisses and clicks of his incantation, and started to scream.

* * *

IV

The Schirr's face filled Polly's vision. Its big hands cradled the back of her head as it opened its mouth, ready to devour her.

But something was wrong. It froze in front of her. Polly got the distinct impression it was trying to close its mouth again but couldn't. Now it was the one paralysed, and she, *she* could move again. Her body was stiff and slow, but she could move.

The Schirr that had been crouched over Creben was frozen too. Creben had toppled back against the console. Though his neat features had started to warp into those of a Schirr, his eyes were still brown and human. Slowly, painfully slowly, he struggled to grip on to the console and pull himself to his feet.

'Tovel,' Polly gasped, turning to face him. 'Quickly, we must finish what we started. What else do we need to…'

He wasn't listening to her. There was little of Tovel left now. His eyes had grown pink and large, fleshy white jelly dripping off them like thick tears. The expression on his broad face slowly shifted into anger, and his hands gripped Polly's throat.

V

The stone angel had upped and gone, and Ben could move again. His arms and legs had cramped up like he'd just swum the Channel, but still he crawled painfully down the passageway, into the light towards the Doctor. The Schirr behind him made no effort to follow him. It still crouched there, shivering so violently Ben thought it might shake itself apart.

He hunted through the rolling indigo swell for any sign of the Doctor. There was DeCaster, spreadeagled against the glass cylinder like it was sucking him in. He writhed in agony, screamed out as glittering blue lightning crackled out from the glass to shake his colossal bulk. The stone angel was peering at him, as if trying to understand what was wrong, as the room began to darken to a stormy grey.

Ben cowered back instinctively as a dark shape detached itself from the pitching shadows. But it was friend, not foe.

'Doctor!' he yelled. 'Doctor, what's happening?'

'Something our friend DeCaster did not allow for,' the Doctor shouted back triumphantly. 'A tenth soul in his black little ritual.'

'Tenth?' Ben didn't understand.

'Shel, my boy!' the Doctor yelled, his words nearly lost over a deafening blast of what sounded like thunder. 'As an artificial intelligence his interface with the webset was far more comprehensive. His outward form was a carrying case only – the real flesh of him is the scripting in his circuitry. His presence in the network is as real as yours or mine.'

''Course it is,' Ben yelled, still puzzled, but enjoying the barmy smile on the old boy's face.

There were footsteps behind him. Ben spun round, ready to fight, but it was only Shade. He looked completely lost.

As he opened his mouth to speak, Ben shushed him and pointed at the Doctor. 'He's your bloke. Maybe you can get some sense out of him.'

'Don't you see?' The Doctor staggered over to join them. He looked a little bruised but was apparently untouched in any other way by the Schirr infection. 'The mere presence of Shel's personality in the neural network DeCaster had assembled was enough to create an imbalance. The ritual could not be completed. It's coming undone, I only hope it's not too late.'

'And what about the Schirr?' asked Shade. He pointed at DeCaster who was bellowing back against the glass. He shook like current was running through him.

'The energy they've expended in beginning the joining has to go somewhere,' wheezed the Doctor. 'If our friend over there is any example, it will travel back into the Schirr themselves.' He gave a brief, malicious chuckle. 'With unpleasant results.'

Ben wanted to cheer, but didn't dare even smile in case the Doctor was wrong.

The head of the stone angel swivelled round to face them.

'What about them things?' Ben cried.

'Give me your wrist. Quickly.' The Doctor grabbed Shade's sleeve and held it to his lips. 'Creben, Polly, are you there?'

There was only static.

'It's no good,' the Doctor fussed, 'there's too much interference here.'

The construct took a step towards them.

'Let's run for it before that stone thing gets us,' Ben urged him. 'It's not gonna be happy, is it?'

'I would never make it,' the Doctor puffed miserably. 'No, there must be another way. Before the network breaks down completely...'

The Doctor shut his eyes, put his hands to his temples. Ben and Shade swapped nervous glances as two more angels lurched out of the billowing brightness.

VI

Pressure roared in Polly's head as Tovel's hands pressed harder and harder down on her throat. Distantly she heard the Doctor's voice, but she couldn't grasp the words. Her sight was dimming, blackness tunnelling in from the edges of her vision. She wouldn't be sorry when the hideous face snarling into her own faded for the last time. After all she'd lived through, this final blackness would almost be a relief.

Then something metallic caught the light, twinkled into the haze falling over her eyes. A knife slashed down and wedged into the back of Tovel's thick wrist. He roared and snatched his hands away, pulling at the hilt of the dagger, trying to dislodge the blade.

She fell back gasping against Creben. He'd finally managed to pull himself upright.

But Tovel had yanked the blade free. Now he slowly advanced on them again, the knife in an outstretched hand, staring down at the blood that spilled from his wrist. His eyes were filled with the same hatred as the frozen Schirr around them.

Polly turned away in terror, just as she heard a heart-rending moan of pain from below her.

It was Roba. Curled up and still shaking all over, his hands covered his mouth. When he pulled them away, Polly saw there was something clamped between his teeth, a sweet or…

She struggled to work the alien tongue in her mouth. 'No, Roba!'

He bit down.

Polly shut her eyes, but the ghastly splitting noise as the force mattress expanded would stay with her forever.

'That's really done it,' Creben muttered. 'Nothing can put that back together. The ritual *can't* be completed now. Look.'

As Tovel shook and spasmed uncontrollably, the Schirr around him were shrivelling up like old balloons. Their eyes glazed over, they howled with frustration as they began to convulse. Then the old wounds, huge and gaping opened up and blossomed again over their bodies, caked with dried blood. Stomachs gaped open. Heads burst. They stood shakily as if in bad imitation of their gory poses on the platform, then collapsed to the floor, bloodless sacks of old flesh.

Polly's head swam dizzily, and then the Doctor's voice was back booming in her head, muffled by static.

'Quickly child,' he ordered, 'look at the panel.' She hesitated. 'The control panel, look at it!'

She tottered forwards on legs she could no longer feel, her vision was blurred, but she tried to focus on the various levers, switches and displays.

'Creben, you must help her,' the Doctor instructed. 'Let me see, let me see…' She wondered which of them he was speaking to, or if he'd lapsed back into speaking to himself. 'Creben. The far switch, yes, that one. Depress it while Polly instigates the reverse thrusters.'

'While I what?' she gasped, panicking.

'I will direct you,' he snapped. 'Now, concentrate child! You must concentrate!'

VII

'What's he doing?' Shade whispered.

'I don't know,' said Ben helplessly, as the stone angels drew nearer.

271

'But whatever it is, we've got to let him get on with it!'

'And what about them?' Shade and Ben fell into shadow as the angels' massive bulk blotted out the blistering light in the glass cylinder. 'They might not be so understanding!'

Ben squared up to the three angels that towered over them. If he could shield the Doctor for just a few seconds longer, maybe that would be enough. 'Just leave us alone!' he yelled in frustration. 'Ain't you done enough to us? Leave us alone!'

The nearest angel reached out both stone-cold hands and gripped Ben either side of his head. He laughed at the monster. Through the accretions of thick Schirr flesh he could barely feel a thing.

The stone hands pressed hard together. Ben knew they could crack his skull like a monkey nut. His mouth sagged open as the pain bit in. All he could hear was DeCaster, screaming and screaming.

From the corner of his eye he saw Shade flung aside like a paper dolly. The Doctor crouched alone on the floor with his eyes closed, unaware and defenceless as the two stone giants bore down on him, hooked hands reaching down to rip him apart.

VIII

'Now, Polly,' the Doctor said, a crackling ancient gramophone voice. 'As soon as you have input those three codes…'

His voice became scrambled with static, then cut out altogether.

'Say again, Doctor,' she implored him. But there was only silence.

'What do you think he said?' she asked Creben.

He shrugged helplessly. Then he pointed over her shoulder, eyes wide in alarm. Tovel had stopped shaking. He thundered over to the console, knife raised, trampling fallen Schirr bodies as he came. The low rumbling in his throat built to a roar.

At the last minute, Creben yanked Polly aside. Tovel was going too fast to stop, he smashed heavily against the console and stared down at the winking displays. He turned to Polly and Creben, then back to the controls. He raised the knife, ready to plunge it into the controls and wipe out their handiwork.

'Don't!' Polly screamed helplessly.

He looked at her. Then down at the shattered remains of Roba.

His other hand inched stiffly over to the controls. Pressed one, two, three buttons.

The knife clattered to the ground.

Polly watched as Tovel grasped a small silver lever and pulled.

IX

Ben heard a crunching noise from inside his ears as the angel squeezed his skull still harder.

Then he fell to the ground, abruptly released, reeling from the pressure pounding at his temples.

It took several moments for his sight to clear.

He was sitting in a cloud of grey fleas. The stone angels had vanished.

'What happened?' Ben croaked.

Shade, flat out on the floor, laughed in disbelief. 'They're gone.'

Ben stared at him. 'What did we do?'

Shade shrugged, and Ben turned back to the Doctor in time to see his eyes snap wide open. He looked about at the thick carpet of fleas before him, baffled, like he'd dozed off and woken somewhere unfamiliar.

Then he jabbed a bony finger past Ben at DeCaster.

The Schirr was stooped and pitiful, slumped back against the glass. He reached out to them as if seeking their help.

'Quickly,' gasped the Doctor. 'Go to him.'

'Help him, after all he's done?' Ben asked in disbelief.

The Doctor stared at him, then shook his head crossly. 'He will help us. Push him through the glass,' he thundered. 'Feed him to the engines!'

Ben stared at him, not sure he'd heard the Doctor right. But Shade set off straight away at a stumbling run for DeCaster. Ben limped after him.

'You, my little Shadow?' DeCaster hissed, with a crumpled smile.

'Come to kill me?' He choked, a liquid sound at the back of his throat. 'You're funny.'

Shade kicked the creature in the chest with all his strength.

DeCaster crashed back against the cylinder. The thick glass sparked and glowed and seemed to part around him, and the screaming tornado of light sucked him inside.

On instinct, Ben threw himself to the ground before the deafening thundercrack could knock him there.

Then it was lights out.

Chapter Eighteen
Curtain

I

'He's looking much better.'

Ben's head felt swollen and sore. Wasn't that Polly's voice? He tried to open his eyes. Golden light from up high shone in his eyes. He was back in the control room.

'Gently, my boy. I'm afraid you were caught in the backblast.'

That was the Doctor. Ben opened his eyes on the second attempt and found Polly looking down at him.

'He's come through it,' she said. 'He's going to be all right!'

She beamed down at him. And it really *was* Polly, barely a trace of Schirr about her now. She looked just as gorgeous as she had done the day they'd met. Her hair was a mess, her face was speckled with burst blood vessels, but it was *her*.

'You still reckon I'm a dog person, Pol?' croaked Ben. 'Got the lives of a cat, ain't I?'

'Looks like we both have,' she said.

'Yes, the power surge has taken the asteroid to the fringes of the Morphiean Quadrant, well out of range.' Things must be on the up, thought Ben, the Doctor was back to his old self, confident and assured. 'With the ritual unfulfilled, and away from the Morphiean influence, the damage to the cells is being undone, and the native DNA maps redrawn. The further we drift, the more the Schirr effect will diminish.'

Ben found he was afraid to sit up, to look round. He might have nine lives, but had the rest of them? He stayed flat on his back.

'What happened to those angels?'

'Retribution.' The Doctor nodded gravely. 'Yes, I think so. Those

Morphiean dissidents presumed to attack their ruling mindforce, under the protection of the amplified neural network. When that protection failed…'

'The mindforce could get at them,' Ben finished. 'And all the angels went to heaven. Good riddance.' He paused. 'You all right, Doctor?'

'Oh, yes, quite well, my boy,' the Doctor said as he turned and pottered away. 'Soon I shall feel a new person…'

Ben felt his face. His fingers rubbed against his cheekbones, eyebrows and his hair, damp with perspiration. They felt almost normal. It was really him. 'How do I look?' he croaked to Polly.

'Horrible,' she said with a beautiful big smile. She was crying. A tear plonked from the end of her nose onto his forehead.

'Clever move.' Tovel leant over Ben, squinting through rheumy eyes. He looked like his face had taken a right kicking. 'Shade chucks some Schirr in the propulsion units to get those blue energy waves really flowing, and you dive head first into them.'

'Glad you made it, Tovel,' Ben said with a grin. 'Honest I am.'

'Reckon those angels did him some brain damage.' That was Shade's voice.

'Ha bleedin' ha.'

'He's all right,' Polly said protectively.

'Yeah,' Tovel said. 'Ben's all right.'

'Likewise, mate,' Ben murmured.

'Well,' the Doctor declared, as he walked back into earshot. 'I believe I've succeeded in rigging some of the equipment in here so it should transmit a rudimentary distress signal. Presumably one of you is acquainted with some universally recognised emergency code we can program into the circuits, hmm?'

'I'll go,' said Shade.

'Far, I imagine,' said Polly softly, 'now all the Shadows are blown away.'

Shade looked at her, gave her a strange smile. Ben saw his face was still a little puffy, but his complexion was clear. The black markings beneath the skin had entirely vanished.

'They won't be calling him a shadow no more,' Ben remarked.

'Another life begins today,' said Polly. 'Good luck to him.'

Ben was too tired to quiz her on what she meant. He pushed himself into a sitting position and grimaced as the world took a few seconds to catch up with him.

The first thing he saw was a body bag.

He looked at Polly.

'Roba,' she said quietly. 'He killed himself. The final straw that broke the back of that horrible ritual.'

'Then at least it wasn't for nothing,' Ben murmured.

'When I saw him there… saw what he'd done… I *had* to hold on.' Tovel straightened up, his voice hardening. 'We'll make sure he gets full military honours, of course. Lindey and Denni too.' He paused. 'And Joiks.'

Ben nodded. 'Suppose his story checks out now we know the angels got Denni.' He looked around dismally. 'So what about the others? Creben?'

'Creben's fine,' said Tovel. 'As usual. Checking the life-support repairs are holding. This place could be home for some time.'

Ben hesitated. 'And Frog?'

Tovel shook his head dolefully. 'I'm sorry…'

Ben looked away.

'I'm *very* sorry, but her new voice is here to stay,' Tovel went on, a smile spreading over his face. 'And Jeez, don't we all know about it.'

'War is hell,' grinned Ben, relieved.

'Miss me, did ya?' Frog yelled as she bounced in through the doorway. 'I've looked all around. You were right, Doctor. Not a sign of them stone things nowhere. Just the fleas, and I'm gonna torch them all. Just in case anything else feels like making a big deal out of 'em.' She launched into a tuneless set of musical scales.

'You couldn't sing before and you can't sing now,' Shade shouted over from beside the Doctor. 'So shut it.'

'I'm gonna learn,' Frog promised. 'And I'm gonna learn languages too. Learn 'em and speak 'em, loadsa languages.'

'You might start with English,' suggested the Doctor, with a malicious chuckle.

Ben gave Frog the once-over. The swelling round her face and neck would go down if the Doctor was right. And the scars that had train-tracked her face were barely noticeable. Shoot her in soft-focus and you'd probably never notice. He was glad for her. 'Course, she wouldn't win no contests – she still had a face like a bulldog licking tar off a nettle – but she looked a lot better as a Frog than she did as a Schirr.

Creben entered the room. His face was red and covered in sores. Ben nodded to him. Creben smiled and nodded back. Quite a show of affection, Ben decided as he got unsteadily to his feet.

'So – now you've done the training… gonna go Elite are you?'

Tovel shrugged. 'I guess. That's what I joined up to do.'

'There'll be other wars to fight,' Shade agreed. He looked at Polly and smiled.

'Yes,' said the Doctor sadly. 'Yes, you've won a decisive battle here today, it is true, but I suppose the war you began with the Schirr will continue.'

'The Ten-strong were heroes to the Schirr dissidents. Meant to be indestructible.' Tovel grinned. 'We've taken them. We can take the rest.'

The Doctor looked disappointed with him. 'Can you not take understanding away with you from your experiences here? Compassion for those whose plight seems desperate? Go to your leaders. Urge them to speak with the Schirr, to take this opportunity to negotiate a peace. You may prevent similar atrocities in the future, hmm?'

'The future,' Ben heard Frog whisper dreamily. 'We've actually got one. Whatever it holds.' She smiled slyly. 'And it might just hold a lot of cash.'

Tovel looked at her doubtfully. 'Oh yeah?'

'We've still got Shel floating round somewhere in these websets,' she reminded him. 'All that top-secret AI stuff… Reckon Pent Central would pay quite a bit to get him back, don't you?'

'I think we'll pretend we didn't hear that,' Tovel said with a smile.

Frog shrugged. 'It was just a thought…' She looked furtively at Ben and winked. 'Well if I can't make a mint off Shel, maybe I'll ask old

Principal Cellmek if Haunt's job's up for grabs. Active service will seem pretty tame after all this.' She did a fair impersonation of Haunt's voice: 'Today you're all school kids and I'm your teacher. So what did we take away from today's lesson, children?'

'Don't judge by appearances?' Shade suggested.

Creben shook his head, actually joining in with the others. 'How about, don't follow orders blindly?'

'Who's got a disk?' Shade called. 'Play him that back when he's the big man in Intelligence…'

As the relaxed banter continued to fly, the Doctor caught Ben's eye. He indicated the TARDIS, steepled his fingers and smiled.

Ben nudged Polly and started to head towards the blue box. Its door stood ajar now, waiting for them.

'Come on then, dolly rocker Duchess,' he murmured. 'Time to go.'

'Hey, I know,' Tovel cried. 'I know what we've learned: Believe in magic. After all we've seen today…'

Shade agreed. 'Magic, must be. Just the fact that any of us are here at all – let alone so pretty.'

Frog laughed and even Creben raised an eyebrow. But the Doctor cut across them sternly as he walked up to his precious ship. 'No, no, dear me, no,' he fussed. 'Believing in magic is easy, the reaction of a cowardly mind to explain away any phenomenon that vexes the intellect. But *finding* magic in the realities of existence… seeking out some hidden truth to cling to from every painful experience we endure… that is never easy.' He looked at each of them in turn. 'That takes courage.'

Tovel cleared his throat. 'Yeah, well, I was actually joking about the magic stuff, Doctor, but… whatever.'

The Doctor looked aghast for a moment. Then his expression softened into a smile. 'Joking, yes, of course. I suppose… Well, it has been an extremely taxing day for us all.'

With that, shaking his head, he walked into the TARDIS.

'What're the three of you gonna do in there?' Frog called. 'And are you gonna sell tickets?'

Polly blushed. She waved goodbye to everyone – her gaze lingering a little longer than Ben would've liked on Shade – and followed the Doctor inside.

'We're gonna clean up, rest up, and then it's on to the next place,' Ben told her. 'Just like you lot.'

He winked and closed the door behind him.

II

Frog – or rather, Mel Narda as she would be known from here on in – watched the blue box start to wheeze and groan. Her jaw dropped as it slowly faded into thin air.

She gave Tovel a wry look as the last echoes of the weird sound died away.

'Don't believe in magic, he says.'

About the Novel

Ten Little Aliens was conceived in Rome in January 2001 by Stephen Cole, then a tired twenty-nine-year-old living in London. After spending its formative weeks as scribbles on pieces of paper and sticky-notes it became a draft outline in early March and an accepted storyline in early April.

After several months of sitting on a back-burner in both Hanger Lane and Finchley, the first chapters of *Ten Little Aliens* were written in late September 2001 in Cornwall. Over the next three months, *Ten Little Aliens* grew very long very quickly in a number of locations, including Miami, Mexico, London, Bedford, Huddersfield, Aylesbury Vale and New York.

Ten Little Aliens was completed in early March 2002. Stephen Cole is now a tired thirty-year-old no longer living in London.

ALSO AVAILABLE

HOPE by Mark Clapham ISBN 0 563 53846 5
ANACHROPHOBIA by Jonathan Morris ISBN 0 563 53847 3
TRADING FUTURES by Lance Parkin ISBN 0 563 53848 1
THE BOOK OF THE STILL by Paul Ebbs ISBN 0 563 53851 1

THE MONTHLY TELEPRESS
The official BBC Doctor Who Books e-newsletter

News – competitions – interviews – and more!

Subscribe today at
http://groups.yahoo.com/group/Telepress